MISTAKEN ENEMY

Mistaken Enemy
by Dennis A Nehamen

Copyright @2016 Dennis A Nehamen

Published by Golden Poppy Publications™
Los Angeles, CA
www.dennisnehamen.com

ISBN 978-0-9890572-3-3

Library of Congress Control Number: 2013947639

Cover and Book Design by Nick Zelinger, NZ Graphics

Nehamen, Dennis A Author
Mistaken Enemy
Dennis A Nehamen

1. Fiction
2. Adventure
3. Suspense

Printed in the United States of America

Second Edition

A Zach Miller Adventure: Book 1

MISTAKEN ENEMY

DENNIS A NEHAMEN

Golden Poppy Publications™
Los Angeles, CA

To my wife Bernice for shining bright
in support and sacrifice.

PROLOGUE

"I'M SORRY. I'LL ALWAYS think of you as my brother."

Those are the last words I recall him saying.

As I lay naked, shivering on the hot dirt floor, I struggled with an awareness that must have taken a bullet. The whirling fogginess was deadening to my senses.

Then in a flash my mind's eye blinked, exhibiting for me a panoramic view of all the events that had transpired to land me…in Hell.

I hadn't betrayed him…but I had planned to.

1

THE TAKE OFF

EL AL FLIGHT 318 to Israel. The announcement sounded like a warning.

Israel? Why in the world was I going?

All I could think of was a hard right turn.

Next I was seven hundred fifty miles from where I intended to shop for groceries.

Finally I was waiting to journey another six thousand miles from my intended destination.

El Al Flight 318 to Israel, the loud speaker pledged for the second time as I apathetically hoisted my carry on bag to enter the plane.

I had a stressful evening before leaving, waking numerous times. Thus, the first leg of my trip, from L.A. to New York, was devoted to catching up on sleep, to which I surrendered much more freely than the night before. The flight zipped by in an instant.

My plan was to relax, enjoy some reading during the second phase of the journey. But first, it seemed I would have to dispose of the pesky neighbor seated next to me who, immediately after takeoff, initiated a one-way conversation regarding his pursuit of a career in Israel as an actor, playwright, director, producer, musical book writer…time for a second snooze.

After bragging up the fame he imagined, he finally shamed me into agreeing to listen to one of his creations, a musical with an uninspiring story line of adolescent love gone sour, with characters arousing as much excitement as the periodic table of the elements in a high school chemistry class.

"Amir Hamdallah," he introduced himself like a celebration after I dutifully complemented his work.

While I had to conclude he would be a bust as an artist, I could imagine him enjoying success as a lady-killer. His black hair was styled into three distinct sections. The longest was on the crown, but still, what most would call short. Trimmed ever so slightly closer was a goatee of matching color. Finally, since he appeared not to have shaved for a couple days, his face was darkly shaded, an intentional act to create the impression of a rugged, untamed man.

"Wish me luck."

"Oh, of course. I'm sure I'll be boasting soon to all my friends that I sat next to you on a plane ride to Israel," I assured him as I took note of his impeccable dress.

His white linen shirt was perfectly laundered, as were the tan casual slacks. On his feet he wore what looked like expensive, burgundy-colored leather loafers. When he returned from a bathroom visit and was about to sit back next to me, three pieces of jewelry he had been wearing commanded my attention—a gold watch with a black leather band, the dial reading Patek Philippe; a large diamond stud in his earlobe, which, judging from the rest of his apparel I assumed was not a cubic zirconia; and a good-sized silver ring with several small sapphires on the middle finger of his left hand.

Our conversation lasted through the entire flight, at times Amir entertaining me with impromptu comical skits; on one occasion he nearly had me laughing.

"Why are you visiting Israel?" he asked, his first probe to find out something about me.

I smiled coyly. "That's the same question I keep asking myself."

"I'm sure you'll figure it out," Amir assured me. "Now, where do you plan to go first?"

"I really have no specific itinerary," I replied, puzzling over the fact that I hadn't even considered his question.

My new buddy proved quite helpful. After a brief historical discourse on the country, he drew up a plan for nearly the first week of my journey. I would spend a couple of days resting in Tel Aviv. Then I would make my way to Haifa, after which I would go to the Golan Heights, before finally looping back to Jerusalem. Then he informed me that he would be leaving immediately for a trip out of the country but he would be insulted if I didn't come visit him at his home, located just outside Jerusalem.

As the plane veered off the runway, we exchanged numbers. Then, inside the terminal Amir stopped to bestow a grand smile and substantial double hug on me, thanking me for making his trip a pleasant one and expressing how joyous it would be to meet me again soon.

We went our separate ways; no doubt both assuming it would be the last we would ever see of one another.

2

WELCOME TO ISRAEL

MY ENTRY INTO THE country was uneventful—at least for the first few seconds. I had my passport in hand, along with the properly filled out entry form to be submitted at passport control. I went along with the other passengers, all of whom seemed to be proceeding without a hitch. However, as I presented my materials to the officer for inspection, she casually, without attention to what I had written, ordered me to step to the side and wait.

I had no idea why but obediently did as I was told. Within seconds, a uniformed man walked up and asked if I was Zacchaeus Miller, which I confirmed. He then requested me to come along with him and bring my luggage. I thought it might be a full body and bag check, one of those random deals where a ninety-year-old woman is stupefied when ordered to lift both arms parallel to the ground so she can be probed.

Not so. I was taken to a small room and "asked" to wait, which I did. I waited and waited, until I started to panic. What if they deported me before I'd even had time to spend a shekel?

The interminable delay did nothing other than heighten my fretfulness over having made the trip in the first place. In fact, I spent much of the period rehashing several times the unexpected encounter I had with my mother when I informed her I was venturing to Israel. I had stopped by the house to let her know I was leaving, and to do something I'd never done since emancipating myself after college, ask for a loan.

"How much do you need, dear?"

I wasn't sure, especially given the fact that I had no idea how long I'd be gone.

"Five thousand dollars." I squinted. "I'm not really sure."

She disappeared for a moment before cruising back into the room waving her checkbook. Then she asked *the* question, quite matter-of-factly, I might add.

"What do you need it for?"

She loved needling me about my dedication to a single lifestyle, teasing me about having traveled more love-roads than can be found in an atlas. On this occasion, she couldn't pass up what she wrongly sensed was at long last my coming of age.

"Don't tell me Zacchaeus the bachelor has gone and fallen in love."

"No, Mom. Sorry to disappoint you."

She giggled, but only for an instant.

"Mom. I'm going to Israel."

"Zach, don't joke with me," she shot out, my words erasing the mirth from her face. I watched as she vehemently threw down her checkbook.

"I'm not, Mom. I'm leaving tomorrow."

"What for? Son, there's nothing there for you."

"I know. It's more like a whim…I mean just some silly thing I feel like I have to do."

"There's nothing silly about that country. Besides, it's not—."

"It's perfectly safe," I asserted, finishing the thought I assumed was on her mind. "I'll be fine."

She hesitated before continuing. "Zach, this is not a good time to go. Look what's happened here," she reminded me, hoping that the couple acts of homeland terrorism might bring me to my senses. "It has to be much worse there."

Imploringly she inspected me. Then I noticed her eyes welling with tears.

"What's wrong?"

She didn't answer. Instead she stood quaking, as if fear had paralyzed her mental functions.

I went over to hug her. As I did she looked up at me and shook her head, a pleading gesture. While embracing her I reiterated that I'd be careful, adding that I doubted I'd be away a week.

What shocked me most was that I'd never known Kaye Miller to be squeamish or meek. She had a fiery personality and nobody would attest to having witnessed her backing up if she needed to defend herself. Still, her reaction alarmed me but not sufficient to do as I wished, forget I was ever conned into making the trip.

Dutifully she wrote out the check and handed it to me.

Before I left she did something peculiar. She went into her desk and took out a leather pouch she kept stuffed with more scribbled entries than a computer could house on its hard drive. Even without the convenience of a file storage or search function, she knew every item and could with astonishing speed extricate what she was looking for from the mass of clutter.

Finding the reference she wanted, she took a pencil and a blank piece of paper and wrote a note, handing it to me. "You probably don't remember him, but there was a fellow I went out with a few times, Zev Feld?"

I laughed. He was a tall, overweight man who'd boldly pointed his middle finger at his premature balding by shaving his entire scalp. How could I forget him? With broad powerful shoulders and a squat neck narrowly rising out of his suit, he was the first man I ever met whose perfectly round head was almost free-kicked by one of my friends who mistook it for a soccer ball.

"The bald Jew!"

"Don't be smart. He liked you a lot. I've kept in touch with him through the years. Here's his name and number; he lives in Tel Aviv and works for the government. Anything you need, he'll help you." She stopped to let the point sink in. "Anything, Zach, okay?"

She wasn't really posing a question. I knew my mother well enough to tell when she was distressed, so I placated her by neatly folding the contact information and putting it in my wallet.

"Thanks, Mom."

I paused, not liking what I saw. Terror-tears were now streaming down her cheeks. "I love you, Mom," I said tentatively.

At that moment, my mother's upset alarmed me. What was it? She understood it was an innocent trip to Israel. She and I both knew that millions of people traveled safely through that country every year, regardless of the risk yet she seemed panicked. The thought crossed my mind how she might have reacted had I told her the true circumstances leading to my decision to make the journey, as well as my own apprehension over going.

By the time I was in the car, I was close to jealousy for those lucky people who allow themselves to use sedative drugs as freely as chewing gum; Valium would have loved my trepidation-bash, and I would have equally delighted, allowing it to vaporize my concerns into airy masses of feel-good bubbles. I wasn't lonely but I felt alone, and that's a rare one for me—*well, if all you have is Xanax, I'll try it, just this one time.*

That evening I jumped into bed, pep-talking myself to prepare for the upcoming trip. "I'm excited!"

I'm also a damn fool.

*****

The room the Israelis were holding me in had a tiny window, and on a couple of occasions I saw various officers glance toward my door, assumedly discussing me. One time, an armed security guard with his back to me received a cell call, and as he answered, he rotated to look in my direction.

I was about to thank my mom for bald Zev Feld's number and thought of giving him a ring when at last another man, this one wearing a plain suit, came in and warmly shook my hand.

"Welcome to Israel," he greeted me matter-a-fact. "You hopefully won't look at the delay as a lack of hospitality." Then, as if an afterthought, he perused the paperwork that he was holding in his hand.

"So, you're a reporter," he announced.

His statement perplexed me. Moments earlier, I'd written "artist" in the box describing my occupation. I'd also distinctly noted that I was on vacation.

"No, if you look at my document there," I pointed, "you'll see there must be a mistake."

"About what?"

"I'm not a reporter," I informed him.

"It's quite all right. You're a cherished guest in our country regardless of what you do for a living." He held out the document for me to inspect. "See, it says right here 'journalist.'"

I stared at the paper. It was definitely mine, but in the space where I had formerly listed my occupation, somebody had written over it, indicating "journalist," just as he'd described.

"That's a mistake," I protested. "I'm a fiction writer...I didn't fill that out."

"Well," he continued, ignoring my last comment, "there is one slight favor I'll have to request of you." I silently awaited what I knew would be a demand. "If you would, we'd like you to register as a journalist. It's quite a simple matter."

I was baffled by the nature of his request. Foolishly, I pled my case. "But I'm in Israel strictly to travel. I'm not interested in reporting on foreign affairs."

"Not to worry," he replied. "It'll only require a few minutes. They'll take care of the registration immediately. You mustn't look on this as an inconvenience. On the contrary, there are privileges you'll have that you may find advantageous. You'll be able to pass checkpoints freely and gain access to areas that would be restricted to you if you were a civilian."

I bobbed my head, not informing him that the last thing I intended to do was test the safety of a zone already designated off limits.

"Mr. Miller, I'll have your luggage secured for you right here for when you return from the Ministry Press Office."

That was it. No more glitches. They seemed to be waiting for me at the press office. There was only one other person there, a male who sat reading a newspaper in the waiting area. I went directly to the counter, and in less than five minutes I was processed and certified.

I made my way back to the airport. As I was ascending a stairway I must have miscalculated the top step by a fraction of an inch because the toe of my right shoe kicked it and I lunged forward, stopping short of a fall on my chin by bracing myself with my outstretched hands. My clumsy action caused the person behind me to nearly fall over my body.

The man didn't look at me. Instead, he nonchalantly went his way. But I recognized him. He looked to be about fifty, was muscular in build, and was wearing a distinguishable Hawaiian-style shirt—he was the same person who had been reading the paper at the ministry where I had just registered. *Strange coincidence*, I thought as I brushed myself off.

Retrieving my luggage, which had been secured as promised, another thought struck me. The episode had one benign consequence. With shocking ease, I had become an independent reporter on Israeli affairs. I might as well have registered as a proctologist as far as I was concerned. I'll admit, however, my first experience with the Israeli authorities unmanned me.

3

SETTLING IN

UPON MY ARRIVAL IN Israel—and without conscious awareness—almost immediately I began to follow the exact itinerary my plane-mate, Amir, had outlined for me. I spent my first day taking a self-fashioned flash course on the region—a task that included a full visceral inspection of the raving nightlife promoted, and in no way exaggerated, by my guide-book on Tel Aviv. That evening, I wandered into clubs with live music and crowds of customers feasting on a party spirit, ignorant of the enmity of the region being debated on news programs at home.

The next morning I took a walk, yearning to find a used bookstore reminiscent of my favorite one in Los Angeles, a cosmopolitan shop with just that name. As a creative writer, I was not an expert on current events. After arriving in Israel I realized how little I knew about the country and its relationship to the Middle East. Sure, like most people, I had heard about wars, negotiations, betrayals, and hopes of peace on both sides. I understood that the Palestinians wanted an independent state, many were refugees, and their position was that Israel was an occupying force since…the 1967 War. But…what really were the issues and conflicts, the historical facts so bitterly important to these embattled people that they would not cease killing one another?

With surprising ease I happened upon just the store I was looking for, a close relative of Los Angeles' Cosmopolitan, called The Book Junkie. I eased my way in and by chance found myself the only customer, making it comfortable for me to amble casually through the narrow aisles cluttered with mounds of dusty books that awaited shelving.

The store smelled musty, precisely as the "junkie" place I had expected. I doubted whether it had been cleaned in decades; some of the books had to be suffering bedsores. The real signature feature of this establishment, however, was the noise. Whoever owned or ran the business must have yearned for a music store, or actually believed that's what it was. The volume of what I assumed was Israel's version of hip-hop music was deafening; I wondered if their specialty item was earplugs. After strolling up and down a few rows, I was approached by a girl in her early twenties, one of the two staff members working.

"Welcome. Can I help you find something?" she perfunctorily addressed me in Hebrew.

"I speak English," I informed her—she then seamlessly shifted language.

She was a skinny thing, shaped like a sunflower stem. Her hair was no doubt very long, but she had wrapped it circularly skyward on the top of her head—the dark color and swirling pattern reminded me of a cup of fresh-machined chocolate yogurt.

"I'm browsing, looking for something to read while I'm here."

"About what?" she shouted above the blasts of sound shooting helter-shelter through the shop.

"Israel."

I don't know what struck her as so astonishing, especially given we were in Israel, but you might have thought she'd just won a lottery. She became animated; the slow, chewing motion on a stick of gum she'd been massaging between her molars quickened in pace and her face toned up from dull yellowish to pink.

"Well, you're talking to the right person. I'm not only Jewish but I've lived here for years; and I've studied the history extensively."

"I'm from Los Angeles."

"Boston for this lady. Yes, I'm American as well," she gaily informed me. "Okay, you'll want to understand as much about the country, and especially the Israeli-Palestinian conflict, as you can. Let's see what we can find for you."

I chased after her as she steered herself like a video game player through a maze of shelves. She stopped and turned to inspect me, as if she were taking me into her sight for the first time.

"Are you here for vacation?" she asked. Her thick-rimmed, black glasses dropped low on her nose; they hinted at a positive trait of high intellect.

"No, I'm trying to figure out myself why I've come here. You know, sort of a spur of the moment, impulsive trip."

Dismissing what she likely interpreted as evasiveness, she turned abruptly, marching forward as she lifted her right arm and waved for me to follow her.

"Nobody comes to Israel on a whim."

It was a jeer, and she lobbed it over her shoulder—in my opinion, intentionally aiming it on my path like a hand grenade.

"Well, to tell you the truth, you see, I'm a writer. I was thinking I might be able to help with the problems here; a fresh, wildly imaginative fiction story that in the end offers the hope of a lasting solution..."

The words popped out mindlessly and embarrassed me; it was a vacuous response, far from the legitimate rationale for my trip. The stick girl rightly took me to task.

"Like a thirteenth century crusader, but instead of recovering the Holy Land for the Christians, you'll be a peacemaker?"

"I don't know if what I have in mind is that grand."

"I hope not," she smirked, "for your sake."

As we browsed books, she emphasized that she prided herself on impartiality in affairs pertaining to the State of Israel. Amazing! My impression after listening to her speak for five minutes was that her opinions definitively keeled her portside. So extremely left was her view of the state created by the Israelis I was almost convinced that she wished to capsize the whole venture.

Still, she lectured me for a good half hour on the history of the country. Then abruptly, as if she lost interest in me, she began tapping on the computer to calculate the charges. She bagged my purchases and handed me the bill. After I paid she ended our relationship by delivering me a luck-to-you-buddy dismissive nod.

As I proceeded down the block, I noticed that a large crowd had assembled. I stopped, attempting to poke my head in to get a view. The group of spectators was densely packed and in my zeal to catch sight of what was happening I must have inadvertently brushed against a lady who was holding several large parcels in both her hands.

She shoved back at me mightily. I stood; shocked by her aggressiveness—she wasn't finished.

"You'll kindly keep your space," she yelled in what to me was a thick, unrecognizable accent.

Shouting her indignity distracted me from the crowd breaking up. The woman walked away. It was then I saw a man whose eyes lingered on me dispassionately. I would have thought nothing more of it except for two factors. First, he was definitely the same man who had been sitting in the lobby area when I went to the Ministry Press Office to register as a journalist, the same man who'd nearly crashed into me after I fell at the airport. Second, my impression was that the object of his interest was me rather than either the encounter I had fortuitously fallen into with the woman or the gathering, the purpose of which I would never learn.

I moved down the street with several others who had been in the audience. In my left hand I gripped the bag carrying my purchases from The Book Junkie, and in my right I clutched an intangible vow to stay the course; whatever that might be.

A few times, I stopped and noticed that same man behind me. I had to believe he was following but, knowing absolutely no one in the country, I dismissed the idea as preposterous. Still, he was there and when I turned deliberately, he casually slowed to glance in a shop window.

Finally I went into a café for an iced tea. I sat down and contemplated recent events—my occupation somehow being changed when I entered Israel, and now possibly being followed. Neither comforted me. But when I reentered the street after a drink and snack, the man was gone. I finally concluded that events of great improbability are still mathematically calculable and therefore will likely occur—I had just experienced an example.

That evening, I had dinner at a restaurant near my hotel, walked the streets alone to digest my meal, returned to my room to read, and went to bed early anticipating...I knew not what.

4

THE HAMDALLAH HOME

I AWOKE THE NEXT morning with the residue of one of the most bizarre dreams I could ever recall having. It seemed to have been inspired by the absurd comment I'd made to the clerk at The Book Junkie about my mission in Israel. In my wild, sleep-induced script, rather than being a writer, I had commissioned myself an emissary sent by the United Nations to meet with the Israelis and Arabs.

I was ushered into a large room, aghast to discover that on opposite sides of the space were groups of diapered infants. They were screeching menacingly toward the look-a-likes across from them, at a louder pitch than their little lungs should have been able to reach. After a moment, I shouted for them to quiet down so I could begin the discussion. The room went deathly silent. A moment later, one of them passed gas and the entire collection of babies started giggling uncontrollably.

"Stop it! Stop it!" I ordered. But my demand only incited greater outbursts of laughter. I was about to walk out, when I noticed each of the members of the two groups holding a rifle—they began firing indiscriminately at their enemies across the room. All the while, they were jubilantly yelling "hurrah," "whoopee," and "yippee." That's when I woke up.

Israel was bizarre to me already and I hadn't even been in the country forty-eight hours.

I assumed my duty as sightseer for the rest of the day. The following morning, I traveled north to Haifa, where I refreshed myself in the early morning coolness of the streets as they lazily climbed upward, preparing to simmer under the afternoon Mediterranean sun. Two days and then I was off again, finally appreciating why Syria never relinquishes its quest to retake the Golan Heights area, while Israel struggles to hold on to as much of this wondrous country as it can.

On several occasions during the trip, I sensed I was being watched. The feelings were dissimilar to those I'd had in Tel Aviv. This time there wasn't anything concrete—just a few different men and, on one occasion, a woman who seemed to be trailing me. I wondered if my counterfeited role of being a peacemaker was getting the better of me. Each time the thought entered my awareness, however, I managed to convince myself that the likelihood of actually being an object of investigation was negligible.

When I awoke on the sixth morning of my venture, I realized that even with all the imagination I was employing to keep up my mood, I had succumbed to a feeling of emptiness. I was alone. I was bored. I was purposeless.

The hotel room I was staying in near the Golan Heights had a phone. My musing about visiting Israel was interrupted by it ringing. When I picked up the receiver, there was nobody there. I hung up. Less than a minute later, it rang a second time. I repeated the same step, saying hello but without a reply.

I set it down, anticipating it summoning me again. This time it went silent. Once more I felt unnerved. Thus, after a couple minutes of deliberating I called the front desk to see if by chance they had an explanation. The clerk informed me that a gentleman had called and asked to be connected to Room 243. He said nothing else. Then a second later he called again. Both times he was put through to my room. The hotel operator had no idea who the caller was but surmised that the person had erred in the room number, assuring me that this was not an uncommon occurrence.

Not wanting to let my imagination get the better of me, I stood up and went into the bathroom to shower. I remember feeling cool and refreshed as soon as I stepped out, jettisoning any concerns about the nature of the calls. I started dressing. As I put on my pants and began loading my wallet and other items into my pockets, I glanced at a small piece of paper sticking out from the corner where I kept my bills. It was the name and number of Amir, the guy who'd sat next to me on the plane.

What the heck, I thought. I wanted company, so I called him.

"Hello, is this Amir?"

"Yes. I recognize your voice. How are you, my plane-mate?"

"Really? That's amazing." I was truly awed. "I didn't know if you would even remember me."

"It was our fate to sit together and become good friends. Why should I forget? Where are you?"

"Near The Sea of Galilee. I thought maybe we could meet. Have lunch?"

"You'll come to my home and stay with my family. I've already told them about you. They're expecting you to be with us."

"I couldn't—"

"Don't make a fuss. My mother will be upset. Here's my address."

That morning I took off for Jerusalem. Amir Hamdallah's home was located in a neighborhood not far from the Old City, Beit Safafa. I traveled by cab. We entered the city, crossing over a short viaduct that led to the main commercial area of town. The traffic was shockingly slow, and we sat for several minutes before continuing on our way. I noticed on the left a large building with a red heart-shaped design painted on its side that, rather than an arrow piercing it, had a yellow and red rainbow pattern streaming from the sides.

Had it not been for a thin green-topped tower rising like a rocket and a few bronze-colored roofs, the sign on the side of that building would have been the single bright-colored feature of the community skyline. All other structures were in shades of tan brick and stucco. Off in the distance, I saw what had the appearance of a grain silo with Arabic writing and underneath the name Hamdallah. It was the only English I observed. I wondered if it belonged to Amir's family.

The nearer we drew to Amir's home, the more I began to feel out of place. I was going into an Arab community, and I was about to stay with an Arab family. Amir had told me that under no circumstances would I be allowed to take a hotel; his house had an abundance of space and his parents would be insulted if I didn't accept their hospitable offer. I assumed I could deal with any potential cultural shock for a few days and then be on my way.

The residential area was to the right of the main road. Land would soon become a focal point for my visit to Israel, but from what I observed initially there was more to bicker over in the ritzy areas of Los Angeles where every square inch of space had astronomical worth. Homes in Beit Safafa were scattered, with open grass spaces between them. The exterior architectural design of all the homes was basic squares or rectangles, lacking the architectural angles, curves, and lines that stimulate the eye.

Then, I noticed something interesting. One house crumbling and abandoned was sitting next to a structure meticulously cared for and seemingly of opulent ownership. Suddenly, I realized that colossal modern home was Amir's. My cabbie confirmed my conclusion by calling out our arrival. He pulled over and shut off the motor, then wrote something on a piece of paper and handed it to me. The charge deserved a comedic swipe.

"My Lord, you must be making a down payment on a planet."

He burst out laughing, taking no offense as he jumped out of the vehicle to collect my luggage, which he insisted on carrying along the pathway leading to the landing of the home. I handed him the fare.

"Thank you, mister," he said with a deep bow.

Amir's home definitely impressed me as the finest in the community. It was a two-story structure, but only half of the top was living space; large glass doors opened to a rooftop patio with what I soon learned was a collection of pricey patio furniture and a garden of potted plants. Atop the second level was a satellite dish, and the exterior walls were all brick.

Before I could ring the bell, Amir flung the door open and greeted me with his signature hug.

"My friend, how has your trip been?" Amir asked, as his arms widened to welcome me.

"So far I'm still in good working order."

He took my suitcase the rest of the way in. The interior space confirmed a fact that no visitor could miss—these were people of marked wealth. The entryway alone was big enough to hold two of my apartment.

After showing me to my room and stowing my limited possessions, Amir suggested we take a walk around the neighborhood. The sun was intense, and I had forgotten my hat in the hotel at the Golan Heights. I assumed I'd find a backup to purchase while out with Amir.

We made our way to a small commercial center. Amir knew many of the shopkeepers. When we walked into one of the small stores, an intense confrontation was taking place in Arabic between the owner and a customer. The boisterous patron was holding a picture. As we stood by the door listening to them argue, I realized I didn't need to know the language to understand that the man was launching a rapid-fire assault of invectives. I turned to leave, but Amir smiled and grabbed my arm to keep me in place.

Abruptly, the yelling stopped. The buyer put down the picture he'd been holding, and he and the owner put their arms around one another in the most pleasant manner. Then, the now-jolly customer gave the owner money and walked out with his purchase.

The owner looked over at Amir and commented in Arabic, which Amir later translated for me, "That's a man there. He's willing to fight the price to the death. He's not like many of those pitiful changers of female diapers."

Amir explained after we left that in his culture a person who doesn't hold his ground bargaining loses the respect of the other person. Nobody should ever accept the first price when buying something, and never walk away without a quarrel.

My new friend smiled at the owner and tapped his right hand to his chest, a greeting of respect that was countered similarly by the shopkeeper. Amir addressed the man in English.

"Omar, this is my friend from America, Zach."

"Then we will speak English," the man said immediately. He came over to hug me. "Let me get you some tea."

The man hurried over to a small kitchenette and poured three cups, one for each of us.

"Zach," Omar addressed me. "What else can I get you?"

"Really, nothing. I'm going to buy a cap later, that's all."

"Where in America do you come from?" he asked in a calculating manner.

"Los Angeles," I responded proudly.

Omar went through his store and came back a few moments later with a Dodger baseball cap. He placed it on my head.

"There you go, Los Angeles Dodgers. I watch them on television."

I reached into my pocket to pay him, and Amir again grabbed my arm, halting me. He looked at me and subtly motioned with his head for me to forget it.

Omar had turned away from us and picked up a photograph. He beamed as he showed it to me. It looked to be a child about ten or eleven years old.

"My boy. His name is Ramzi."

"He's handsome." To compliment him, I added. "He looks like his father."

I could tell it meant the world to him. His smile might have purged mankind of enmity. But to keep us from having to linger too long, Amir addressed him.

"Praise be to Allah. Your family is well?"

"Thanks to God. To your father."

That afternoon we stopped into several other stores. Every person was as gracious as Omar. Amir had different relationships with each of them but was always gentle, cheery, and amicable, nearly enchanting. By the time we ambled back to the house, it was getting late and I was starving. I didn't have to wait long to eat.

Hibat, the family cook, had a feast ready when we arrived. This lady had no Michelin rating, but I can attest to the fact that she was a five-star master of gustatory ecstasy—that night we dined like princes.

Reading my mind, Amir remarked. "We live well. My father owns real estate and is an investor. His properties are in East Jerusalem, Jaffa, here in Beit Safafa, and a few other communities in Israel, and some in England and America as well."

"Yes, when I arrived I noticed your name on a building."

"That belongs to us, as does the shopping center we walked into today. The owner of the shop would have been insulted if you had tried to pay for the Dodger hat."

"I was prepared to show him I was no diaper changer," I said, proud to demonstrate I had already learned a cultural lesson.

"That's why he gave it to you. You're a guest, and he didn't want you to bargain. By giving it as a gift he avoided that."

"That was really nice. So, Amir, I assume your father's position allows you to devote fulltime to your career?"

"It does, yes. I appreciate it, but at the same time I'm not proud. You see, what I mentioned to you when we met on the plane about being Israeli citizens, I've never respected my father's doing that. After the 1967 War, the Jordanians retreated from the West Bank and Jerusalem, leaving the land to the victorious Israelis. It was then they made the offer of citizenship, but in exchange for allegiance to Israel."

"So you didn't agree."

He then curtailed the discussion. "You'll see."

I was about to, very soon.

It was only an hour later—we were about halfway through the South Park movie we were watching and a bowl of popcorn Hibat had prepared for us—when Amir's father came in.

"I hope I'm not intruding." His voice was gentle and his smile as charming as his son's.

"No, Papa, this is my friend I told you about—Zach, who I met on the plane."

"Oh, yes." In the kindest manner he came toward me, and as I rose to shake his hand, he embraced me as a long-lost friend. "I'm so pleased you came. Amir told me all about the long journey you shared on the plane. Isn't it wonderful traveling? Years ago, in Switzerland, I met one of my best friends, before I was even married, when I was on holiday for fun in Europe. He invited me to stay with him on his family farm." His eyes begin to twinkle as he added, "The best food I've ever had in my life."

"That's saying something, sir, after the meal we just had." I was still drooling over the dinner. "It's good to meet you too, Mr. Hamdallah."

He made no offer of informality, and I would never address him other than "Mr." for the remainder of my visit.

"Well, I'll leave you two to finish your film."

Before he took off, however, Amir instigated trouble.

"Papa, I'll prepare Zach for what to expect in a blasphemous home."

Laughing, Mr. Hamdallah took the bait and spat it back playfully.

"Please, and don't forget an Arab home of Israeli citizens."

Click. It was time for a movie intermission.

This was to be my introduction into a rift that never ceased to be an assault point for Amir on his father. Amir was unforgiving that his father "sold out" and accepted the conditions for citizenship set by the Israelis. He was equally miffed that his father made the decision knowing that his first cousin had been killed while fighting for the Palestinians. Amir believed it was an insult to the relative that his father conducted his life without sympathy to the Palestinian plight.

One occasion when Amir mentioned the topic of the deceased cousin I recall distinctly. In response, Mr. Hamdallah shrugged before sorrowfully addressing the loss. "I can't bring back my cousin's life. It was decades ago. He did what he felt was right. I loved him and would have taken care of his son like my own, but we never had the chance to know the baby."

Later Amir embellished, filling in for me that the cousin was a newlywed and the wife was pregnant when her husband died.

During these conflicts that unfolded almost routinely, and never reached resolution, Mr. Hamdallah would gently remind Amir that it was owing to his prescience on the issue of citizenship that the son enjoyed a Yale education and that the home growing up was frequented by dignitaries.

As the son passionately ridiculed his father, I was surprised that the elder Hamdallah never scorned his boy—the intentional affronts by Amir left his father unruffled. In fact, he never manufactured a bead of sweat on these humid, warm, late spring Jerusalem evenings, whereas Amir produced enough moisture under the arms to discolor his fine tan cotton shirts.

5

GETTING TO KNOW SISTER BAHLYA

FOR THE FIRST THREE days after my arrival at the Hamdallah home, it was only Amir and Mr. Hamdallah in the house; Mrs. Hamdallah was on vacation with the daughter. Any apprehension I had about being in an Arab dwelling quickly dissipated, mostly due to the fact that this one bore only minute resemblance to the typical Middle Eastern residence; it was as western as any house in my own neighborhood.

During those days, Amir and I enjoyed the luxury of free time, spending two of the afternoons at the beach in Tel Aviv—swimming, reading, and conversing. One morning, we began with a tour of Lion's, Herod's, Jaffa's, and a collection of other gates to the Old City of Jerusalem. We visited the Dome of the Rock, Al-Aqsa Mosque, and a host of other sites near the city center, the trek eating up most of the afternoon. I noticed, however, that we never entered, nor did Amir mention, the Jewish Quarter. Amir, intermittently along the guided excursion, infused me with history, as well as a superficial political education.

Several times while we were vacationing during these first days, Amir received calls and would talk freely in my presence. Yet, as I listened to these conversations, I would have guessed them to be coded; they lacked any of the detail one would normally hear; such as names, places, or specific issues.

I never asked him about the cryptic conversations, assuming he was talking business and his side of the discussions did not require anything more than perfunctory response. Still, as I glanced his way, I noticed tautness in the muscles of his elongated jaws as well as flexing down the sides of the neck. His grave expression confirmed that whatever he was addressing was stressing him, but after the conversations he became friendly and cheerful once again.

When I came down for breakfast on the fourth morning of my stay, I noticed Hibat had set two extra plates. Within moments, Mrs. Hamdallah and Amir's sister, Bahlya, took their places. When my eyes set sight on Bahlya, I imagined her absence had been deliberate; Mr. Hamdallah was intent to determine whether or not I could be trusted in the same house as she. I couldn't.

Either Mr. or Mrs. Hamdallah, or perhaps both, must have possessed moments of clairvoyance before her birth, for they had selected the name Bahlya for its Arabic meaning—beauty and radiance—qualities no man would question when looking at her. In every respect, Bahlya was a princess. Raised as a wealthy girl with all the luxuries money can secure, she needed none of it to purchase pure beauty.

"Zach, what brings you to Israel?"

"Everyone I meet asks me that," I smiled. "You're Mrs. Hamdallah, I assume."

Amir interrupted. "Mother, I'm sorry; I should have introduced you as you came in." His apology for the oversight lacked no authenticity.

"I don't mean to be evasive, Mrs. Hamdallah, but the plain explanation is that the nature of my visit is unknown to me."

"That sounds intriguing."

These were the first words I heard from Bahlya, my ears tuning in to a melodious, sensual voice packed with contrivance, charm, and a most stunning, unashamed swirl of tease.

"To me it's disconcerting." I responded shyly, like a teen praying he could find the boldness to talk to a girl. "It seems I was sent on a mission, like a child on an Easter egg hunt."

"Yes, I know what those are; how fun," Bahlya said breezily. I silently complimented a face like none I had ever seen—a perfect oval, angelic, creamy, and without a single wrinkle, line, or blemish. "Perhaps Amir and I can help find the Golden Egg our little guest is looking for."

I laughed nervously, staring at her large, dark, deep-set, alluring eyes. She swished her head slightly to the words "our little guest," and as she did her long, thick, light-brown hair, combed straight down to the small of her back, swayed like a silk scarf.

I had no opportunity to reply, Mrs. Hamdallah taking her turn asking questions of me. "Then, you don't know how long you'll be staying?"

She seemed to be sneaking in the query, and I presumed she expected my stay to be brief. I responded accordingly.

"No, I really have no agenda. Amir kindly invited me to stay but I'm sure I'll be continuing my journey soon."

I was warned by Amir that talk of not staying in their home would offend her, and it did.

"We wouldn't hear of you leaving. You'll be our guest until your destiny takes you elsewhere." Mrs. Hamdallah spoke gently but emphatically. "You're a friend of Amir and you must stay in our home."

The "offer" from this puffy-cheeked, tender woman with tiny slit eyes to house me felt strangely similar to the custom agent's request at the airport that I register for my press credential. This time, however, I had no interest in objecting—I was quite comfortable in their home.

"Thank you. I'll try not to be an intrusion."

"Maybe you'll become part of the family," Bahlya put in. "My new brother." She hesitated, as if furtively reading a poker hand. "Odd, very odd. I already feel like you are part of our family, though we've hardly met." She stopped again, this time to deliver a gentle admonishment to Amir. "After all, my brother never introduced us."

"If it will help, Zach, my sister Bahlya, and sister, this is my friend, Zach."

"Well done, big brother." Bahlya commended, after which she addressed me. "Amir and I want to take you out on a journey today," leading me to conclude that my visit had been discussed beforehand with her brother. She then added with a seduction that turned my white skin to an embarrassing pinkish tone. "It won't be an Easter egg hunt, but I'll see if I can get you something better."

Before we left on our outing, Bahlya explained that often when outside her home she behaved strictly in accordance with Islamic law, offering some details of her traditions.

"To Americans, the phrase 'don't leave home without it,' refers to a credit card. Muslims who are serious about their faith apply it to clothing. Now, Zach, you have to understand that hijab is more than a head covering; it's an entire code of dress. The word actually means 'curtain' or 'covering,'" she proudly explained. "A Muslim woman must be modest and exude morality in public, so no part of her body but the face and hands are to be shared."

"I'm not sure that's a custom I would vote for," I bantered to her.

"You simply have to use your imagination."

"I'm not sure if mine's in good working order."

"Then I'll assume I have a job to animate your senses."

"I'm not sure I'm ready for that." I swallowed nervously.

She simply smiled. Whatever game we were playing, she knew she had the winning hand.

That morning Bahlya, Amir, and I went off for a full day's activity. They promised it would be a surprise, and that is exactly what it turned out to be. The only clue Bahlya told me was to be prepared to be outdoors and to bring sunscreen, hat, and a bathing suit. I donned my new Dodger's cap and was ready to go. On the way to wherever we were headed, they stopped suddenly.

We pulled into the parking area of the open mall owned by their father. Glancing to my right, I noticed another car parked across the lot. If the man driving wasn't the same one who had trailed me after I first arrived in Tel Aviv, he was surely his twin brother.

He never looked up or directly at me. He sat in his vehicle while Bahlya and I went into a café to pick up a large bag of food they had ordered in advance. When we left the store, the man was still there, now glancing my way. I couldn't help but bring it to her attention.

"Bahlya, do you see that man in that car over there?" I said, trying not to point but instead using my head to lead her eyes. "I swear he was following me when I first arrived here."

To my surprise, she didn't give the man a look. "Israel can be a scary place," she said nonchalantly as she pranced across the lot. "Many people when they first arrive get suspicious and start imagining things that are not real. I promise…nobody cares to hassle you."

"But somebody changed my career on the papers I filled out when I entered Israel."

"Don't make more of it than it deserves. Everyone thinks the Israelis are flawless, but they're constantly making mistakes."

We got back in the car, and by the time we'd driven a few blocks, I had managed to comply with Bahlya's advice—the man was out of my mind.

We drove into Tel Aviv. Near the Carlton Hotel was a marina, where we pulled in to park. I was informed that the Hamdallah family owned a sailboat and we would be spending the day at sea. I knew nothing about the sport and had to place my trust in their proclaimed expertise. Thankfully, both were knowledgeable in the craft. In fact, Amir had competed in some fairly long races as far back as high school. I helped as best I could to prepare the boat, but they seemed to have perfected their routine, and in only a few minutes we were setting sail.

The boat was about thirty-five feet long and roomy enough to hold several more people. The main sail was a pleasant pink, pale blue, and yellow geometric pattern; the name painted in red letters on the side of the white hull was *Bahlya's Baby*.

The day was clear, warm, and mildly breezy, just enough for us to be moving along at a fine clip. A short time after we set out, I innocently asked how it happened that the boat was named after Bahlya.

Big mistake! Bahlya looked on the verge of dumping me at sea to swim for home. "Why are you so surprised?" She stabbed the question into me like a stiletto. "Are men supposed to have all the power?"

I tried to correct course with her. "Bahlya, I was just curious, that's all."

"You were curious because since men dominate women, you assume the boat might better be named something like *Zach's World*."

I really wanted out of the debate I knew was coming, but I could tell this lady, whom I hardly knew, was in the mood for a quarrel. I tried to avoid the inevitable by making light of it. "I like that name—good idea."

"Zach, you're not escaping the issue that easily. Admit it, men run the world. That's why we have to fight for the rights of women."

I tried to appease her any way I could. No matter what I said, however, I was staring into those magnificent eyes. I noticed her snout snarling as she glared at me.

I wonder, I recall thinking to myself as I deliberated how to diffuse a potential disaster, *if she's calculating whether I'd drown or be eaten by sharks first after she tripped me off **her** boat.*

I even agreed with her that men run the world. But when I added that it was women who run the men, she bristled.

"Then who runs you?" she volleyed back at me.

"I haven't found the right woman yet."

I was off balance and she sensed it. Plus…it was the wrong answer—end of conversation.

She refused to even look at me for the next hour, and the worst part was it troubled me. All through lunch she shunned me, and even when Amir tried to ease her foul mood, it made no difference. Little did I know she was deciphering my words, actually raising the value of the stock she held in me, while at the same time deliberating what strategies she'd have to employ to eventually crush me.

I was surprised how it ended. She came up unexpectedly behind me and put her arm around my shoulder, whispering with her lips nearly kissing my ear. "Zach, are you finished pouting?"

It was such a relief to be back in her graces, I agreed. Then, for extra dressing, I played a second line like a stage character. "It hurts so much when we fight, but I love making up."

"Then, my little visitor, we have to fight often."

Lustful. Sensual. Bahlya could reach in and take out your heart, and it would still be pumping in the palm of her hand.

We spent the remainder of the afternoon sailing, enjoying what for the most part was a grand day together. Bahlya had her edges, but they were what made her sensational beyond any other girl I'd ever encountered.

As I was basking in the splendor of the princess' grace and the wonder of a diamond-glittering sea, every bit of hesitation I had regarding coming to Israel dissolved. For the first time since leaving home I felt…at home, safe and thrilled. A sweet love bug might have bit me.

6

LOOK, MOM, A REAL TERRORIST!

AFTER SEVERAL MORE DAYS of playing with sailboats and lounging on Mediterranean beaches, I placed a call to my mother. She was ecstatic, unusually and alarmingly—to hear from me. I had been out of contact for weeks in the past, receiving nothing more than a welcome greeting upon calling her, but this time was different.

"Where are you?" she demanded.

"Did a little traveling through Israel. Now, I'm just outside Jerusalem."

"Give me the name and number of the hotel."

"Actually, I'm staying with an Arab family."

"You're what?! Zach, get a hotel and don't rely on the locals. They're all warm and charming, but they'll knife you in the back the first chance they get."

"Mom, what is with you? These people treat me as if I'm family. It's the first time I've even felt like I have siblings. Just a fantasy…I'll get over it."

"Who are these people?"

"Mom, let me handle this. Besides, you'll be relieved to know the father is a devout atheist."

Expecting bonus points for Mr. H's lack of religious conviction, I was surprised yet again to find it did nothing to appease her.

"I don't care what he says, assume it's a lie. Don't forget Zev Feld; anything you need, he'll help you," she said, her voice weakening.

"It won't be necessary."

"When are you coming home?"

"I really don't know."

She bawled, yelling through her tears, "Just get out of there safely."

She hung up. Her dramatics might have upset me had it not been for my desert darling swaggering into the room in one of her intoxicating outfits.

"Today we're going to visit a small neighborhood not too far away," Bahlya announced just as her brother joined us.

"Bahlya and I think you should understand more about our lives," Amir added, his sister aiming a curious eye-twinkle toward me.

Unbeknownst to me, the outing to Silwan, located just outside the Old City of Jerusalem, would signal the commencement of the second phase of my journey in the Middle East.

While in the car, I thought about a few matters that I had been deliberating earlier but never addressed. Brother and sister were remarkably united, and almost without exception

I now spent all my days and evenings with the two of them. I began to wonder about their friends, as well as their pursuits separate from one another.

If Amir was, as he told me, dedicated to an artistic career, where were the signs of involvement one would expect to see? I also questioned why he and Bahlya devoted so much attention to me in the first place. It was merely a chance occurrence sitting next to Amir on the plane. At most, I would have anticipated us having lunch or dinner together upon my arrival in Jerusalem. Could it be nothing more than a cultural display; was their graciousness a demonstration of hospitality typical for these people?

What I did know was that beyond the occasional affectations of Amir, overall, I felt deeply welcomed by the whole family, who extended a genuine sense of warmth toward me. But beyond that, deeper than the surface attraction I had toward my lovely amber-skinned girl, there was an affinity between us—a current passing both ways—one I failed to comprehend.

There were many occasions I sneaked a peek at her dark, mysterious eyes; the eyelids and lashes, bewildered, captivated by a distinct familiarity for which I had no explanation. Strangely, I perceived her features as a part of me, as if a piece of her was contained within me, a missing ingredient I yearned to possess.

All these impressions weighed so heavily on me that as time went on there were many periods when my sexual interest faded in favor of a love transcending corporality. At moments, I insisted that it was my imagination creating a fantasy of soul intimacy simply to relieve me of the pure, raw, passionate libidinal drive I doubted would ever be satisfied. Yet all along I reserved suspicion that it was not that, especially when I stared in the mirror and saw her features reflected back upon me. I wondered if the mystery would ever be answered.

"Amir, you haven't mentioned anything about the projects you're involved in," I mentioned as we made our way to Silwan.

"Things are going well," he answered, patting me gently on the shoulder. He smiled widely, but his reply seemed intentionally evasive. "You'll see. I'm due to be traveling several times soon. Don't worry; your friend is on his way to fame."

"Just wondering. I know how important your career is to you."

"The highest importance," he affirmed.

Then he added, as if mindlessly pouring ketchup on a plate of fries. "Since you came, I've wanted to spend as much time with you as possible. It's been wonderful having you at home. My parents adore you, too."

Bahlya said nothing. She let Amir bestow his elusiveness on me. Then she began to brief me on the history of the area we were visiting.

"This land has changed hands over the centuries between Jews, Yemenite Jews, Arabs, and Christians. It's a very pretty area, isn't it? The lower levels are fed by water from the Gihon Spring, and most of old Silwan slopes upward, directly facing a new Jewish settlement and archeological extravaganza built over the past several years called the City of David. Growing up, I used to come here often and had friends living close to the area. It was a peaceful place at one time, but not any longer.

"If you had come here early in the twentieth century you would have found that the Arab population outnumbered the Jews ten, even twenty, to one, with a few Christians as well. Today, it is still mostly Arab, over forty thousand. Obviously, the town has grown in size, not only in population but land mass."

By now, we had climbed in elevation. We parked and exited the car, looking to the valley below. Once again, most of the structures, multi-storied and stacked like crates atop one another as they competed up the hillside, were all of varying shades of tan. The elevated earth looked as if it were shrouded tightly in dwellings. As the eye followed naturally downward, the upper structures seemed to be coughing out a thick, slow landslide of monotone buildings—only a few with pastel orange roofs—two adjoining knolls at the bottom squeezed them to arrest.

While I continued to gaze, Bahlya redirected my attention.

"That third peak you see, over there with the groves of olive trees, is the southernmost of the three that are part of the Mount of Olives, an area with many Jewish sites, including the Hebrew University on Mount Scopus. Then, all the way over to the southern wall of the Temple Mount is Silwan today. Below you're looking at the Kidron Valley, an area of the city proposed for development into a garden."

She paused, sneering before continuing her speech.

"If you had been here a short few days ago, you would

have witnessed Israeli security forces brutalizing my people for objecting to the upcoming demolitions in Ras el Amoud and the City of David; several were sent to the hospital with injuries. Fortunately, this time, there were no fatalities."

Her voice began to take on a tone of restrained rage. I noticed tautness in her face. I'm sure, had she been wearing one of her in-home outfits rather than her Arab robe, I would have observed tension creeping along the muscular pathways of her neck and into her chest. Her hands, still visible, balled into murderous fists that were raised chest high in such a way that as she talked they moved vigorously in repetitive piston-like motion and seemed to have the authority to order simultaneous bobbing of the head—an invisible string might have tied the extreme members to the chin.

"You know how they justify raping us of our earth, our soil, our life blood? One of their esteemed lunatic leaders said it, 'The Holy Land, including the West Bank, was given to the Jewish people…by God!'"

She shouted so loud the valley below trembled.

Understand that this was early in my introduction to what would become textbook-length lectures on the Palestinian-Israeli issue. At that time, I owned no resistance to smugly parading my nonpartisan robe. This permitted me a predictable reply, but one repressed not by discerning judgment so much as a literal bite to the end of my tongue. Had I not gripped down with adequate force to let blood, I would have retorted as I willed.

Lots of people argue that if you believe in God you can have it any way you choose.

Bahlya was drifting into thoughts. But she had said it. Here were people—the Israelis—heisting property from others because they believed it sanctioned by God. I knew also that in response, the perceived victims—the Palestinians—were sending out deadly projectiles that God had ordered them to fire on the offenders with mortal intent. Was there sanity here? Was "here" any different from "there" or "anywhere" man dwells?

Engrossed in my own thoughts I nearly neglected her next sentence. So powerful was her statement it would be enshrined in a chamber in my head, echoing so that had I missed its first articulation, a lifetime would be left for me to capture her words and then contemplate them.

"Amir and I were responsible for organizing that demonstration."

If that were not enough, like one soundtrack playing without interruption to the next, she added quickly and proudly, "We endorse resistance of the most militant type. In your country, we might be called terrorists. Here, we are heroes."

The statements first waltzed andante without measurable emotional registration, canceling out any residue of my theological deliberation. Yet, within an instant, they gathered charge like ions urgently rummaging the vastness of atomic space in quest of a missing electron, launching my heart to an unmelodious cyber-grinding speed.

All I could drool out was one feeble word. "What?"

They understood I was jarred. Coming to my aid as sturdy bookends, shouldering the weight of a row of novels about to domino and scatter to the ground, they each as one and at the same time put their arm around me. We stood silently for what seemed to be a few minutes. When we did finally break out of the linear embrace, both were looking at me with memorable kindness. It was Amir who spoke first.

"Now you see I have interests besides my art," he said. "But when I travel it's pertaining to my career. Like when I couldn't meet you right away, when you came to Israel, I had a meeting in Amman, Jordan about making a movie."

What I didn't know at that point was that whatever he told me was undiluted rot.

Bahlya, hoping to impregnate a latent Palestinian sympathizer within me, was to oversee what I will refer to as my indoctrination. She tutored me meticulously on many details regarding the contest of will and might that had ignited between the two parties hundreds of years preceding the State of Israel's inception; the conflict had escalated and become increasingly bloody and violent as new generations were birthed.

Silwan deserved a protest and, if necessary, the loss of as many lives as was required to force "the occupying Israeli oppressors" not simply to bend, but to snap. That had to be the core theme threading together the education she imparted on me when we were with one another on outings. I used the discussions as opportunities to ask questions. I wanted the whole story.

One afternoon, the three of us were visiting Pisgat Ze'er, a Jewish settlement on confiscated Palestinian land. The spot appeared quaint and innocent yet according to Bahlya this piece of land had been the scene of may protests and acts of violence. As we approached, I noticed the community peeking above the concrete separation barrier. It was as if the gradually rising hill offered the opportunity for the tan structures to crane and stare at what was on the other side, though they decided to retreat and settle away from the foreboding wall. The undifferentiated tan buildings shrouded the low rolling hillside like a dust cloud.

"So the Palestinians protest, toss bottles, and homemade bombs, but what do they accomplish?" I inquired as we were getting out of the car.

Amir followed as Bahlya and I walked on ahead, Bahlya proceeding like an elder, taking questions posed by a child at the Passover feast. "First, we employ the means I mention because what munitions we have are hard to come by and must be used sparingly; many we must make ourselves. Why we actually demonstrate is to let the Israeli government know that we are united—each and every one of us—and ready to fight, forever if necessary, to stop the illegitimate incursion into our land. We are going to continue our battle until we regain what was taken from us."

"But really, how much of what you call illegal land-grabbing is there?"

"Silwan, which we visited the other day, and Pisgat Ze'er, are just two of over a hundred and twenty examples of what is happening throughout the West Bank and Jerusalem. We have systematically and deliberately been robbed of what is rightfully ours."

"How much land?" My questions were persistent; at times, I could tell they were irksome to her.

"Zach, we have only a few kilometers of space left to live on, if you call it living, having to endure conditions under the domination of vengeful occupiers. Does that tell you how much?"

She paused. I noticed a reconfiguring of her facial expression as it fell under the authority of emerging hate. Each time this side overtook her, my own emotions would reel; I recognized unfiltered fear rising to the surface of my veins. I had never encountered a female, nor for that matter a male (except as characters in movies or fantasy cartoons), with as explosively accessible potential as I perceived in her. That afternoon in Pisgat Ze'er she was firing on all cylinders.

"The riot we last orchestrated was in protest of the Israelis getting ready to bulldoze Palestinian homes in the valley to make room for a park and garden. You see, that's what they say, but in the end what they'll do is change the permits to incorporate more Jewish settlements and homes. What's wrong with that, you wonder?"

It was standard procedure during these lengthy, swift-paced, and informative lessons for her to ask questions without pausing for me to answer.

She proceeded, elucidating how the Israelis made special arrangements with the U. S., how they received loans never expected to be paid back, and how they used the source of endless funding to "bulldoze, bulldoze, bulldoze" for new settlements. She rattled off names of communities I'd never heard of, where homes were confiscated routinely. In spite of families occupying them for years, evictions occurred when it was discovered there were no permits. Or, when an owner thousands of miles away in a foreign country was offered a huge sum—funded by wealthy Americans—without the tenants' awareness, the house was sold.

"Imagine someone arriving at your home, where you've lived for decades, often generations, with your wife, children, parents, grandparents, and great-grandparents, sisters and brothers, telling you to leave…that it's not your house. Would you fight, would you throw stones, would you defy the devil threatening your family?"

Her vitriol rose feverishly. "You're a man, tell me! What would you do?"

I had no answer, my silence serving only for her to grimace.

"What could permit people who are supposed to be decent human beings to do this to their fellow man? They want us gone, every one of us, that's what they seek. They want it all to themselves, and when they have it they'll move on to the whole Middle East; that's why we have to stop them now.

"Never mind we were living here long before they came, never mind we have tilled the soil, planted our seeds and moistened the ground by sprinkling it with our spiritual hearts and souls, never mind our ancestors buried our heritage far into the earth to give us strength, courage, and pride. They mind nothing of the disrespect they do to us."

She stopped; a full halt. She looked so exhausted that I thought she might break down. As it turned out, she was nowhere near finished; with boundless stamina she continued, losing only one breath. Yet during the ceasefire, I observed something I hadn't noticed before: an appeal for me to do something.

Unexpectedly, she posed a question that floored me. "Zaci!" she shrieked. "Are you a Jew?"

I had already shared with her the origin of my name and my lack of religious training. I had told her I was raised minus most of the things others took for granted, such as father, siblings, extended family, traditions, religion, or allegiances to causes, entities or beliefs. My slate was clean. I'd assumed that she had trusted what I'd said. But she was distraught, overcome by the depth of pain and humiliation she felt for her cause.

"Bahlya, I told you…"

I tried to repeat what I'd shared with her prior to that day about my background, but as I spoke I started hearing sounds, trampoline pounding vibrations atop my words, repetitions of my name tumbling, bouncing, and flipping, timed perfectly as Bahlya had spoken it…Zaci, Zaci, Zaci. Zaci, Zaci, Zaci, over and over.

But her mouth never moved. The portrait of her sorrow remains embossed in my permanent memory, ready to be revealed on short notice—as I'm doing presently, reclaiming a memento from the past, a sound recording cherished—for it was not of accusation but absolution. She was expressing full exoneration from any doubt she might have had in my regard, making a plea as I heard her call out my name, Zaci, Zaci, Zaci.

Associates in the past had taken the liberty of familiarity with me much like a conductor tends a member of his orchestra. Bahlya climaxed to this intimacy out of desperation; there was no need to respond.

"Of course you're not," she said at last. "Don't you get it? You feel; you have compassion; you bring kindness and love into our home; you have none of the ugliness these monsters have brought to Palestine. They were persecuted, victimized, exterminated, and what did they learn? Nothing! Not a thing except to purge innocent people from home and land, grinding their spirits to powder and then rejoicing as the dust dissolves into the air. They strive to enslave the few remnants of a proud people until all memory of their lot is lost; then they'll move on to conquer another new territory and tear the carcass off more helpless souls."

I had questions I knew I'd have to pose later; she had whipped herself into a trance.

"Why, I ask again, why? I'll tell you. More settlements, more Jews, and the figures change. Their proportion increases, and it's easier to puppet a democracy when dissenting views are eliminated.

"That is why Silwan is bustling with new areas for Jews. That's why soon there'll be no more Palestinians in Pisgat Ze'er and many other communities. Go. Try applying for a permit to build if you are a Palestinian; then see what happens. They're squeezing the remaining inhabitants as a boa forces the breath out of its victim; but at least we can respect the snake that hunts to survive. Unless you're my father, who eats at the same table as the Jews, you'll age and die waiting for them to process your application."

Amir hadn't said a word, instead deferring to his sister's zeal. As we all walked back to the vehicle, he put his arm over my shoulder.

"It's true," he whispered.

That's all he said on that subject for the rest of the day.

As to why I stayed after absorbing the revelations pertaining to my hosts' professed occupations, I'll confess to being fascinated with what I termed the idea of light "resistance." For after the initial shock of hearing Bahlya utter the "T" word, that's all it seemed to be. I perceived them to be rich kids who enjoyed labeling themselves as terrorists, but since I had still not witnessed one shred of evidence to validate it, I was able to mitigate what they would have liked me to believe. To me, they were harmless.

Regardless of the justification I used to pursue my association with Amir and Bahlya, I decided to continue along a path now beginning to be illuminated by scattered particles of nuclear dust. I was living in the midst of two Palestinians who were professing to be Zionist and Israeli-haters, who were rich, handsome, and beautiful, and who were calling themselves terrorists. Further, I had no idea what—if any— role I might play in their unfolding game.

During the rest of the ride home Bahlya's shared more about her background. She was educated in England at the London School of Economics, after which she worked briefly for her father—she was disillusioned as she learned of his associations with businessmen around the world and thus retired before completing a full year of employment. Still, she professed her love for her "papa," though it bristled her that he was a "devout chauvinist."

Bahlya was a warrior, and I pegged her to be the one I would be reading about in future negotiations between Israeli and Palestinian interests. She showed no sign of intimidation dealing with men; her deference to her father was not duplicated with other males I witnessed her interacting with, including myself. But I would soon learn that her goals, while lofty and heroic, were playground games compared to her brother's pursuits.

Amir would always remain the enigmatic figure, one not to be underestimated, obscure as an ancient hieroglyphic. As our relationship matured, he would become increasingly mysterious, always kind and effusive with feelings, but slipping and sliding like a skilled boxer. He had things to say, aspirations he was gloating over but would not, could not, ever reveal.

7

MY FIRST TASTE OF VIOLENCE

ONE MORNING ABOUT A week after our visit to Pisgat Ze'er, Bahlya came out of her room and walked into the den. Her hair was wet and pulled back. She was wearing a sheer, cream-colored sleep top, screeching for attention, two subtle buttons on both sides of the chest making it clear that this was a bra-off-duty morning—she had to know she was killing me breathlessly, but this was a moody blue wakeup and she cared not for my erotic fantasies. She walked up to me, gritting her teeth.

"I need some air," she growled. "Let's take a walk."

"Where are we going?"

"Just to get out; I'll throw something on and we'll go."

Mercifully, when she came back less than two minutes later, she was in her out-of-the-home garb, covered head to toe; and off we went. Remarkably, she had transformed not only in dress but temperament during that short interval, and whatever had raised her choler had dissipated. I complimented myself that the thought of going out with me had soothed her.

We must have covered half a mile, chatting about movies, music, and food—categories of benign content people gravitate to when avoiding intimacy. With Bhalya, however, everything was intimate; it was inescapable.

"If you had come to my room this morning while I was getting ready to go out —"

"You didn't invite me," I interrupted in a kidding manner.

As I began my response, I realized what it was that was putting me in a more teasing mood than usual. The previous evening, after we ate, Bahlya and I went alone on a shopping spree in Tel Aviv. She treated herself to a wardrobe of new clothing from a few chic boutiques and was wrapping up, trying on a pair of pants at one of the shops. She went into a changing room, and I was wandering just outside when I heard her voice.

"Zaci, can you come?"

It seemed odd she'd be calling me when she might not be fully dressed, but I followed the voice that led down a short hallway. She had her head out the door of one of the small dressing rooms, her arm waving for me to join her—she had a naughty smirk on her face. I went in and there she was, stripped down to her underwear and bra. This was definitely setting up to be one of those fraternal-love-misappropriated deals—buying all those clothes must have stimulated her juices. She drew me toward her.

I stepped up to the plate like a long-ball hitter, brazenly warning the imaginary fans sitting in the stands of my intent to sprint around all four bases—my knees were wobbling. Was I going to be safe at home, called out at the plate?

I'll never know. I heard steps on the wood floor, followed by the intruder's voice.

"How do those feel, darling?" asked the saleswoman.

"I feel great," giggled Bahlya.

"Let me know what else you want to try. I'll wait right outside here."

Bahlya was hardly able to contain her laughter. I didn't know whether to thank the saleswoman or shoot her.

"Zaci, wait here until I get her to the register. Then you come out," she'd whispered.

She quickly dressed, leaving the old baseball star with a bat but no glove.

"You didn't invite me," I repeated playfully the morning of our walk. "Besides, Amir already laid down the rules about Arab women."

He had, in fact, warned me previously of the dangers dealing with local women and had not singled out Bahlya as an exception.

"Oh, yes, but I don't consider myself totally Arab. You have to be clever enough to know where the Western and Arab parts of me fall."

"I hope I don't get seasick watching."

"Well," she said, dismissing my insinuation that she was adept at wiggling the cultural border at will, "had you come by, you would have been treated to some great music; it was Count Basie who pulled me out of the funk."

It bewildered me how she discovered Count Basie; then I remembered she had been educated in the West. Regardless, I couldn't even properly credit myself for her mood change…

and I was supposed to predict what was or wasn't Arab about her?

"What do you think?"

"About you or Mr. Basie?" I responded, still perplexed about her interest in big band music.

"Stop teasing. The Count, of course."

"I like him…but I'd definitely prefer a medium rare steak with crispy French fries and tartar sauce."

A tiny smile curled Bahlya's lip. "That's a close call for me. I see we have similar taste in some areas."

Then her brow furrowed with doubt—about what I had no idea, but I suspected that it had nothing to do with steak and fries.

"Zaci, I have to bring something up to you," she said finally. "Just for your opinion."

"If I have one, I'll be glad to share it."

"It's about Amir. I'm worried."

"I guess that's the end of the conversation about us."

"Us? Yes, interesting. We can do that another time, but now I want you to be serious."

"One of my least favorite states, but for you, anything."

"Good. Now, have you ever looked at Amir's work?"

"He shared a bit on the plane when we met, but most of it I've never seen or heard. Why do you ask?"

"What did you think of what you saw?"

"Between you and me?"

She assured me she wouldn't be sharing what I said. While I knew she adored Amir, I also was confident she was a person not prone to violate trust.

"I didn't see much there. But it was only one piece."

She nodded as though this was exactly the answer she'd been expecting.

"Now that you bring it up, I'll tell you. What's curious to me is that he couldn't stop yakking about his projects when we met, but since then he's never once brought them up."

"Yet he says he's traveling for his career," Bhalya said. "And, Zach, his trips have been far more frequent during the last year than ever before, even more so lately. I hope he's not in trouble."

"If he is, he's not bothered by it; he seems chipper most of the time, wouldn't you say?"

"Yes, that's Amir. I'm still concerned. He's not himself. To me, he's distracted, like something is on his mind. I know he's intense about our work and he worries about it, but it's more than that. My instincts are usually good when it comes to my brother."

I believed her. Bahlya and Amir had their sibling spats, but there was a genuine closeness between them. The fact that she was questioning her brother raised suspicions to me that he might be hiding something—something shameful, embarrassing to the family, or worse.

"Are you thinking what I am?" I asked her.

"I'm not sure what you mean."

"Well, is it possible he has a woman and perhaps a family but for some reason can't say anything?"

"I have considered that because I haven't seen him go out much lately. There was this girl, Ghayda, but something happened several months ago and it ended."

"Have you seen her since?"

"No. It ended abruptly. Then she disappeared."

"It might be best to keep an eye on him for a while and see what happens," I carefully replied. "If I get a chance to subtly sound him out, I will."

By now we had traveled farther, probably two miles or so. We came upon an Israeli settlement, Har Homa, one of those allegedly built illegally on land appropriated from the Palestinians. We had been walking swiftly, the concern about Amir quickening our pace. Once the discussion ended, we began to move more casually.

It was surprisingly quiet out and we slowed to a stroll. Bahlya looked at me and smiled. It was an atypical gesture of pure gentleness and it left me feeling tingly—unfortunately it was a short-lived sensation.

"Shit," Bahlya shouted as she yanked my arm. At the same instant she was pulling on me, I heard loud gunshots. "Follow me," she ordered as she dragged me through a door leading into a small building. I still didn't know what was happening, but I could hear multiple screams and the sound of vehicles racing along the street. "Now you'll see what life is like for a Palestinian," she snapped as she led me up a stairwell to a landing from which we could peek out to the street below.

From the safe lookout, I was able to see swarms of people racing frantically down the block to escape armored Israeli vehicles.

"Look!" Bahlya's teeth were gritted as she pointed me in the direction of one of the jeeps.

The driver of the vehicle, with a mounted machine gun atop, was operating like a hunting animal trying to separate weaklings from a pack. He'd isolated two men and veered them off from the throng. Just as they were about to duck into an alley, two companion Israeli vehicles sealed their escape and joined in the attack. Several soldiers jumped out and slammed the pair to the ground. Once they were secured, a plastic tie was used to bind the men's hands behind their backs. They were then thrust into the rear of an awaiting paddy wagon.

My heart was pounding so hard that a kilo of tranquilizers wouldn't have calmed it. Adding to my distress, I noticed a man talking with one of the Israeli military. I was sure it was the one who had been at the ministry office, who'd spied on me after I first arrived in Israel, and who had been at the shopping center.

"Bahlya, that's the same man," I whispered while elbowing her on her arm. "I'm sure that's the guy who's been spying on me."

She never looked at me nor did she acknowledge she had heard what I said. I crouched low, fearing he'd notice me. I was able to see that he looked around, as if searching for something. Then he hoisted himself into a vehicle and drove off with the other Israelis.

"Pigs," Bahlya spat under her breath.

"Bahlya, that man...did you hear what I said?"

She stood transfixed in grief; I was certain not one word I said registered with her. We stayed a few minutes until the street was silent again. Then, she seemed to rejoin me.

"Come on, it's clear now."

As we exited the building she led us back toward the house, reversing the direction we'd been traveling. But after only a few steps, she reached to hold me back. A single figure was rapidly closing the distance between us. I noticed the person was wearing light blue jeans, black tennis shoes, a black Nike sweatshirt with white trim, and a pale blue keffiyeh with white print wrapped around the head.

As he approached us at full speed, I could see he was a small male who was carrying himself several inches taller than his actual height; his frame was rigid and his tiny chest pushed outward and upward to compensate for a deficiency of time to develop his manliness.

"Ramzi," she called out. "It's Bahlya."

The man-boy slowed for an instant, slipping back his head covering, revealing his dark, crew-cut hair. His face was void of the childlike features I expected to see in a boy his age. His eyes were intense and deep-set, his cheek, chin, and forehead musculature taut with the awareness of mortal danger.

What he did upon greeting Bahlya was shocking in its potency and ferocity. He raised his right arm and saluted while vehemently uttering a militant single word, "*Alyawm*," which I was able to translate myself as meaning "today." He proceeded on his way, leaving Bahlya in a rare state of free-flowing tearfulness. She didn't speak until she was able to compose herself. In the meantime, I had been delivered another *very unexpected* jolt.

"He was on his way back from a demonstration. 'Today,'" she declared, "meant he was willing to give his life at that moment. But he's only a child! Why do you think this has happened to our youth? Because their fathers were killed in the intifadas or are hopelessly imprisoned by the Israelis. They are boys!" she shrieked. "Look what the enemy has done to us."

"Bahlya," I interrupted. "I recognize that child. The first day I came here, Amir took me to the mall and one of the storeowners, Omar, the one who gave me the Dodger cap, showed me a picture of his son—it's Ramzi. I'm sure of it," I told her with astonishment.

She glanced mindlessly at me, ignoring what I had said. "Our roots and our culture are gradually being decimated; they want to poison the souls of our youth."

"You didn't hear me," I persisted. "The boy is Omar's son. His father adores him. Why would he risk his life like that?"

She hesitated answering but finally did. "That's not his father. Ramzi lost his father during the second intifada. That's his uncle who raises him."

"Still, he's only a boy," I protested.

"Zach, it's because Ramzi and others like him are willing to die for their cause, because they will avenge the deaths of their fathers at the hands of the Israelis, because they have fierceness that will grow stronger and fiercer still, because they will have children of their own to build the numbers of men fighting for freedom, it is for those reasons we will win."

Her tears ceased.

"He's only a boy," I kept muttering. Bahlya paid no interest to my fluster.

Every cell of her body stood at attention like a soldier in full battle gear awaiting the charge. There was conviction in her voice, with *fait accompli* quiescence. She reminded me of a triumphant statue, the culmination of an illustrious career of an artist set in a museum to demarcate a momentous historical era.

*****

For the rest of that day, I couldn't get Ramzi out of my mind; I was going to have plenty of time to dwell on him. When I awoke the next morning, Amir had already left, disappearing on another of his brief, unexplained sojourns. Then Bahlya announced she was off for a visit to Egypt for a couple of days. I was left to delve deeper into the troubling matters separating the Israeli and Palestinian people.

In their absence, I had nothing to do but read, eat, and enjoy the fine benefits of wealth that even my well-raised bones had never soaked in before. I took advantage of the time alone to delve into some of the books the clerk at The Book Junkie had picked for me, which I still hadn't reviewed.

One afternoon, I decided to take a walk to the shopping center Amir and I had visited on my first day with the Ham-dallahs. My intent was to do no more than get out for a cup of coffee. I was inside a café, doing just that, when I heard sirens. Along with several other customers, I went outside to investigate the commotion.

Within seconds, several armored Hummers screeched into the lot and a platoon of rifled men ran into Omar's shop.

A knot of people had formed around the area, blocked off by the Israeli military, and I had to push a bit to get a full view. Shouting and yelling emanated from inside the shop but, thankfully, no gunfire.

Then, two soldiers emerged dragging a body. Within an instant, I recognized it as Ramzi. I stood speechless as they threw him on the ground before using a strap to restrain his hands. A third soldier came out of the store carrying a rifle and a fourth with a box of what looked like explosive materials. His uncle, Omar, was screaming and weeping all at once, but Ramzi held his face in angry defiance and never displayed a sign of weakness as they hauled him into a vehicle and sped off.

I was instantly sickened. How could they take a mere boy and treat him like a criminal? As Ramzi disappeared in the dust of the convoy, I wept. It was my first tearful episode since leaving home, my first that I could remember since childhood.

*****

I recall it was a Wednesday when Amir and Bahlya came home.

"I see you've been enjoying yourself," Amir announced upon entering the den. He was in typically pleasant spirits.

I related the scene with Ramzi and told him that because of it I wasn't in such a grand mood. When I asked him what had happened, what might be the fate of the boy, he shrugged.

Evidently, he had already learned what had occurred but was ignorant of the eventual conclusion and powerless to influence it. Our brief exchange on the topic never developed into a conversation.

"I've done a lot of reading," I said, knowing there was no reason to question further about Ramzi. "Just trying to educate myself more on the affairs of Israel and Palestine."

Amir applauded me in so far as he beamed proudly. I thought it might be the right opportunity to bring up a topic that had been nagging at me.

"Amir, why are you going to all this trouble for me? I mean, I'm staying in your home for weeks and you spend all this time with me. You must expect something in return."

His response was voiceless at first, but his facial expression reminded me of the absolute joy of a teen at a hip-hop concert. He leapt up to me, close, embracing me with more familiarity than on any prior occasion and with greater liberty than I was accustomed to from a man. He proceeded to kiss me alternatively, twice on each side of my cheeks. All the while, his eyes glistened as if I had just presented him his first Academy Award.

"You are my friend," he finally answered. "When I met you on the plane, I knew we were to become like brothers."

He went about the same touch-feel routine he'd just completed; I was not a smidgen more relaxed with it the second time around. I'm sure he recognized my abashment from the dead freeze in my skeleton. He might have been inclined to repeat the act a third time but my reaction likely permitted the answer to my question to butt to the front of the line.

"So what do I want from you? First, I want your friendship. Second, you are a writer. I want you to write. I want you to tell the world the story of what is happening here. Go home after you have learned everything. We will introduce you to other people who will tell you of their experiences dealing with the Israelis and what they are doing to fight for our cause. Then, you'll be able to tell everyone that we will not stop. You will be able to let them know that Amir and his sister will fight to the death…that we Palestinians don't care about the cost in lives and property. We must have justice."

I wasn't sure either Amir or Bahlya would be pleased with what I might have to report, in that while I was sympathetic to their cause, I wasn't sold on the belief that it was as cut and dry, as one-sided, as they portrayed it—they were understandably biased, yet still, their position needed to be represented in such a way that the urgency of statehood for their people might be accomplished without further bloodshed.

I thought my next question might be more confrontational. "Amir, I know you and Bahlya are committed to the Palestinian cause and participate in anti-Israeli actions. Still, I haven't seen any direct involvement."

"We work behind the scenes."

"But when?" I couldn't help pushing the matter, because it seemed to me they had no time unaccounted for, unless when they said they were traveling they were misleading me.

"We'll get to that."

We never did.

As I assessed that situation at that point in time, I realized that Amir was a far more reserved, composed orator than Bahlya when the Palestinian cause was the topic. I stopped short, however, of mistaking him for having a shortage of zeal. His personality exuded a forcefulness as powerful as water; he was unrelenting, pressuring, and had undying patience.

There were times I would grin, listening to my friend reciting an exposé on one subject or another. Wearing Ferragamo shoes, Lorenzini shirts, and cashmere sweaters from Harrods, he had the presence of a movie star. Yet, here he was, drawn to fight for the liberation of his land as the proverbial moth to a flame. The better acquainted with Amir I became, the more he reminded me of a Pokémon character, Doduo, the two-headed figure.

For Amir, one head bowed to the principles taught in the home and later in formal education—the rational, thoughtful, modern, and cultured man ready for achievement and accomplishment. His other head was cemented with Gorilla Glue to more primitive influences. For better or worse, both shared a single heart. For the phase of life I experienced with him, the heart had forsaken the first head like a priest does fleshly pleasure.

"Now, changing the subject," Bahlya's sweet voice unexpectedly interrupted from the corner of the room where she had been listening, "we have a short family trip planned for later in the week and would all be insulted if you refused to come along. We're going to see our sister."

I blinked with surprise. Nobody ever mentioned a third Hamdallah child.

"She lives with her husband in Gaza City," Bhalya said. Then, with gleeful eyes, she made a disclosure about the nature of the upcoming visit. "She's about to bring the first grandchild into the family."

8

A VERY BRIEF VISIT TO GAZA

THE MORNING WE WERE scheduled to visit their sister, Lilya, as I walked downstairs I noticed there was more commotion than usual. Mr. Hamdallah was carefully inspecting a handful of documents and small folders resembling passports, questioning each family member to be sure they had their personal identification in order.

Within a couple hours we all piled into Big Daddy's fully equipped Mercedes sedan and off we went, on our way to the Erez Crossing, from Israel to Gaza Strip. On the way the atmosphere in the car was joyous, especially for Mrs. Hamdallah.

"We're going to be grandparents. Right, honey?" Mrs. Hamdallah sung out to her husband.

"I think Lilya is going to make me the happiest man in the whole world when my first grandson is born," Mr. Hamdallah rejoiced.

"I wonder, dear husband," Mrs. Hamdallah responded, staring as if marveled by her husband's partiality. "Here you are, with three of the loveliest women in the world in your family, and all you can think of is that your grandchild will be a boy."

The topic appealed to Bahlya, enough to step into her parents' dialogue and take a playful jab at her father.

"Papa can't help his Arab values, Mama." Bahlya patted her stomach as if it were carrying the baby. "Perhaps this little fellow will be the first liberated male in our family."

"I can't see where my attitudes have suppressed you in any way, my dear daughter," father countered merrily.

"I discovered a small male deep down in my spirit and brought him to life," Bahlya disclosed. "You know, father, they say all men have a little lady buried in their personality. Likewise, women have a male dwelling inside their psyche."

"I'm all man, I promise," Mr. Hamdallah said with the only expression of immodesty I ever witnessed from him. "Ask your mother."

"Stop it, Hal. You're embarrassing me," Mrs. Hamdallah giggled. "Darling, I think sometimes you have no discretion. These are our children…and Zaci our guest. What will he think of us?"

I'd never seen the family so happy.

As we approached the crossing, I noticed to the right of the road was a pillbox with machine guns, armed by Israeli soldiers. We stopped at the guard station and the family was detained for twenty minutes; every pocket of their clothing, bags, and shoes on their feet were examined, not to mention the massaging the vehicle went through—even then the family was pelted with a secondary barrage of questions.

As for me—well, all I had to do was flash my journalist credential and I strolled through like an Israeli big shot.

When I was a boy, my mother took me during a summer break on a trip to Europe. We traveled to Germany and into East Berlin. I must have been about ten, and it was just before the wall came down. All of my impressions remain in tones of gray. The streets were eerily void of foot traffic. The faces of the few people walking outdoors showed no sign of emotion; they looked worn and stern. Peoples' voices were spiritless. Like a tragic spill of oil on the sea, gloom and despair spread unmercifully.

Going into Gaza, I expected to experience a similar sense of dreariness. But I was pleasantly surprised. It may have been one of the most overpopulated spaces on the planet but there was life; there was commerce, people moving about the streets wearing colorful clothing, and there was even a brushstroke of smiles on faces.

We drove along the shoreline on our way to Amir and Bahlya's sister's home. It was a beautiful day; patches of pure white clouds sketched shadow designs on the water's glittering surface. Many crafts of varying sizes lounged in the harbor, with a few fishing boats lazily bobbing offshore. A short distance from the crossing, we came upon a stretch of white beach with little children running to greet the incoming waves. Just a few yards away, larger waves were bullying a group of amateur surfers.

The vehicles were mixed, like in any city, but included Mercedes and BMWs. There were clusters of large, modern buildings, and streets wide enough to handle the flow of traffic. Street vendors were selling food, and in the business and shopping districts there were many people carrying parcels, milling in and out of establishments. Bahlya pointed out a large, tall structure as the Parliament Building, in front of which was a wide open park-like space with bushes, blooming flowers, and knots of palm trees.

It was promising to be a splendid day—so much for promises. We were only a couple miles from the sister's home when the tranquility and lightness of the day rapidly transitioned to fright and threat.

It began with a sound I recognized most unhappily—rifles firing. The noise level equaled an infantry assault. When I glanced ahead, not more than a hundred yards up the road toward a main thoroughfare, I noticed a crowd of several thousand men, women, and children. They were marching.

Many of the men had boys on their shoulders. Some of the youths were shooting weapons, the blasts sharing the airways with militant chants to compose a chaotic pitch. The noise level was sufficient to divert all of our attention from the delight of the moment.

The traffic came to a near standstill. As the car approached the periphery of the action, I noticed some of the participants wore varying colors of t-shirts and jeans, many with green bandanas around their foreheads. But the more militant band wore full body coverings of varying shades of green, from moss to emerald to shamrock. Around their waists were munitions belts, and they all wore black hoods; they reminded me more of pest exterminators than soldiers, except they were holding rifles aloft—all by the right arm…no lefties allowed. Scattered like portable trees swaying in the breeze was a collection of large flags, all green as well.

Then we heard loud roaring sounds as the sky filled with armed Israeli helicopters. Almost immediately, a convoy of troop transport trucks and tanks rolled down the highway toward the mob. In seconds, the road was cut off and cars were being inspected and turned around. We were escorted, along with numerous other vehicles, back to the crossing at Erez and out of Gaza—I'd never revisit the city; I'd never meet the sister or brother-in-law either, though I'd have an indirect and profound influence on both of their lives.

*****

Returning from Gaza demarcated a subtle transition for me. The process of what I perceived to have been a contrived indoctrination on the Palestinian-Israeli issue was being advanced. What surprised me was how impassioned I found myself becoming about the issues pertaining to both the Israeli and Palestinian people.

First, I had never shown interest in political matters in general. Second, to have developed a personal investment in affairs of state was quite remarkable. I love writing, and my stories included absurd to gruesome to inspirational accounts, but you would not have witnessed me lunching at a presidential, congressional, state, city, or county fundraiser. Now, if I could believe it, I was breathing the air of human injustice, sweating the juices of man's freedom quest, drinking the sorrow of humankind's oppression to one another. To be honest, seeing the boy Ramzi aggressively hauled away by the Israelis won no points for their position. I wanted to lean in the direction of my friends and the Palestinians, but what kept my heart teetering between the two sides of the conflict was a known probability that Ramzi had committed murder.

Resisting taking a side allotted me a window of relief, and I widely opened the pane. When I did, a convenient insight blew my way. I'll admit the idea breezed past me a few times since coming to Israel, but this time it stuck. *This has to be it, to write from an intimate, and hopefully unique, perspective on this seemingly irreconcilable chaos.* The thought repeated in my mind, providing me with a meaningful explanation for why I swallowed the bait that subconsciously hooked me into coming to Israel. *It must be my good fortune to have come across such a worthy pursuit, to devour whole the affairs of these people and regurgitate a profound commentary that might alter irreversibly*—I hoped in a positive direction—*the fate of these combatants.*

Thus, at times I basked in a state of undeserved glory, waltzing left, whisking, then accelerating tempo to foxtrot right, to promenade…oh, feeling so proud, relieved, and back-row-center-on-a-chess-board royal that *I got it.* For an otherwise circumspect soul such as myself to take off on a whimsical trip half way around the world needed a goal, and now I had one. It was my job to stash my satchel full of the ingredients I needed to create a one-of-a-kind story meticulously delivering to people at home the nature of the insanity in this region.

I'm certain it was the intoxication of a dormant humanitarian desire, as well as the lingering need every child harbors for siblings to love and to be adored in return, that facilitated these drunken fantasies. Regardless of motive, I was now on a quest for any knowledge I could attain that would arm me for my task.

Amir and Bahlya bragged that they were responsible for organizing demonstrations, orchestrating the manufacture of badass, blow-up-in-your-face cocktails, and training the next generation of suicidal fanatics. My duty, which I deemed of equal or greater importance, was to influence hearts and minds, and I was earnest about the goal. In fact, my enthusiasm worked wonders because my friends began introducing me to new comrades who were significant in furthering my education, at least of the Palestinian position. This entailed many visits into the West Bank.

What I never disclosed to them was the objectivity I swore allegiance to. I was aware during what I might reasonably refer to as a "methodical inculcation" that the Palestinian perspective was being injected into me like a drug. At times, I thirsted to hear the Israeli side of the conflict.

"Bahlya, it might make my position more credible if I also had a better understanding of the Israeli side of the conflict," I remember bringing up to her after one of my educational lectures.

"Do you think I'm lying to you?" she retorted, but without recognizable offense.

"No, it's not that. It's just that when there are conflicts that the parties have taken to extremes, where there are two juxtaposed positions, it helps us to understand—"

"After you hear what we have to say, if you're still dubious, I'll get you all the Israeli propaganda you want. Is that fair?"

"Sure," I acquiesced.

She wasn't finished with my request. "You might be looking for a ground close to the middle, Zach. My dear, you'll never find it if that's where you want to be. Sometimes, sadly, things are painfully and plainly one-sided—evil does not play fair by distributing itself evenly."

I said nothing. I knew there had to be a middle ground, a place where truth is pounding the canvas of a trampoline, bouncing skyward to capture the combatants' attention, but unable to seize their awareness. Yet that halfway spot might serve as a secure perch for those impartial beings that realize they are powerless to permanently curtail the tragedies of the human condition—for those with such wisdom will find in the center a safe cushion from which they can view the drama, and if necessary, weep.

One way or the other, I had to get the other side of the story.

The tutoring Amir and Bahlya promised me took place in the West Bank. Each visit I found myself increasingly awed by the barrier erected by the Israelis. Two neighbors so mistrustful of one another that a physical separation was the default means of security made for a sad commentary on humanity: the central fences and walls with parallel, unoccupied spaces on both sides for Israeli patrol vehicles was a constant reminder of hatred.

A Palestinian man, Salem Hadecka, conducted the educational sessions I attended. Amir or Bahlya, usually both, would transport me to meetings with him. Some of the lessons were private—either one of the siblings or both would sit in—but frequently there were others attending with me. Since his twenties, Hadecka had been involved in the diplomacy of the Palestinians but had since removed himself from politics. He was introduced as a very bright man who had been educated as a lawyer. As he progressed into his sixties, he became increasingly more forceful in his views; he had firmly gravitated to a hard stance on Israel—"total refusal to negotiate," to quote Amir.

There were many things I recall about him, one of which was how he'd lecture sitting in front of a small table at his home, burrowing his chin downward. While he spoke, his loose facial skin drooped like a bead of fat about to splatter onto a fry pan. I noticed he rarely invited eye contact, especially with me.

Hadecka was a fastidious teacher, religiously keeping his hand on the throttle, never decelerating, frequently pacing his material but at equal regularity racing, with me all the while attempting to takes notes. Usually when he completed a segment, it was unannounced and abruptly ceased; he would simply leave without a word other than to inform me, and any other student present, when the next lesson would be.

Only on rare occasions would he joke, and I highlight this fact because he was a harsh man, his eyes glistening not with glee but with disquieting vengeance. The more time I spent in his presence, the more I became in touch with fear. He definitely knew the purpose with which I was employed, and while he endorsed me insofar as he stuffed me full of information, I could tell he had no faith that I would come to be of any substantial value; and frankly, he made no attempt to conceal his opinion of me.

His hair was maintained consistently shorter than a buzz cut but longer than shaved bald. He had a full beard that was trimmed to a medium length; there dwelled the largest collection of visible hair on his body, though with the top two buttons of his dress shirt open, the patch on his chest was competitive. As unappealing as he appeared, at least to my taste, his wife, who served us refreshments each time we were at his home, was a pretty, petite, and sweet lady who would come over and gently kiss the top of his head and whisper endearing comments in his ear. "Sweetie, don't let yourself get too tense; it's not good for your heart."

Often after she left, I'd wonder if these were affectations of a woman as fearful of the man as I, but I sensed only authentic concern. Still, it did nothing to assuage my own awareness that he would slit my throat as casually as zip his pants.

After one of the early lectures during which Hadecka discussed the "Zionists acting like animals…sharpening their weapons for the intimidation and violence they excelled at… dishonorably taking land from the Palestinians," Amir and I were on our way home rehashing some of the details.

"The fellaheen, the local farmers, were ignorant of their rights," Amir proceeded, embellishing on Hadecka's talk. As he was speaking a vehicle traveling at high-speed passed. Inside was a young couple. I recall being moved by the joyousness I perceived in both of their faces; "ecstatic" would be the best word to describe their common expression. Amir's eye quickly scanned the car, and then he turned away; I know now why he took a deep inhalation and then held his breath.

He didn't say a word but the silence was quickly cleaved when, in an instant, a ghastly drama concussed in front of us. That vehicle with the cheerful couple had crashed through a parapet and was headed pedal-to-the-metal toward the next checkpoint, precisely the one we were approaching. Prepared for the commissioned lunatic, the Israeli soldiers opened a barrage of heavy fire. They managed to halt the bomb-on-wheels only feet from where they were controlling the traffic. However, the car dutifully maneuvered close enough that when it turned to flames it burst into an earthquake force convulsion, completely lofting skyward two adjacent vehicles that in turn transformed to fiery enclosures, undoubtedly trapping the passengers inside to a gruesome and immediate death—I know I saw a limb fly out the window of the car with the couple that had raced ahead of us.

I don't know how many others were injured but I do know two facts. We were delayed getting home by more than two hours, and I was so frightened I passed on my dinner that night and the following morning's meal as well. Amir was, as usual, a calm, cool customer. He looked over at me, and I'll never forget his words: "These are the types of acts the Israelis understand. Imagine the sacrifice these young people made. Do you think it feels good to know you are part of the reason things like that happen?"

My tongue dropped so far out of my mouth I could have tied it in a knot.

"Did you have something to do with planning this?" I asked.

He looked at me blankly but never answered.

Violence was brazenly stepping out from dark corners and hidden passageways, crossing my path like black cats; foolishly, I didn't stop to contemplate how many evil omens I could stare down before being scratched.

*****

Later that night, we went out to a café in Jerusalem. We met a couple of Amir's friends whom I'd not been introduced to previously. Amir greeted one with the gripping of hands, hugs, and bilateral kisses; there was an air of comradeship between them. The other, I noticed, kept more to himself, merely glancing at Amir and bobbing his head up and down a few times.

These two men were diametric opposites. The first, Esam Kattan, was outgoing, friendly, and light-hearted. He eagerly welcomed me, inviting me upon arrival to share in the hookah. The second, Faisal Alawi, made no attempt to shroud his dislike of me. Why did he aim dagger-eyes toward me before even making my acquaintance? His reaction did not endear him to me but I will say that this man deserves a special introduction.

I recall contemplating his name when I first met him, even asking Amir if it had any particular meaning, which it did not. I privately referred to him as Fang. That nickname was derived by virtue of an uncorrected birth deviation whereby his two top front center teeth were abnormally long, dropping below the adjacent outer incisors so prevailingly that any more appealing physical property he possessed—and he was not a bad-looking guy—would never be noticed; the trait could be of no known benefit other than munching a carrot. I deliberated Rabbit as his fictitious name but passed—there was nothing fuzzy or soft about him.

Faisal, a man slightly older than Amir, was the type who preferred to let his eyes do the talking. They were a quintessential pair of bullets, drawing the portrait of a tortured soul entirely unfamiliar with fundamental human trust, kindness, or compassion.

His silence allowed him to peer discerningly about his surroundings, scouting for signs of human incongruence, inconsistency, or infraction. The few times I met him led to a conclusion I believe to this day—that he was a classic paranoid psychotic with psychopathic personality, which would place him in the elite company of such famous American monsters as Charles Manson, Ted Bundy, and John Wayne Gacy. Alawi was not the kind of guy you'd introduce to your eighteen-year-old daughter.

He displayed a bright intellect when he did utter sounds mimicking recognizable words, a necessary but not sufficient trait for the type of atrocities I sensed he could commit. Why Amir associated with a character of such outstanding viciousness and unpredictability, I surmised to be due to the fact that he and Amir were joined by the similar nature of their activities; Amir was stuck with him like a wick to dynamite.

There was one occasion when by chance I overheard Faisal in a sustained dialogue, and I was the topic. I had visited the men's room, located only feet from where we were all puffing on the smoking machine. Only a short wall separated the bathroom door and the table. It was early, the café was near empty, and the music was unusually low.

"Amir, we don't know anything about him."

"He's been with us for weeks. I'm telling you he's a good man."

"He's a foreigner, and I don't trust him; and you shouldn't be taken in by people so easily either."

"He can only help," Amir responded, as if making a legal defense. "There's nothing he knows that can hurt us."

Faisal expressed unmitigated irritation with Amir. "You tell him nothing, do you hear me?"

Faisal was persistent in his objection to me. Amir, on the other hand, seemed indifferent to his concerns. He responded with a vague and ominous statement.

"Look, it's not that urgent, so don't worry. Soon, you'll see, our problems will be over."

"You keep dreaming, but we have work to do in the real world." Faisal made no attempt to conceal his annoyance with Amir's cavalier attitude.

Then, Amir added a curious comment. "Faisal, if you're really concerned about Zach, let my sister know. She's handling most of this."

"I would, but I never see the bitch."

After I returned to the table, another man took a seat. I had never seen him before but would later recognize him as one of the other students who showed up at Hadecka's from time to time. Eventually, I would know him by the name Demian.

The study of politics was a major issue for most of the people I met. This gentleman had just finished reading an article for one of his classes. It was from an opinion paper, and he was eager to share it and then debate with his comrades.

"People, listen to this; it'll only take a minute." After capturing everyone's attention, he pulled out a document from a thin valise he was toting. "I found this by chance, browsing at the library; it was written by Hadecka several years ago."

Demian went on to incite the group by discussing how America pandered to Israel to create "a monstrous child disclaiming wrong or responsibility for its demonic behavior and in the end forming a perfect partnership between an all-powerful parent and devilish child." Demian continued, quite excited by Hadecka's words. "Hear what he said. 'They form a two-headed snake, the Israelis on one end and the Americans on the other. It's not enough to cut it in half: we have to kill both heads, preferably at once.'"

Alawi stood up and commented while pointing at me irreverently. "This is an American, Demian. He represents one end of your snake!"

He then walked out.

There was no further discussion on the piece Demian brought with him. On the way home, the thought of Alawi choked me like tear gas. Not wanting to be seen as delicate, I refrained from bringing it up. Amir seemed to sense my discomfort and attempted to attenuate his associate's words.

"Alawi seems more dangerous than he is."

"He has it in for me, Amir."

"He's harmless," Amir insisted, making light of the matter.

"I don't feel good around him. The less I see of him, the better."

"You won't have much to do with him, Zach; I'll talk with Bahlya about it."

Even with his kind assurance, I retained my own impression of Alawi as a horned-devil.

9

MEET ZEV FELD

IT WAS THE NEXT MORNING when I again called my mother. I tried to reach her every couple of weeks to let her know I was doing well. Each time she was atypically quiet, her silence a strong objection to my staying for a prolonged period in Israel.

I noticed that for the entire time I had been away on this trip, she had never expressed interest in what I was doing, which was unusual for her. Normally, she would read every piece of work I wrote. Often, while I was developing a story, she would display curiosity to the point that if she believed she saw a developmental weakness or character incongruity, she would volunteer a criticism.

Not this time. I would have needed boiling water and a wrench to pry open the rusty cap closing in her thoughts. I left it alone, knowing there wasn't much I could do about it at this point. My reasoning was that I would square it with her when we were next together.

I admit I had doubts about my safety. Given the proximity to danger I had found myself and the professed occupation of the people with whom I was associating, how could I not? But the last thing I wanted was to worry her. The conversation ended as each preceding it. "When are you coming home?"

Her tone worried me more than ever. After we hung up, I finally placed a call to her friend.

"Mr. Feld, this is Zach Miller, Kaye Miller's son. Do you remember me?"

"Of course. Your mother told me you were on a trip to Israel."

"I didn't know she had informed you, but yes, I've been here for some time now."

"Where are you staying?" he questioned me.

"I'm in Beit Safafa, with a family."

"Wonderful. I hope you're enjoying our country."

"So far, I am, Mr. Feld."

"Well, tell me, is there anything I can help you with?"

"I'm doing great, but it's my mother. I know she admires you as a friend. In fact, she insisted I take your number when I left. The problem is I know she's worrying about me, and I was wondering if you might give her a call, just to let her know all is well."

"Do you think it would be best if we met briefly before I get in touch with her? That way I could tell her I saw you directly."

"Unfortunately, I don't have any immediate plan to come to Tel Aviv. Look, I think a call would be enough, but I'll definitely reach you as soon as I know when I'm coming; we can meet then."

"That's fine. Don't worry, Zach. I'll reach her and settle her down. Doesn't matter what age you are, a parent always worries."

"I guess so. Thanks."

During the week after talking with Feld, I noticed I was restless. I had started thinking of going home. The meeting with Faisal Alawi weighed on me. The demonstrations and gunfire alarmed me. I was increasingly worried about my mother. Cumulatively, it added up to an arsenal of ammunition I might use to legitimize heading out in search of the quickest road home.

*****

I was contemplating at most a few more meetings with Hadecka to complete the tutoring I needed, plus gathering information about the Israeli perspective. I knew by then, I'd be prepared with substantive material from which I could craft some sort of story with a message—I assumed when I finished, it would be an easy sell.

It so happened that one morning I was informed that Amir and Bahlya were both leaving for a day. I decided I'd call Feld back, this time to ask if we might meet if I came that day to Tel Aviv—the instances when I believed I was being followed, the altering of my entrance papers when I arrived in Israel, and the violent episodes I'd witnessed all contributed to a sense of unease I thought he might be able to relieve. I believe I was hoping a neutral outsider's opinion might help me gain perspective.

He immediately agreed without questioning the reason for the visit. I traveled by cab, calling the company first and getting the price worked out in advance. The driver was an Arab man and not very friendly. His skills behind the wheel were frightful, and I spent most of the ride calculating my chances of surviving. When we finally arrived, I handed him the set fee, plus a tip deficient enough to let him know I wasn't pleased but sufficient to avoid a conflict.

Feld was waiting for me at a small eatery, Café Michal on Dizengoff Street. I might as well have been on Montana Avenue in Brentwood, California. The restaurant sat on a corner and was walled off from the street by a two-foot-high concrete floral bed. Abutilon—blood red, bright gold, and pink—assaulted my senses; two birds were flitting from bloom to bloom to collect the sweet nectar.

The table arrangement tested the dimensions of the interior, the designer diligent not to waste an extra square inch of space. No doubt I was in a high rent district, but it worried me none since I had spent a pittance of what I thought I might have needed up to that point.

After lunch, Feld picked up the check—a minor contributing factor to the rather absurd twist to this story that allowed me not only to return every cent borrowed from my mother, but also to arrive home with excess funds. How I pulled off this hat trick without a hot run at a casino will be reserved as a very interesting footnote to this experience.

"Mr. Feld," I began, as the server cleared our plates. "When I arrived, they forced me to register as a journalist. I don't understand why. Does it seem strange to you?"

"Not really," he said, with no sign of disingenuousness. "When it comes to security, we do things differently here. I wouldn't give it a thought."

"I see. But I was concerned if I need to recertify to maintain my entry papers in proper order. I wasn't sure who to call."

"It's not a problem. The certification is good for the same duration of time as your passport, six months."

"Oh, that's great. And thanks again for talking to my mother."

"Sure. I just spoke with her a second time and she's assured me she's healthy, physically and mentally. Her only concern is you coming home, mainly when." I noticed a mild stammer, suggesting not irresolution but deliberation about when to bring up a subject on an agenda. "Zach, what made you decide to come here?"

"Believe me, you're not the only one who's asked me that. You're going to get the packaged response—I really can't say for sure."

"Well, it doesn't matter. What is of importance is why you're staying and how long you'll be here."

It was strange to me that he would be gently suggesting I leave. Then again, under the circumstances of him trying to lobby for my mother, it made sense.

"I've met people I care about and who care for me. Nothing to do with politics, I assure you."

I knew Feld worked for the Israeli government in some capacity, so I didn't want to seem too interested in anything to do with policy or state affairs. As far as my own opinion on the subject of Israeli politics, the last thing I needed was a heated debate on Zionism and Israeli mistreatment of Palestinians.

"Girlfriend issue, I presume," he probed.

"Not really. I'm sure I'll be returning home the same bachelor I left," I smiled uncomfortably.

"Sounds good."

As Feld was responding, I looked up. Just past his shoulder and to the right, toward the street, my former cab driver was standing. He had a small video camera in his hand and was indisputably filming me. If this was meant to be a stealth operation, the fool was not up to the task. He stood out like a streaker racing down Fifth Avenue in New York. So intent was he on photographing me, even while I was looking at him, he didn't notice I'd discovered him. He kept on shooting.

I jumped up and started for the door. Finally, he did see me and dissolved into the street crowd before I could get to him. I went back to the table.

"Mr. Feld. The cab driver that brought me here was filming me through the window. I also know that another man has followed me several times."

"The Arabs are strange people—a bit paranoid I might say."

"But the other man was definitely not Arab," I informed him.

"Zach, do you mind if I give you some advice?" I signaled for him to proceed, assuming he would, regardless. "Israel can be a fun country for vacationing, but a dangerous one to get involved in internal affairs. It's best to be careful about the company you keep."

"I'm not sure I understand what you're saying."

"I'm trying to tell you that it's easy to get into trouble here. That's what your mother is worried about."

"I'm not in any type of predicament," I retorted, my words now revealing a mild vexation I preferred to keep from coming to his awareness. "People are watching me for no reason."

"I'm trying to help you, that's all," Feld said, taking on a paternal tone. "We all have forces of varying kinds in our life, some preying on us from our past, and we can get swept away trying to resolve them. You're a writer; surely you know what I'm talking about."

"I don't see how that applies to me," I responded sharply.

"Be careful, that's all I'm advising."

"It seems to me you're saying that I'm an object of investigation. Are you suggesting that I leave?" I asked point blank.

"Yes. Before anything bad happens."

Feld had permitted himself to go a few steps beyond subtle counsel, all the way to deliberate intimidation. Again, all I could surmise to account for his behavior was the influence of my mother.

There was no way he would have any interest in my relationships with Amir and Bahlya—first, they were the children of a prominent Palestinian and a man who openly dealt with the Israelis; second, to my knowledge neither were even known to the Israelis as opposition leaders; they proclaimed to be working covertly.

Up to that point, I'd seen nothing to contradict this. In fact, I'd still not observed any sign of involvement for either of them that would have classified them as terrorists—and even if they were, I had done nothing other than imbibe knowledge leading me to sympathize with the Palestinian situation while at the same time maintaining my own personal objectivity. Furthermore, I had every right to voice an opinion on the issues contested between the Israelis and Palestinians—specifically, in written form when I returned to my country. As far as Feld was concerned, I took offense at his tactics, even if he was trying to muscle me on behalf of my mother.

"You're a good friend to my mom. She's always cared for you. Thank you for taking the time to meet with me and treating me to lunch," I said respectfully. "I'll let her know how kind you were to me when I get home."

I swiftly departed. The meeting with Feld hadn't provided me with what I wanted, but it did give me what I needed—it was time to leave. I didn't want to credit his admonitions with advancing my timetable for exiting Israel, but along with the factors I was already deliberating and then the newly added wrinkle of the Arabs following me as well, he did have an influence. I began deliberating a schedule for my trip back to Los Angeles.

I grabbed a cab to return to the Hamdallah home. On the way, I made two calls. The first was to the transport service that had brought me to Tel Aviv. When I confronted them about the behavior of their employee, they responded as if I were a dunce, telling me it must have been my imagination. When I insisted on speaking with the driver, they said he was a temporary man and they couldn't reach him.

The second call was to my best friend Preston, who by the way played an indirect role in my coming to Israel. I talked softly, making sure I couldn't be overheard by the cabbie. I hadn't been directly threatened, but the repeated events made me feel I was in danger.

"How are you? It's your friend from Jerusalem."

"Thought you joined a kibbutz or converted," he kidded. "What have you been up to?"

"Not much, just plotting to overthrow the Israeli government."

"Bullshit. Who's the lady that's about to have her heart broken?"

"There is a lady, but if any heart is going to be cracked, this time it's mine."

"Then get the hell out of there. You've been to the station enough times to know there's always another train coming down the track."

"Seriously, getting out of here is exactly what I need to do. Things can get dangerous in the time it takes to strike a match, and I'm not talking about heartbreak."

"I heard that's how it is in the Middle East. So when will I be seeing you?"

"No date yet, but my guess is within a week for sure," I estimated on the spot. "Just need to wrap up a few items and I'll be on my way. Look, I'm in a cab going back to my place, so let me get in touch soon. You be well."

Pondering my conversation with Preston, I knew all signs pointed to a speedy exit, and I was planning accordingly.

10

PREPARING TO DEPART

WHEN WE ARRIVED AT Hadecka's home the following day, the attendance had increased. Demian, Faisal, Esam, and a couple of others I had never met were sitting around the room. Our teacher wasted no time, zooming ahead full speed as soon as he landed in his seat. He then proceeded to go on for hours, addressing everything from United Nations peace offers to terrorist squads of Zionists fresh out of the holocaust attacking Palestinians, and then war, the Israelis taking on the whole Middle East.

I noticed Demian loved to display not only his knowledge, but also a need for Hadecka's attention. Whenever his leader paused, he interjected a comment. "They expanded the land mass of Israel six-fold after the 1967 War."

Hadecka looked as if he were about to spit, unable to disguise his repulsion.

"Yes. You should all learn that there's no such thing as temporary when it comes to possessions. Once somebody has something in their grip, they come to believe it is theirs, and not only will they fight to keep it, but they will lust for greater ownership, whetting their appetite to seek more and more. The Israelis have no intention of stopping."

Demian's voice shot out. "That's why we will destroy them. That's our mandate, and we will not stop until we succeed," he proclaimed, pounding his chest to express intent. "The whole Arab world wants them dead. Say what you want about the Arab leaders, but remember that none of them has broken ranks with their brothers except Sadat."

The mention of Sadat was like a hot rod shoved up Hadecka's rectum. "He was a silly man, talked into Carter's delusions of sainthood…what a team. The only rational man at the Camp David meetings was Begin."

Demian was fully engaged with his mentor, but outraged by the comment. "Begin? The leader of Israel? He fleeced us worse than any of the Jew scoundrels."

Hadecka followed his own line of thought, undeterred by Demian's impulsiveness.

"Begin returned land taken from Egypt in the Sinai, but what did he really pay for peace? Nothing. Sadat will always be an outcast in the Arab world; he sold out the Palestinians. By agreeing to recognize Israel as a state, he damaged the image and influence of the entire Arab community." He crimped his lips as if about to puke. "He was and will remain a disgrace to his people."

Hadecka stopped to emphasize his next statement, one he had repeated like a soldier's oath. "Do not negotiate on a matter you know you should never compromise. Negotiation by definition means to bargain, settle by agreement. We were misled to meet on such terms. This is something we can never do in the future."

"Then why do you compliment Begin? I don't understand," Demian pled.

"You didn't listen," Hadecka jeered at his faithful devotee. "Begin recognized an opportunity to get a huge return and pay nothing for it. We must be objective if we are not going to repeat the follies of the past. Sadat was a pathetic puppet, and Begin pulled his strings like any master would have done." Hadecka smirked at the folly.

"My suggestion to you, the younger people upon whose shoulders our hopes rest, is that you find new solutions. No more roulette wheels or blackjack tables. The problem has to be solved, once and for all, the old-fashioned way, but dressed in modern style and design."

Faisal was irked. He had none of the adulation for Hadecka the other students conveyed. "You're talking in riddles. What is this 'dressed in modern style and design' supposed to mean to us?"

Hadecka took no offense to the hostile tone, but he did turn his head to eye Faisal, a gesture I wasn't sure was curious or foreboding.

"Figure it out," he said. "You can't compromise, so you must use the powerful tools of destruction at your fingertips to implement a final solution."

I refrained from asking what "final solution" meant. The words did cause me to squirm in my seat. Protests and violence I understood to be unavoidable events in this part of the world, but what "tools of destruction at their fingertips" he might be referring to definitely left a residue of worry for me.

Hadecka didn't pause to give me time for further deliberation. He moved on to what he summarized as a "lamentable" subject he would have preferred to ignore. From my own reading, I had noticed the cast of organizations that had represented the Palestinians over the decades and wondered why the polarity and splintering. Amir and Bahlya had addressed the topic several times before, but Hadecka went further.

"On any point, you are going to have varying opinions and perspectives. This is the way it is with humans. It can be a blessing, because out of the sea of ideas the most advantageous can be selected. A problem arises, however, when the points raised on a subject cannot be evaluated with objectivity, when personal advancement, attainment of power for the sole sake of control, and individual stupidity are calculated into equations. We have had our share of all of these, much more than we would be proud to admit. And don't forget that our adversaries have successively exploited our weaknesses. Divide and conquer has worked like a charm every time."

The gathering ended on two sad points. The Palestinians were spending more resources fighting among themselves than with the Israelis and that there was no solution to right all the wrongs short of acid washing the land of the Israelis.

After the group cleared out, strangely, Hadecka's wife came into the room and for the first time offered me an embrace. If her husband was offended, there was no way to tell. Without announcing his exit—he never did anyway—he had already parted, his work with me over for the day.

I recall having an unusual feeling leaving Hadecka's on that occasion, as if I wouldn't be returning.

In addition to gathering information from the Israeli perspective, an assignment I committed to addressing before venturing home, there was only one question lingering: where was I going with Bahlya? I assumed I'd take a bit more vacation time to explore if there was, after all, going to be romance for the two of us. As it turned out, I was not the only one thinking of Bahlya and me.

*****

The following morning, I was informed that both Bahlya and Amir were again leaving for a day or two. There was no explanation for Amir's trip, but Bahlya was going to Haifa to celebrate the birthday of a close friend. She instructed me that if neither she nor Amir were back by the following day, I should call Hadecka to notify him we wouldn't be coming to the next lesson.

I devoted the early hours of the morning to organizing my notes. I was surprised when Mr. H. came to my room and suggested we spend some time together. He said we could have lunch. Since I had never been alone with him, I eagerly accepted the invitation.

After I'd showered and dressed, I found him waiting and we immediately took off. Why a man of his stature would make time for me I didn't question; in spite of the fact he was rich and powerful, I always experienced kindness from him and perceived him as a shy, reserved character. While he had many associates, and not infrequently I saw him entertaining men in his home who I could tell by their dress and manner were cultured and important, that was business. Still, I was inclined to believe he was short, even devoid, of true friends—a lonely man whose life revolved around his wife and children.

Mr. Hamdallah had his black hair slicked back and smelled of sweet spice cologne. He was dressed in a pair of black slacks and a white linen shirt, and around his waist he had tied a thin grey cashmere sweater—he might have been going to the club for a round of golf. He announced he had to make a stop before we ate, and he drove me to the outskirts of an Israeli settlement where a development was going up. There were at least a couple hundred dwellings under construction. I smiled, thinking it was just the type of "progress" Amir and Bahlya would have spat on after delightfully fantasizing about blowing it up. Yet, their father was proud to be making a bundle off of it.

It touched me, having a meal alone with the father of my friends. He was a keenly intelligent man, not at all ignorant of the psychological and emotional struggles young people have—their quest to formulate an individual identity and then to achieve a means to potentiate the discovery of their talents, personal temperament, and spirit.

"Amir speaks to me often about how pleased he is to have made a chance acquaintance with you," he said as we ate. "He told me he'll be making a trip to America to visit you after you return home."

We had never talked about it, but short of Amir hauling a dirty bomb through customs, I would look forward to it. Nevertheless, I played along. "I hope he will, and bring Bahlya as well."

"That's another story. She worries me. She passed twenty a few years ago and she's still not married." He followed this statement with a zinger, presumably the reason for the unexpected lunch. "She likes you. I can tell. I'm not a matchmaker, and I don't need to inform you she's a pretty girl. I'm sure you've noticed."

She's a damn knockout, for god's sake. If we're talking about her appearance, she's a sex pistol, accelerated through all the stop signs of my mind, the transmitted messages compressed, and then panted in three vacuous words, "Yes, I have."

"Zach, I'm going to do everything I can to stop this mixed up son-in-law of mine from taking away my daughter, and my first grandson too." Bahlya had explained to me a detailed story of her brother-in-law's plans to take her sister and the new baby to Syria, where his family lived. "Many years ago, I let my guard down and lost a male in our family, and I'm not letting it happen again."

"May I ask what happened?" I sensed he wanted to tell the story.

"Amir told you some of it. My cousin, who I loved as dear as my own brother, chose to get wrapped up in the battle against the Zionists and was killed. Months before, he met a lovely lady, a foreigner, and as you know, things happened… she was pregnant when he died.

"Zach, you'd have to understand us to know that when I vowed to look after the unborn child, it was out of reverence to my cousin. I might have made a mistake, looking back," Mr. Hamdallah painfully admitted, "because I refused to let his wife leave until I knew if the baby was a boy or girl."

I prayed I wasn't showing disrespect, but my emotions prevailed. I couldn't help snickering as I challenged him. "You mean if it was a girl you wouldn't have cared?"

"I can't apologize for how I was raised," Mr. Hamdallah responded without taking offense. "I'm a modern man, but I accept that there are Arab values deeply rooted in my character. Had it been a girl I would have supported the child just the same but not objected to the baby leaving with the mother."

"Well…what happened then?" I asked eagerly.

"Nothing. I never heard from the mother again. I have no idea about the boy who would be cousin to my children. End of story."

He paused for only enough time to let me know the issue was buried and his attention was on here-and-now matters.

"Back to what we were talking about. I don't know what to do about my son-in-law, but he's in for a war if he thinks he's taking my family away. Bahlya, on the other hand…well, if she wanted to live halfway around the world, if she were with someone who made her happy, I would endorse it."

His message was passed to me like a baton, with me assigned to run the last lap of a relay. I remember thinking I owed it to him to at least explain that I didn't have a steady job, but I said not one word. I was...stunned. Thankfully, he went on without wresting a response; he was a sensitive man.

"You think about it. And please, can we keep this between us?"

"I promise." I wanted to fall at his feet and beg his assistance. How could I handle a package like Bahlya?

I couldn't produce a word other than my pledge to not disclose what he had mentioned to me. The thought that raced through my imagination is another story. I might have candidly said, "Sir, I don't even know if I love your daughter, but what a ball finding out. Then again, she frightens me. I'll admit it. Well, okay, I'll do it, but could you talk to her and tell her that if she decides to become a teacher, she has to promise not to incite a class of eleven-year-olds to plot the overthrow of the United States?"

He took the opportunity of my company to free associate further about Amir and Bahlya.

"Both of my children still at home are good people. As you would say, they have their heads squared away. It will take them some time, but I expect they'll both find success. I don't know if you have read any of Amir's writing or looked at his artwork, but he is good. It's not an easy field he's chosen, and I don't think it wise to interfere on his behalf, because it's the public in the end that has to weigh the worth of creative material."

I made no attempt to disagree with his opinions and fortunately he didn't ask for my thoughts on the subject. He went on with his great power of insight, wrapping up with Amir. "He's a strong-willed young man. He had the best of education and he's determined, so I think it's only a matter of time; that's why I give him the leeway I do."

He smiled proudly before he turned his magic wand to his darling daughter. "Bahlya is another story. She has a gentle disposition and…really hasn't found her calling yet. If you ask me she's no different than most women her age and would as soon find a mate and have a family, though she never mentions it." He looked directly at me. "We'll talk more about it, I'm sure," he added with a wink.

Wedding plans? Bahlya had shut me down more times than I could count. Could I purchase a road test first? I wondered.

Mr. Hamdallah took me home after our tete-a-tete, me thinking about what I heard as a proposal, a sort of arranged marriage for Bahlya and me. I was quick to discover it was common practice for unions to be orchestrated in this fashion in Middle East countries. I was thinking about it all the way to first base, but wondered if Bahlya would agree.

*****

The afternoon following my lunch with Mr. Hamdallah, Bahlya came home. Amir had called and wasn't expected until the following day. I don't know if it was by intent—owing to Mr. Hamdallah's quest to bring us together—but he and his wife left for the evening, allowing my Arabian queen and me the uncommon experience of being alone. We ate dinner together and then sipped our way through a full bottle of wine, both of us cozying up to the kind of gentle mood only a moonlit, balmy twilight can evoke.

Even without Mr. Hamdallah expressing it, I had suspected her attraction to me. And mine for her must have been howling like a stormy winter wind. We reclined in the backyard patio on a double chaise—the precise piece of furniture I had fantasized many times sharing with her—laughing at things neither of us thought were funny, deliberating if we really "should" open another bottle.

For me, that lasted a miserably long time. Would a mere kiss be too much? I casually slipped my left arm around her shoulder—quite a move. She didn't object, but she looked at me…and that's when I realized she had flipped on her Arab side and I was staring at a foreign creature. I'm certain she knew what she was doing, testing me to see if I'd risk taking command or let her dictate the play.

It was that split second hesitation on my part that allowed her to stop me in a most unpleasing manner. "I suppose you want to talk about the near calamity at Hadecka's the other day," her referring to an outbreak of hostility between two of the students attending one of Hadecka's lectures.

Why she chose this inopportune instant to blemish what I was beginning to think might be the crowning experience of my trip to Israel, I couldn't answer. My hope was that she wanted to pick up where we left off in the changing room at the boutique, but without the saleswoman. It was about time she seduced her American guest. I saw only one chance for that to happen: put Hadecka in deep freeze.

"Forget it! Hadecka's lectures are the last thing on my mind right now," I asserted with a sip of wine.

"Well, it was scary, wasn't it?" she asked solicitously.

Fear? No. I needed courage. It was time for unfiltered, raw organic bravado. "No more so than outrunning Israeli armored vehicles."

"It's hard to believe you took it so lightly," she said, as if trying to tread gently on a little boy's ego that was about to be burst.

Give me a hand here, darling, I silently appealed in my mind. *Where's all the allurement, seduction, debauchery inciting fantasy of defloration?* It was all gone, stolen away like sight in a thick fog.

Did she have a precognitive insight that my destiny and hers were as ephemeral as the sunset we had put to bed together hours before? Did she possess this great awareness and the strength to act mindfully, heedless of the fact that I was working myself up to not giving a hoot? If recapping what had taken place at Hadecka's were to slow down my sexual thunder—if it was her defense against future regret—she couldn't have picked a better strategy. As she persisted bringing it up with greater force than I mustered to seduce her, my appetite for romance was deleted like listening to Peter, Paul and Mary singing, "If I Had A Hammer." The girl wasn't intent on breaking my heart, just icing my testicles.

Where was Mr. Hamdallah when I needed him?

We talked, talked, and talked about Palestinians, Israelis, and Arabs. In retrospect, I think it turned her on more than any method I had archived in my repertoire. Had I the courage to follow her lead that evening, instead of petering out in defeat, I might have found her obsession with politics to be the only means to her dropping good sense, and her pants too.

Is it possible the reason she was still a virgin—as Amir had assured me—was that no man had discerned all they needed to do to light her fuse was to pant red-hot blazing ejaculations of, "I hate the Jews, God punish the Zionist pigs, I'll kill every Israeli oppressor for you, oh yes, let me, let me, let me be your servant and I'll bring justice for your people," in her ear?

Such a fool she must have taken me for, instructing me faithfully on her brand of pre-lust stimulant for almost two months, only to discover she had picked a wood-headed dolt who couldn't fumble his way through the first step. If only I had known…

I recalled in college being handed a book by a buddy. He thought he had discovered the ultimate answer to being the Don Juan of our generation. For some reason, he magnanimously shared it with me. The key premise of the work was that there are an infinite number of secrets that can be used to excite the erotic drive of a woman, but every lady has only one chosen preference of her own, like her special and unique scent that is dispensed when she is ready.

The great author of that text suggested that the guy better read the signs or he'd be on that chaise lounge, a nitwit like myself, discussing lectures inciting violence by grubby, slovenly, brutes like Hadecka—if only, if only...I had the power to go back in time, she would have been tossing her clothes in the air, yelling to the man of her dreams, "You do it, get those damn Israelis, Zaci, wow, am I hot!"

Dr. Elmo Wilcox, author of *A Woman's Scent*—where were you when I needed you?

My failure with Bahlya that evening had set me free. I was ready to mosey on my way.

11

HOME ALONE

EARLY THE NEXT MORNING, I was surprised when I discovered Amir had come home sooner than expected but had to leave immediately on another two-day trip. He was vague but told me there had been an "emergency" that necessitated him coming home before he'd anticipated, but he'd be on his way again immediately—his schedule was becoming increasingly more erratic. Fortuitously, Bahlya had been called to help an ill friend not far away and would be gone for the evening and the following day.

I had a need to push it again with Amir, to get some idea where he was off to and why. "Amir, I have a great idea. I have nothing but time, and I think I'm close to having acquired what I need to start my work. I was considering a series of articles, each compelling the reader to be awaiting the next, like a television serial. Anyway, what I was wondering is if I could come along with you. I've not seen any of the other countries in the region. Where are you off to, anyway?"

This evoked another round of elusive embraces.

"This is important business. I wouldn't have any time to treat you the way I want to as my guest."

I had never heard him mention a woman, but I still had suspicions that he had a lover he traveled to see; it made more sense than any other explanation for his secrecy. By now, my imagination had graduated to the possibility of him actually having a family he supported in some far-off, or possibly close-by, land. I decided to raise the issue.

"You've made me curious. I'm thinking it has to be a girl. I promise, I won't tell a soul."

"No, I have no time for a girlfriend right now."

"Then you have to be traveling for one of your projects?"

"Of course," he said to quell any doubts on my part.

"I hope we'll be celebrating when you return."

He responded with what seemed to me like an omen. "September, my friend, I promise huge festivities." He closed by asserting, "At last, there will be vindication."

"Amir, are you sure you're not seeking approbation, rather than vindication?" I quipped, assuming he had erred, a rare misemployment of a word by him.

"I think we'll have both," he proudly proclaimed.

Later that evening, after Amir had left, Mrs. Hamdallah came down to the den where I was reading. She was all glammed up and ready to party with her hubby; they were off quickly, the lady of the house calling out haphazardly to the adopted son, "Zaci, take what you want to eat. Hibat is off for the night."

There I was, home alone. I felt like a real rich kid, house full of fancy, ultra-modern furniture, a kitchen flush with conveniences my apartment version would be intimidated to allow; trash compactor, center counter-level pop-up toaster on a touch-glass top, automatic can opener, knife sharpener, intelligent refrigerator—be nice or it refuses to open—warming drawer (an appliance I didn't know existed), built-in BBQ stovetop, wall-installed microwave and, the best for last, a dishwasher so quiet you could hear the purr of an idling Prius next to it.

I made a snack of hummus and crackers with a Hire's Root Beer—all this in Jerusalem—and in heavenly delight went to the balcony garden to see if I might dig deeper into my reading material. After about half an hour, I had to relieve myself and went to my room. As a guest I had nothing to complain about: my quarters were larger than the Ritz-Carlton provides dignitaries, plus daily room service and all the food I could eat; it was a bargain at zero cost per night. The bathroom was spacious, with a tub that might double as a lap pool if it was too cool outdoors to dip.

Upon exiting my room, an errant thought ran through my mind. Everybody at one time or another has impulses they may or may not act on, but ones that if they did, could alter their future course so radically they might rise to unimaginable success and esteem or flop unceremoniously into disastrous infamy, or even death.

I had been in the Hamdallah home as a guest going on two months, and my good friend Amir had never invited me into his bedroom. We had talked many times in the sitting area of my quarters but his had remained out of bounds. That was about to end.

I had no intention of doing anything more than taking a peek. I swear on the souls of any children I may someday beget that the compelling voice ordering me to go inside his room had no mission of prying into the privacy of Amir's life; well, not in a bad way. I solely wanted to take a closer look, to gather a few clues about a friend who was becoming a progressively more mysterious figure.

I did know what I was doing was wrong, but I venture to guess my ungovernable urge to take an uninvited visit to his room was one most people would have owned, and the majority acted upon; humans all have a dark side and need excuses to exercise its potentialities in relatively benign experiments, like sneaking around when the odds of being caught are negligible.

It was a nice room, about the size of mine. His bed was a thin mattress sitting on a frame about eight inches off the ground, covered by a white comforter with a wide, dark yellow stripe wrapping around the lower end of the bed; the headboard was wood but with detailed Arabic carving. The entire collection of furniture was matching dark brown, highly glossed hardwood, and included a large cabinet in the corner. The walls were white and the windows, which looked out to a neighbor's home, were covered with white shades thin enough to allow filtered light. There was a valence color-coordinated with the bedspread.

His domain was of geometric shape. Along with its neatness and precision, the room made a strong statement. Every item was in what seemed a prescribed order; odd for an artist, I thought. His desk, which also was of the same material as the other wood objects, was cleverly designed in that it was a large round table with two chairs but also accommodated several drawers and capacity for a printer and computer; off to the right was a file cabinet.

The two nightstands were cut low, and each housed a cast iron lantern that was tubular in shape and composed of dark red shades; they looked like giant candles. Mirrors dominated the walls, such that he could never lose himself in his own space.

As was the case with most of the house, his floor was hard-wood and covered with a Persian rug. I was never able to understand the intricate patterns woven into these beautiful pieces of art, but the one in Amir's room was unique for its octagonal shape—the pattern looked to be of various creatures crawling over the landscape, which was dominated by deep gold but with a multitude of shades of purple, brown, and rouge as well.

On his desk was a stack of documents. As I meandered about, I noticed the one on top had his name on the cover page. It was a script for a play, written in English. I picked it up, granting myself the right. I had already taken the leap—and that was the problem. Another human characteristic of universal proportion: we don't know when to put the brakes on our imagination. Once we take a first fateful step, we find the successive impulses indomitable to the power of persuasive entitlement as we convince ourselves that what we are doing has no potential for injury. We conclude, therefore, that it's not bad after all, or at least not improper enough to warrant ceasing.

I started skimming the first few pages of a story about a lawyer evidently morally conflicted after becoming convinced his client was guilty of the murder he was defending him against. It was mediocre in style and lacked reverence to the primal principle I understood for screen or playwriting—show, don't tell. I rated the piece no better than the work I'd read on the plane when I first met Amir.

I went on to examine the pictures on the wall, all reflecting unpracticed artistic methods and with the initials A.H. on each. Most of them were graphic with mechanical-looking themes, though I couldn't tell what the messages might be. They were cold and evoked no emotion or mood in me other than frigidness, and the colors and shapes were without unity or rhythm; generally they were elementary and without traces of the mental excitement and inspiration we reverently bow to in great painters.

I felt badly, not as much for the illegal entry to his space as the misguided direction of his life in terms of becoming an artist. I wondered if terrorism might be a better vocation for him, but my assessment of his work in no way compromised my appreciation of his graciousness and kindness to me.

It did discourage me from desiring further venture into his world. In fact, I was about to leave when one more time the same inducement to peek aroused me like a red light in a district of houses of ill repute is certain to excite a man's libidinal drive—this time it was a dark green calendar book on his desk.

What captured my attention was not so much what it might contain as why it would be there in the first place. Few under fifty use anything to organize dates and personal information other than an electronic device. So, I nonchalantly opened it.

Empty. I flipped several of the pages. Not an entry. That would have been it had I not reached July, specifically the week of July 2-8, which included what I knew was his birthday, July 4th—America's Independence Day. There, I noticed boldly written on the top of a page six numbers with several letters: R 45, L past 1X 81, R 27. That was the entire contents of the ledger.

Nothing suspicious to most people, but to a man who once researched home security systems and in-home safes for a thriller story he was writing, the sequence was a dead giveaway. One would think Amir might have employed better safeguards with the combination to his safe if it contained items of great worth; I assumed it was where he kept his jewelry and a few personal items. Curious George was irrepressibly in pursuit of an answer.

The problem was finding the thing. If one wonders what possessed me to make an unrelenting exploration of the room looking for a safe—the contents of which I had no knowledge of or reason to suspect finding anything of value—I was weaseling, but no way in heaven would I have stolen an item worth even a cent—I believe the initial answer would be instinct.

Beyond that, however, I was motivated to see if I could glean some understanding as to what secrets Amir had that he alluded to so often, as well as why he frequently disappeared, and where he went. It seemed innocent enough, especially given that I already planned for the near future to politely say adieu and be wished Godspeed.

Locating the safe was no easy task. If he had no worry that anyone would be seeking the combination, he was painstaking in his effort to make any criminal interloper work to find the booty. I nearly surrendered the search, and would have done so if not for the fact that I had to satisfy my urge to know that the number and letters represented what I suspected.

I opened every drawer, took them out to check what was behind them, inspected the wall behind every picture, lifted rugs, pulled at bathroom tiles and fixtures, searched around every article of clothing in the closet, and looked carefully at the air conditioning vents…for my efforts, the only rewards were a hidden box with a pair of women's underwear and a small baggie of pot in a drawer, all of which I left unmolested.

Then I noticed in the corner of the closet, near what appeared to be a storage area, a suit rack with a spot where the paint, otherwise perfectly clean, was slightly blemished; it appeared as if a hand had over time soiled it by rubbing repeatedly. I tapped around the area, but nothing happened. In so doing, however, I caught an acoustical disparity, a hollow sound where the soiling was, as opposed to the full, solid resonation one would expect to hear. I pushed instead of tapped. A large piece of wood paneling eased back without great exertion against a spring-loaded force. I angled it right and it slid about a foot, allowing access to the hidden treasure chest.

R 45, L past 1X 81, R 27; turn dial right to 45, then left past 81 one time, now spin it around again to 81, and finally back the opposite direction to 27. It opened like the puss of an alcoholic visiting the boys at Mickey & Minnie's Joint for Monday night football.

12

AMIR'S DIRTY LITTLE SECRET

WELCOME TO THE INNER world of Amir Hamdallah.

I estimated the interior dimension of the strongbox to be about a cubic foot, with two horizontal felt-lined red shelves that partitioned the space into three separate sections. Numerous items of jewelry were carefully placed on the bottom, and I quickly dismissed them. The second level was home to several items. On top was a thin file folder. I pulled it out, and the entire contents were two letters, both from a female, Ghayda—the woman Bahlya had mentioned to me. They were short, thankfully, because I would have never been able to report them verbatim. Still, I am blessed with a fairly sound power of recall, so the following is close to the original documents.

The first read as follows:

"Amir:

I don't understand you. We had so much fun on our dates, yet you show no manly interest in me. I hope my appeal is not a disappointment to you. Please don't get me wrong. I'm not the type who would ever jeopardize my standing in my family or in any way embarrass my parents by so much as a hint of promiscuity, but if one has amorous feelings toward another, as you professed toward me, there are subtle gestures that a woman will embrace no differently than a jewel presented as commitment to a lifetime of love and devotion.

I know you have spent many years abroad and may have acquired a more liberal attitude on these matters, and if this is the reason for your recent distance and coldness toward me, I would never behave unfaithfully to my beliefs, but I'm sure our talking would result in an understanding of our feelings that would translate into a working union for now and the future.

My heart throbs with yearning for you,
Ghayda."

The letter was touching; a lady's precious effort to tenuously balance what she believed to be two value systems by proclaiming there would be no action on her part to jeopardize her honor, yet at the same time courageously opening her heart to being broken. The first letter was dated April 22nd and the second was written only a few weeks later on May 14th.

"Amir:

I cannot write to you without admitting tears have drenched several prior attempts I have made over the last week to send you a note. I am terribly torn, between reproving myself for being such a fool and expressing my sincere understanding for why you never leveled with me.

I can't help but judge myself harshly for my unwillingness to see what was as obvious as a dark dove flying in a white flock.

Perhaps it is my age, a young woman searching for the right partner to spend a lifetime with, but I genuinely believe regardless of your inclinations, my heart and soul had bonded with yours.

My dedication and respect for you will never be compromised by what has now been confirmed beyond a doubt to be true. In our culture, the path you choose to follow might be terribly painful, and possibly dangerous, and I appreciate the extent to which you have, and likely will continue, to keep it a secret even from your dear family. I wish you and Faisal nothing but the best, and should you ever need to talk, I will always be a sensitive ear. God will bless, I know.

Your true friend,

Ghayda."

I don't make gay love, but I don't make gay hate either. It truly mattered not a whit to me what his sexual preference might be; he was kind to me, and that's what was appreciated. Then again, Faisal, a homosexual—he seemed to be about as effeminate as a torpedo. I spent no more time deliberating the theme, the letters having the effect to torque my spirit in terms of getting on with the rest of the findings in the vault, anticipating at last I would have definitive answers about where Amir was spending his time.

Under the first thin file was another much thicker version and under that, a rubber-banded series of pictures. I went to the latter first, several shots of Amir and Faisal during what appeared to be a trip to a seaside resort. Faisal was smiling like a boy who'd just forked a piece of cream pie.

The other file had far less effect on me. There must have been over a hundred copies of letters sent to prospective agents and producers. Each had attached a response, almost all similar in content. "Thanks for submitting your screenplay, *Legal Pad*. We're sorry, but it's not a genre we're interested in currently. We wish you luck finding a home for this worthy project."

These rejection letters were of no surprise to me, with one exception. The submission was to The Plume Agency in New York, New York. The response I'll share as close to verbatim as possible, not as a smug told-you-so boast, but instead because it seemed to have demarcated a turning point in Amir's career plans.

The letter, signed by C. Willard Plume, must have been received by Amir at about the same time as the highly revealing piece of information shared by Ghayda, for it was dated May 6th by Mr. Plume, and Amir's response to him dated May 16th, just after his dear friend scribed her "now-I-understand-why-you-can't-love-me-but-I'll-still-be-your-friend" letter.

"Mr. Hamdallah:

I sincerely hope my candid commentary will not be mistaken as anything other than an act of kindness. As you can understand, I am a very busy man, but by chance your screenplay arrived on a day our mailroom clerk was ill. In order to retrieve a much-awaited document, I went to sort it out myself. I couldn't help noticing your envelope—clever! I don't think I've ever seen a script delivered wrapped in maroon paper and bright pink ribbon with 'I'M REALLY HOT' embossed on the outside.

I was about to leave for a lunch meeting, but was a bit early. So, intrigued, I took out your work to review it. I'll admit to only having read twenty pages, and after doing so felt I would be remiss if I only sent a standard rejection letter. You can imagine, I've read thousands of scripts through the years and have a fairly good idea, regardless of my personal interest in one topic, genre, theme, or another, what has merit and what does not, which writers have talent and which do not.

Sadly, I would suggest you devote the immense energy and dedication it takes to produce an artistic piece such as this and find another outlet. We all have to find our calling in life, and I can only speak for myself when I say this is not yours.

That said I do wish you success in your life. I can tell you have a deep sensitivity to human issues and admirable imaginative resources.

Respectfully,
C. Willard Plume, President."

Amir must have been deliberating the point even prior to the bold yet compassionate letter by the agent and later having responded with a short note. After the letter from Ghayda, he no doubt was feeling vulnerable, and thus the two correspondences in rapid succession finalized his sentiments.

"Mr. Plume:

I take no offense to your blunt and well-intended criticism of my talents. For months now I've wrestled with similar concerns but lacked the courage to call it quits. Your words only validate thoughts I feared I would have to confront eventually.

Fortunately, I do have other interests and am presently dedicated to what may be the most important project of my life, one with profound importance for the Palestinian people; I'm sure time devoted toward earning a name for myself is better spent on my current endeavor.

Sincere thanks for your time and mercy,
Amir T. Hamdallah"

This material was sufficiently revealing and gave me several helpings of food for thought that would have been amply rewarding if the top section of the safe had contained nothing more than doodling. For my friend to be homosexual and a confirmed failure as an artist would have no influence on my assessment of him as a person. To the contrary, as I sat for a moment sorting out what I had just learned, I thought I understood him better, and that encouraged a greater generosity toward him.

I wish I could say it was deserved.

13

CAUGHT IN THE ACT

I WAS ANTICIPATING NOTHING Earth quaking from the still unexplored section of the safe. Assuming I was correct, I would therefore be wrapping up my clandestine operation shortly. My goal was to get back to the den. The room was elevated and a telescope had been positioned in a perfect observational post in front of a massive glass window.

I'd grown enamored of a toy I'd never had growing up. I had taken it upon myself to learn the stars of constellations such as Andromeda, Pyxis, and Aries. In fact, earlier in the day I had read an article about two large galaxies colliding in constellation Corvus. The core was described as a heart-shaped birth of new stars with pinkish-colored ribbons of cosmic debris streaming off both sides.

Why birth was intriguing me I couldn't explain. I knew my mom would be jazzed; she wanted to be a granny—even more so if the newborn was to be a star. It was a pristine evening and I couldn't wait for the adventure. But first...

I had come this far and felt compelled to reach for the top shelf, where a single thick folder I estimated to be four inches high rested like a napping babe. I was about to disturb the snooze of this seemingly benign packet, one in truth filled with millions of recluse spiders lusting to inflict their necrotic toxins on an unwelcome intruder such as myself.

That's when I heard a sound as startling as the effect anticipated by the insect's bite. I froze. Steps were tapping on the wooden stairwell. My heart leapt out through my throat and ran for safety. I was left short this most vital organ with a remaining head losing function as fast as oxygen burns. My brain was capable of no more than counting paces one by one, as I knew someone was getting closer and closer to discovering me. I literally fell on the floor, out of sight from the view of the partially open door. Now the movement paired with a perturbed voice. I quickly recognized it as Mrs. Hamdallah's.

"One of these days, I swear I'm firing her. How many times have I told her to turn off the damn lights?"

I regretted my lungs didn't have the cowardly nature of my tin heart to considerately abandon me because I was suffocating to near asphyxiation, fearful a molecule of air feeding my respiration would uncover me as the cheap sneak I had become. Still muttering about the absent culprit, a housekeeper who in the morning wouldn't hear a word about her dereliction, Mrs. Hamdallah reached into Amir's room to switch off the light and then close the door, with force equal to that with which she wished one day to punish the irresponsible maid and loud enough to mute my lifesaving exhale.

I heard her call out to me as if I were her darling, never considering I could be anywhere but my own room, "Zaci, honey, I forgot the tickets. We'll see you later."

It makes me teary thinking how much these people cared for me; they never understood just how close I was to them either.

I lay still, resuming my breathing and listening until the receding sound of the engine assured me I was once again alone in the house. Even after the near disaster, I was compelled to continue the covert operation.

I took the file out and on the top in large writing were two words:

TAKING REVENGE

I stared at the cover. Before I could even open it, my heart sensed drama and again it commenced to dash out. But this time I caught it at the mouth and stuffed the fraidy cat back. It began a tantrum. I was in no mood for disobedience and kept the sucker in place behind a locked jaw.

When I did open the file and looked at the first page, it made me want to cry. My gut tightened. I felt a sick, nauseating sensation. This was more than a dirty secret—it stank a worse malodor than all the sewer systems of the world squeezed together at the same time.

TAKING REVENGE.

Below were the numbers *9-11*.

It didn't take me long to contemplate what to do. The file was open on the floor with me sitting in front of it. At the most benign level, it was memorializing the horror to America of September 11, 2001. It was further a not-so-wholesome celebration in advance of what was being planned for a similar date in the future.

I began reading and never looked back. The content of the other files I'd found in the safe dropped status like a pedophile politician. As I delved into the reading, I noticed my thoughts knifing back and forth. One moment my timid heart would pound like a punk drummer stuck in blast beating as I ventured into material of unimaginable horror. Seconds later, I found license to dismiss as wild imagination a project that was to my estimation as loony as Jack's Magic Beans.

Indeed, was there some sort of magic at work? Was the explanation as to why I ventured uncharacteristically so far from home locked in a safe in a distant land over seventy-five hundred miles from home, waiting for me to discover it? Destiny. Fate. Divine organization. I never placed a bet on any of them—I never gambled.

Then a cautionary thought waved frantically to catch my attention. Given the nature of the material I had stumbled upon, the last thing I wanted to do was to leave any clue that I had made an uninvited visit. I knew that there were no cameras in the house but fingerprints were another matter. By some remote chance, if anything were to happen, I'd be fried.

I dashed downstairs to where I knew Hibat kept a box of latex cloves. I took a pair and put them on. Since I had thus far only touched a few sheets of paper from that file, I carefully wiped them to guarantee I left no evidence. Then I proceeded with the remainder of my investigation.

I had never heard the name Hamdi Jawiris until reading the first page of the file; I quickly appointed him "Master of

Doom." Amir referred to him as his "mentor," a term revolting to my taste, given my assessment of him as a monster.

For starters, I searched him out online and was able to discern that he was an Egyptian in his mid-forties, trained as a medical doctor at Harvard University Medical School. He then completed his residency in otolaryngology at, of all places, a Jewish hospital, Mount Sinai, in New York. After returning to Egypt he was involved in public medicine, at one point responsible for overseeing the entire health system in Egypt. He had traveled extensively throughout the Middle East and was acquainted with most influential dignitaries and businessmen. He openly professed his devotion to Islam first and the destruction of Israel second. In spite of his vengeful posture toward Israel and his sense of deep humiliation for the bruising losses inflicted by the Israeli forces on the Egyptians, I found no references to his being credited for or suspected of terrorist involvement.

Amir, for one, knew better. Jawiris had birthed a scheme of giant proportion but kept it in incubation in a laboratory of evil as he furtively solicited the elements required for a successful delivery. He needed money, hundreds of millions, and it took two years for him to raise the funds. From what I pieced together, Amir had been recruited first by Jawiris. Amir had the qualities Jawiris needed. He was highly educated and had a respected gift for intellect; he had financial independence along with the capability to travel extensively without arousing suspicion, due to his stated artistic career aspirations and family connections.

I believe there was other reasons as well, ones implicit in the notes taken by Amir. Jawiris was also the product of an extremely wealthy and powerful family. Like Amir, Jawiris bickered bitterly with his father. The junior Jawiris perceived his father similarly to how Amir judged his, in that the elder Jawiris also supported Sadat's vile decision to be "defrauded" into peace with Israel, an unforgivable sellout to all Arabs, in the opinion of both sons.

Hamdi never forgave his father. Their political positions were more severe than between Amir and his father—a point of departure in the backgrounds of Jawiris and Amir—in that the Jawiris men couldn't tolerate being in the same room together. A recent marriage to a much younger woman, now about to give birth to the first grandchild for Jawiris senior, had done nothing to ease the rift.

Early on in the correspondence to Amir, Jawiris promoted the lofty objective of the plan: kill all residents of Tel Aviv, Haifa, and several other small but important military, commercial, and manufacturing populations within Israel, effectively destroying the capacity for the remaining fragments of citizens to operate as a state. Then, as revenge for complicity, annihilate the populations of five major U. S. cities: New York, Washington, D.C., Chicago, San Francisco, and Los Angeles.

During my initial reading of this enormously evil intent, frankly, I fancied Jawiris a quack. I presumed anyone else beginning to peruse the material I had at hand would have concluded similarly. Sadly, he was not mentally unbalanced.

Amir was my friend. Sure, I was aware of his political ambitions and hatred toward Israel. But this went beyond anything I could have ever conceived. We had sailed together, spent evenings socializing, laughed at funny movies, dined, and played chess to pass time. I slept in a bedroom next to him. Now I had discovered that he was filled with more horror than a serial killer, and without conscience—he was willing to be party to an act promising to kill my mother. I went to the bathroom and threw up. But it was dry heaves and did nothing to relieve the sense of revulsion that had overtaken me.

When I sat back down in front of the file, I had no idea what to do other than read on. I was still hoping that along the way there would be evidence that I'd poked my head into another of Amir's fantasies, an outline for what he hoped might have been his first novel.

Jawiris' plan was scrupulously crafted into phases, with checks and balances as well as precautions he'd ingeniously incorporated to assure that last-minute sabotage would be impossible—he was the only person aware of all elements of the operation.

As my review of the pages continued, I finally came to understand how this egregious drama was to play out. I had several times second-guessed his method of destruction and concluded it had to be a form of nuclear explosion, but that was not the dandy choice of mass destruction this man had invented. Actually, I could have never anticipated his method-ology, even considering Jawiris' background.

He intended to use sound to create atomic explosions—and yes, when I read it I nearly laughed my guts out. On the surface, the project seemed like the vaporous product one would expect from a group of college freshmen intoxicated by billowing clouds of laughing gas wafting from smoking ends of Zig-Zag-paper-wrapped reefers. But as I read on and found that the file included actual published documents on the topic, not only by Jawiris, but also by his friend, a Dr. Efron, my condescending snickers ceded to sickened acknowledgment.

I knew Dr. Eyal Efron, professor and reputed genius in biological and chemical engineering, to be the husband of Lilya, the third Hamdallah child. He was the man whose remarkable history Bahlya, after the thwarted visit to Gaza, had recounted to me. He had been raised in an Israeli home and assumed to be Jewish. In truth, as he discovered much later in life, he had been adopted as an infant by an Israeli family. His biological parents had lived in the Golan Heights during the 1967 War. In the chaos of battle they were separated from their infant, and it was only by a most miraculous coincidence that his identity came to light decades later, by which time his family was all living in Syria. After the revelation of his true heritage, he vowed to leave Israel with his wife and soon-to-be-born baby to be with his biological family.

It was this intended act of taking a potential grandson out of Israel, to a country they would never be allowed to leave, that raised the ire of Mr. Hamdallah. Nevertheless, the duel advantages for Lilya's husband were irresistible. Eyal Efron—a man born Makrom Quteish of Druze heritage, a man up to his eyeballs in terror as a co-conspirator with Jawaris in a plot against Israel—could time his exit to avoid being present when the fatal attack was launched and at the same time reunite with his family of origin.

I couldn't believe what I was reading—I couldn't help not believing it either. Amir had expressed to me a fondness for his brother-in-law. No wonder. The papers I was about to read would shed light on the essential contributions Dr. Efron had made to assist Jawaris and the intimate working relationship between Efron and his brother-in-law.

As I read further, the early pages of the manuscript detailing how the plan was to unfold, I vaguely remembered stories either in science fiction movies or novels in which schemes to employ sound as a weapon had been entertained. More remotely, I recalled references in military journals describing research on using sound for crowd control, but I had no understanding of the physics of acoustics, nor how frequencies of waves or volumes of sound might impact the human organism, even to the point of death.

I was about to be educated when I had my second scare of the evening—talk about black cats. By then, it was around one o'clock in the morning. I had my light on for reading, with papers carefully ordered on the floor where I was sitting. Mr. and Mrs. Hamdallah were coming in from a late date. Mrs. H. had taken off her shoes so she could come up quietly and not wake me.

When she reached the landing and turned toward her room, down the hall from mine, she must have noticed my room illuminated and rightly assumed I was awake. In a half call and half whisper I heard her voice.

"Zaci, what are you doing up so late?"

"I'm catching up on some journals I need to look over."

"Can I come in? I want to show you something."

I knew she'd never open the door. Quickly thinking, I decided it would be my best strategy to tell her I wasn't dressed. Frantically, I began to put everything in a drawer, while calling out to her, "I'll throw something on."

"I'm dropping off my coat in my room and going down to meet Mr. Hamdallah for a snack," she sang back in what I read as a merry mood. "Come meet us when you can."

It wasn't unusual for them to be out late, but I couldn't imagine what she had to show me that couldn't wait until morning. When I met them in the kitchen, both were having a glass of milk with a piece of the cinnamon date cake I had sampled earlier in the day.

"Look at these." She handed me several photos. "My sister found them and gave them to me before the show."

I knew they had seen the Jerusalem Symphony Orchestra at the Henry Crown Symphony Hall in the Jerusalem Theater. I was fortunate they had accepted my refusal to accompany them. I'm somewhat of a lowbrow; Beethoven and Handel are great, but I soar higher listening to Eminem or 2Pac.

"How was the performance?" I asked as I scanned the pictures.

"Wonderful. We heard Handel's Water Music," Mrs. Hamdallah cheerily informed me.

"Actually, that's one of the few classical pieces I know well."

"Mrs. Hamdallah loves the classical sounds. Mostly I sleep," Mr. Hamdallah ribbed at his wife.

"I have had that experience as well."

"Stop it, Zaci…and don't listen to him tease. Besides, Hal, I'm sure Zaci's an expert on the classics."

Mrs. Hamdallah refused to esteem me lower than the high perch she'd chosen for me to rest. Plus, she had this innocent endearment, the kind you'd rather lie to than heartbreak with truth.

"Of course, I've seen my share of symphonies," I offered to humor her. "Now, what are these pictures I'm looking at, Mrs. Hamdallah?"

"Your friend with a couple past girlfriends at family parties," she giggled.

"Hasn't been out on a date for months. Does he ever mention a girlfriend to you, Zach?" Mr. H. posed the question more out of a muse than expectation of an answer. "He disappears often, and I'm certain he's taken a lover, but I'm not going to be the one to pressure him. I'm sure when he's ready he'll introduce us to her."

"He hasn't disclosed a clue to me," I stated, certain this was not the time to advise them that for the groom's party the knights would be suited, but the Hamdallah family would be buying a bridal gown for queen Amir.

"Well, I can't wait," Mrs. Hamdallah said excitedly. "It's time we have lots of grandchildren.

Mr. H. looked away. The comment by his wife aggravated the peevish matter with his son-in-law. I managed to manufacture a yawn, the perfect gesture to excuse myself.

"Both of you sleep well. I want to finish up my work and then get some rest. See you in the morning."

"She's a doll, isn't she?" Mrs. Hamdallah swooned, holding one of the snapshots for me to see.

"She's adorable, you're right," I agreed.

I wondered what Mom might have to say when Amir told her The Fang was coming for dinner. More, how was Papa going to deal with it?

14

TURNING UP THE VOLUME

I SCAMPERED UP THE stairs. I realized I desperately wanted to go home. That was before Jawaris' document further horrified me.

Unwittingly, I was about to take a plunge into an area thought by most serious scientists to be chimera. To Jawiris, however, it was an operational reality close to full beta testing, a weapon soon to be released with disastrous consequence. I'll do my best to summarize his approach.

Jawiris wrote that during the early phase of medical training he was intrigued by studies of soldiers found dead during World War I near an explosive site; shortly after that, he wrote a paper on the find, a copy of which was included in Amir's file.

"The controversy regarding the cause of the fatalities has never been resolved, the debate primed by the fact that these men suffered no visible sign of injury, whereas internally, hollowing of ear, lung, and gastric organs was observed. What is in question is not so much whether or not the blast itself

accounted for the deaths but what was the organic mechanism leading to their passing.

The theory most probable, in my opinion, is that lung embolisms developed from the blast pressure on the chest. As the lung tissue ruptured, there was admission of air molecules into the arterial pathways routing directly to organs, including the heart and the brain; most likely reaching the primitive brain stem medulla oblongata, which as we know controls many vital functions."

Studies had shown that this type of anatomical reaction would occur at sound levels close to 200 decibels, which is about the maximum possible. By way of sound comparison, a normal conversation is between 60 and 70 decibels, city traffic about 85, standing within a few feet of a power tool 110 decibels, and a KISS or Manowar concert tracking in the 135 range.

Jawiris, in the same paper highlighted a specific medical condition, one he had done research on during his doctoral training.

"Long QT Syndrome is not only life-threatening but can also be triggered by loud noise; syncope and then sudden death occur when an abnormally rapid heart rhythm resists blood being pumped to the heart, depriving the brain of blood and oxygen. Estimates vary, but it is believed to account for thousands of deaths each year in the U.S. alone, where most of the research is being conducted."

Jawiris' boastful handwritten annotation on the file copy proclaimed the number would soon be in the millions. Just to prove he was a cheery chap, he closed with a dose of his own humor.

"After 9-11, I think there will be more grants to study this condition than doctors left in New York."

The procreator of this plot was dead certain Allah was going to welcome him in person at the gates of heaven. While I lacked the sophistication to comprehend his approach by using the complex principles of physics needed to understand what he discovered, I would learn that the concept boiled down to blowing up canisters of highly compressed oxygen and nitrogen and then utilizing free atoms of these elements in the air to trigger repeated, sonic-like blasts lasting sufficient time to kill all humans within a one-mile radius of the site of release.

He referred to his method as an "atomic acoustical bombing," noting his plan was to set off as many of these as required to cover the cities identified; he limited the larger geographic urban areas, like Los Angeles and Chicago, to the core central city—what a sport.

Would it work? He'd written to his prospective backers in marketing his "business plan":

"I've already tested the method in enclosed laboratory conditions, and yes, with human subjects. The outcome was precisely as I anticipated. My next test will be in an open setting with a larger number of test cases. I'm certain we have an inexhaustible supply of volunteers, unlimited as the very molecules of air we breathe."

So alluring was this devil's handiwork that based exclusively on the preliminary results and his great esteem he was able to assemble a prestigious group of backers for the project. These were the people Amir was scuttling to meet periodically—answering at last where he was mysteriously disappearing to so often. He was also scheduled, from the time I intruded into his safe, to be coordinating the remaining testing, as well as assembling the numerous personnel required to execute the plan.

The silent sponsors of this demonic crusade constituted a prestigious team of individuals, collectively putting a vast wealth of resources and money at Jawiris' disposal. There were a total of six, and beyond dedication to their cause, they all shared common entitlement to a subscript after their name: billionaire. They also concurred in their commitment to an apocalyptic venture they believed to be obedient to god's revelation.

Pleasant dreams.

15

TAKE THIS HOME WITH YOU

AFTER RETURNING THE FILE to its safe hiding place, every piece of paper in perfect order, I went to my room and lay in bed for several hours. I still couldn't repress the urge to deliberate whether, by some slim chance, what I had discovered might be a pipe dream hatched by a clever doctor seeking euphoria by gifting himself heavy doses of a mega-amphetamine as opposed to a real attempt to definitively remedy the problems of the Middle East. I had no doubt it was the latter. My inability to sleep was solely the product of sheer terror.

One of the realizations that I couldn't get over was that Bahlya had no awareness of what Amir was doing. In fact, I concluded indisputably that there were two separate and totally distinct paths being followed by Amir: one concrete, verifiable, and without his sister (his project with Jawiris), and another, unsubstantiated and likely fanciful, with his sister (their claim of being terrorists for the Palestinians). When I went back over my own journal, charting where I had been each day and what events had taken place since my arrival in Israel, I noticed that indeed each of the times Amir had disappeared corresponded to a meeting he'd had regarding his duties for the project.

Bahlya's doubts about her brother and my suspicions were all well justified. His apparent lover, the monster Faisal, had to have been kept at arm's length from his involvement with Jawiris. Likely, many a spat between the couple took place with Faisal accusing Amir of unfaithfulness to a romance in some far-off enchanted land. Faisal's immediate enmity toward me may also have been due to him imagining Amir two-timing him with me, a fantasy Amir may have unconsciously nurtured in a lover who was capable of letting his mind venture far beyond what Amir ever would have wished.

The next morning, Mr. H. informed me that both Amir and Bahlya were due home soon—that was bad news. After I'd finally put the file back in the safe I realized that I should have used my phone to take pictures of each page. I didn't want to risk going back into his room that evening, and I was fairly certain I wouldn't have the opportunity the next day. My only choice was to employ my memory as best I could to retain the most critical facts.

Even so, I realized I had a problem. I couldn't sit in neutral, idling along, without taking some sort of preventive actions. But what options were open to me? Who would I turn to? Who would even believe me without proof? Is there a sane person who would not write me off as a prankster?

What I concluded was that I had to get out of the Hamdallah home and to a safe haven where I could think. How could I be in Amir's presence and not let on that I was aware of his role in this planned endeavor? I didn't trust my poker face—

I wasn't even sure I had one. Further, I assumed if I did slip up, if Amir became aware of what I knew, he'd turn Faisal's attention to yours truly like a laser beam intent on slaying a cancer cell; I was as seriously addicted to living then as I am today. No, I simply needed to invent an excuse to leave… that day.

I began packing. By the time brother and sister arrived home, I extended my sincere gratitude, explaining that I had spoken with my mother that morning and she was seriously ill, necessitating my departure as soon as possible. I expressed confidence that I had enough material to begin a campaign of some sort to support the Palestinian position in America. I had made a flight reservation for late that afternoon.

In addition to phoning the airline, I placed a call to Preston. I had an uncanny sense of needing someone to know I was about to make a swift exit. At the same time, I didn't want Preston to think I was in trouble, which I sincerely believed I was not.

"Preston, how's it coming along with the new love of your life you mentioned in your last email?"

"Who?" He laughed, assuming I'd have already figured out it was over.

"That was quick," I returned. "One of these days you'll run across a lady like the one I've just spent time with and then…"

"Don't disappoint me, buddy. The last time I recall a young lady putting a hurt on you was junior high school."

"I'm a grown man, Preston. I guess I'm overdue. I think I may have been played a fool but good this time. Honestly, I don't think she ever cared to do anything other than torment me."

"I'm sorry," he said with genuine condolence. "But if that's the worst, you'll get over it."

"It's not the worst," crept out of my mouth like bad breath. "But I'll leave that subject until I see you. I'm going to need some serious counsel."

"I'm at your disposal."

"Good. Now I'm getting ready to come home."

"Fantastic! Did I tell you I've missed you?"

"No. It's never been your style," I joked. "But I'll tell you it's not as much as I've missed you."

"I'll pick you up."

"Great. I'll send you my flight schedule after we get off."

"I was starting to worry about you."

"I've been staying with this family most of the time, but I have to leave immediately," I responded, knowing I was ignoring his concern because I didn't want to go further with my story. "I can't explain all the details now…I'll fill you in," I quickly advised him, wanting to move on to a preliminary plan I'd outlined before calling him.

"What I need is for you to promise you won't open an email attachment I'll be sending you later today. Can I count on you?"

"I don't like what I'm hearing, but sure, I won't open it."

I knew Preston to have a damn good scent about people in general, and he knew me like a song. I wanted to set him at peace.

"Listen. Despite the issues I have to deal with, I'm really great. I'm in one piece and plan to keep it that way. Just a couple of loose ends to take care of, then I'll be in the air."

"Did you call your mom?"

"Preston, there's nothing to be concerned about. Leave her out of this. I'll let you know if I need her. Trust me, okay?"

"I really don't this time, but what choice do I have?"

"None. I'll see you soon."

When I'd informed Amir and Bahlya that I was leaving, they couldn't do enough for me. Amir insisted immediately on taking me to the airport. Bahlya countered that she would take me. This resulted in a brother-sister tussle, one of many witnessed during my stay; this one easily won by the superior manipulative and girlish tactics of sister. What fun would it have been if the geniuses had concluded they both could have taken me?

There were a couple hours before we needed to leave. I took the time to thank Mr. and Mrs. Hamdallah, who unwittingly shamed me for my false exit; they were genuinely concerned and assured me that if I needed anything I was to call them and they would help.

I liked to think I had become like one of their children, but then again, after contemplating the monstrousness of what their son was orchestrating, I reconsidered and was singularly pleased they had acquired the fondness I trusted they both had for me.

Then something out of the ordinary happened. I was in my room putting a couple of items together for my trip home when Amir came to my door.

"Zach. Can you come here for a minute?"

I anticipated we'd go downstairs and talk. Instead, he motioned me to follow him into his room. I nearly panicked.

Why at this moment did he choose such an unprecedented invitation?

"Have you ever been in my room before?" he asked innocently.

"No. You've never invited me."

"That's strange, isn't it?" He seemed deep in thought, pausing before his next statement. "That was rude of me."

"It's nothing, really. You've been an amazing host." I punctuated my appreciation with a solid and unprecedented Arab hug. "I hope you'll come soon and visit me at my home, Amir."

"I have to ask you something," he posed while I contemplated why his body was tightening to my embrace. I sensed he was investigating rather than asking out of curiosity. "Have you ever visited Israel before?"

The question perplexed me. It wasn't that I needed to lie, for it was my first trip to this country. Was he asking because he didn't believe me?

"No, this is a first for me," was my bewildered response.

"Well, I hope you accomplished what you set out to do," he said, but with none of the lightness and warmth I was accustomed to from Amir.

"Since I had no agenda, I guess I did. I'm sorry I have to leave."

"Nothing is more precious than family. If you were my brother and I knew you were a traitor, I would kill myself rather than you."

It was the most bizarre statement I could imagine coming from him. I hardly processed it before I heard words flowing from my lips. "My mother is all I have. I see how you are with your family and I know how important they are to you."

I assumed we would have more time to talk if he ended up coming to the airport, or before I left, so I was about to dismiss myself and finish packing. Unfortunately, Amir had another question. I could tell he was troubled.

"You'll leave about two." He turned away from me but then glanced back in my direction as if adding an afterthought, one that nearly caused me to drop my load. "Oh, Zach, I had this odd sensation when I got home and went into my room. I noticed a couple of the drawers were partially ajar and my clothing in the closet was disheveled. I'm one of these orderly people, so—"

"Probably Hibat," I interrupted, cursing myself for the rapidly contrived indifference.

"No, she knows how I am," he chuckled to acknowledge his obsessive trait. "Okay, probably my imagination."

He seemed to be dismissing me, so I left. I felt like a crumb. At worst, I assumed he suspected me of entering illegally and it raised an issue of trust. That he thought I might have found and entered the safe was beyond my imagination. More than likely, he wondered if I had inadvertently discovered his stash of drugs or the underwear and was embarrassed. Still, now in possession of knowledge about the ruthlessness of this man, I was frightened.

I was the most popular person in the house that day. As soon as I got back to my room, Bahlya appeared. I had little time to ruminate on the talk with Amir, but I carried with me a sense of alarm, mostly owing to his questions about prior visits to Israel. Where was that coming from?

Bahlya wanted to talk "where we can be alone," and took me to the den. She had her own agenda of doubts, far more flattering than Amir's.

"I hope you're not leaving because of me."

"Why? You're sensational," I complimented. I noticed what I thought was a twinge of fright on her part. "Bahlya, I adore you," my choice of word reflective of not really knowing what to say.

"I think it's more than that between us." Her candor rendered me speechless, but it didn't matter. Bahlya was transforming in front of me, and in fast motion. "I know I wasn't fair to you."

"What are you talking about?"

"The other night. You know."

"I'm really not sure what you're getting at."

"Zach, stop being naïve. I've been a cruel tease all along." I tried to swallow, but my throat constricted. This was not the "girl" who had been toying with me like a pet—she was pure woman. "The car that day, on the way home from sailing, when I sat in a revealing pose, in the changing room at the store in my bra and underwear, and then the other night when we were alone on the patio—"

"You did confuse me." I was amazed she had catalogued every instance when she'd shot me down.

"It's because I was confused myself. I've been horrible." This was going to be a full revelation whether I was ready for it or not. "Zach, all along I've been fearful of what's happening at this very moment, you having to leave."

I noticed wetness forming on her corneas, and for the first time ever, her facial expression beckoning. We were sitting on a small loveseat, and to my astonishment her lips parted and I saw a streetlight flashing green. She was giving me my first "GO" signal. She took her own cue.

As if in slow motion, her face began a journey of only a foot, but the trip seemed like the infinity of distance in an eternity of time. Her eyes remained open as she voyaged, and I guess mine were too, because we were visually embraced until the final instant when her mouth locked with mine. Her arms, far more resolutely reached to pull me closer and then closer, the firmness of her breasts pulsing against my deep breathing chest left no doubt we were lifetime members of the "me Tarzan—you Jane" crowd and not the "me Neil—you Lance" order.

"When you come back or when you call for me to come to you, I'll be ready."

There was no restraint now. Her emotions were dancing off her sleeves like miniature angels from the Quran, tempting her to pardon the liberation her body was petitioning. I have no idea how far this carnal connection was destined to go, but the ticking wall clock reminding us that I had a scheduled departure was not going to terminate it. No, we would have lingered in intimacy, dangerously close to me missing my flight, had not a shout from down the hall abducted our clutching limbs.

"Bahlya, please come here for a minute." Amir's call sounded like a superior's order.

Bahlya looked perplexed, but after glancing docilely at me, as if experimenting with a form of obsequiousness foreign to her, she followed his request. I had no idea what had happened, but they were definitely arguing. I couldn't make out the words. The tone, however, was different from their usual playful banter. It ended with a door slamming.

Amir came out a minute later and casually announced that he would be taking me to the airport after all. It was a very peculiar last minute change of plans that did concern me—Bahlya had been victorious earlier when she argued that she would be taking me, yet there was no explanation why that was no longer the case. Still, I convinced myself I had no reason for angst, in that there was no way Amir could know I had found his safe.

Quickly, my bags were loaded into the car and off we went. My alarm bell started to sound softly when I realized the grieving Bahlya would not come out for one last tender moment with her charming beau. *Will there be a next time for Bahlya and me?* I wondered. I attempted to get an answer to my question while in the car with Amir, but I would soon discover his response was another lie.

"What happened to Bahlya?"

"She had to take care of something important for my mother."

"Oh, it seemed strange she left so abruptly."

He had resumed his typically jovial style. If his intent was to assure me all was well, it didn't settle right—not that it mattered.

"No, she said to tell you she's coming to Los Angeles to visit you."

Amir drove briskly. After that exchange he went mute.

I noticed he passed an entrance to a road that read "Tel Aviv" and wondered why he hadn't taken it toward the airport. Then, he pulled into a parking area in front of a store.

"I'll be right back. I have to pick something up," he told me.

I sat only a few moments before he returned carrying a wrapped package. He started the car and off we went. He drove a few blocks and slowed down.

"The tire feels funny. I better check."

He pulled over to the side of the road and then glanced over at me. His eyes were moist; similar to the way I had seen Bahlya's. He reached for me and I thought I saw something in his hand.

That's when I went to sleep.

16

ZACCHAEUS, THE ISRAELI SPY

TO THIS DAY, I cannot claim a full understanding of where I was taken. I believe I know under whose captivity I was held. I am certain where I landed differed from hell to the extent that I had hope of a finite end, death.

When I faintly dabbled with conscious awareness, I was lying on what I recall as a dirt floor, a burlap sack around my head and my feet and hands bound together tightly by a thin coil. My body was aching from the reduction of circulation. My mind was foggy from the effects of whatever substance had been used to render me unconscious for a period of time I could not begin to estimate. In my semiconscious state, I heard voices—all Arabic—and made out enough to understand that my jailers were anticipating my coming out of the drug soon and laughing about the joyous surprises they had planned for me.

I lay motionless, helpless to arrest the images of torture I must have crafted in my imagination in anticipation of what was coming my way. The visions flashed in succession, first at an accelerated pace, so quickly I thought them blinding, and then, as if viewed through a stroboscope, the pulsing began to slow, forming distinct pictures, each parading a short time in front of me, as if at a fashion show with the models on stage posing for an audience, but instead, in a theatre of the grotesque. With each reflection, I shuddered. I noticed the images, one followed by the other, receding like random-colored visual floaters dissolving behind closed eyes.

Each of the figments of my mental playground sadly proved to be prescient, mirroring the vicious treatment that the tip of a whip snapped on flesh would command to wake me to senses stored deeply in primordial hidden cavities of my soul.

The circus was about to begin. I was starring in the big tent.

My first imaginary tormentor had a fetish for teeth. He adored extracting mine, one by one with large pliers. The heartless monster tossed my incisors over his shoulder like worthless pebbles. All the while, I screeched a hideous sound I would soon recognize as one I was indeed capable of producing.

The sadist was dressed in a fancy white tuxedo shirt with red tie and red slacks. He surveyed my mouth, realizing he'd run out of ivory parts to play with. He casually picked up his sport coat that was sitting on a nearby chair, and while hold-ing it, took a bow to an invisible applauding audience. The stage was brilliantly lit. There was so much light that to look outward was blinding. Thus, whoever was appreciating the festivities was vaporized, as if swallowed in the sun's gaseous clouds. He stood next to me for a proud encore before turning over the stage to the next act, a magician.

The magus was costumed entirely in black. In my semiconscious dream state he presented with long, thin, pure white hand grabbing a club of smooth wood. He gently held the bat-like object up to display it to the seated fans and then rotated it so they'd be convinced they'd had an opportunity to examine it. He then pointed it toward me as I sat petrified, strapped to a chair that was tilted back at a sixty-degree angle.

He surveyed the situation. When he was satisfied that the bottoms of my feet were in the correct setting, outstretched toward the viewers, he sharply wrenched the club. That's when I noticed small nails protruding from the wood. He proceeded to smack the bottoms of my feet until they turned bloody. After several bludgeons, he flicked the stick again and the nails disappeared, such that the object looked once more like a smooth wooden stick. Boastfully, he motioned to my bloody feet. Then, he raised the bat, rubbing his hand over the surface to prove its inability to cause the lacerations I suffered. The crowd cheered him mightily.

The magician man was replaced by an electrician, one of those master craftsmen in the practice of slow-roasting human tissue and organs. I was hanging, my hands tied with a rope secured to an overhead hook, my body naked, and my mouth tightly shut with masking tape.

His pleasure was using an electrode to probe parts of my anatomy; his wish was no greater than to watch my eyes speak the same language a lobster might if he or she were capable to express how they felt after being dropped in a vat of boiling water. He was a cooer, toasting me like a toddler left exposed to burn in a boiling hot summer heat. At will, he employed his power stick to demonically discipline any random violations he invented on my part.

These grand visions—which I could no better stop than I could run a marathon on hot coals—gradually merged with a living sensation of extreme cold suffusing my entire body. This brought about the horrible awareness that in reality I had been stripped of my clothing. My stomach sickened, and I vomited on the floor.

My gut-puking act endeared me to my jailors. They were delighted that my awakening allowed them the opportunity to begin without delay my education in the real-world art of physical and mental pain. It started with several brutal kicks into my gut and groin. I squealed. Hearing my voice in such distress upset me all the worse. Since I couldn't see any of them, I had to rely on my auditory skills to count to three; triplets, each eager to get on with experiments in cruelty and degradation.

It was my thinking—if you can call the primitive symbols and sounds gasping for recognition in my head thoughts— that I must have overlooked something while putting back the contents of the safe. Amir had to have found me out. That being the case, I assumed I would be tortured first as a punishment for trespassing trust and then killed because of the danger I represented. With that in mind, there was no choice but to surrender to the hurt and hope it would end soon.

I tried to speak as little as possible. What purpose was there in trying to defend myself when I was known to be guilty? The few times I did raise a question or make a request, it inspired my captors to beat me more savagely. I quickly learned to give up on any strategy designed for leniency or empathy.

One may wonder why under such circumstances, where one knows they're going to suffer for no purpose other than to die, they wouldn't behave so as to force an early settlement, provoke the guards to lose control and overdose the brutality. I entertained that question numerous times. The only answer I could conceive was that the human drive to survive will, under any condition, employ hope that somehow a miracle might permit them to be spared death.

The convict sentenced to die and requesting to get it over with or the mental patient attempting suicide is acting out of no impulse other than to be saved. No man professing he wants to die is truth-telling, unless his sickness is terminal and he has reached a point of enduring pain where hanging on can only cause further harm and suffering to those he loves.

That's my two pennies on the subject; I believe my experience qualifies me as an expert up to a nickel's worth. So, while at times I could be heard groveling in pity and praying to be allowed passage from this life, sincerely I might add, at the same instant I could have just as easily been standing in front of life's giant wheel of fortune and, like every other sucker, hope for that one-in-a-million chance that it would land on my lucky number.

I think the first kick to the abdominal area was the most momentous act of abuse of any during my incarceration; it's the one I'll forever recall, for it acquainted me for the first time in my life with true humility. To helplessly receive an insult of this magnitude, to not be able to defend myself, to not even know who was inflicting the harm or why, to weep only to receive harsher treatment, to experience restraints preventing the natural impulse to reach out and try to protect oneself from further injury, that is a degree of degradation demanding one to question how it's possible that those who impose mistreatment on others are often the very ones who have had the worst abuse inflicted on them.

I can attest to the fact that it is not an experience of great transcendence, one a person wants to share with others, and thus accounting for a person repeating the savagery they themselves suffered. The guards who were mistreating me had definitely been victims of the same type of behavior, making comments to that effect as they invented new atrocities to test on me. In fact, it was through a few inadvertent statements they made that I was not only able to prove the point that they had been violently manhandled but also to understand why I had been taken prisoner in the first place.

Early in my confinement, Jaber, by far the most brutal of my initial jailors, was punishing me. As was often the case while I was beaten, he had worked himself into a thick lather. He started yelling at me. "You fucking Israeli bastards think you can torture me and I'll forget?" He screamed frequently and seemed to have inhuman endurance when it came to assaulting me. "You're a lousy spy, Israeli spy, and you'll die for your crimes!"

His words inspired him to remarkable acts of vengeance. While he was working me over, I snuck a short break to contemplate how I had been deemed a spy for Israel. He had no interest in my quest for order and logic, continuing with some of his favorite tricks. What he liked best was having me sit in a squatting position for hours on end. It was impossible to sustain this. Usually, he would call in one or two other prisoners, ones I learned were actually Palestinians accused of conspiring with another faction, or worse, with the Israelis. He'd position these men close to me and instruct them to watch and wait. The first inclination I showed of falling required them to begin attacking me.

It has to be revenge that induces a person to do unto another what cruel things have been done to them. The experience made me wonder, had I the opportunity to pay back the tormentors for what they took from me, would I react in like form? There is an awful anger that seeds in the soul from that type of torment. If allowed to mature, it could easily evolve one into a repulsive and repugnant animal—I'm grateful I've not since been put in the position of exploring those parts of my being.

The cell I was kept in, worse than a dog cage, was small, and I was only taken out of it for more elaborate forms of mistreatment. With very poor ventilation, and due to the outside heat, the temperature inside was stifling. Most of the time, I was kept in the dark, and it seemed my abuse was administered at all hours of day and night; I lost complete track of time along with the number of days that had elapsed.

As the period of my incarceration advanced, I began to have an entirely new type of experience. It gradually entered my awareness that these transformative "trips" were rooted in my stay at the Hamdallah home. It had started one evening when I was alone in the den at my host's home. I was gazing out, through their telescope, billions of miles past the night sky of Jerusalem. I had dabbled with the toy on several occasions prior, but during this particular exploration, I was launched into a vast and infinite world with no dimension or signpost other than what looked like a star I had never noticed before. It was at that moment of wonder that I first spawned a fondness for the idea of space travel—thereafter, I'd visit the room as often as I could, and these excursions became an infatuation.

I believe it was during the first week of my confinement that a sapling emanated from that incipient concept of being able to voyage willfully any place in heavenly space I wished. Under confinement, that skinny sprout would grow into an immense trunk with giant branches reaching beyond our universe. I first climbed upon these strong, powerful limbs and then used them for launching myself to hitherto unknown realms of eternity.

At the time I didn't comprehend the potential for what I had begun, but as the exercises in travel continued, I soon came to understand that I was being instructed on the vast adaptive capacity of the psychological survival instinct. Initially, it was a realization of being able to distance myself from my physical and mental processes, as if I were a guru capable of travel to distant planets in an instant of time, leaving behind any relationship to normal connections in reality. During these detachments, I lived temporarily in a dream state from which I could drift into or out of, depending on the tolerability of the events unfolding in the cell.

One of my most favored excursions was to an imaginary planet I credited myself with discovering while first using the telescope in the Hamdallah den. I was charting the stars, looking for some of the constellations, and fantasized there was a land at the outer reaches of our solar system that had never been identified.

Amazingly, while imprisoned, I rediscovered this identical wonderland. It proved to be the planet most similar to our earth. More astonishing, its inhabitants were capable of speaking, hearing, smelling, touching, and feeling. I might one day write an entire story describing this marvelous land, but for now, it will suffice to note that the creatures on Zmyvs differed from earth humans in a single fundamental and life-altering manner: they had never conceived of god.

This vastly impacted their lives, most notably in that they had never fought a single war. In fact, while I related successfully with them on many topics, these deprived souls had no language to even conceive of what war or killing would be like.

Oh, I did my best to have them comprehend what I was talking about, but all for naught. To make matters worse, they showed no interest in my persistent attempts to find common symbols describing the cruel, inhuman and violent acts we on earth routinely enjoyed, ones I explained as having many benefits, not the least of which was controlling population growth. There was nothing I ever did that could convince them they were missing out on something better than pastrami on rye.

Perhaps the most confounding manifestation of godlessness was that these people knew as little about their own mortality—and they did die, no different from us—as war and killing. How is it possible, I quizzed them repeatedly, to cope with death and the vagaries of life mounted to the future like diamonds in a bezel, without a supreme power, without a force greater than their collective mass and greater still than the whole of the energy in the universe? They laughed, not to mock me but rather because they had never thought of such a bizarre idea.

The inhabitants of Zmyvs were not ignorant fools either. The seniors immediately recognized I was schlepping with me painful concerns and fears about dying, and without a means to lighten my load—they wanted to help me. Here I was worried they might see me as unsuitable to their population and refuse my landing in the future. But they had no punishment for my derangement—only compassion.

These friends, and that was precisely what they were, worked as hard trying to ease me of my suffering and worry as I did trying to explain to them that most of my fellow humans on earth would argue they were depriving themselves by not embracing god—as many as they could dream up if they liked. But in the end, they failed to impart to me the peace they achieved so effortlessly on their own.

Whenever I visited these people they welcomed me and, recognizing I was hurting, attended to me kindly and lovingly. Never did they attempt to proselytize. They preferred to do what the wisest of psychologists knows as the only effective therapeutic approach—they provided a healthy environment of honesty, trust, empathy, and respect to facilitate my growth and rehabilitation.

Every time I'd land on their planet, I would get a dose of their simple blend of humanity—I was addicted. I thought nothing of traveling millions of light years for a touch, smile, or caress, never calculating the fuel costs. Each time I'd return to the torment of my cell, I couldn't help wondering if our version of mankind hadn't made a single, fatal turn—simple as that. I know my opponents, including the masters I now owed every second of my suffering existence to, would sit in council to conjure new methodologies of cruelty toward me for the slightest mention of the heretical idea that man has erred in his orientation to faith.

I'd endure worse still if I mentioned that consideration be given to at least voting on one god only, a singular entity capable of whitewashing hate and killing from man's conscious- ness. I was certain this would warrant a little trip for me to Milton's Pandemonium, the wild and crazy deeply buried den designed by Satan to punish the lives of evil humans.

Bonkers again? But my circumstances entitled me to dream a little dream of goodness—without paying a penalty. And no, I had no sense of psychosis. For me, fantasy and reality were well demarcated.

What was in my possession through this new hobby of time and space travel, however, was a process of escapism. I had cultivated a way to access a pump handle that allowed me to draw at will from an archaic well of psychic waters a means of protecting myself from insanity, enabling me to cope with conditions not only intolerable but destined to otherwise produce madness. I'm doubtful my jailors understood intellectually that their torment easily reached a point where I would have no choice but to escape to this narcissistic cavity. However, I believe intuitively they sensed my capacity to disappear and this fueled their uncanny tact to randomly deliver the pain-infliction sessions.

Thus, at unpredictable intervals, after I would make return landings to earth, reclaim my heart and mind, reacquaint myself with the aches of my head, limbs, torso, feet, and hands, and relive the tears and fears of what was happening and what would happen to me next, with no real hope of ever seeing my mother or my friends again, they would begin tormenting me. The latter idea of forever losing the love of those intimate to me was dreadful. I noticed that even during the times I reconnected to the key elements composing what I call "me," I stopped thinking in terms of any of the matters familiar to my personal life—it was too painful.

My thoughts consolidated around those pertaining to bodily sensations of hunger, fatigue and pain, and mental experiences classified as depression and anxiety. I noticed my appetite receding, as if my esophagus was choking off admission of nutritional matter to my stomach, the latter aching endlessly with spasm, cramping, and nausea.

Sounds? At all hours, they would be hideous in amplitude and tone, their only redemption being that they assured me I was not the only victim of abuse in this non-anesthetic institution. I would hear screeches, shrieks, and the guttural rasping of a voice hopelessly pleading before dying out like the speechlessness of an aphasic.

I was not alone.

17

A NEW FRIENDSHIP

ONE DAY I MADE AN astonishing discovery. While listening to one of my prison mates being tortured, I heard something different from any of the other noises. It seemed the sound was oozing into my cell like air thrusting through the slot of a whistle.

I began pacing on my knees around the small space like a dog searching for his bone. Finally, my ear found the origin of the intruding shouts and screams. It was a tiny circular area about the size of a dime at the base of the wall. As I inspected it, I saw something I'd never noticed—the dirt was loose. As I crouched down and touched it with my finger, I was able to brush some of the particles aside. Then I gently blew. As I did, more material scattered out of the hole. With only a few more shots of air, the hole opened so that I could see slight illumination from what I assumed correctly to be an adjacent cell.

I waited until I was sure there were no guards around. I put my mouth to the hole I'm sure the prior tenant of my quarters had worn his fingers drilling; I whispered through to the other side. It was silent. I offered a "pssssst" sound to try and attract the attention of anyone imprisoned there. I heard what I thought was a cough. It was definitely a human sound coming back my way. My excitement equaled discovering a vein of gold.

"I'm Zach. I'm an American. Who are you?"

"Adar," he whispered. "I'm an Israeli. I'm a soldier."

"What are you doing here?" I asked.

"You don't want to know."

"Please, let's talk. I need to hear a friendly voice," I pled.

"Okay, but it's unbelievable. We were working on a project to bring the Israeli and Palestinian children together. You know, a program to teach tolerance rather than hate." The cynicism in his voice was unmistakable. "The youths had been working for weeks together, planting a huge vegetable garden just outside one of the settlements." Adar went silent for several seconds.

"Why did you stop?"

"It's pathetic."

"What is? Please go on."

"The children were having fun. They got along as if there was no hostility between our two groups. Finally, there was an abundance of ripe food and we were preparing for a feast. The children and their parents were all scheduled to attend. That morning all the Israeli families showed up, but there were no Palestinians."

"Why?"

"The parents refused to attend or to let their children come. Then, for extra insult, they started launching rockets. I don't know how many civilians were injured or killed, but there were three army vehicles, and I was in one of them when it blew up. I guess I was taken prisoner."

"I don't understand," I said, uttering an inane response because I really didn't know what to say.

"If you lived here you would," he said caustically. "The Palestinians will never give up the hate. They won't take a chance that their children will grow up without it."

I didn't want to distress him further by mentioning what I had witnessed with Ramzi. Besides, the story he told was so disconcerting all I wanted to do was change the subject. It highlighted in my mind, however, that my prior pledge to be impartial and complete my research to get a better grasp of the Israeli position as well was essential.

"They're mistaking me for someone I'm not." I blew the words through the hole to him, foolishly thinking he might be able to give me an explanation for the bizarre imputations made by my jailers. "They keep telling me I'm an Israeli spy."

"Are you? You can tell me. I hate these Palestinian bastards."

"No. I told you, I'm a writer. But, I discovered something I have to get in the hands of the Americans or Israelis."

"That's probably why you're here," he reasoned.

"No way. They would have brought it up by now if they knew; and they would have killed me already."

"Good luck getting it out of here," he said despairingly.

"I'll tell you everything. Then, if you make it out you'll be able to do something with it." I urgently shoved my hushed words through the tiny life tunnel. "Millions of people are going to die soon."

I was awaiting a response but instead I heard a door slam and then yelling. I pushed some of the soil back into the hole to block any light coming into his cell but could still hear loud voices and then screaming. It lasted an endless period. Finally, I heard my new friend, Adar.

"They kicked my teeth out. I'm bleeding all over. They're animals," he whispered tearfully. After a break lasting an eternity, I heard him again. "Tell me the story."

"Okay. Remember the name Amir Hamdallah. In his room is a safe and inside is a folder with details of a plan to kill people throughout Israel and five American cities."

"They're trying all the time. We can defend ourselves," he said proudly. "Don't worry."

"You don't understand. This is different. Have you ever heard of names like Rami Majeed, a Syrian, or Ali Halaby Laylaz, an Iranian?" I queried him.

"Yeah, the Laylaz name. He's some super-rich Arab."

"Adar, these men and several others are backing the plan with hundreds of millions of dollars…"

"What's your name?"

"I'm Zach, Zach Miller."

"Zach, just hearing a friendly voice is like a treasure to me. I don't want to offend you, and I can't laugh because it hurts too much. You must have some drugs in there."

"I don't do drugs," I assured him.

"The way you're talking it wouldn't surprise me."

"Sorry to disappoint you, but the answer is no. Anyway, I'm not a scientist, but I checked out the research. The method they're planning for the mass destruction can work. Just hear me out," I pleaded.

"Okay, go ahead. But if you're holding out on me and have a joint I'm going to be pissed."

"No drugs," I repeated. "I lived with Amir for months and never knew the evil he was up to."

"That's how these Arabs are, Zach. You think you know them, but you never do."

"You have to get out of here. The mastermind of this scheme is an Egyptian whose name is Jawiris. I'm going to give you all the names and you can memorize them like I have."

"Is there a date?" Adar asked.

"Yes. That's why it's urgent. My mother is going to die in Los Angeles."

"I'll try to send her messages."

"How?" I asked with astonishment.

"Telepathy. You understand?"

"I hope it works," I said dubiously. Then, to add to the absurdity, I informed him of my hobby. "I've learned to space travel. When they torture me, I leave my body behind and go to this planet…"

I noticed myself laughing, anticipating his reaction when I told him about these wondrous people I'd met. But before I could begin sharing with him my adventures, I heard him frantically whisper.

"I hear someone at the door."

I plugged the hole again and waited. I heard nothing for quite some time during which I shuddered at the thought that the distance between life and death was no more than a single pulse of the heart: I counted mine ticking.

Hoping I'd hear from Adar soon, I contemplated the four walls of my cell. I counted the number of tiny grooves left in the mud barriers of my home. The shoddy craftsmanship of the contractor who had erected my square box enclosure with uneven sides would have been evident to a child.

For some reason, the walls, dirty, thick and splattered with what I humorously considered the designer having prided himself for his faux technique, stood out to me as a sign of perverse culture. They incited laughter; even if one used all their imagination, they could not conceive of such an ugly a space.

As I lay waiting, I loafed into a moment of wry conde-scension toward my keepers. Just then, my door screeched in worse pain than I myself was used to experiencing, taking a nasty bang as it flung open. My guard must have heard me; unconsciously I'd been giggling. He entered peeved, thinking there were still lessons to teach me, but all he did was scream at me, smack my face several times, and kick me in the balls.

He rushed out and again whacked the door closed, so hard it produced a whanging sound that vibrated for several seconds afterward. It was then I had a breakthrough—I knew I had won. I was no longer afraid, not of them, not of dying, not of anything, and it was then that I knew they were not ready to kill me.

The experience of his rushing out and my momentary sense of empowerment must have excited my mind. I thought of one of the first times with Bahlya. One of her haranguing sermonettes on how Israelis were abusing imprisoned Palestinians came to mind.

"They're holding our people illegally in over two dozen prisons in Israel, outside Palestine, and therefore in violation of international law. These people were placed on trial by military tribunals but without legal defense…and guess what? Every single time they were found guilty. Usually, there were signed admissions, but these confessions were extracted after the prisoners were tortured.

"Within prison, there has been continued abuse documented in the form of shackling, deprivation of food and water, beatings, threats of rape and attack by dogs, threats of retaliation to family members, and long periods of isolation. These Palestinians are often held without contact with family members and without anyone knowing their whereabouts for months, even years."

This hardly differed from how I was being treated.

The noise returned to Adar's cell. I heard commotion and loud voices. My limited Arabic made out the word "dead." It was repeated several times…I knew I had lost my last friend in the world. I wept like a child. When my eyes were dry, I screamed insults until I collapsed on the filthy floor.

18

THE RETURN OF THE FANG

WHEN I CAME TO CONSCIOUSNESS, several pictures of decapitations were lying on the floor. This photo exhibit had no doubt been orchestrated for effect, timed to the opening of my door. I looked up. I froze in horror. I was staring at Faisal Alawi, Amir's colleague and lover. In turn, he stood glaring at me.

It was obvious he wasn't in a talkative mood. I judged it a bad time to assure him that, while I would have taken barium enemas for a week straight to sleep with Bahlya, romantic fantasies of Amir were as appealing to me as soaking my underwear in kerosene and torching it—while on me.

"You can save us all a lot of trouble by telling us why you are here. I'm not going to spend much time on this, and you will not have unlimited opportunity to answer. Keep in mind that neither Amir nor Bahlya will be permitted to see you again and neither can do anything to help you. Now, make it easier on yourself and tell me what you were assigned to do."

I thought of disclosing to him about the safe and explaining how sorry I was, that if he let me go I would never tell a soul.

However, I realized again the stupidity of that approach. Nowhere in Amir's notes had there been any mention of Faisal being involved. It was not only that fact convincing me Amir hadn't divulged to him the program he was working on with Jawiris. I specifically recalled one time overhearing an argument between Amir and Faisal regarding one of Amir's spontaneous trips. Faisal was irate that Amir wouldn't tell him where he had been. No, Faisal knew nothing of that matter.

There had to be another reason my imprisonment was sought. Still, I had no answer, other than to imagine that it was nothing more than envy on the part of Faisal, who mistrusted me and wanted me out of the way, or that I had genuinely been mistaken as an Israeli spy with an agenda harmful to his interests. Instead of answering his question about what assignment I had been given, which I knew I couldn't, I followed with the only statement that seemed logical.

"You know what I was asked to do. Amir and Bahlya wanted me to use my writing skills to represent the Palestinian ca..."

That was as far as I got.

"I'll be back to give you one more chance. I hope by then you'll be in a more candid state of mind."

Faisal turned and walked out, motioning to the men to continue abusing me.

The torment began again, this routine commencing with my head being pushed down repeatedly into a bucket of water until I nearly drowned, my chances of survival mitigated by the fact that my tormentors were amateurs and could have easily erred and killed me. Other perversions I would prefer not discussing followed. I journeyed often to far-off lands, leaving behind the agony I would have endured had I not.

During the phase between Faisal's departure and his later return, I had no idea how many hours, days, or weeks were subsumed in torture. At times, I felt that I was beginning to lose the most vital ingredient I needed if there would be any chance of survival: my identity. There were stretches of time when I couldn't recall my name, where I came from, who my mother was, who my friends were—I laid prostrate for vast periods, trying to recite my address, cell phone number, or who won the last World Series.

When I did occasionally grasp a crumb of what comprised the person I thought I had been, I would repeat my discovery over and over, thousands of times, as if cradling an amulet that protected me from death by evil spirits. These were the most distressing times, because the vessel I used to escape on cosmic journeys would vanish. My attention would be sucked up by the whirling vortex of my missing self, and without my identity, there was no purpose in leaving.

How terrifying is it to lose one's sense of self? One would have to imagine the passing every relative and friend they had in their lifetime, all in a single instant—the force of suffering is greater than that. It makes facing death seem like floating on a cloud on a cool, breezy day—it's the nearest equivalent to being dead that humans can experience without actually dying.

Needless to say, once I confronted this phenomenon, my energy increasingly focused on retaining "me" at all costs. My mother was particularly critical. I associated myself with her, such that at times I could talk to her and hear her voice. While I still had awareness that she was not there—I was not hallucinating—these sessions with her reinforced my tenuous sense of being alive as a unique being, with a history and specific earth address that distinguished me from all other people.

Oddly, I must have repeated my social security number enough times to be awarded a medal of honor from my government. The United States of America would never have to worry in the event I suffered permanent impairment from my confinement—I'd still be able to pay my taxes.

Kaye Miller. The sound sweetly spoke to my being a member of the Miller family. I was Zacchaeus Miller, a person. My childhood came under inspection and I cried and cried. I had been a happy boy. I'd felt secure and full of confidence. I'd had energy, vitality, curiosity, and intellect; I'd had imagination for Christ's sake. I could sing from atop the moon at night, sprout wings and fly with birds, live in the sea and play with dolphins, and perform feats of strength greater than Batman. It was so fine a life. I saw no logic in it ending so abruptly and rottenly.

Where was my mother? Where was Preston? Where were all the people who cared about me and had to know by now that I was missing? Was it possible they couldn't find me, that my ego had diminished to such a tiny proportion I was now invisible?

Familiarity with my past, harmonizing with the vice my captors kept tightened about my being, at times cracked me like a walnut, broke me down to a puddle of divorced molecules of liquefied humanity evaporating from the dirt of my cell.

Each time, however, I crawled and scraped, did anything necessary—with determination I could never have known a human capable—to fight back.

Bahlya was one subject that came up repeatedly. My hope was that she loved me and it would be she who would come to my rescue, and then we would go off merrily ever after. Would she be able to plead with Amir and Faisal for my release? That possibility tightened my grip on the elusiveness of prayer.

Faisal Alawi did return. He came armed with a small folder, throwing it on the ground along with a thin jacket he took off as he entered.

"If you want to save your life you'll start talking now."

I knew he was lying.

19

FAISAL—HALF OF THE TRUTH

"FAISAL, I HAVE NOTHING TO tell you other than what I tried to discuss with you last time."

He picked up the file, staring at it. "You think we are all stupid just because we are Arabs? Is that it with you fucking Jews?"

He bitterly smacked the folder across his opposite open palm, his dark skin concealing the blood no doubt dashing in the opposite direction as if halted by a stroke.

"They even tried to conceal you years ago. We have our spies too," he sneered before pausing. His hideous eyes stared at me to let the point sink in. "That's right. How many times before have you infiltrated…Mr. Ashrawi?"

This was the first time since my imprisonment had begun that I wondered if maybe I was going crazy. I didn't recognize the name Ashrawi as mine, but I wanted to agree, to embrace it as a part of me.

My mood and emotions were swinging like a pendulum and when weak, I might submit to anything that would possibly afford me an advantage, an extra few moments' sleep, another spoon of broth. I was in that dangerous state as he mentioned the name, and the more I deliberated the more familiar it seemed.

"Ashrawi, is that it? Yes, that's me…I think."

"But your file has the name Miller. That's your name, too, isn't it?"

"Well, I think I'm Miller. Yes. Could I be both?" I answered, genuinely dumbfounded.

"You are both. It says so on the file at the Israeli ministry. It says Miller and in parentheses, Ashrawi. Your file is understandably sealed and has been for some time. Only those at high levels of Israeli security would be able to see the contents," he smirked. "But obviously you know all that, right?"

"I can't remember for sure. Can you give me a minute to think about it?"

Faisal was not patient, smacking me for the first time. The heavy gold ring worn on his middle right-hand finger grazed my left eye, causing a profusion of blood to pour onto the ground below me.

"Don't toy with me, Miller, you bastard. Now, who is your contact at the ministry?"

"I don't know if I have one. I came here for a vacation."

"You are angering me, Miller, Ashrawi, whatever the hell your name is. I'm going to give you one more chance. Who is it?"

"I don't know what ministry you are talking about, really, please, I don't."

This was not what he was looking for. Faisal pitched invectives at me like an annuity salesman, before lancing me with a familiar name.

"It's Zev Feld, Zev Feld, Zev Feld. Should I say it again? Zev Feld, Zev Feld, Zev Feld!!! You really play me for a fool, and I don't appreciate it. Are you denying you met with him, called him twice in addition, since you began your stay at the Hamdallah home?"

Of course I knew who Feld was, but what difference did it make to Faisal that I had called him? He was a friend of my mother's. But I recalled my mom telling me to call Feld if I had a problem, so I excitedly suggested it to Faisal.

"Yes, Feld. Can we call him? He'll be able to clear up this matter for you in no time. He knows who I am. Yes, I'm Miller, Zacchaeus Miller. That's my name. My friends call me Zach, and a few who adore me call me Zaci," I said like an eager child.

So possessed by the insight, beaming from a perceived return to order, sensing well-being brightening my cheeks and feeling the flow of juices throughout my body, I boldly— proudly—shouted like a superscription on a legal document all that was left of Zacchaeus Miller, "Yes. I am Zacchaeus Miller!!!"

Faisal had retained the roughness I would have expected from the brutish type he was, but after my outburst he showed a side I had not anticipated, a part of himself I would have bet against him even possessing.

He calmed and put his arm around me, comforting me like a babe. I panicked at the thought of being a free-of-charge sexual treat for The Fang—I could only pray he wasn't interested in reaming me raw. Fortunately, that wasn't his motivation. Soon, I noticed his generosity inflicting me with a sense of wanting to please him. I wanted him to like me. So, when he proceeded with a soft voice, I melted to him.

"I want to go over this with you one more time, okay?"

"Yes, of course," I answered obsequiously.

"We know you went some time ago to see Mr. Feld in Tel Aviv. Do you recall the visit?"

"Yes, I saw him for lunch…in Tel Aviv."

"Good. Now, what was the reason you contacted him?"

"My mother gave me his number. She said if I needed to, I could call him any time. Zev Feld is an old friend of my mother. When I grew up, on a few occasions, he came to visit her." I giggled shamelessly. "He had this fully shaved head. I could never forget him."

"Sure, but why did you meet him?"

"I really don't know other than I thought I should ask him about my visa."

"What did you want to ask him?" Faisal prodded.

"I'm not sure I recall. I think it was mostly just to say hello. That was it. Oh, yes, I know now. Each time I called my mother, she seemed worried about me. I'm an only child and we are fairly close. Usually when I travel, she has no problem with it, but coming to Israel for some reason spooked her.

"Then each time I called, all she seemed to care about was when I would be coming home. The last time I called, she appeared more upset. I thought if I saw Zev Feld and he knew I was well, he could speak to her and then she would feel more comfortable." As if assuring myself at last that I had struck on the correct answer, I added, "Yes, that's the truth. Do you understand now?"

"And the two times you called him, what were those for?"

"Just to let him know I was here in Israel and that I was doing well, Faisal," I explained. "Since my mother had mentioned him as a contact, I felt I would check in periodically. Oh, yes, and to have him call her to reassure her I was fine."

"You were very close with Amir and Bahlya at the time, right? I mean you were with them most days. Now, the day you went to see Zev Feld they were both out of town, correct?"

"Yes, as a matter of fact, they were. That's why I went."

"Did you tell either of them you knew Mr. Feld?"

"No, why would I?"

"Why wouldn't you? That's the question. You're staying for a prolonged period with the Hamdallahs, *that* we know. We also know that you are being groomed by Amir and Bahlya to report for them on the plight of our Palestinian people," Faisal plodded meticulously. "This necessitates you being apprised of fairly sensitive material, including the fact that Amir and Bahlya are involved in what the Israelis would consider terrorist activities. Are we agreed so far?"

"Yes, Faisal, we are."

"Wonderful, now we're getting someplace. So, when I ask you the next question I would appreciate an honest answer, all right?" he asked with a smirk stretching his lips and chin slightly. "How can you justify this role with your new friends,

Amir and Bahlya, when you have an association with a man who is known to be a top security official at the Israeli Ministry of Defense? Now, Zaci…"

His use of my familiar name was transparent, but I was still so charmed by the benevolence he was displaying toward me that I clutched it in a bear hug.

"This is very important. All I want to know is what you have told Mr. Feld about all of us. You have to understand that it is not only your life that may be at risk, but your good friends, both Amir and Bahlya, as well as mine, Esam's, Hadecka's, and who knows how many others may be in danger. I know you're tired, but I want you to think carefully because you may save the lives of people who care about you."

Again, I began tearing up with frustration, owing not only to my wish to comply with his request but also my inability to do so. I had said nothing to Zev Feld, other than that I was staying with a family in Jerusalem and they were welcoming and gracious to me.

I knew Faisal was going to be upset with me, but I had no defense, no solution to the dilemma, and no resources to draw on for a strategy to postpone an answer. Faisal had come for business. But now I further understood he was scared as well, for his own safety and for the others whom he believed were in harm's way. They had concluded that their endangerment was because of my deception, an act that could not be proven and was untrue. I'd had no idea as to the occupation of Zev Feld or what position he held with Israeli security. Yet I had no proof of my innocence either. I tried asking questions to postpone the inevitable disappointment I knew was coming Faisal's way.

"I didn't understand what you said about the Israelis having a file on me. I've never in my life been to Israel before this. It makes no sense. And ever since I arrived, they've been spying on me. Is it not just as likely that there is a mistake?" I reasoned to him. "After all, you said the record was sealed, so wouldn't it be reasonable that what is in the file could prove I am not the person you think I am?"

"Please, now, we were doing much better. Your identity as an agent of Israel is not what we're deliberating. That is an established fact," he said casually. "That file says Zacchaeus Miller; it was originated many years ago by Feld. Yes, Zev Feld himself. We know that."

"I don't understand," I said with desperation.

"We don't know why the name was changed. Most likely, Ashrawi is the name you have used for various infiltrations. Then, when it was compromised to the point of irrelevance, they switched to your birth name."

"No. There's a mistake. I promise." My words were pleading again.

"That's my supposition, but I was hoping you would clear it up. Let's end this sham. It will only cost you further discomfort. Zach, if you come clean now, I promise you can leave. We'll never see each other again."

Another obvious lie—there was no way he was letting me walk, knowing I could identify him and possibly set off a series of retaliatory actions by the Israelis. I was screwed in an ocean of unblemished smooth blue. He would accept nothing short of an admission, yet even that would not provide the assurance he was looking for.

Faisal gave me one last slim hope as he continued speaking to me.

"Zach, we know everything about you. I ask you again if you think us stupid. You have a Foreign Journalist Accreditation, correct?"

I nodded agreement.

"We both know this does not come easily. You need a letter of assignment signed by the chief editor of the service in whose employ you are, and it has to designate the type and length of your business. You need your own valid journalist credential from America. You need to submit an extra copy of your passport picture and pay a fee of fifty shekels."

Faisal was becoming impatient again. His rising voice of indignation clued me into his perceived ingratitude on my part. "You did none of this, is that true?"

"I don't even have a journalist credential in America," I added agreeably.

"I know that. I have a friend who happens to work for the Israelis in the Foreign Journalist Department. He was baffled when he checked and saw that you were issued the accreditation on the spot, that very day. He said he'd never heard of that before.

"You went to Gaza. While even Mr. Hamdallah was kept waiting for clearance and his vehicle carefully inspected, you trotted freely through the Erez Crossing. How could this be?

I'm sure you know. It was your friend Feld who authorized the issuance of the accreditation," Faisal declared victoriously.

It was all becoming perfectly equivocal, a jumble of loosely connected facts merging randomly into one obscurity trailing after another, a series of mosaic pieces composing the innards of a phantasmagoric museum, offering me no logical clues as to how all this mess evolved. It didn't really matter any longer. My king was checkmated and I knew it.

"Faisal, there is nothing else I can tell you."

Faisal's façade of gentleness evaporated in the still heat of my sweltering death cell. He made clear my destiny was about to play its final act. His booted right foot had been ordered to strike and with precise aim honed in on my left kidney first, followed by similar pointed-toe kicks to the hip and buttocks.

"Five more minutes for you to talk and then we're ending this," he fumed.

He stormed out. I knew I'd soon be fertilizing a camel park. I wondered if my head was round and would roll once severed. Shock burned my limbs, my heart pounded fiercely, and every thought I'd ever imagined in my entire life was sucked into a single atom of fear. I sat. Then, as if the horrid state lost motive to torment me, it left. I recall an enveloping, unexpected sense of calm coming over me. That's when it happened, what I had searched all my life to find—I was at peace…I was ready to die.

20

NEW MASTERS

IT WAS PAINLESSNESS, NOTHINGNESS, and sweetness. I rested on the ground, not waiting, but in the purest state of being. I had no will to die or to live. That decision had to be assigned to forces beyond my influence.

On that day, I was ordered to live.

It started within five minutes of Faisal leaving my fine home, a space measuring about five by nine feet, hardly enough room to house one human, let alone three. I heard volleys of bullets, screams, and shouts. It seemed in an instant there was mass chaos up and down the halls. The calm I had purchased was stolen. I was again reduced to trembling. All of a sudden, the door to my cell swung open and Faisal, along with one of my tormentors rushed in, slamming it shut and holding it in place with all their strength. Faisal had a revolver, but the other man was unarmed.

I curled up in the corner, neither of the men paying attention to me. I had no idea what was taking place, only that my two new cellmates were terrified. While they secured the door, gunfire started to tear into the wood structure. I peeked from my cradled position and saw bullets ripping the boards apart.

Faisal and the other man had taken several shots and while the stranger had fallen and appeared to be dead, Faisal was standing with his gun poised to fire. He seemed weakened, blood gushing out of his neck like a broken sprinkler. He stumbled backward, only two tiny steps required for his spine to engage the wall where I was in fetal hiding.

The door was kicked fully open. As Faisal randomly fired off shots, the two men at the entrance to the cell discharged several well-aimed bullets. Faisal dropped to the ground; his dead body slumped across my still living one.

I looked up at the two gunmen. I was awaiting the fatal bullet with my name on it. Instead, I heard one of the men speaking in Arabic. I had advanced in my comprehension of the language such that I could understand full sentences at times. "It's the Israeli spy, the American," one of the men announced, and with that statement, shut what was left of the door and rushed off.

I surveyed the cell and noticed at least twenty holes in the wall where shots had been fired. Several bullet casings were scattered on the ground. As I lay, I literally began taking an inventory of each part of my body to determine if they were all present. I made a cursory inspection to see if the blood now covering my abdominal area was mine or belonged to Faisal. I was numb and could have been hemorrhaging and not known it.

I shoved Faisal's corpse off me. I propped myself in the corner of the cell. The rapid firing had stopped. Still, while crouching I heard intermittent single shots that I assumed were being discharged in other cells, owing to the reverberations that seemed to emanate from the walls of adjacent enclosed spaces.

It might have been a minute. Then again, I could just as easily have been waiting on the ground several hours. Someone had to be coming to finish the job on me. It really didn't matter, for I had reclaimed the detached peacefulness previously snatched from me.

I heard the door open. Instead of looking, I closed my eyes. I heard footsteps. Then, I felt a burlap sack being placed over my head. No words were spoken, but the hood was secured. Someone lifted me up, and I was led out of the cell.

I walked some distance. The smell reminded me of what it was like after a terrible earthquake I had lived through years earlier in Los Angeles. Every item in my kitchen had been shaken out of the cupboard and splattered on the floor. The air was thick with the most hideous blend of fragrances I had ever experienced. During my exit from the cell to another unknown location, the only difference between the stench in my kitchen and that moment was the distinct scent of death.

It was enveloping me. Each step I took was over or around what I was certain was a body, and on a couple occasions I started to slip on what I was sure was life's fluid. I may have vomited but wouldn't have been conscious of it.

I was taken to another part of the prison and thrown into a cell. I didn't dare take off the head covering. In fact, it was hours before I did remove it to discover that the new dwelling was identical to the former one, except that the door was intact and there were no bullet holes.

I had no idea what was taking place but later I came to understand what had happened. The treachery between the factions of Palestinians was a terrible weakness in their hope for international respect and recognition, and ultimate statehood. A group that was loyal to Hamas had been holding me. While that organization had authority in Gaza, they were unable to secure official rule in the West Bank, where the Palestinian Authority was deemed the official representative by Israel and the Western powers.

The raid was by the Palestinian Authority, a violent takeover of a prison where Hamas was holding a few of the PA's leaders. It was like a large-scale reenactment of the conflict I had witnessed at Hadecka's home during one of his lectures, the one Bahlya employed to snuff out my sexual charge.

What forestalled my being killed, at least for that moment, was the unfolding of just one tiny battle between the two groups. How they knew who I was or that I was there I didn't know. I believe that at the time they hadn't even calculated what value I had to them; I wondered why they didn't shoot me on the spot. But whoever was in charge of the attack didn't deem it fruitful to eliminate me without first considering the options.

My new jailers were initially no better than the prior thugs. In fact, they must have attended the same institution for human indecency and degradation, in that many of the same forms of abuse were used on me. They were aware of who I was, an American citizen but also a spy for the Israelis. That was sufficient for them to hold me hostage, to inflict more suffering on me.

I was interrogated and asked for an admission of guilt, which I refused. I knew it would serve no purpose. Several times again I was threatened with pictures of decapitation, the choice method of execution. I was told that unless I admitted to my crimes I would be executed summarily. Still, I calculated no advantage in consenting to what was not true.

Then after what I estimated was a brief span of a few days, and quite abruptly, a strange thing happened. The mistreatment stopped. I was moved to a larger cell. It had a window through which light shone all day. I was given a cot to sleep on, offered regular hours of sleep and edible meals. For the first time I had the opportunity to go outdoors for exercise in fresh air. I was spoken to without threats or intimidation.

For the hundredth time I was confused.

The kindness went on for quite some time, and I noticed much of the bruising on my body starting to heal. I was beginning to walk with less of a limp. But there was no change in my weight, owing to my appetite having abandoned me like a wildcatter would a dead oil well. I was at the point that the mere sight of food made me ill.

In this new environment with such unexpected conditions, I had an even bigger problem; I was in a constant state of anticipatory dread, not knowing when the torture would start again. I had no idea when or if my life would be snatched. It was the same curse; I wanted to live.

21

JAIL BAIT

AFTER A COUPLE OF weeks, I was visited for the first time by what appeared to be a high-ranking official of the prison, a man others called General al-Pirani. He was a small man, about fifty years of age. His uniform attracted my attention for its disproportion to his body; it looked several sizes too large and had it not been for a belt tightly cinched, he would have been naked-assed. He was notably bald except for grey sprouts on the sides of the scalp that were meticulously combed back and oiled flat to his head.

He wore thin metal spectacles and sweated enough to display both old and new saturation marks under both armpits. He had smooth but greasy skin and a pleasant-looking face. But when he turned to reveal his right-side profile, a jagged scar about five inches long wrapped sinuously from the top of the ear down to the middle of the neck, the work of an incompetent surgeon or, more likely, the result of a violent assault; it looked dark and seasoned, a relic the general wore with no diffidence.

"We have looked over your file, Mr. Ashrawi…or is it Miller?" he asked in a slow, monotonous style. I soon recognized it as a repetitive pattern whereby sentences were tiresomely delivered in what I interpreted as an acquired habit, with the purpose of compelling others to hang on his every word.

"I'm Zacchaeus Miller," I spontaneously proclaimed with an air of pride.

"Yes, yes. But you are also a known Israeli spy sent by your benefactor to implant yourself in the Palestinian community to convey information about our operations back to Israel. You assume we are going to kill you, right?"

I stared at him with a vacant look. The idea of verbalizing the inevitable act of me being murdered was taboo.

"You are wrong. We have no intention of harming you. As quickly as we can make the arrangements, we are going to return you to your agency in Israel. We have already made contact with the appropriate people at the ministry. Our hope is that it will not be long until you are released. Do you have any questions?"

Again, I stood mute. I was unable to speak and still in disbelief.

"There is one favor I will be asking of you. Could you grant me something in appreciation for what I am doing for you, giving you back your life? It turns out your detention has created quite a stir. Your mother has been inquiring about your whereabouts."

"My mother," I muttered mindlessly.

"Your prior hosts were quite unwilling to offer any information regarding your condition. Fools. They even refused to let anyone know you were in their custody. Your mother is a persistent lady. She's managed to get the American embassy looking into your disappearance. They've been demanding an inquiry, which of course won't be needed now," he pleasantly informed me.

"There is one small glitch. That is what I'll need you to assist me with, if it won't be too much trouble. As you know, we are the representatives of the Palestinian people. The world needs to understand that we are humane and reasonable, not brutal or unjust like Hamas. We must let them know that we do not conform to the image so many in the West especially think of us.

"So, before we turn you over to your employers, the Israelis, I'll ask if you will do a television news program letting everyone know you are healthy, that you were treated fairly, and that the Palestinian Authority realized that in spite of the fact that you are a spy for Israel, your release is justified because you can no longer harm us.

"Most importantly, you will convey the message that we, the Palestinian Authority, are seeking a lasting peace between what we hope will be the future State of Palestine and Israel. Mr. Miller, I'm sure you wouldn't mind doing this minute gesture for us."

Faisal was a veritable liar, intent on excising from me what I knew and then killing me. The general was speaking the truth; he was offering me the option to barter for my life. The average person might rightly say that what he had proposed would compromise their values. He was asking me to proclaim to the world that I had not been tortured. I was to admit to being a spy working for Israel.

It took me less time than peeling a banana to accept his offer. I could have cared less what anyone thought. I wanted to leave. I knew I was not the first, nor would I be the last, to sell out for the privilege of returning home to hear my newly married next-door neighbors shout insults at one another at two in the morning.

I was about to be released from the brutal authority of the Palestinians, looking forward at last to civilized and humane treatment by the Israelis. I assumed they would immediately divest themselves of me like a sour investment, dumping me on the doorstep of the American embassy and wishing to never see me again.

I rejoiced in the thought that I would soon be on my way home. That's all that mattered to me.

The media circus was actually swift and finely orchestrated. I was presented with a script and told I was not to deviate or improvise in any way. All I needed to do was parrot the words the general had prepared for me.

I was taken into a small pressroom with a long table set up in the front. Al-Pirani led the way and suggested I sit in the center, where numerous microphones shot out like fists in every direction in front of me. The general was sitting directly to my left, and next to me on the right was another uniformed man I had never seen before. Standing behind us were several suited men purposelessly lingering and trying to look grim.

The reporters were crammed into the body of the room, each eager to interpret the event according to their own fantasy. Bright lights shone from a set of high windows on the wall opposite where I was sitting. Around the sides of the room, television screens were mounted. Cameras were flashing randomly.

I might have fancied myself a celebrity if some great achievement on my part were being rewarded instead of me being shamed by doing a promotional worse than endorsing chewing gum for children. The formulated responses to questions were typed on papers set in front of me. Al-Pirani was running the show.

"Welcome, everyone. We want to share this momentous occasion with the world, a gesture of peace and friendship to our neighbors. Next to me is a young man who has been in the employment of the Israeli government for many years. He has been serving the function of infiltrating Palestinian organizations so as to funnel information back to the high command in his country. May I say he is a spy?" al-Pirani subtly jested.

"When persons committing similar crimes have been discovered throughout history, they have been made to stand trial and usually severely punished. That is not our intent with Mr. Miller, who also goes under the name Ashrawi. We want to use this great opportunity to stop the fighting between our two countries. We want to ask our neighbor to work with us in establishing an independent State of Palestine. As a good faith gesture, we have arranged to return Mr. Miller unharmed back to Israel.

"I would like now to give Mr. Miller an opportunity to speak." al-Pirani turned to face me. "May I ask you, how have you been treated since you were taken into our custody?"

"I have been shown respect at all times. I have never been abused nor deprived of any of my rights. The Palestinian Authority has provided me with a clean, safe environment, with regular, nutritious meals and exercise."

"Do you admit, Mr. Miller, that you have in the past, and up to the time of your arrest, been an Israeli agent?"

"I do. While working in the role of agent, I have been able to embed myself into several Palestinian organizations. The information I have provided to Israel has resulted in arrests and deaths of numerous high-ranking Palestinian officials."

There were a few more redundant questions to which I responded with equally vacuous and transparent answers before al-Pirani asked the audience if they had anything to ask me. I was certain the questions were screened as well. However, the well-known news source Al Jazeera must have made a last-minute change of reporter. Their man posed an unrehearsed question.

"I'm Danish Nasir with Al Jazeera. Mr. Miller, it sounds like your incarceration was comfortable for you. I presume you had quite a bit of contact with the other prisoners, right?"

General al-Pirani rose abruptly. In the process, he practically pushed me off my chair. He looked at the reporter with vengeance, a stare cautioning the renegade to cease with his line of inquiry. The man would have no part of it.

"What I'm getting at is your impression of how the other prisoners were being cared for," Mr. Nasir proceeded.

He narrowly finished the sentence, al-Pirani cutting him off and motioning to another reporter to proceed with his question. But Nasir was undaunted, raising his voice.

"All I want to know is if Mr. Miller has received special treatment. There have been reports of torture. If we are going to be democratic we have a right to address…"

"Mr. Miller is not here to discuss other prisoners. Now, Mr. Nasir, thank you."

The reporter had nerve. After several more heated exchanges, he was impolitely escorted out of the room. This was followed by a few other banal questions—I was able to dispose of them quickly.

General al-Pirani must have been overwhelmingly pleased with my tinny, dumbed-down performance on national television; he hugged me. The big shindig ended quickly. In no time, I was passed like a hot torch to the waiting, scowling faces and gritting teeth of the Israelis.

22

KAYE MILLER GOES
TO ISRAEL

IF I LEARNED ANYTHING from my ordeals it was that
the origin of the word madness is a derivative of the word
government. Only a miniscule percentage of humans go crazy
and end up in institutions, but I'm convinced that not one
single entity representing a group of people, no matter what
name is ascribed to it, has existed since the evolution of man
that has not ended up in whatever is the equivalent for organizations of the human nuthouse. None of the various sects
vying to speak for the Palestinians or the State of Israel were
close to convincing me that they would be the first exception
to the rule.

Had I arrived at this wonderful insight before my delivery
from the Palestinian jailors to the Israelis, I would not have
expected anything other than what took place. The Israelis
had drawn their own conclusions on the matter of my identity. Anything I said would be dismissed as lies.

The Israelis held me under what they called administrative
confinement, a nice way of saying I would not have a lawyer,

not have a trial, not have contact with family, and not have any rights for an indeterminate period of time. Officially, I didn't exist.

Why? Because I was a spy sent by the Palestinians in what the Israelis considered a grossly obnoxious, devious, never-before-attempted ploy by the enemy. The Israelis thought it was a scheme dreamed up by the Palestinian Authority to dummy up an Israeli spy that they knew all along was one of their own, with the purpose of smearing the Israelis in a global public relations campaign. If it were true, I would fit the description of a suicidal fool, for I would have had to accept at a minimum that I'd spend the rest of my life imprisoned. At a more likely maximum, I would be executed for… falsely admitting I was a Palestinian spy?

What the Israelis believed were "facts" proving I was an extreme idiotic fanatic who would stop at nothing to take personal revenge on Israel, were no more than conjectures inspired by a witch-hunt-paranoid mentality. However, in order to convince me of their brilliance, several astonishing revelations would be brought to my attention by my new masters.

I should mention that, unbeknownst to me, long before my release by the Palestinians to the Israelis, my mother had begun mounting an assault on the Israelis. It began in America and continued without a break after she landed in Israel. I'll outline the stream of events as she ultimately disclosed them to me.

It was Preston who first pressed the old panic button, never believing in the first place that everything was going well. When the email I told him I was sending didn't arrive as I had specified that day, and then the next, he was over to my mom's in a flash. Immediately, my mother started trying to reach me and after a couple days of my not responding to emails, text or phone messages, she rightly assumed the worst.

Like a fool, I had never mentioned to them the name or address of the Hamdallah family. Why should I? I'm a grown man…I should have. As a result of my negligence, they had no idea where to go to find me.

Her first call was to Zev Feld. He assured her that when he had last seen me I was well. Unfortunately, he claimed he was not able to make any headway pertaining to what had happened to me. As a result, I was just another missing person statistic—except to my mother and Preston.

My mother went on the offensive. She was certain I was being held in illegal confinement. How she concluded this she could never explain, except to say that she knew I was not irresponsible regarding my safety and if some accidental tragedy had befallen me, she'd have been notified. Therefore, she reasoned that there had to be a mischievous explanation to account for my disappearance.

Whoever was responsible for my bad fortune was guilty of no small infraction in the mind of my mom. She instinctively understood without benefit of a degree in etymology that governments not only bite, but they can be poisonous. The Israelis may have been victorious in repeated wars against multiple national foes simultaneously, emerging unscathed, but they were not going to step out of the ring after a conflagration with my mother without at least a firm belt in the face. She had it fixed, wrongly at first, that they were the culprits.

She began her campaign to discover what had happened to me from her home. After weeks of painstaking effort to put out the word that I was missing she made a trip to New York, followed by a visit to Washington, D. C. She had during the entire time of my being missing tried to secure a meeting with an official at the State Department. Finally she was able to arrange to see Undersecretary Phillip Kessler. After a surprisingly short wait, Kessler greeted her and she was welcomed to his office.

"How can I help you, Ms. Miller?"

"My son has been missing for weeks. The Israelis issued him a foreign press pass, and I have no idea why. My son has never been a reporter. Besides, I checked on the requirements to be issued the press permit. He could have never qualified. I have a friend over there, Zev Feld, working for the Israelis in security. I called him, and he advised me he doesn't know a thing about it. I don't believe a word of it."

"Did your son ever indicate he was in any type of trouble?"

"My son's a grown man. I've never known him to run home for help. I know my boy, and he can take care of himself pretty well. The one thing significant here is that just before he disappeared, he called his best friend and said he was sending an email—it never arrived; that's very unusual for him. When Zach says he's doing something, he does it. After that, he never returned any correspondence. He said he was staying with a family near Jerusalem, but I have no other details."

"I understand. What have you done so far, so I can avoid redundancy?" Kessler queried.

"I've been to the Overseas Press Club in New York, and they're trying to use their contacts in the region to get information. They notified the Washington Foreign Press Center, and they're up in arms. For some reason, probably because he is a published writer, they believe he might have been falsely arrested because of the journalist issue, but they can't determine anything so far."

My mom then produced a bundle of papers, ones she later showed me. It seems every newspaper in the world was wondering what happened to me, none able to discover that Hamas had been torturing me in a filthy prison. As she addressed Kessler, her posture was undoubtedly erect and her speech sharp. I had witnessed her nobody-is-getting-in-my-way insistence in the past, and she must have conveyed it to the undersecretary.

"This is the beginning. Over twenty American papers are running stories, and they've got their foreign bureaus making inquiries. In the Arab media, as you well know, only a few will help." She loaded both barrels. "I need you to torch the rest of their derrieres if necessary. Do you have children?" she rifled his way.

"Two. But they're quite young."

"This is my only child. My next stop is Israel, a dung hole I'm as interested in visiting as a morgue. But let me tell you something. I'm coming back with my boy, and those assholes are going to know Kaye Miller's in town."

Kessler cocked his head and squinted his eyes, wisely taking this distraught woman at her word. "Let me see what I can do. I'll make calls today, I promise. Is there anything else you need?"

"Call that shiftless Zev Feld and have one of your agents drill him until he gushes. I know he's lying to me."

"When will you be leaving?"

"Tonight. I'll call you as soon as I get there…if that's okay. This is a mess. I apologize if I've been disrespectful in any way, but Zach Miller is a good man. I can bring you reference lists of people who will vouch for him."

"You have every right to push. I'll do everything I can to help."

He did. It was too late.

Kaye Miller was on the plane at the exact time my public appearance and release to the Israelis was taking place. Thus, upon landing, she had a message waiting from Kessler.

"Ms. Miller, this is Phil Kessler from the State Department. Zach's alive," he informed her. "He's now under the authority of the Israelis. I'm attempting to gather more details." Kessler's voice turned somber. "Ms. Miller, your son is under tight security. I'm sorry to tell you this because it's not a light matter. They're detaining him. They say they have evidence of Zach's *nefarious activities* against Israel. There's some issue about his identity not being as he presents it. They say he has known associations with Palestinian terrorists.

"Call me when you can. If Zach is innocent, of course, we'll do everything we can. But I'll level with you…this is not going to be easy. When it comes to security, as you can imagine, the Israelis are unyielding."

Unyielding? That's an understatement if there ever was one.

23

YOU'RE A JEW,
YOU SCHMUCK

I COULDN'T WAIT TO unload the potentially devastating information I had found in Amir's safe, material I had all but forgotten while rotting in the Palestinian jail. I anticipated being drowned in gratefulness and quickly released. The Israelis had a different agenda. When I brought up to my new hosts what I had discovered, they were sufficiently intrigued to smirk at me. Then, they left me in confinement for two days before talking with me again.

The Israelis were big on interrogations, far more sophisticated than the Palestinians in terms of gathering data. Their approach was to stone the mind as opposed to the body. While at first I was relieved I was not being beaten, in due time, I began to wish I were; the mental anguish was far more distressing than the physical abuse I'd undergone with my prior captives.

After I had been softened up with days of isolation in darkness, without sound, smell, or touch, and food so bland that what sense of taste I had left was decimated by another

214 | MISTAKEN ENEMY

ten percent with each meal, I met my first interrogator. He expressed his disappointment in me. How could a nice Jewish boy with a name like Zach turn into an anti-Semite? So appalled, he assured me, I'd most definitely have a fresh point of view when he finished.

I was beginning to think that I was Jewish. The Palestinians were convinced of it, the Israelis knew it to be a fact, even Bahlya had inquired about it. What a hack I was.

"Please, this is important," I voiced in an attempt to let the fellow know what I had learned in Amir's safe. "They're going to kill millions of Israelis and Americans."

"Miller, here are the ground rules. I ask questions and you answer. Otherwise, shut the fuck up."

This drill sergeant guy, not much beyond my age, was named Lt. Col. Mordachai. His given name, by the way, was Guy, which I heard occasionally when he and a fellow officer conversed outside my cell; he was quite a guy. Probably owing to his youth, he was devout in conducting his work, proceeding with tenacity and durability I found remarkable. He hated wasting a moment he might otherwise devote to badgering or frightening me.

"Today, we cut all the bullshit, okay? I level with you and you with me."

"That's what I want. I'm trying to tell you…"

"Remember the rules? Shut the fuck up and listen."

Torment I had become accustomed to through my earlier imprisonment. But it was Mordachai who finally lowered the boom, allowing all the pictures on the open windows of the slot machine to show identical, a jackpot tumbling the mystery and madness of my life in intelligible order.

Mordachai was a tall, very dark-skinned man with wavy thick black hair, not outstanding on its own. But it was his face that distinguished him, a mug never to be forgotten; and, I might add, one any common thug would have the good sense not to choose. The head was long and thin, the nose a vertical fault line separating two giant cheeks that would fail to belie a likely prior career as a professional boxer who'd lost too many fights; they jutted out, puffing like the tops of cupcakes, and the sheer bulk as they flowed into the cap-size chin gave the impression that the latter would have dropped off his face if not secured equally from both sides of the jaws. The eyes were set deep into the skull. The way the eyebrows protruded forward offered a canopy, as if to protect the eyes from rain.

"You watch movies, I'm sure. Did you see *The Godfather, Part II*?" he asked as he bent over, for what reason I couldn't imagine, other than to stare at his shoes that he maintained at the highest level of shine. In fact, they were so reflective that if he were gazing into them he might be seeing Rocky Balboa beaming back, for he appeared a near-perfect replica of the punch-drunk fighter.

Both parts I and II were my favorite movies. The mention of it saddened me, in that it was one of those items from my past I tried not to dwell on. I acknowledged his question with a head bob.

"Now, Vito Corleone as a boy watched his father and brother, then mother too, get killed by the mafia boss.

Remember? And what did Corleone do as soon as he had the chance? Right, come back to Italy seeking revenge for the death of his father…especially. That's how we humans are designed, irresistible impulses, psychic apparatuses we are incapable of repressing, and then acts of violence to cleanse the emotional filth infecting the body and mind. Now, you understand what I'm talking about, right Ashrawi?"

He must have taken his playbook from Faisal. I wanted to ask him whose invention this Ashrawi business was, but that would have broken a rule. I shut my fuckin' mouth, offering him the same flat face I did Faisal.

"I say we straighten all this out today. I want you to know why you'll be spending the rest of your life in an Israeli jail. Yeah, you'll have your damn trial and all the lawyers your mother can hire, but it won't be worth a whit to you."

That was the second time my mother had been mentioned. It gave me a surge of hope, despite what this Lieutenant Colonel had to say.

"We have the file on you, created even before you were born. It was classified, but since you decided to return home with vengeance in your heart, we had it opened." He stopped to clean the dark glasses he religiously wore, seemingly never attentive to the dull light of a prison needing more illumination—as I said, quite the guy. "No, you will not get the chance Corleone did, because we are not careless. Your potential for harm to our country was anticipated long before you birthed your first atom of hate; for us, caution is survival. You simply underestimated us," he boasted.

"Did you think you could come here and in a matter of hours get a credential as a foreign correspondent? Did you think you could live with the Hamdallah clan all that time and that we would have no idea what you were up to—getting educated on how to attack our country, crafting skills of retribution and terrorism?"

I observed that there was a similarity between these interrogator types. They loved being right, hated disagreement, and were so convincing to themselves that they easily worked into a rage; voices raising, hands slamming about angrily, faces shoved right up to your nose—a couple with foul breath—and building impatience that might convert to wicked tongue-lashings without warning. Mordachai was steaming.

His neck, long and thick like a tree trunk, revealed pulsing arteries running like ropes top to bottom. His physique left no doubt he was a powerful man, but I had to laugh to myself in that his voice betrayed him, a natural countertenor who might have filled in for Michael Jackson on an evening he were ill with laryngitis—which might have accounted for his propensity to shout, an exercise to hide a perceived defect behind a lower pitch. He shrieked at me.

"We know why the Hamdallah family took you in so graciously, offering unlimited lodging, and you do too. I told you, the jig is up. You want to tell me about it?"

"I really don't know what this is about, but if you would tell me, I would appreciate it," I said eagerly. I was awestruck by his allusions and waited for him to finally unravel a mystery everyone seemed to understand but me.

"Oh, don't worry, I will. I just can't understand how you can be so stupid to continue claiming innocence when the evidence is all packaged and tied with a pink bow. Anyway, you can stop the charade. Hamdallah was first cousin to your father, which would make Mr. Hamdallah your second cousin, and his children, I believe…third cousins or cousins removed?"

I don't mean to make myself seem like a sniveling ninny, but I was beyond containing emotion. I broke into an oceanic water show, crying hysterically, which, by the way, meant nothing to my interrogator other than confirmation that I had been discovered and there was no place left to hide.

Had he heard my thoughts, he would have journeyed with me back to my talk with Mr. Hamdallah when he had mentioned losing a baby so many years ago, a male, because he let his guard down. *It couldn't be.* "No, not me!" I cried. "Please. Stop it. Why are you doing this to me?"

Mordachai proceeded unsympathetically, ignorant to an association that kept my tears flowing.

"Your father was Abbas Ashrawi, a Palestinian living in Jerusalem."

I must have shrieked a sound startling even to my heartless leader, for he stopped. This had to have been the man Amir had mentioned to me, his father's first cousin who had died fighting for the Palestinians. The possibility of these concurrences being true ferociously smacked me in the face, my body thrusting downward as I buried my head with my hands and arms in an attempt to cut off incoming stimuli.

Mordachai delighted in what he interpreted as contrition. What I had been concealing as a secret that would incriminate me, in his mind, was finally admitted.

"Now, Miller, you see we're not ignorant. There's no use. We've known all this since before even you found out. Your father was a man of words, like you, a writer, correct? And what was his favorite subject?"

He paused, as if a conductor, motioning for me to fill in the blanks with pieces of history he believed I knew. What he didn't understand was that I was the ignorant one, a man about to fail a course supposedly of his own history.

"If it's too painful for you to admit, I'll do it for you," he said, smirking as if he were about to bestow on me a magnificent gift. "Your father's favorite subject was material inciting violent opposition to the Israeli state. Oh, sure, he professed no enmity toward Jews, which he ridiculously believed to be true. In fact, to prove it, along comes a cute little American Jew, visiting the birthplace of her parents. That's right. Your mother came to see where your grandparents lived, where she had been conceived, and low and behold, she and Abbas fall in love.

"Tender story, but not that phenomenal. There have been Jews and Arabs marrying for centuries. What made their story unique was that his new wife, while Jewish, opposed statehood for the Jews and sided with her husband. Quickly, your mother became pregnant. That's you, Zacchaeus."

He couldn't resist mocking my formal name.

"Shortly after, their fairytale came to a tragic end when your father was killed; yes, by Zionist settlers during a sneak attack," he said, the last word coinciding with him stamping his shoe on the ground.

"It was orchestrated by your father," he lashed at me. "Did you ever get the details? Your father led a team of Arab militia on a mission to destroy a five-vehicle *unarmed* convoy carrying doctors and nurses to a settlement on the border of the West Bank." His words were punctuated by his voice raging. "By the time help arrived for the defenseless drivers and passengers, they had all been killed. It was during the attempted escape that your father was shot.

"Oh, here I am again, wasting your time telling you tales you've already heard. But here's one you may not have known." It must have delighted him, thinking of heaping more suffering on me. He was beaming. "Zev Feld was a friend of your mother's from grade school. He was the only person in her life who knew the whole story."

"Zev Feld," I mumbled, still bemused about what role he played in this production.

"It's been very hard on him, because he likes your mother and hoped this would never happen. But he had to do his job. By the way, he never in all these years let on to your mother that he knew the identity of your father."

"Zev Feld," I repeated at a nearly inaudible volume, the outline of an evil apparition coalescing.

"He cleared your credential and made sure someone knew of your whereabouts and activities at all times. What did you think? That you could get even for the death of a father you never knew? He died for a cause he believed in. It was a lost one, even before he gave his life. Now, you'll rot away the remainder of yours in jail, claiming you had no choice but to do what you did…and you may be correct."

"What you're saying is I'm half Jewish and half Arab?" I asked in disbelief.

"That's right! And welcome home, for good. It's time to surrender. Be a good lad. Admit what you've done, and take your punishment like a man."

"But my mother raised me without religion. She avoided organized faith," I countered, bemused. "I had no grandparent. It was only the two of us."

"You never know when to stop. You're unconscionable, ready to take the lie to your grave. So be it. It's your prerogative."

"Are you sure this is correct? I was born in America."

"Indeed, you were. But you were to be the first-born, a male, to an Arab. Do you know what that means to these people? Mr. Hamdallah, according to our records, was very close with his cousin, your father. He vowed that if your mother's child were to be a boy, he would be raised with the family in Jerusalem. If it were a girl, your mother was free to leave."

His words punctured me. Amir…Mr. Hamdallah…both talking about my father…still very much alive for Amir…a man I had never heard of before.

"Your mother, for all practical purposes, was a prisoner herself, waiting to give birth. But she outwitted Hamdallah and escaped, going for help to the American consulate and then securing a flight home. I'm sure by now you are aware that we know everything." His cockiness offended me. "You would want us to believe it was by chance that you ended up in the Hamdallah home with your relatives?"

Effortlessly, I appeared muddle-headed. But it was of no consequence to him. He delighted in salting the jumble of my mind with an insult intended, no doubt, to inspire an outburst on my part.

"I hope you weren't screwing that tramp cousin of yours."

"No, I'm afraid I struck out on that one."

"Nothing about you would surprise me. Unfortunately, you won't be improving your hustling skills where you're going."

He curtailed speaking for several minutes as he looked over his notes. Then he resumed.

"I'm about to turn you over to Captain Alon. I do want to let you know we have the journal you kept. Not very detailed for a man of pen. I assume you were too busy plotting the destruction of Israel to write the way I'd expect based on the stories you've produced in the past. I've seen most of your work and it's not too bad.

"We are going to be asking you for some factual material soon about your accomplices, including the cousins. The senior Hamdallah knew nothing about his children's involvements until we paid a visit to his home, expecting to put both of his darlings under arrest.

"I'm sure they would have been squealing like scared squirrels, but they had already been tipped off and escaped, at least for now. Their father is actually a straight man. I feel for the sorrow he has to go through now. Some children bring nothing but grief to their parents, you included."

He took a breath, and I used the opportunity to pose an inquiry about Amir and Bahlya, but it was to no avail. "What's going to happen to Amir and…"

"I'll ask the questions. But you can forget them. You'll never see them again."

"You said you don't know where they are, so how do you know that?" I wanted to challenge his audacity, but he simply grinned arrogantly.

"You understand that what you did put in the journal will be enough to convict both of them, and yourself."

I had intentionally documented nothing about Amir's plan in my journal, for fear of the outside chance he was conducting counter-espionage on me and would have discovered my treachery.

Mordachai was interrupted by one of the guards whispering in his ear.

"Well, this is goodbye for me. Captain Alon is here and ready for your re-education and debriefing."

24

THE BLOND JEW

IT WAS SOME TIME before Alon entered. I was grateful for the respite. It had been weeks of imprisonment under deplorable conditions. While my body was continuing to recover, I was still suffering from what I knew were untreated fractures to the arms and legs; abdominal cramping along with alternating bouts of diarrhea and vomiting; severe headaches accompanied by nausea and perception of small black spots floating gently in front of my eyes, causing dizziness; and a croupy cough where I couldn't breathe enough oxygen and felt I was going to pass out—other than that, I felt like taking a jog.

My mind was worse than my anatomy. As I said, the Israelis had elevated themselves to the level of genius when it came to mental torture. Between the sessions I was treated to, educating me about my background, I was beaten down by psychological abuse. In response, I voluntarily took my sojourns to distant planets and imaginary grottos where pet dogs licked me adoringly, Queen sang to me nonstop, and women held me to their bosom to nurture me.

When I was here on earth, however, I had episodes of severe anxiety. My extremities trembled, I experienced terror without any external stimulus, my heart raced uncontrollably, and a swelling sensation choked my throat. At times I noticed myself sweating profusely, even during cool evenings, and I shivered despite the external temperature being comfortable. Dread often overtook me unexpectedly. At those times of depressive episodes I wanted to run, hide, or even kill myself to escape the sensation of deathlike doom.

I was aware my baseline mood was subnormal, but most memorable was the periods of despondency that peaked high like mountaintops, craning above the mist and cloudiness concealing the misery below. My power of concentration was poor. My mind would dissolve ideas like soap bubbles blown from a child's wand. I yearned to be alone; the insecurity stemming from the thought of being around people was petrifying.

Occasionally, I experienced a senseless unleashing of elation, supplanted instantaneously with the feeling of dropping free-fall down an elevator shaft, my heart pounding and tears streaming. I had no ability to master my emotions. In a flash, I could go from calm to slamming my hands against walls and pounding my chest or head. I'd say that the cumulative impact of my despaired states taught me to become a champion at feeling sorry for myself, skilled in the practice of self-pity to the point where my supply remains abundant. While I've been informed it's unhealthy to wallow in misery, I find it oddly comforting.

Listening to Mordachai, I couldn't resist looking at the almost irrefutable evidence in favor of the facts recently presented to me about my past. But the last thing I needed was to be told under conditions of imprisonment that all along I had been staying with close relatives but didn't know it, that I was half Jewish and half Arab, that my mother had been deceiving me all my life, that I hungered to embrace my sweet cousin, and that I had come to seek revenge for the death of my father. I battled with all my might not to believe them. Why wouldn't I? Couldn't they all have been reading script notes for the wrong story?

Since I had been incarcerated, every single person I'd come into contact with had lied to me, except al-Pirani, who told me the truth—only to use me to his own advantage. Now, I was supposed to believe this far-out tale because people who had nothing but ill will toward me were saying so? It was my turn to tell them all to screw off, and I did, the first instant I met Alon.

I don't know if he was surprised or not, but he said and did nothing. He simply waited for me to finish my rampage and then proceeded as if I hadn't said a word. As I mentioned, my status was as a nonexistent being, and he did nothing to contradict that rank.

Alon practiced patience like a professional golfer. An errant shot might require hitting five hundred balls to correct it—he'd whack a thousand more to be sure his point was hammered in. He was interested in the specifics I knew regarding Amir and Bahlya—who their accomplices were and what I knew about their network and planned activities.

When I explained how little firsthand knowledge I actually had, other than that they claimed to have been involved in resistance and were avid about the destruction of Israel as the only solution that would salvage the dignity of their people, he would go back to the beginning, asking the same questions he'd started with that I had already answered. I couldn't help feeling sorry for him and at the same time wondered when his tolerance would take an about-face and he'd resort to extreme measures. It never happened.

He was a tall, gangly man in his mid-forties. His blond hair was wavy and without sign of balding or graying. Most women no doubt would label him a stud. His uniform, a long-sleeved shirt and slacks, was impeccably pressed. As I inspected the entirety of his physical presence, I concluded that he was as close to a faultless male specimen as I'd ever seen; had Hitler found Alon along his rise to power on a platform of Aryan supremacy and racial purification, he would have been the perfect poster boy. Yet, here he was, a fair skinned, blue-eyed Jew.

The wonder of his appearance did not belie the elemental flaw in his character, one he shared with the rest of the Israelis I'd had contact with in prison, that he was a liar. I prejudged him to be perpetuating the same stories about my family that I was trying to convince myself were fabrications. When the topic would come up, I'd resist him, telling him he was intentionally deceiving me. In response, he would patiently assure me that I would in time come to my right mind. To shut him up, I'd occasionally admit I had known the truths of my family all along. Usually, he'd tell me he didn't believe me. He always had an agenda, but it was the same one: scramble my brain. He'd play his routine over and over until I wanted to scream, which I often did.

He carried a small chair with him to each visit that he placed in the middle of my cell for his comfort, insisting I stand at attention throughout his talks. I assume he thought that would prevent my mind from wandering, but my proficiency in the art of space travel was far beyond what he could have conceived. As a result, I was able to be absent, without his knowledge, for portions of his discourses.

What nearly killed me was that he was asking for more detail of what I had learned since coming to the Middle East. Yet, every time I tried to tell him about Amir and the scheme to destroy Israel, he'd shut me up. One example of a talk with Alon will serve to illustrate what continually drove me to unimaginable feelings of helplessness and impotence.

"Zach, we know Amir was faithful to Hamas. What we need to know is who in that organization he reported to." His voice was sonorous, with the remarkable capacity to turn common prose to lyric. I was impressed as I witnessed him use it like a whip assigned to extract truth from me. "You had to have been with other people since you were with Amir most days."

"I told you, the only people I met directly who I can name were Faisal, Esam, Hadecka, and a fellow named Demian."

"No, Faisal and Esam are minor players. Faisal is dead anyway and Hadecka is harmless. Amir, however, was too important to not be taking orders from higher up. We need those names. I know you're trying to protect him, and I respect it. You're a fine man. But would they do the same for you?

"Really, we're going to do this until you clean out your bowels. I promise, you will feel better after you take a good crap. Nobody will know. You needn't worry about retaliation by the other prisoners when you go into the general population."

The thought of a regular bowel movement appealed so finely that I considered making up information to take him up on his promise. My body functions had gone into a messy revolt.

"Sir, I've tried to tell you a hundred times that there are lots of names and people, and they're all collaborating to destroy Israel. I saw the details. It's for real—I'm trying to help!"

"You are a shifty one. All this conspiracy theory you keep trying to peddle is not what we're looking for. The Palestinians have stuffed you full of lies. We know that; it's common practice. Do you think you are the first person I've had here who tries to sell me on some grand scheme only they know about, a secret plot to destroy Israel, one that if they could explain to me would save thousands of lives? You're not the first to offer to divulge this invaluable information to me at a discounted price, in exchange for your freedom."

"But this is different," I argued. "I found what I was not intended to see. When I imprisoned by the Palestinians, before I was turned over to you, they never once asked me about it because Amir was the only one who knew. Just let me..."

"I think we're losing direction. Now, tell me about some of the contacts Amir was hanging around with."

That's as far as I was able to get, with anyone. The thought that I could do nothing to save myself from death at the hands of Amir's group was distressing. As muddy as my mind was, I held on believing that what I had read in Amir's file was true. Therefore, sitting in jail in Israel, I expected within weeks to be a victim of Jawiris' deadly atomic boom.

As time passed, and I listened to people like Alon telling me my story was commonplace, I did revisit my own doubts. *Could my finding have been no more than Amir's fictional story?* I noticed that I made fewer and fewer attempts to confront Alon with my profound knowledge of the doom that was coming to Israel and cities in America.

One morning, however, everything changed. Alon told me my mother would be visiting the next day. I imagined she muscled her way in by holding a loaded pistol to Zev Feld's hairless head. As I learned later, it wasn't exactly a pleasant exchange between them. I'll describe it as it was related to me.

"I didn't orchestrate this mess; Zach did this to himself," Feld remorsefully explained to my mother.

"No, you did it! You set him up with this damn press permit, and that's why the Palestinians took him as your agent. Paranoia. Zev, you people can't grow past it."

"I'm going out on a limb here, but let me tell you something. A week before Zach decided to come here, Amir landed in Los Angeles. Are you aware of that?"

"How the hell would I know? I never wanted anything to do with those people," she shot back.

"We don't know his itinerary, and frankly it's impossible to trace it now. We assume he had meetings with Zach, not only because they flew out of Los Angeles together, both making their reservations at nearly the same time, but because he was staying at a hotel blocks from where Zach lives. In fact, Amir even paid extra at the ticket counter in New York for a seat change to be next to Zach—granted it was for an extra leg room row...but directly beside Zach, his cousin?"

"It was chance, nothing more than that. You know it."

Feld smirked, unable to restrain astonishment at a mother's perceived naïveté.

"For God sakes, Kaye, your son could have flown nonstop. Instead, he takes a flight and changes planes in New York. Then, Amir does the same. Hamdallah has more money than Gillette makes razor blades, so he wasn't going for a discount fare."

"Laugh all you want, but I know my boy," she bitterly proclaimed. "Zach never knew a thing about my past. There was no way he and Amir could have known each other."

"Kaye, I've always cared for you and respected you. Be honest with yourself and tell me this could all be coincidence. With the Internet today, people can find anything. You think you cloaked the history from him? All he had to do was get curious and start looking into his grandparents and the story would have opened like a movie premiere."

"So, your theory is that after all these years, he finds out about his past and takes off to fragile little Israel to seek revenge for his father?"

"Precisely, and it's not the first time it's happened."

Kaye Miller's light skin turned fire engine red, the vascular arteries knotting at the throat. "This is crap and you know it!" she shouted. "Nobody is buying it. I've got the press demanding an explanation from you people. You'll have to answer for what you've done."

"During his stay with the Hamdallah family, he's done nothing but attend anti-Israeli meetings and been in the company of terrorists. We let him have freedom to do what he wished while visiting. We didn't tell him what to do." His voice rose out of frustration. "Go ask him yourself, if you don't believe me."

"Good, I will. When?"

So it happened that Feld had enough clout to arrange for my mother to see me, for all of a five-minute visit. She was outraged with the conditions, but at the time she didn't dare argue the gift to abolition. She knew it was the Israelis' way of appeasement without cost. They could shut up the rumors of an illegal detention, extend the period of time they held me without rights, and at the same time display sensitivity toward a suffering mother.

I didn't want her to see me. I didn't want to see her either. I wept thinking of her sorrow, felt profound guilt and shame, and knew the likelihood of ever seeing her again after that would be slight to nothing—it was all more pain, and I couldn't tolerate added suffering.

I found myself scripting conversations, even confronting her about whether what I was being told about my background was true. Was I part Jewish and part Arab? But a big piece of me felt indifferent; I was Zacchaeus and that thought was the only one that made me feel alive.

I did start to dwell, however, on the moment of reflection I'd had shortly after meeting Bahlya. In the mirror, I had sworn there was a portrait of her projecting back from my own eyes. Was I seeing a piece of Zach in Bahlya because we were blood to one another? Or was it an impersonation, a more general acquaintanceship with my anthropomorphic archetypal anima that might as well have been offered by any female I allowed myself to peer into as intimately as I did with her?

This episode of contemplation came to an abrupt halt.

25

NO TIME FOR TEARS

IT WAS EARLY IN the morning. I heard a bang on my door and assumed Alon had knocked his chair on the frame. Instead, it was a guard I'd never seen before. "Let's go," is all he said. I followed him. He took me out through a locked metal door and into another section of the prison.

He opened the door to a small room with a desk and two chairs. It was void of windows, objects to write with, or telephone. The sterile space was a ten-foot square; the walls were flat white and the floor carpeted in a tan weave. I remember it was cold, the air conditioning duct pushing frigid air into the room with impunity.

"Your mother will be here in a few minutes," he told me and walked out.

I had vowed to withhold emotion when she arrived, rehearsing repeatedly how I would handle seeing her weeping and broken. I concluded it was far more important to use the precious time to arm her with as much of the material the Israelis had refused to listen to as I could. If my discovery was the real deal, I knew she'd mine it for every ounce of worth it had.

I doubted she would be allowed paper and pen. What I did in preparation for her coming was to take the first letter of all the last names of Jawiris' accomplices and make it into a phrase. It was a trick I'd learned in junior high school to prepare for tests, like "*a rat in the house may eat the ice cream,*" to spell "arithmetic."

She had excellent power of recall. She also read like a glutton and had a mind that could hover over any topic like a helicopter to gain a unique perspective and then manipulate the material into infinite combinations.

The lady stood about five foot eight. Her bones were strong. She had an athletic frame that might have found satisfaction in sports had the arts not dominated her interest. Her hair was colored brunette. I never saw a grey strand in her fifty-some-thing-year-old head; what am I supposed to know on that subject?

Usually she preferred jeans, rarely blue, and it was bright sweaters in winter and Lacoste tops in summer. She loved to laugh and tell jokes, and I recall many times growing up when one of her friends would visit for a couple of drinks and they would clown themselves to tears.

Please don't cry today, I rehearsed in my head in preparation for her arrival.

She was escorted to the room by a guard, but also accompanied by a male in a suit who peeked into the room and looked at my mother. She motioned affirmatively to him.

Later, she would tell me his name was Phillip Kessler from the U. S. State Department. He had flown in to help her. The Israelis had insisted that he accompany her in order to confirm that it was I at the meeting and that she was permitted the allotted time.

He waited outside. As she entered, I was amazed at her strength. I didn't notice a flea-sized sign of feeling except a warm smile and nice hug. The brief discussion, which I'll paraphrase as best I can, took place, to my surprise, without a staff member present, though I suspect the room was bugged. There was much to cover in a short period.

"You listen to me, son. I still have no idea what evidence there is to hold you; these people are very tight with information. Even Feld. I held a fist to his fat head and threatened to pop him like a zit, but all he'd tell me is this rot about you and Amir knowing each other in America and you coming here to harm Israel."

What amazed me was her balls-to-the-wall assurance that I had done no wrong. I never felt the need to defend myself.

"Anyway, I have lots of people working on it. I will have you out of here soon," she insisted. Then, as if she had forgotten where she left her car keys, she asked, "Are you okay?"

I'd sworn on my own soul I wouldn't let on about what I had been through, yet I couldn't imagine that she wouldn't see it. Actually, I hadn't looked at myself in a mirror since the ordeal began and had no idea if I showed signs of beatings and mental anguish, but I imagined I had to. She displayed no indication that she was looking at a scarecrow or hideous figure. I still had to hang on for dear life to the slippery reigns of a galloping emotional beast to arrest the flow of tears eager to pour out.

"I'm hanging in, Mom. They think I'm a Palestinian terrorist. But just to keep both sides even," I chuckled ironically, "the Palestinians were equally convinced I was an Israeli spy. I'm sure you saw it in the news."

Before I allowed myself to waste precious time spewing my emotional gut, I briskly moved on to the business I knew I had but one chance to transact with her.

"Mom, I wish we had more time, but there is something I need you to know. They won't listen to what I'm telling them. I need help."

"You just go ahead and tell me everything Zach."

"Listen carefully. I'm going to give you a sentence and then a list of names. What's the date today?"

"August 22nd."

"Okay, there is still some time, but you'll need every second. I'm not making this up. On September 11th, millions of people will die in Israel and America. I'm not sure what, if anything, can be done to stop it at this point. If I've gone insane or if it's a sad mistake, I'm sorry. You're the only hope I have. If you can find any clues that what I'm saying is real, then you'll have to get somebody to pay attention. Time is running short."

"You're not crazy. You know that. And what sort of mistake could there be?"

"That what I read was actually nothing more than documents to be used for a screenplay; but I don't believe the source I got it from has the imagination to invent a keychain. You'll know what to do. Check out the names and get any informa-tion you can on them. I know they are all real characters be-cause I did my own research the morning after I came across the material. There's just one more thing. Will you promise me something, I mean unconditionally?"

"I will. What is it?"

"No matter what happens, you leave Israel by September 10th. Then, you don't go back home until after September 11th."

She stared at me and then gave a slight nod of assent. A knock on the door broke our eye contact. A head peered in, a most polite voice informing my mother that time was up. She rose like steam from a boiling kettle, ready to scald her way through any obstacles placed in her path.

I felt confident she would find something that would help, but the optimism was short-lived. I realized I might be send-ing her on a goose chase with radicalized prey, carrying heavy weaponry more likely to kill her than let her catch a draft from a crack in their plan.

"I love you, Zacchaeus Miller. Don't forget who you are. That's all that matters." That was just what I needed to hear. "Remember, I'm here. I won't stop until you are out of this mess."

Where she was off to I didn't know, but for me it was back to my cell.

Of course, as soon as she left, I started ruminating about everything I should have said. I never told her I loved her and how much I appreciated her. I began to sob again, the depres-sion swooping in like black storm clouds on the day of the last game of the World Series. I lay for hours, temperamental to the point that when my lunch was sent in, I threw it against the wall. I pounded my forehead to my knees so many times that I drew blood and had to be taken to the infirmary for bandaging. I guess the visit hadn't done much good for my spirits. Now, I was worried that I might have put the person who cared most about me in harm's way.

Later that day Alon returned. He had read a few comments I had scribbled in my journal, thoughts on what Bahlya and Hadecka had been telling me about the Zionists and Israel, their intent to drive out the Palestinians by any means, legal or not. It was time for a rebuttal.

Why he wanted to spend time refuting them, I couldn't imagine. When I asked him that very question, he said it was a matter of principle, that I shouldn't spend the remainder of my life, or whatever sentence I received, with misconceptions about his country. It was the first comment I'd heard since this most recent incarceration—though off-handed and with no real substance from which I could suck an ounce of optimism— suggesting that my sentence might not consume the remainder of my life.

He also said something else I might have interpreted auspiciously, had I been able to swallow the depression lodged in my throat. He quipped that someday maybe I would be able to write sensible material explaining the Israeli position. I was starting to feel like a Ping-Pong ball being smashed by iron paddles to see which pro was capable of putting more spin on me before finally whacking me hard enough to burst my celluloid skin.

It was his opinion that Jews are safe and secure in America, and because of that, some have taken the liberty to assault the Zionists who accomplished a near-impossible feat of building a thriving economy and vibrant country for millions of Jews—out of sand, dirt, and scorching sun. He was miffed at what he called "unappreciative, spoiled-brat Jews" who would never understand that the respect they enjoyed as members of their religion was earned through sacrifice of the lives of their relatives. He labeled them "intellectual weasels, Beverly Hills limousine liberals, writing anti-Israeli books while their aunts, uncles, and cousins were having their innards blasted out of their casings by people with no motive other than hatred for Jews."

I was sure some of the reading suggested to me by the clerk at The Book Junkie had been authored by individuals fitting the sentiment Alon was preaching. I had no time to contemplate, however, because my leader whacked me with another eye-opener.

I was tired and needed a rest. I wasn't going to get one.

26

GRANDMA AND GRANDPA

"DO YOU KNOW THE story of your grandparents?" Alon chirped to begin a session.

"I mentioned to you, or someone, I was never told much about my grandparents," I moaned to counteract his morning gaiety.

"Your mother could have never disavowed her faith. She knows full well she is a Jew." In spite of his dandy mood, his scorn for my mother was without mitigation. "The Palestinian blood in you is no more than a gnat on a lion's ass and years ago you should have swatted it off. You were raised with a Jewish spirit in your home. Now, are you ready for the story of your grandparents? By all means, stop me if I'm being redundant and you know this already."

"No, I'm ready for the saga of my grandparents." I knew he had no intention of giving me a choice about hearing a thousand times over the documentary he had produced for my entertainment. "I hope you don't tell me he ended up a serial rapist and she a stripper."

He ignored my foolish attempt to lighten the upcoming news I imagined would further confuse me.

"Both your grandfather and grandmother on your Jewish side were Zionists who came to Israel before we were a nation, arriving from the Black Sea port of Odessa in Russia. They wanted a place to live peacefully, to be free from the oppression and discrimination Jews were subjected to in their country.

"Your grandfather was a soldier during the first Arab-Israeli War, a conflict that spanned a decade and only ended after World War II and the creation of the State of Israel—we became a nation on May 14th, 1948. The woman who birthed you, by the way, was born one year later…to the day.

"Your mother would be the only child for Rose, your grandmother, who aged prematurely from the arduous lifestyle and constant threat of attacks by the Arabs; she kept a weapon close by at all times and knew how to use it.

"Why am I telling you all this? Because you come from proud Zionists, the people we owe our country to. Your grandfather went on to become a diplomat for a country still in its cradle, finally traveling to America as the first Ambassador from Israel."

I wanted him to stop, to give me a moment to process the startling information he was presenting, but he ratcheted the delivery of this historical account.

"I didn't know any of this."

"Sure," he said, seeming not to believe me.

"Great. Look, I'm getting to where I don't give a shit about all these stories of my family. It's my family anyway, not yours."

"Glad to see you're finally owning it."

"I don't know anything about it. I'm just sick of you teeing off on what is none of your business. And that's it. You don't listen to me, I don't listen to you."

It was amazing. I could have told him Lady Gaga was coming to strip to the flesh and he would have proceeded undeterred.

"Your mother never had the strongest bond with her parents. These early settlers had it rough and were hardcore people. They had to be. They spent as much time fighting for their lives as living them. Their convictions were unwavering and they were met with nothing but hate and rejection by the Arabs. It was not just the Palestinians. It was the whole of the Arab world. They had always held the Jews in contempt, judging them inferior and subservient. Landing in Palestine with the intent of reclaiming land they understood had been gifted from God was reproachful to the Arabs, for no reason other than that they needed to keep these people down.

"Kaye Miller was nineteen when she took her first and only trip to her place of conception. She had argued bitterly with her parents about religion, always questioning the beliefs and traditions. In the end, she proclaimed to reject Judaism. No doubt her protests were proportionate to the fervor of her mother and father's reverence to their faith, not untypical for most young people acting out against the beliefs of their parents.

"It was a compromise that led to her coming to Israel. Your grandparents agreed to withdraw their demand that she attend college if she took the trip to her birth county. Presumably, the thought was that she would discover herself. Instead, she met your father—setting the stage for the mother of all acts of rebellion.

"Can you imagine how your grandparents felt, their only daughter, a Jew, falling for an Arab, a man whose roots dictated that he must murder every Israeli in sight? How is that for a mixed-up young lady? You know the rest of the story, except that not long after your mother ran for her life, pregnant, her parents were both killed together in a plane crash on their way to Israel on business.

"Your birth surname is Levy. Your mother changed it to Miller before your birth. Had you been raised properly, proud of your roots, you might not have been so anxious to meet your Palestinian relations and made it your life purpose to kill Jews."

He wouldn't let up. I was trying not to listen.

"Think it over. If you're interested in how we know all this, it's simple. Your grandfather, Abraham, as you surmise, was a fairly important man and left extensive correspondence; some day if you'd like, you can read some of it. I'll see you tomorrow. There's a lot more to talk about. And by the way, if you don't believe any of this, ask Zev Feld."

Something snapped, likely the mention of Feld. I was ready for a showdown at all costs.

"You may see me, but I won't be here. Do what the hell you want. You can lock my body in this cell, you can try to make me stand at attention, but you can't control my mind and spirit; I'm out of here. That's right. I'm done with all your mental harassment and intimidation. Throw me in jail for the rest of my life. Go ahead. You'll do what you want in the end regardless."

"Your sentence will be what a court determines is just," his smirk one of entertainment rather than offense.

I took to my pulpit again, bellowing my reproof, while Alon was gathering his belongings. I saw his contrived indifference as intentional, to wave a banner of antagonism in my face.

"No. Justice is admitting you have no right to be holding me in the first place. You think I'm making it up about Amir, right? Right? Right??"

The louder I screamed, the wider his mouth spread with unconcealed delight. But I kept it up, higher pitched with each word.

"Right? Right? Right? You people deserve what's coming. We'll all die here together because of your ignorance. Yeah, go ask your asshole friend, Zev Feld, why he set this up, why he insisted I register as a journalist. He did this to me!!"

By the time I finished he was out the door.

No story is worthy of the paper it's written on unless there is a villain. I'm partial to the view that if the miscreant does not atone for his sins in the end, it'll be all the better; the ogre is a convenient outlet for undiluted contempt, with no guilt or regret. Zev Feld was and would always be a reprobate rascal to me; I wouldn't forgive him if he let me shave his scalp.

I'd felt better knowing none of my past. My life had been cozy and secure. My mother had always been there when I needed her. But even after having all these historical facts dumped on me like a load of manure, I still had no sense of disillusionment or any anger toward her. These people were judging her life based on their set of values, with no consideration or regard for why she had made the decisions she had, no respect for what she'd accomplished, no idea pertaining to her character— it peeved me.

I did, however, appreciate one insight from his recent disclosures about my mother. She retained the fire and determination of what a Levy must have owned; it made me proud that she had instilled a good-sized dose of the same in me. It might be what had helped me endure the agony up to that point.

There may have been more I owed to my grandparents. The extensive attention the Israelis were showing me might have been an act of respect to my family roots. I might have been indebted to these unknown ancestors for any leniency granted me—but only for crimes never committed: yes, the pestilent thought that I had done nothing to deserve my suffering rarely abandoned me, a free pass for all the self-pity I wanted to gorge on.

As for the next morning debriefing Alon was promising, I couldn't wait. I'd set in my head to play with the fellow until he was a broken toy; and as for any of the content he had imposed on me, I would have just as well traded all the lectures I'd received to date for a tube of toothpaste—I had been a fiend about brushing and feared a mirror's view of what must have by then been a mouthful of yellowing enamel.

27

INDOCTRINATION, ISRAELI STYLE

WHEN EL CAPITAN ARRIVED in the morning, he was in an even more chipper mood, no doubt delighted that he had been assigned the task of counter-indoctrinating me. I noticed his attire had changed; he was wearing a short-sleeved shirt and shorts, the upper three buttons of his top open, showing no hair but displaying a large Star of David.

I had no idea what day of the week it was but wondered if it was a day of rest. Could my Nordic prince be the hardworking type who comes in voluntarily on his day off to work me over? He could have been on a drug, smiling at me, a lousy Arab sympathizer, like I was his best buddy, even after my last harangue.

His discourse took off like a slot car; he was in his groove. He called out "Attention!" to get me on my feet even before the door eased its way into the jam, clanking as it always did. He was ready for combat. Shamelessly, I snapped upright, as if the trash talking I directed at him the day before had never happened. Had I no self-respect left?

As soon as he began speaking, for some reason, I was hooked. I'll admit I was impressed with a philosophical bent I didn't suspect of him. After prefacing with a comment about how I had been "drinking hogwash from the Palestinians that needed pasteurizing," he continued with the Israeli version of the controversy between Israel and its enemies.

"Modern history, the history of mankind, is about strength and adaptability. Should people feign weakness, become careless and then inadequate, so they can permit themselves to be defeated and subjugated? Would that not contradict the laws of natural selection, survival of the fittest? And if so, if we violated such an elemental law as gravity, would that not spell certain doom for the human species, more absolutely even than nuclear bombs, natural disasters, or holocausts?

"Ah, the socialists work from this model, professing equality for all. But they do it out of fear, guilt, and shame. Fear of facing the ferocity of the fire within man, the power and force inherent to humans; guilt stemming from man's natural, inescapable inclination to subordinate the weak and inferior; and shame that some possess authority, imagination, and invention lacking in others.

"Great talents have been lost to the quest for eternal mediocrity of mankind, all due to these frailties I describe. No gang is more dangerous than one chanting lyrics of equality, none more destined for certain defeat, because in the end man's true nature will always rule. Yes, the lilies will be pulled from the earth and their bulbs smashed to pulp by those harvesting a hardier crop."

I thought I was listening to a lecture on the philosophy of Ayn Rand.

"When you hear our story, beginning with the birth of Israel, the transposing of weak vegetation to make room for the transplantation of more durable genus, there is a different resonance, a full orchestration of man and his elements. You will not hear us proclaiming to be victims. There will be no cry for others to rescue us. We do not groan that our mistakes are to be blamed on anyone or anything but ourselves.

"Let me know if you witness griping about outsiders corrupting us against one another. Sure, we argue, vehemently in fact. We have greatly divergent views, ideas, and interests, but we manage to work out our conflicts for the betterment of the whole. May I add that you will not be reading about us killing one another, murdering our kin, decapitating those who are of differing philosophy or belief, using our bodies, the bodies of our children, as weapons of mass destruction against innocent civilians?"

As I listened to these words, I thought back on Hadecka's lectures, in particular his lament about the infighting and betrayal by Palestinian factions—it was a point for Alon. It caused me to wonder why the Palestinians handled the situation as they did, with futility, desperation, and chaos. I had no time to dwell on the matter because Alon was in an unusually hurried state.

"Am I saying we Israelis are all good? No. We do not profess to be. We are at war, a struggle where our survival is at stake every day, and perhaps that is the best place to begin—even before the State of Israel came into being, a time when things were no different than presently in that we were unwelcome and threatened with expulsion by the whole of the Arab community.

"And let me clear up one point immediately: we have been here for thousands of years, no different than the Palestinians. When you assess it, as I began today, the stronger, smarter, and more determined will always prevail. Their only possible weakness, potential for defeat, is to be ashamed of what was accomplished, of the talents and strengths used to achieve designated aims."

Curiously, he paused. As he did, I noticed a slight movement of his right buttocks followed by what I'll describe as a long puffing sound, indisputably that of him passing gas. As his posture shifted back to fully balanced on his chair he looked up at me disgustingly, shaking his head so as to infer that I had executed the act. Shamelessly, and indifferently, he went on with his brainwashing session.

"Zach, we make no excuses or apologies for expansionism, which has been a cornerstone of Zionism from the beginning..."

There were times I would debate an issue, directly confronting him with a view contradictory to what he was professing. "But the Zionists had options to build their state where they wouldn't have had to expand at the expense of other nations."

Alon refused to dignify my challenges with displays of irritation or consternation. Oh, no. Usually he'd punish me by going back to an earlier point in the lecture and make me listen endlessly. "I see you might have missed a key concept. Let's try it again."

If I was lucky, he might offer a sterile retort, handling me like a pitiful germ. "To have gone elsewhere could have violated God's wish. You'll understand better when the Jew in you comes to life."

"I'll never be a Jew. You can't force beliefs on a person," I protested indignantly.

"You are quite right but you'll discover it on your own. Now, shall I continue helping you to do so?"

It was useless to resist.

"What do you say we go back to these heroic Zionists? They began buying land at skyrocketing prices…"

Then he'd go on about land, the Arabs selling to the Jews, more settlers arriving to build roads, hospitals, manufacturing businesses—the elements of an advanced society. All the while, in his opinion, rather than appreciating them for improving the quality of life, the Arabs hated them.

It was the same story of war, betrayal, enmity, and mistrust.

I remember one occasion when Alon's lecture was interrupted by his cell ringing. He stopped to answer, then immediately he walked out the door. It was odd because usually I would hear the door lock as soon as it was exited, regardless of whether or not someone was returning. But on this day, no doubt owing to him leaving unexpectedly, it was left unlatched.

It seemed I hadn't learned my lesson about snooping. The urge to peek outside overtook me. I eased the door open and craned my head just enough to peer out and down a long hallway. Nobody was there. Then the thought rushed me like a mugger, "I could escape." My head took off speeding down the hall in a full sprint, but my body refused to execute the command to move.

It was a humiliating experience. When I realized I was too frightened to leave the safety of my cell, I let loose of the door, dropped to the floor inside, and cradled myself in fetal position as if I were an infant, rocking my body to tame the shivering and tremulousness, just like I remembered my mother doing to me as a baby when I was afraid. By the time Alon returned I hadn't moved. He must have been accustomed to these displays of regression because he didn't comment. Instead, he picked up his line of thinking as casually as a smoker lights a cigarette—after, of course, he called me to attention.

"Now, after the division of Jerusalem, close to when we were attaining statehood, there were communities like Silwan…"

"Silwan? I remember Bahlya telling me how the Israelis were displacing the Palestinians. That was one of the places where she had been active during a demonstration. See, I do remember…but I already told you that, didn't I?"

"Of course you did. They've made a big stink about Silwan…"

And he jetted on about…land. What else? He might go on for hours but seemed to know precisely when to scan his watch. "I'll see you after lunch." Off he'd go, later returning for the next session.

Tormenting me may have stimulated his appetite, but mine was stubbornly absent. Stomachs must have memory, and between the head dunking in filthy toilets and meals with live insects crawling heartily through slop, it would be some time before mine faded and I could coax a peanut butter and jelly sandwich into my mouth without reflexive regurgitation.

I'll admit that based on my prior incarceration with the Palestinians, I was now being treated to VIP service—I had a cot with blanket and pillow, a clean toilet in my cell, meals that were nutritious, and outdoor fresh air once a day—and I noticed a yearning to read. I surmised my impulse to do so was attributable to another fear I had developed, that I was going blind.

I think atrophy begins to set in when you don't use an organ of your body. My sight was constantly blurry, and when I was outdoors for my brief sessions of fresh air I noticed I was straining to keep them open. Also, they were tired most of the day. It was to the point that I craved keeping them shut, which I did most of the time Alon kept me heedfully on my feet.

As the ocular defects came into psychic focus, I confronted the possibility that my future vision would be irreparably damaged. Thus, my interest in reading, both to test the extent of injury done as well as to experiment with a list of exercises I surmised I needed to vigilantly practice if I were to improve my prognosis.

Out of devotion to my teeth, and in the absence of a brush, I cleverly discovered a strategy to at least keep my gums as healthy as possible by massaging them twice a day with my fingers. As far as both my sight and teeth were concerned, I was motivated by the remote possibility I would eventually be released to freedom, in which case I would have salvaged at least a couple of my physical faculties.

No, what almost every male likely considers their most vital organ had passed its last rigor mortis exam quite some time before—it had not officially been declared deceased, however, until one awful morning when a fantasy crept past the guards and snuck into my cell. What must have been an apparition was a hip cat who immediately aroused my jealousy because he was happy: I saw him as the epitome of a free spirit. He had a shaggy beard and long brown hair protruding from a green knit cap. He was wearing old jeans fraying at the cuffs, with lots of holes and a piss-yellow t-shirt that heralded him a beatnik.

His upper garment plucked my heart like a sour musical note, bountifully proclaiming "ALL IS COOL" in bright pink across the front. He was smiling gleefully but must have traded his guitar for the *Hustler* magazine he was holding in his hand. He was a bighearted dude, opening the centerfold to show it to me. It was a dead ringer for Bahlya…and I threw up.

I thought of asking Alon if I could get some material to read and vowed by the end of the session to do so, but in the meantime I vomited another portion of my lunch as soon as he came back. He in no way appeared insulted, my captain— unless his rank was promoted for boring me worse than measuring the speed in which sunshine melts glaciers—for he took no notice of my gagging.

"Hamas, essentially a resistance movement, was established late in 1987. It took them about an hour to make the official mission of their organization the destruction of Israel, stipulating absolute proscription from negotiation or compromise, from any form of diplomacy with Israel. To justify their hardcore stance, reinterpreting history as fascists are so talented at doing, they concluded not only that the Jews had single-handedly caused World War II but the big one before, the revolution in Russia, the fall of the Ottoman caliphate… then our tiny portion of earth beings were responsible for lice, rattlesnake bites, bee stings, hot temperatures, snow, deluges, world poverty, the man in the moon, old age, and finally, sneezing. You get the point."

What a comic. I had been given no license to express humor and feared it might be taken as a sign of joy, which of course would necessitate his backing up and repeating the lecture, so I refrained from laughter. While dousing the urge, I did grasp on to the remote memory of levity. From an earlier life, I recalled when I had enjoyed wit while in repose, lying on a couch, probably because it was a movie or television program entertaining my now perishing sense of humor.

For the remainder of the afternoon, he bored me with rerun discussions of the intifadas, the various peace processes, and dealing with Palestinian leadership. As he was concluding that day, I had the sense he was wrapping up his work with me. He never directly addressed my hunch.

"If you'd like, I'll have those records from your grandfather sent over to you."

"Sure. But if you don't mind my asking, might I have some books, perhaps a novel?"

"What do you have in mind?"

"Anything by Tom Robbins, James Steinbeck, John Fowles. Fantasy." I would have dropped to my knees and begged if I thought it would help. "I need to…use my eyes."

"We'll see. It appears you will be having a trial not too far in the future, so I would imagine your attorney will be coming to see you."

"I didn't do anything!" As I said the words, a profound sense of sorrow came over me, for I was innocent.

"You had no business coming to this country with the intent of hooking up with relatives dedicated to overthrowing Israel. You may now have a different reference point to comprehend how magnificent this country is. It's a miracle that from wasteland we have built a dynamic model of freedom, industry, and intellect, that we have advanced services for our people, making us competitive with any nation, that we are growing in a world mired in economic chaos."

He continued with a sentimentality I wouldn't have expected. "Zach, I like you. I hope for leniency when your sentencing takes place, but mostly I hope you understand what you have done and how misguided you were. You are a Jew. I hope you will find a way to be proud of it."

And this is a democracy? I wondered. I've been deemed guilty without a trial, imprisoned as an enemy combatant of the state without an official hearing, denied any rights, and I'm to have a new perspective, to love Israel and be proud of my Jewish roots; I'm to eviscerate the bowels of the Palestinian in my soul, go to temple every Saturday, become a Bar Mitzvah?

I could only imagine redressing him with expletives. But what would have been the use?

28

MOMS: BETTER HOPE YOU GET A GOOD ONE

EVEN WITH THE REORIENTATION sessions sponsored by my new hosts, I had far too much time on my hands to think. Fortunately, Alon was kind enough to arrange for several books to be sent to my suite, including *Skinny Legs and All* by Tom Robbins. Why this novel was permitted I'll never figure out, since it directly pertains to the Middle East region and is an obvious indictment of modern culture, especially Western society.

I made a disciplined effort to read at intervals each day. While I was battling an ocular dust storm—my eyes fluttering and twitching—trying to imbibe the unexpected jewels Alon had delivered to me, my mother was overwhelmed, attempting to collect facts based on the information I had provided her. Most of what her early labor reaped would not come to my attention until the finale of this adventure. Nevertheless, it seems appropriate at this juncture to commit an anachronism. It permits critical information to be disclosed at the most opportune moment.

By the time my mother arrived in Israel, she had been shaking political trees for weeks. As she'd made clear to Kessler, she was setting her plan into motion for inundating the media with information about her son who was imprisoned and denied basic rights. While most of the Arab media turned a cold shoulder, that reaction was not universal. Shortly after setting down in Israel, she received an unexpected call.

"Ms. Miller, my name is Danish Nasir. I'm a freelance journalist covering Israel and the whole Middle East." (Indeed, it was the same Mr. Nasir who had boldly stood up to al-Pirani at my media show. He was also a man fluent in not only Arabic and English but French and Russian as well.)

"Then you must know by now what I'm up against," she commented to the stranger.

"I've written quite extensively about Ron Rosen. Do you know who he is?"

"Vaguely," she answered. "He's a journalist who was expelled from Jerusalem—initially only Jerusalem, but later from Israel entirely. But I don't know details."

"What we're told is that he was writing anti-Israeli material. That really doesn't appear to be the case. The Israelis simply didn't like his views and deemed him unacceptable. It's about journalistic freedom and I'm an advocate. So, what I'm interested in is whether your son's case may be related."

"I don't think so, because Zach never wrote a word while in Israel. I doubt he had any intention of reporting on anything of a political nature; at least he never has in the past. He was set up and now the Israelis are saying he's a Palestinian spy.

They're charging him with being a security threat. They're accusing him of intending to conduct acts harmful to Israel. Do you know what that means?"

"I do. Really, though, this doesn't sound like a story I'd want to get involved with. I appreciate your taking the time to talk with me," Nasir stated, about to hang up.

"Mr. Nasir, I need help," she urgently pleaded. "My son is innocent and I can't do this alone."

"I don't see how I could be of any assistance."

"I'm going to tell you something I haven't discussed for over thirty years. Nobody I know is aware of this, but I'm desperate so I'm going to disclose it to you, a man I've never even met. Why? Because you called me…and you know this region of the world…and I can hear in your voice that you are a man of principle and compassion. If it's okay, I'll continue?

"Of course," he courteously replied.

"I was married here in Israel to a Palestinian man who is dead; nevertheless, he's father to my son. I'm born Jewish," her phraseology crafted to emphasize that the manner in which she addressed faith was not commanded by her background. "What's happening to my son is because the Israelis…listen, there's so much more going on…and I promise what I have will put your Rosen matter in diapers; anything you've ever reported on in your career will be child's play in comparison to this. Please, at least meet me for coffee and hear what I have to say—I'll buy!"

Nasir was reluctant but he agreed to invest at least a few minutes. They met down the block from my mother's apartment, at Forelin Café. It was late in the afternoon and the restaurant was close to empty. They sat at a table for four, facing a large window looking onto the boulevard. A white cloth was draped over a bright yellow tablecloth beneath, matching the yellow walls and the large pleated white curtains secured with sashes. The chairs were an amber shade and made for a distinguished setting. Kaye Miller, wearing a tan and yellow Lacoste top with white jeans and brown leather flats, blended in as if she were a piece of the décor.

Nasir noticed that she ordered a full entrée—roasted peppers with goat cheese wrapped in slices of eggplant—but only occasionally nibbled while sipping grapefruit juice. He also saw her as distressed, seemingly tired, and a tad jittery. The man had never had children but had been around relatives enough to understand that this woman was fighting as much for her own life as her son's. As the conversation progressed, he also was able to gain a better sense of her character and personality.

"Zach doesn't know any of this. After his father was killed, I wasn't allowed to leave the community we were in; the family was sure I was having a son, and the cousin, Mr. Hamdallah senior, volunteered to oversee my detention. I was staying in his home at the time and not permitted to leave. Well, one day I managed to get his sister to take me out shopping. We were at a store and I ditched her. Then, I stole a car and headed straight to the American consulate. Until the recent incidents with Zach, I thought about them as little as possible."

"You never remarried?" Nasir asked.

"No. I'll tell you, I think I was traumatized. I was pregnant; my husband who I adored was dead, and right after that my parents were both killed in a plane crash. My fate was to raise my baby alone. I had to dig deep, and it was the only time I was grateful for the stubborn determination my parents had unwittingly infused in me. I dedicated my life to being a mother…and I really don't regret it."

It is doubtful Nasir had anything contrived in mind, but his line of questioning might suggest otherwise.

"But you've been done being mother to a child for many years."

"True…but look, we're getting off the subject."

"Of course we are," he said kindly.

During the meeting she shared all she had gathered from her brief contact with me. Then, she launched an unabashed entreaty.

"Mr. Nasir. One week, that's it. I'll pay you whatever you believe is fair for your time. If, after that, you find nothing to offset the suspicion that my son is concocting a story to escape a charge the Israelis will prove in the end to be true, you're free to quit; and I'll double the fee for the week."

Later, he'd assure her it wasn't the money—he was nicely fixed as well—but who she was that convinced him that Zach Miller didn't come from the type of background that would breed an individual willing to come to Israel to do damage to the country. What he shared with me later was another factor influencing his decision: my mother was desperate and he felt compelled to assist her.

"You've got yourself a deal," Nasir submitted. "It happens I was planning a week off, so this will be my vacation."

She wasn't in a strong position to bargain, but my mother wanted no misunderstanding. "This won't be restful, trust me."

The first finding Nasir made was an article that appeared August 17th in Etala'at, an Iranian newspaper. During a political rally held for President Ahmadinejad, one of his staunch backers, Ali Halaby Laylaz, was uncharacteristically chatty and took to the microphone. As an addendum to his short speech praising Ahmadinejad, he addressed the Palestinian problem to a crowd deliberately crafted so as to exclude any opposition and thus inclined toward a hard-line attitude.

"We are a people of destiny. As our president has courageously asserted, we will drive the Israelis into the sea. This is a prophetic mandate that must be honored by the Iranian nation."

The journalist continued his report: *Mr. Laylaz had the crowd cheering at his insistence of Iran's great historical fortune. This is a man not known to appear often in public and less frequently to speak openly of his politics or business affairs. He further excited the audience when he reminded them of the devil's due America had suffered on Sept. 11, 2001. He then targeted his next comment toward that date the following month, adamantly professing to have inside knowledge that Israel would be America's partner in crisis this year.*

After the speech, a young reporter of the aforementioned journal, spotting an opportunity, rushed to Laylaz with pen and pad in hand, begging a few minutes' time for further commentary that he might use for his article to be published only in Arabic. Laylaz (one of the billionaire backers of Jawaris' scheme) must have been in a charitable mood, taking the fellow aside and answering questions at length.

"Mr. Laylaz, I'm sure all of Iran would like to know more about what you say is *inside knowledge* of impending attacks on Israel and America. Is Iran finally ready to take action?"

Laylaz might have patted the eager newspaperman on the shoulder, pacifying his avidity, or sent him on his way with a seductive wink. He did neither. Instead, taking the occasion to stoke his own zeal, he expounded upon his hatred of both Israel and America in general and on the inevitability of their downfall.

"The time is ripe; history is on our side. We are pregnant and ready to give birth to tragedy. Did they think we would never find a way to cripple them?"

Several days later, the story showed up again, this time in an Arab political weekly, Ain-Al-Yaqeen. The author, Wali Mirza, mentioned that he had tried, unsuccessfully, to contact Mr. Laylaz, hoping if nothing else that the otherwise keep-to-himself man was starting to open his personal life and Mr. Mirza might possibly earn an inside track on a biography. No follow-up was ever found regarding Laylaz' divinatory remarks.

There were, however, two other items related to the research carried out on Laylaz. First, Laylaz—one of two sons—had a brother, Duha, who was a successful businessman (but far less so than he) living in America—New York, in fact. Several months prior—in what appeared a rushed decision—Duha had sold his group of five women's clothing stores, as well as the properties on which they were located.

The second finding was that over the past year, Laylaz had made large transfers of funds to a Lebanese bank, Fransbank. Nasir was able to ascertain the amounts and the account they were deposited into but could not find the beneficiary of the account entitled "Mafaz," "victory" in English. Noteworthy was that the man was not known to have had any enterprises or potential investments in Lebanon.

What would be brought to light later regarding Laylaz' past and his potential motivation to fund Jawiris' plan was that his family had owned large parcels of coastal property in what is now Israel but had fled for their lives after the Zionists had attacked the area where they lived. Laylaz hated the Israelis and believed that since his ancestors were deceased, he'd have an easy time reclaiming the property in a reconstructed Palestine.

I had given my mother all the names of the parties involved with Jawiris, along with as much factual material as I could convey in five minutes. With Nasir, the first vein of gold had been struck. The initial findings pertaining to Laylaz tweaked Nasir's imagination, inspiring him to redouble his efforts. That was a huge break for my mother, in that Nasir was a seasoned reporter with extensive experience as an investigator. He was able to delve into material that would have required extensive translation, plus he had a vast network of impartial contacts throughout the Middle East.

Further, he had knowledge of all significant media outlets and understood how institutions, especially those involving banking, operated in the region. He was known as such a charmingly tenacious pest that he could penetrate the offices of princes and magnates with no more than a smile. Finally, he had guts and wouldn't back down if political pressure were to be exerted on him.

Kaye Miller, self-appointed investigator, rented a two-bedroom apartment in a suburb of Tel Aviv, using one of the bedrooms for sleep and the remaining space for work. She furnished the extra rooms with desks for herself and Nasir, and there was a spare bed in the second bedroom.

Nasir frequently worked late into the evening and often slept over. In fact, it was subsequent to the next breakthrough that he realized he might be on the threshold of a story with the potential to make Watergate seem like a detergent commercial. Thereafter, he never left the apartment except on business.

The temporary dwelling was just across the street from the beach, on HaYarkon Street. Off the living room was a superb large balcony with a small table, two chairs, and a lounge. It had an unobstructed view of the Mediterranean coastline; there was also an equally enchanting scene of the ocean from the main bedroom. One could lie in bed in the morning and watch the sunlight tap dance gleefully on the water's surface, then in the evening from the same spot witness the spectacle of pink, red, and yellow on the horizon vaporize to a dark mist as the sun dove into the sea—and at the same cost enjoy it from the outdoor balcony.

I mention this priceless feature—and it took a chunk to rent it—only because of the fact that not once did either of the inhabitants of the apartment step out to appreciate the beauty. The monotonous, flat-painted, cream-colored walls and basic wood and fabric furniture in brown and red tones were equally ignored. With the exception of outings to purchase supplies, they knew nothing of what was occurring outside the spellbinding partitions.

So entranced was my mother by their cause that when she did finally have occasion to vacate the temporary workstation, for the first time noticing cafés, restaurants, and the ocean, she commented to Nasir, "How come we never went out to dinner?"

Nasir laughed at the irony and hugged her, his head of full, thick gray hair cropped just short enough that it prickled naturally upward in an array of silver sparkles, stood six inches above my mom's. He was only two years senior in age to his new partner. He had lived around the world, for the last twenty years in the Middle East, and made his home in Dubai, where most of his family still resided.

Nasir always dressed formally. He proudly purchased his wardrobe during trips to Italy. Grey- and black-toned sweaters with white dress shirts, slacks, and dress shoes were typical attire. He was careful to shave daily and prided himself on keeping a tidy appearance, arguing that good work habits begin at home and the man who neglects his presentation will be sloppy and careless in his career, something he believed potentially disastrous in his field.

Right after the wetting of his tongue on the Laylaz story, an associate journalist who actually worked for *Ain-al-Yaqeen*, the weekly that had referenced the Laylaz article, called Nasir. The man, Jibran Baccus, insisted on absolute anonymity when he disclosed that Rami Majeed, the Syrian backer of Jawiris' project, had a parcel of land outside Damascus that had been used as a training facility—it had been impossible to penetrate the security during that time.

He informed Nasir that as of the past week the facility had suddenly been abandoned, leaving numerous buildings and equipment unattended. His investigation discovered that Majeed was the owner of the land, but Baccus had no information as to who had leased it and for what purpose. Nasir had been knowledgeable of many suspicious facilities in the region during the past several years. Most, he assumed to have been used for secret military projects or terrorist purposes. He appreciated the news—Baccus had contacted Nasir to see if by chance he had any information of his own on the subject— they had shared data many times in the past.

Nasir was acquainted with Majeed only because the man had married the Syrian president's daughter. Being an astute businessman, he was able to acquire wealth such that by the time he was thirty he owned a position on Forbes' list of the ten youngest billionaires—number three to be exact.

Scanning the Arab portal, Al Bawaba, for Majeed, Nasir noticed the man was referenced with respect to an article in a Syrian newspaper, *Alforat*. Not unexpected was the fact that the paper was owned by Majeed and essentially served as a mouthpiece for President Bashar al-Assad to express his views as regional secretary of the Ba-ath Party. Majeed had written his own editorial condemning Israel for bad faith in negotiating the return of the Golan Heights. What floored the team working on my behalf was that in the article Majeed expounded to those Syrians with relatives still disenfranchised in Israel.

"Let me assure our people trapped illegally in land occupied by the Israelis that you will be reunited with friends and family in Syria soon. I'm leaving in a week for vacation in Iran and I'll be returning September 17th. In my absence, the anniversary of September 11th will be celebrated. By the time I return home, I expect our army will be marching unopposed into what was briefly Israel, to liberate our land and people."

After reading the short editorial, Nasir sat down across from where my mother was busy making nagging calls to news outlets and informed her of what he had found.

"Kaye," Nasir chuckled, "people of prominence in my culture all like to envision themselves as prophets, auguring the future, foretelling of disasters they claim to have been delivered to them by God. Lucky for us, they also can't keep their mouths shut." He stood up, nodding his head confidently. "Soon we may be ready to get the attention of the Israelis."

He had a habit of imitating a golf swing when he was elated. He refused to call the sport his hobby, but he did own a set of clubs and was known to shoot a round on occasion. He was modest, and rightly so, admitting his game rarely broke ninety. On this occasion his torso rotated excitedly.

"I'd run a check on Majeed's accounts but he owns the whole damn banking system, so it'll be impossible to get anything," he said, watching his imaginary ball soar into the Mediterranean Sea. "What I think I'll do is take a shot, see if by chance he's conducted any activity through Lebanese banks."

After uncovering four equal deposits for twenty-five million and one for ten million over the past year to Byblos Bank, Lebanon—deposits that were later transferred to the same account Laylaz had used at Fransbank, with no record of land purchase or business investment in the country—Nasir was convinced I was telling the truth.

"That's it, Kaye. Your son is legit. Let's get working," he shouted across the room.

29

THE ARAB BILLIONAIRE'S CLUB

MY MOTHER WAS SPENT, physically and emotionally. She assumed he was joking that they now needed to get down to work and responded in kind.

"You mean we haven't started yet?"

"Nope!"

She looked over at him and laughed, but he was dead serious. "Are you sure you don't have children?"

"Maybe it's not too late," he winked one of his small eyes. "We have to put all this together and make sure we have every conceivable fact on each person involved. Time is short and if we don't organize meticulously, they'll find cause for doubt."

I can only imagine the savage dedication for both. They had already devoted every minute of the days and nights they were together to reach the point they were, now the next few days were going to be equally as tiring as they collected the added material Nasir sought.

Jawiris had kept his lips sealed in public announcements. However, he telegraphed a clue by traveling three times to

Syria during the prior six months. Then, after arriving in Damascus, he was chauffeured out of town, his destination undisclosed but definitely proximate to where Baccus had indicated the facility was located. His last visit was two days before the desertion of the camp.

Additional incriminating evidence came by way of emails sent by Jawiris to a very close friend in Israel, Dr. Efron. Speaking in obvious intentional riddle, he suggested that if the doctor was planning to reunite with his family in Syria, he might want to advance the date a tad. I'll quote one of the correspondences.

"*What a shame about our friend* (he had to be referring to Amir, specifically to a fact I'd later learn, that he had to flee from the Israelis). *Fortunately, his work was completed, but I must express concern at this point for the safety of you and your family.*"

For some reason, Efron did not heed the warning. He kept to his anticipated date of departure between the 8th and 10th of September.

The travel records for Amir were also obtained. They showed visits to each of the cities where the six backers lived and to the same region in Syria where the training was being conducted. His phone records also documented many calls to all of the partners and to a host of other accomplices involved in the planning stages.

One of the other donors, Basem Uddin, an Iraqi, was well known to Nasir. The journalist had written a story about the miraculous history leading to Uddin's wealth. As a small boy, his father had abandoned the mother, brother, and him and was never heard from after that. The brother, a dull-minded fellow, took off in his early twenties on a brainless journey to find their father.

What he discovered was that the elder Uddin had farmed for a period of time in Palestine on a plot he had purchased. Subsequently, the Zionist threatened him off his land. At that point, he took a position on a freighter and made his way to America, where he died a few years later. He also learned that his father had accumulated an unclaimed estate of fifty thousand dollars, a huge sum at the time.

The brother was making his way home with the fortune and somehow ended up in upstate New York, where he was swindled into buying a large parcel of worthless land; he was then killed on the voyage home.

Years later, the younger Uddin received correspondence from a party looking to purchase the land. Uddin, having worked in land and real estate at home, decided to come to America and investigate himself. What he found was a bonanza in real estate development where his brother had made his purchase. He decided to handle the improvement of the property himself, and this launched him on the path to financial success.

It was the land in Palestine that he believed was his inheritance from his father that most riled him. He sought revenge against the Israelis. That motive—proving the indestructibility of hate—made him a perfect partner for Jawiris' plan of destruction.

Nasir recalled hearing of the vitriol expressed by Uddin toward Israel. Finding his name on the list I had given my mother excited his interest. Contrary to Laylaz, Uddin had pressed upper and lower lips tightly together, not letting out a line on the inside track he held on this soon-to-be implemented plot.

But what he did do—similarly discovered through the research by Nasir and my mother—was to make deposits into Bank Med Lebanon and then subsequently, in smaller denominations, to transfer the money into an account at Banque Misr, also in Lebanon. Finally, the entire sum was transferred again to the same account in Lebanon used by the other conspirators.

Nasir calculated it was near a billion dollars that had been deposited and placed at the sole discretion of Jawiris. As an interesting side note, the most consistent patterns between the parties investigated were the large money transfers into the Lebanese bank and arrangements to move family and friends out of harm's way.

For example, Uddin, a boy raised in poverty, treasured education. His oldest son was a graduate business student at Northwestern University's Kellogg School of Management, living in Chicago with his wife, who at the time was in her final month of pregnancy. They were excitedly awaiting the birth of their first child.

The son had spent the summer in an internship position with an international consulting firm. After registering for classes for the fall semester of his second year, he unexpectedly withdrew to postpone his last quarter. The act was obviously orchestrated by his father, who in anticipation of the grand event, arranged to have him flown back to Iraq to be with the family.

Coincidently, Uddin also had a nephew for whom he assigned himself to fill in as father figure, owing to his older brother having been killed on his journey to find their father. This nephew was a businessman living in Gaza with his family. Uddin used his own contacts with American companies in Iraq to gain favor with the Israelis and was able to obtain a special permit for the man and his family to join him in Iraq.

This took place in August. The explanation given the Israeli authorities was that Uddin himself was ill and wanted his family close to help him with his business, to take over in the event that something happened to him. It was a consummate fabrication.

Once Nasir determined the enormity of the threat, he discreetly placed trusted people in proximity to each of the key conspirators to gather critical tidbits of information. These were facts that when bundled together wrapped truth about the Jawaris project as fatally as a rope around a hanging man's neck.

This seems to be a fitting place for revealing a secret I've debated disclosing before the completion of the telling of my adventure. Nasir, an Arab who abhorred violence and who lived by the principle of human worth irrespective of race, color, or religion, proved his point to me, falling in love with my mother. To be honest, I was thrilled to have my mom finally move on to a relationship. I'll also admit that when I found out, it unleashed in me what might have been a dormant drive for an old-fashioned, lasting, secure bond with a mate: I found myself yearning for it for the first time in my life.

I think up to this point, each of the roads I had traveled were excuses for me to shrug off responsibility. I'm certain that along those well-traveled highways I had left some good women, furtively reaching for their hearts with my left hand and pushing them away with the right, racing off like a rank shoplifter.

How they had time for their love story is astonishing, given the volume of work they were producing. In addition to what I've described regarding the fruits of their research to this point, they also studied in depth the other three donors, Asif Pervaiz from Pakistan, Hussein Al-Mostafa from Egypt, and Jaffer Al-Yassin from Saudi Arabia. In each case, the investigation found unusual and incriminating evidence.

By the time the team had compiled this information, they were overwhelmingly convinced I had not wandered upon fictional material. To the contrary, they were alarmed and recognized that they needed to take action to arrest the planned assault.

As they debated what step to take next, they lingered on questions they couldn't answer. Here was a collection of bright and highly successful men with influence and power. They were savvy about how the world of politics and commerce operated, yet they carelessly allowed themselves to be linked to one another.

What Nasir and my mother didn't understand was that each of these men had no awareness they were connected in support of the project. Furthermore, there was not one single act uncovered by the investigative team that was worthy of attention on its own. Unless someone like me stumbled onto the landmine of information I had found in Amir's safe, there would never have been reason for suspicion and no motivation for anyone to try to connect the numerous disparate dots making up the puzzle picture.

One could question their judgment. Men of high status openly fomenting anti-American and Israeli sentiments in English press would be foolish. But their outbursts were to the Arabic media, where the same words would earn them respect and notoriety: presenting opposite faces in the Western countries and Arab world was common practice.

The only issue somewhat questionable was the movement of money. Yet, even there, several banks were involved before all the funds found their way into the "victory" account for Jawiris to parcel out as required. And there was nobody who would have been concerned with the transfers. They were large, but not atypical by the standards of the rich institutional banks being used.

My mother and Nasir were at a disadvantage trying to muscle their way through apparent inconsistencies. They couldn't have known many of the other details I hadn't had time to convey to my mother during the only meeting she was permitted, critical considerations such as knowing that none of the partners had even the slightest control over the project.

Therefore, stealth commando operations arresting and bringing them to Israel would accomplish nothing.

There was the possibility that even if I could step in and provide further assistance, there might be no interdiction that would prevent the disaster. Jawiris had placed many safeguards to prevent a short-circuiting near the September 11th date. I wasn't sure if even he could call off the attack.

Nasir, with the findings he and my mother assembled, knew they needed to act but didn't know what path to pursue.

"Kaye, if we encounter Israeli officials who refuse to listen because they assume we're trying to influence Zach's upcoming trial, which would be considered tampering, the word could spread and doors will categorically close to us without a chance of bringing the facts to their attention. Then again, in careless hands, the information could result in disastrous consequences," he reasoned out loud.

"What if there were to be a leak? If the press were to catch wind of even a whisper of suspicion of what might happen, it would place Jawiris and his people on alert. That's dangerous. They might panic and accelerate their execution date, leaving fewer vital moments to create a plan to counteract them. Not to mention, Kaye, if the public was to sniff a rumor of this sort, the chaos would be unimaginable."

In the midst of their deliberation my mother received a phone call.

"Hello," Kaye said, hearing a voice only remotely familiar. "Yes, it's Ms. Miller."

The female party on the line introduced herself and then continued.

"I've been away for the last two weeks on a project that's kept me out of touch with the news. I just heard about Zach."

"How did you find me?"

"If you're in Israel, I can find you." The voice at the other end of the line chuckled. "I want to hear what's happening."

"This is so strange. I remember you had a crush on Zach," my mom sobbed.

"Problem was he didn't have one on me," the caller jested. "I'm sorry, Ms. Miller. Can we get together?"

"I'd love to but truthfully every second of my time is consumed with trying to help him. I have a partner who…"

"Please, I work for the Israeli government. I can't do anything if the allegations are true, but if anyone can help, it's me."

It was one of those fortuitous, hard-to-imagine, phew-phew-phew contacts that might be needed repeatedly in a lifetime, comes only once, but you're so happy to have it on that occasion that you forget about all the times luck ducked you in a dark alleyway.

30

DIDN'T I KNOW YOU IN
HIGH SCHOOL?

I HAD LEFT THIRTY behind and was by now early thirty-something, thirty-two years old to be precise. I'd graduated from high school at seventeen. Like every other person my age, I've lived almost a complete second life since that memorable event: I recall only snippets from the first half of my existence.

Lots of people look back in horror, reflecting on fifteen to seventeen as a crummy period of identity crisis, rejection, and relational experimentation resulting in pain and heartache. I remember riding Tony Robinson's motorbike down Pico Boulevard on the way to a Friday night party with no helmet on and the cool breeze making me feel invincible. I recall working as a busboy at a restaurant and the first day on the job being accused by a waitress of ripping off her tip; the vehemence of her reaction until the coins were recovered from the dish cart they'd accidentally been tossed into reflected how precious money is when you work for it—from that day I could do no wrong with her and was adored by the rest of the crew.

I can still reminisce about the time two of my friends and I drank an unfathomable volume of liquor. I came home in time to vomit on the back porch, my mother awakening, surveying the situation, indifferently taking the hose and washing off my puke, and then going back to sleep without expressing a word to me.

There was another experience from junior high school I'll never forget—the first time I danced with Stephanie Eisenberg, her neck so long, smooth, and soft, I wanted to burrow in and hibernate the winter away smelling her gardenia fragranced body oil. I've never been able to get over stretch-version necks. To this day, I love to let my eyes climb slowly up the trunk, awaiting the thrill of exploring the cheeks, eyes, lips, and hair that sit atop.

As I tax my mind to examine my past, what stands out most is the awareness that the bulk of the experiences I lived through have decomposed, as though shoved through a sawmill in my cortex, only to be blown away with the wind to fertilize the collective unconscious of generations to come; I know they're gone only because much had to have happened between the few events I do recall. Of those surviving as memorable phenomena, they can be retrieved with varying degrees of effort. A few are redeemable with cheap coupons, but the most obdurate demand double- or triple-value certificates. The memory of the party calling my mother that day would have been pricey. Still, it was a fateful occurrence that the lady landed back in Israel when she did, playing me a true royal flush, in spades.

The girl who phoned my mother was my classmate from high school; in fact, the pretty chick—the term we boys used when referring to the lovely ladies—had the smartest head of anyone in the school, probably even in the state or country. She also happened to be my senior prom date. I can't explain why that wondrous event was put to sleep within a week of our graduation.

"Okay, Josea. Let me tell you what's happening," my mom expressed to my prom date during the unexpected first call. "When I went to see Zach, he told me he had come upon information about a terrible scheme to harm Israel and America this coming 9-11. I've been working with a journalist, Danish Nasir, and we've uncovered what amounts to proof that what he's saying is true."

"I don't want to upset you but lots of prisoners make up stories," Josea interrupted.

"Maybe you should see what we're talking about," Kaye Miller replied hotly, trying unsuccessfully to hide her irritation.

"I'll have a car pick you up within an hour. Put together what you have."

She hung up. Both my mother and Nasir soon arrived at Josea's flat, toting three large folders they hastily bound together, each crammed with meticulously organized notes and documents compiled since the beginning of their research.

Josea lived very close to my mother's place and also enjoyed the blessing of a full ocean view. Why she spent the extra money for the amenity is a mystery; it was apparent she enjoyed it as little as my mother. There wasn't even a piece of furniture on the panoramic outdoor patio. The inside of her apartment was also sparingly decorated, with just the basic essentials in the living and dining rooms. She had occupied the same unit since her arrival in Israel, yet neglected the walls and made no attempt to furnish the place with the little items one buys inexpensively at Pier One. She lived in a minimalist manner, but it was not necessitated by lack of funds.

There was an upright studio piano. On the top was a series of family pictures. Otherwise, the rooms lacked character or personal expression. It was obvious to my mother that Josea had a crash pad and spent most of her time working; she surmised Josea needed a partner who wanted to play home-maker.

It was deep into the morning hours when my mother fell asleep on the floor and Nasir on a chair. Josea was engrossed in every morsel of data, skimming, categorizing and compart-mentalizing, memorizing and storing it; synthetic analysis would follow—all this was done without the aid of scanner or computer. Under normal circumstances, she would have availed herself of modern office equipment out of consideration for others who might need the information at later dates, but contemplating the options, she decided it was best the informa-tion be kept tightly packed where she had confidence for its safety. Later in the morning, when the couple awakened after a brief sleep, the parcels had been repackaged. When my mother saw nothing to indicate Josea had made copies, she broke down in tears, accusing Josea of foolishness for not believing the evidence.

"What the hell is wrong with you people? Let them blow you to Texas for all I care, but get my son out of that rat trap!"

"What are you talking about?" Josea queried, dumbfounded by my mom's outburst.

"You're giving everything back. You never made a copy… you don't believe this, right?"

"I think this is indisputable," Nasir calmly tried to mediate. "If you don't do something quickly…today is August…27th. The clock's not stopping."

"Mr. Nasir, Ms. Miller, I agree. I'm trying to determine what course of action to take. I don't need to tell you how sensitive this is."

"Then why didn't you make your own copy?" Kaye demanded.

"I did."

"Where?"

Josea laughed, pointing to her head. "Things like this I prefer keeping to myself. I don't want to take papers as potentially explosive as these to the office…yet. You need to guard those files with your lives."

"You're telling me you memorized all that?" Kaye asked.

"Yes."

That was the last time my mother questioned Josea. Over the course of the few days that followed, during which time the three worked together intensely, Josea referenced the material off the top of her head with perfect and instantaneous recall—later my mother would be heard jesting, "Now that's a freakin' elephant."

Josea's mind was racing through every possibility. "Ms. Miller, suspicions are going to run rampant. There may be questions about Zach's forthrightness. The Israelis will rightly be concerned that what he's reporting is nothing other than a fiction fed unwittingly to him as a counter-terrorist ploy, the Palestinians releasing him to the Israelis, knowing that once they heard of the plan they would overreact and create an international embarrassment that could be used against Israel—so the Palestinians could then bargain for statehood and God knows what else.

"You have to understand that the perfidiousness in the relationship between Israel and the Arab world is so gross that no conceivable act can be dismissed. This is what I work on every day. It would not be beyond the masterminds of the entire Arab world to align for this type of project. That's why the Israelis won't listen to Zach."

Her next statement didn't set well with Kaye Miller, who wanted no part of aspersions suggesting a lack of innocence on my part.

"Let's not rule out yet another possibility. What if the Israeli position is accurate? What if it was only due to the Palestinian betrayal and abuse that Zach has decided to disclose what he discovered?" Josea presented as a supposition. "In other words, he could have been involved in terrorist activities and at the same time have credible information about the security of Israel that he is now hoping to trade for his freedom."

"You believe that could…"

"I'm only telling you what I know they'll be considering, what I would take into account myself. This is exactly the type of project I'd be called in to investigate, so I can't approach this carelessly."

"Yes, but do YOU believe that could be true?"

"I doubt it, but it's conceivable. I have to account for even the most remote probability." Josea stopped to deliberate. "Does it make sense he'd all of a sudden become a radical in any faith? No. But I am aware people have sharp reversals of allegiance through their twenties. It is not impossible that he discovered something within his being that led to him going through a mental upheaval," Josea astutely cautioned.

Josea knew nothing of my family history; much of it had just been introduced to me. But my mom knew she had to be informed. After a full disclosure, Josea was intrigued, but her response was not pleasing to my mother.

"That's powerful history. It ups the stakes for the theory that Zach was researching independently to become aware of what you're telling me. What else could have caused him to come to Israel, especially on such short notice, and in spite of your objection, insist he was leaving? Then he stays for a prolonged period with absolutely no agenda or mission? Ms. Miller, I'm not trying to discourage you, but these are critical potential motivators. I need to talk with Zach directly."

Josea Roth had cruised through the SAT with a score the rest of the student body drooled over, a perfect 1,600. She chose MIT and graduated with a dual major in math and physics. She was working for RAND Corporation on high-level government projects and graduated Harvard Law School before she could vote for president. It was during her legal training that she met Samuel Levine, an esteemed professor. He would later introduce her to the Israelis, who in turn would offer her a top post in their security network.

That both Josea and her high school prom date would be in Israel at the same time was no miracle. Nor was it shocking that she, an esteemed jewel for whom the Israelis were willing to pay ten first-round draft choices to coax her into coming, had a greater worth than I, a traitor to my people—I wasn't worth the price of the box they'd just as soon send me home in.

That was the score when Josea came to pay me a first visit. She wanted to be sold on me. She wasn't.

31

HEY, JEW BOY, YOU HAVE A VISITOR

THERE WAS NO GAME of twenty questions challenging me to guess who was coming to visit. Instead, there was a rap on my door.

"Hey, Jew boy, put on your Sunday clothes. You have a visitor," one of the guards yelled to me minutes before Josea arrived.

I couldn't imagine who would be coming other than my attorney, who I still had not met. Immediately, I tried to collect an orderly accounting of what had happened to me in prison. I wanted to have the information I believed he would need to defend and clear me of the false charges in a timely manner. But the thoughts muddled and every time I tried to join two together I fumbled. Exasperated, I stood pounding a wall, the damn thing so sick of me beating it senseless that it started spitting flakes of paint in my face.

That's how Josea found me when she entered my abode. I turned to her voice, realizing that other than the few minutes I had spent with my mother, hers was the only female sound

I'd heard since the morning I'd left Bahlya. The softness of her greeting, the unexpected hope that only a women's tone can deliver, not only startled me but forced me to stifle the vitriolic, acidic temper I was on the verge of threatening the wall with again.

Josea wore her black hair pulled back into a bun, a nest secured by a gold clip. Her skin was pristine, white in tone, accenting the smallness of her eyes that were heavily painted with black mascara, a nose with the tiniest of nasal cavities, and a mouth coated with bright orange lipstick. She was dressed in an orange blouse, closely matching the lip color, a black knit skirt, and black high heels with long, pointed toes. She wouldn't have been conscious of it, but she looked like an oval-shaped pumpkin, dressed months early for a Halloween trick-or-treat.

She strode in as though she owned the place. The instant her eyes met mine, I saw unmistakable shock. This was not going to be a reprise of our only date, when together we watched MC Hammer singing of hopes for a better world—I had long ago given up lapel buttons, and lately, just about every fantasy they advocated. She had to see my despair as clear as she could zero in on the proof of the Pythagorean theorem or Euler's formula.

She stood facing me for the time it takes moons to orbit planets, an eternity for a man in morbid humility with no place to hide. I could tell she was about to cry. I felt horrid; all I could imagine doing to console her was to crawl into a crack in the floor—that would have been a big mistake.

Josea's universe had always been either too large or too tiny for adult-sized objects. When she later disclosed to me that she hadn't gone out with a man since our single date, I understood that any prospective suitor would have had to blow himself up to the size of a planet or shrink to amoebic proportion to gain her attention—my best chance of invisibility-to-avoid-humiliation was to stand as still as possible.

"Zach, I'm Josea." It was a good thing she spoke, because I might have let her leave without saying a word and then tried to pretend I had imagined her. "I'm Josea Roth. Do you remember me?"

The entire collection of thoughts and memories of Josea that I had unconsciously hidden away for future recall coalesced in the amount of time it would take one of her quarks to travel across a yardstick. I smiled. When I did, I noticed my lips cracked; for what seemed like a century, I hadn't expanded them in an expression of emotion remotely close to happiness. This feat was followed by another spectacle: I talked. I wanted to talk.

"I do, Josea. I guess I've never told you that I had a great evening grad night. What luck Pam Mintz and I broke up... and you...would you try to convince me it was fate?"

"It had to be destiny...didn't it?" she smiled.

"Why are you here? I mean...I can't figure any of this out."

"Zach, I just finished reviewing your file. You're being accused of terrorism, conspiring against the State of Israel. I don't have to tell you it's serious. If you're innocent, I'm going to try and help you."

"*If* I'm innocent!" I shot out, expressing my consternation on the subject. "Nobody has asked me."

"It doesn't matter what you say," she replied curtly. "It matters how we can prove you're being held unnecessarily. I work for the Israeli government, but I'm not the president. I can't just pardon you. Frankly, I wouldn't, if what they say is true. We have a lot to talk about."

Josea carried nothing with her other than a handbag, one I recognized by the pattern as an expensive designer model. It was large, like a floppy leather sack. I had an urge to open it, just to touch the contents and feel the texture and shape of objects a woman considers companions. She reached in. After fumbling blindly through the interior, her hand exited holding a chocolate See's sucker. She reached out to give it to me. I felt like an animal subject in a reinforcement training experiment—I grabbed it without hesitation.

"I bring boxes of them when I come back from home; I'm surprised I haven't been arrested for possession with intent to sell," she joked.

I tried to be casual. I still couldn't resist savagely pulling off the thin covering and popping the sweet treat in my mouth to suckle it.

"Zach, I want to know why you came to Israel."

"I wanted to tell my mother when she was here, but we only had five minutes. All I could do was give her the information I thought most important."

"I know that. What I'm interested in now is a detailed accounting of your story."

My explanation took only moments. Her verification of my words was going to require a longer period of time.

"I've never told anyone this because it sounds…not like me. Anyways, it's not all that shocking except for the ending. Preston won a contest, a weekend at this spot on a Mescalero Indian Reservation in New Mexico. It's called the Inn of the Mountain Gods Resort & Casino. The date was set but in the meantime he had to do a gig out of town and couldn't go. So, he asked me to take it. I had nothing going on. In fact, I had just finished a couple short pieces that were being published and was getting antsy about finding a story line for a new novel.

"When he called I was on my way to the market. His excitement when he told me was infectious. The next thing I recall was driving. I don't know if you've ever been there but the California-Arizona-New Mexico desert seems so vast I was thinking of a few countries that might get lost there and never be found. Well finally I came to mountains. Then up and up, and before I knew it I was there, Mescalero. I noticed a road with a small sign for a restaurant called Kuruk. I headed north a short distance before I saw the old run down place. I parked. I remember laughing. The lot was full of vans and pickups, not a single sedan like mine. They were all covered with grime and dust, a tedious tone of rusty brown…collectively they made my bright red vehicle appear to be hemorrhaging."

"Very poetic," Josea chuckled.

The last thing in the world I was trying do was be funny; I was eager to get on with an account that I assumed would lead to my release. "Anyways, a moment after I took a seat at a table this barrel-shaped girl in her early twenties who had a beautiful but stern face approached me." It was odd because as I was talking to Josea the images were so vivid they translated into sentences that might have been coming from other than my mouth. "Her lips were unusually small and the few words she spoke breezed out of her nearly immobile mouth like a whistle. Watching her reminded me of a ventriloquist, and she undoubtedly could have made a famous one.

"I recall as she was taking my order there was this huge fellow staring at us; he looked mean, his eyes fixed on both of us. I paid him no attention but then as I glanced past the giant I noticed this young boy. He had beautiful long thick black hair, the type most women would kill for. He appeared to lack appetite for rather than gulping down his food like most of the kids I knew growing up, he used his spoon to take measured portions of what looked like a broth—I thought I might bring him a bagel and cream cheese.

"Wow. It's all coming back as if I were there living it. I ate and was about to leave to head over to the hotel. That's when it happened. The boy stood up and walked over to where I was seated. He placed the palms of his hands on the tabletop and looked at me."

His words startled me. "If you're looking for a story, this is not the place."

"I squinted my astonishment that he'd read my hidden frustration over finding something compelling to write. 'You hit it on the head; lucky guess.'

"He laughed like Santa. I didn't think what I said was funny. Then he spoke the sentence that embarrasses me to repeat. 'If you took off for a place like Israel I think you'd have a lot better chance of scoring. By the way, my name is Jivin.' Then he walked away. I never saw him again but I denominated him, *The Little Dude.*"

"That's why you came to Israel?" Josea queried with understandable astonishment.

"That's why I never told anyone the reason. I know it seems inane but looking back there were two factors that sold me. The first is that I had no reason not to go. To the contrary, since I was seeking something that would arouse me, get my juices going, I had every reason to do the unexpected. Where better to visit than what many would call the nucleus of civilization? Then second, I will never be able to explain it but there was something in his eyes, his speech…his presence that snagged me. That's the whole truth and nothing but the truth."

"I know after reading your file that you ended up at the Hamdallah home," she shot at me. Her lips parted and the tip of her nose aimed skyward—I took it as a sneer, a sure sign that I was not winning her over. "How can we explain this?" she asked, no doubt digging for that one incongruity or inconsistency to confirm my guilt. "I mean he's the cousin of your father. The Israelis have nothing to prove that Mr. Hamdallah or his children had any prior direct contact with you, but Zach, we do know Amir was in Los Angeles at a hotel blocks from your apartment for the week before you came to

Israel. Then, he intentionally changed his ticket to sit next to you on the plane. How do you explain that?"

"I don't. It's the luck of the draw, odds of billions to one coming in," I responded haplessly.

"That's big odds. It's a stretch for me to believe you ended up of all places at the Hamdallah home, then you closely bonded with the family, and it all happened because you won about ten lotteries in a row. It makes no sense."

Her doubting me, near mockery, irked me; and discouraged me. "What makes sense is that this kid named Jivin suggested I come to Israel. That's it. No more and no less. I had nothing to do, so I…took off," I protested wearily, but with irascibility. "That's what young people do, isn't it? We seek out the world rather than retreat from it."

I sensed I was losing her. Knowing that this might be my one chance to have somebody advocate on my behalf before the dreadful day of September 11th arrived, I stepped on the assertion throttle. "Right now, I don't think there is anyone else who is more likely than I to assist in saving lots of innocent people. Look, I'm telling you what happened, but we haven't even covered the facts I hold in my head that were in the safe. Get me out of here because I can't take much more…and I'm no good to anyone dead. I'm not threatening…"

"What is it? What are you saying?" Josea looked surprisingly disquieted.

"I'm having furious dreams…like visions. I'm despondent too; I feel like a suicide in a hurry to gulp a bottle of pills. If you tell anyone and they hospitalize me to keep me alive I'm finished. You'll never get another word out of me."

Abruptly, she moved toward the door. "Zach, I'm leaving," she said, her neck craning over her shoulder.

"I hope I didn't put you in a compromised position," I answered, hiding my worst fear that my bluff had failed.

"Not at all."

"Will you tell my mom I'm okay and that I love her?"

"Of course," she replied as she paused to turn toward me. "Pardon my hurry but I'll be heading out for New Mexico if I can this evening. I'm going to meet this Jivin character. As soon as I return I'll come see you."

She slung her purse downward as if it were a yo-yo, and then as she popped her body upward readying to leave she abruptly stopped. Almost as an afterthought she reached into her purse and took out a book, handing it to me. Of all things it was on Israeli history and the Israeli-Palestinian issue—as if I hadn't had enough of those subjects.

"I came to Israel because I love this country. I believe in our purpose. Zach, we Jews are a lousy fourteen million people on earth, two-tenths of one percent of the world's population. Imagine. There are one point two billion Arabs, about twenty percent of all people living today. So now think about this. There are seven Nobel Prize winners who are Arab. How many Jews are winners of the most esteemed award a person can receive?"

"I never thought about it."

"Read that book. There are one hundred twenty nine. Get the point? It's has nothing to do with an attitude of superiority. What is important is that if mankind is to survive on this planet, which is in jeopardy today, than the greatest minds are needed to dedicate to that objective. I'm here to guarantee that we have a safe and secure place on earth to continue making contributions to humanity."

As soon as she left, I began calculating her trip. If she did leave as planned that evening, she would have to fly from Tel Aviv to New York and then catch a flight to Albuquerque, at which point she'd have a long drive to Mescalero. Under the best case scenario, I figured she could be there shortly after the same time it was when we'd just talked, moving backward in time. Although, she probably had access to military transport and her travel schedule could accelerate accordingly.

While still lying on my cot contemplating her itinerary, I had an odd sensation. At first I couldn't place the feeling, but then it dawned on me—I'd experienced it before but this time was more intense. I felt lonely. Mostly, I had been steeped in gloom and doom, far too weary to weep over this-world losses. I was an ocean removed from the absence of familiar faces or the yearning for the billboards, street signs, and buildings that I had once recognized, and that had allowed me to sleep peacefully in the comfort that they would be where I'd left them when I awakened. The thought I might be set free curiously saddened me.

Later, I looked over the book she'd left. Most of the material seemed dreadfully familiar, so I scanned it, casually looking at the quotes. I came across a beauty by Israel's Prime Minister, Benjamin Netanyahu. My memory may err with a word or two, but the message was remarkable:

If the Arabs laid down arms, there would be no more violence; if we Israelis laid down our arms, there would be no more Israel.

I surmised the Arab response would be:

If the Palestinians laid down their arms, the Israelis would take the rest of our land; if the Israelis laid down their arms, there would be less bloodshed as we drove them off land that is not theirs.

Frankly, I wished they'd all leave me alone. I hadn't asked for this.

32

YOU HAVE ONE "GET OUT OF JAIL 'UNFREE'" CARD

WHEN JOSEA ACCEPTED A position with the Israelis, it was in a staff-consulting role for Mossad, a group designated with responsibility for overseas intelligence. The assignment, originally estimated to last two years, was completed within months.

Her boss, Major General Uri Hazut—the director of this independent department, the overarching agency for military intelligence for Israel and subordinate to no one in the military, reporting only to the defense minister—quickly learned her exceptional competencies. Her successes were rewarded. By the end of the first year, she was Hazut's first assistant. That earned her freedom to come and go at her own discretion, with any form of transport she required to maximize use of her time.

With the clock moving backward and forward as she traversed continents, Josea returned to Israel in the wee hours of August 29th. She had work to do before revisiting me. Her first meeting was with her boss. It ended up being a two-hour discussion. After leaving his office, she went to my mother's apartment to pick up additional materials.

The Miller-Nasir investigative team had not gone to sleep on the job. Rather, while Josea visited Jivin, they had continued their research, hoping that other clues would be revealed. Nasir had assigned people he trusted to assist in his investigation of each of the consortium's members—yet none of his cohorts knew the reason for Nasir's request. After Josea agreed to see me, he increased his efforts, arranging for full-time surveillance of Jawiris and each of the billionaires.

While he was awaiting feedback from his colleagues, he continued his quest to trace the movement of funds. It was a skill he had acquired over the span of his career. Specifically, he wanted to know where the money was disbursed from the Lebanese banks.

What he uncovered, which he soon would share with Josea, was that Jawiris was clever in shuffling the money, circuitously moving it about so that most of it ended up back in Syria in banks controlled by Rami Majeed, while the remainder was kept in Saudi banks. After they were withdrawn from Lebanese and Saudi Arabian financial institutions, all funds controlled by him were then deposited to accounts corresponding to what he referred to as "institutions."

For example, there was an Institute for Arab Development with a corresponding account; in total it received over sixty million dollars. This particular so-called "institute" was a front for the training site in Syria. The Institute of Regional Commerce had an account as well and had purchased vast amounts of equipment from around the world, including

Israel and America. Most of the materials were forwarded to the training facility in Syria, but huge quantities were also sent back to Israel and America where they rested for months at a time before being claimed.

Later, as part of the Israeli investigation confirming the material Nasir was providing them, the Syrian training site was accessed. Sample materials corresponding to what I described from the file, pertaining to acoustical testing, were still there. Most horrifying was the uncovering of a burial ground with over fifty bodies. After testing the victims, it was concluded that the cause of death was consistent with what had been found near the explosive site from World War I, which had been of so much interest to Jawiris: lung tissue ruptured, additional damaged organs, including the heart, and grossly compromised primitive brain structures. Beyond the obvious comparison to the bodies believed to have succumbed to sound death decades earlier, it was staggering that the final stage of Jawiris' testing had been performed on humans—and so many of them.

Adding to the overwhelming evidence being compiled in support of my claim was the fact that all these materials were shipped to the very cities in America and Israel targeted for attack. What Nasir hadn't the time or resources to do was follow up on who had claimed the equipment being held. He presumed they would have used false names so that further tracking would be nearly impossible.

There was more that was delivered to Josea as soon as they met. As the date of execution approached, Ali Halaby Laylaz must have been experiencing anticipatory ecstasy. On a whim, he traveled to Saudi Arabia and made an impromptu visit to Jawiris, surprising him at his office. Nasir's man was an excellent investigator, able to grip Laylaz in a sound vice without him realizing that he was an object of surveillance. Thus, when the unannounced visitor walked in and surprised Jawiris, the response by the latter was recorded on an iPhone, the contents streamed as an email attachment with a few simple keystrokes.

"What's wrong with you? You can't come here. We can't be seen together, ever."

"What? We're not going to celebrate?" Laylaz joked.

"Never with one another. You have to get out of here immediately. Don't come back, and don't contact me. If I need you, I'll get in touch," a miffed Jawiris said as he pushed Laylaz out the door.

On August 29th, near the time Josea was landing at Ben Gurion International Airport, a private jet had just parked. The man exiting the plane was not recognized but proved to be a real estate consultant hired by Mr. Basem Uddin. His visit would not have been noteworthy had it not been for the fact that he went directly to the area where land once owned by Uddin's father—which according to Uddin had been stolen from his family—was located.

The real estate expert made extensive notes pertaining to what presently stood on the land. He inquired at the Israeli Land Administration as to details about the parcels: none were for sale. He then flew back to Iraq and met immediately at a swanky restaurant with Mr. Uddin, who according to Nasir's source, looked fit as the proverbial fiddle.

The selection of a public place made it convenient for the sleuth to overhear the conversation. It was a briefing by the man of unknown name, for which Mr. Uddin expressed his gratitude. The man then asked out of curiosity what interest Basem would have in land already developed, and in Israel of all places. He responded that he was looking at a redevelopment project. According to Nasir's operative, the conversation ended as follows: "But Mr. Uddin, that land is not available for any projects…it's owned by the Israeli government."

Uddin seemed irked at the suggestion that it was not his land, responding indignantly. "It is *my* land! I will be developing it, starting in the next couple weeks. You'll see."

After reviewing the cumulative findings from my mother and Nasir, along with the information attained from her trip to Mescalero, Hazut was on the phone to the facility where I was being held. In minutes, papers were issued for my administrative release. Late on the morning of the 29th, Josea arrived at my cell. Immediately, I could tell that her attitude toward me had changed. She came in and hugged me warmly, and for a prolonged period. Then she began to outline the experience she had at Kuruk.

Her discussion at first frustrated me. Irrelevant events seemed to have thrilled her, the excitement baffling to me.

"With the time changes everything was all off and the helicopter ended up arriving at five in the morning. It was hysterical. We scared the shit out of the bears shopping in the trash barrels. Then in no time the lot filled up with rifled locals coming out to protect Preeti."

It turns out that Preeti is Jivin's mother. Josea was ecstatic filling me in on how she'd developed this close bond with the Apache women. On the surface they appeared opposite in every way but they connected. I failed to understand the relevance. All I recalled of the women named Preeti was when Jivin was eating and had started coughing—a deep, hacking, sickly sound followed by shortness of breath and wheezing. While he was gasping, a beautiful woman rushed into the room and masked his face with a cloth. She looked as though she was in her early thirties, close to my age. Her hair was long, dark brown, thick and meticulously combed. She was wearing a white sleeveless top and blue jeans. Her feet were housed in artfully designed, tan buffalo-hide moccasins up to the calf.

In a few seconds, her son's breathing returned to normal. The woman bent down to hug him tenderly—her back to me—and I saw his face in a serene smile. She craned her neck, glancing incuriously in my direction, allowing me a peek at her honey-shaded skin shining from the application of lotion. She then turned back to Jivin before disappearing into the kitchen.

Most important regarding Josea's trip was that Jivin had confirmed everything I had told her. Yet when she explained to him what had happened as a result of his suggestion, he shrugged as if to say it was none of his concern. Suspicious that it could have been more than a mere coincidence that he would mention Israel and as a result this astonishing series of events unfold, at one point in what sounded like a full interrogation she asked him if there was anything he could think of that would help in terms of interceding in this potential crisis situation. His reply was off-the-cuff, flippant: "Ask Zach. He'll know what to do."

When she told me that I had to laugh.

"There was something weird about him...I don't mean in a bad way, just odd."

She shook her head to signal that she didn't disbelieve him yet at the same time she harbored concerns that there was more to his story than even he was able to report. My encounter with The Little Dude had been so brief that I couldn't add anything to help her resolve her doubts.

Finally she addressed getting me out of jail, sheepishly noting that in order to do so there were a couple "conditions" I would have to agree to. After everything that had occurred, I knew if they were dropping charges I could set my own terms of freedom, but I let her do the talking.

"I can get you out of here immediately if you agree to a few minor provisions."

"Provisions?"

"Zach, I know you have a right to be angry and it has to come out. But this is their way of telling you they need you."

"No wonder they're in the mess they are. I learned more about effective communication in elementary school," I jeered.

"All they're asking is that you agree not to leave Israel until this is over so you can consult. My boss is waiting now to start the debriefing."

That was not what I wanted to hear. "Debriefing!" The word demyelinated my neurons harsher than the sound of fingernails scratching a chalkboard.

When I asked her if I was expected to stay and risk being killed if things went other than how we wanted, she had a response prepared.

"If we get to September 10th and this thing is still pending, we have safe bunkers where we'll be able to protect you; and by then your mom will be placed in safety as well."

"So I get V.I.P. lodging along with the other important people. What happens to the other few million people?"

Josea never flinched; not one muscle flexed. Then she made the slightest gesture, one I can confidently translate as, "Isn't that the way life is?" I couldn't deal with that ethical mess at the moment. Frankly, I was relieved I'd have an admission ticket to wherever important people would be taken.

There was another big sell inducement for me to accept my terms of release. "It's your story, Zach. You can write it as fiction. You'll be in on all meetings, even with the highest officials, so you'll know the characters first hand. It's what you always dreamed of, isn't it, a tale like this?"

"Sure. But don't you see, I'm in a bit of chaos mentally, and physically I'm not in much better shape?"

"Time will heal. Now, I'll be with you all the way. I promise. Just try, okay?" Josea tenderly urged.

Josea brought with her a small suitcase she had placed in the corner of the cell when she entered. I had no idea what had happened to the possessions I'd packed to take to the airport from the Hamdallah home. Apparently, after the takeover at the Palestinian jail and my being turned over to the Israelis, they had found their way to a storage room in the detention center where I was kept.

She took out a change of clothes. I was given time to groom myself properly and change into my own pants, shirt, and shoes. The bathroom I used was just down the hall. When I examined myself for the first time in a mirror I was startled. I truly wouldn't have recognized the man peering back at me. But I pointed at the forlorn figure in the mirror and spoke the words, "You're Zacchaeus Miller?"

He mimicked the gesture right back at me, at the same time imitating the precise grin I was wearing. If I wasn't mistaken, he said, "Yes," and peeked back at me with a cunning glance. Then he rifled words to me that I will forever hold him to, "I'm the one who will always be there for you, buddy."

I showered and shaved. I knew it was Zacchaeus I was examining but the emaciation still alarmed me to tears. I had no shame sharing my shock with my reflective friend still hanging in with me on the wall. My face was drawn in and my cheeks and chin were more pronounced due to facial tissue thinning. My body was gaunt; the bones of my chest arching so as to form what looked like a birdcage.

Slipping into my pants I noticed they were at least three or four inches too big at the waist. Since I avoided belts like cyanide pills, they fell off twice in front of the mirror before I figured out I had to keep holding them up. As I was leaving the bathroom, one of the guards noticed the problem. Kindly, he ran to a storage room and found one of the hated leather straps that reminded me of being beaten. I agreed to wear it temporarily as an alternative to finding myself on the street bare-assed.

I cleaned up decently. With the vestments covering my dilapidated frame, I didn't look half as bad as I thought I would. My head was another matter. It was more than the apprehension of leaving. The very morning following Josea's meeting with Jivin, I started having visions. These were not the fictitious type I had deceived her with earlier.

Instead, these were the real deal. I wish I could have dismissed them as fabrications, but they were distressing signals rising like geysers from a source buried remotely in my mind. They were stronger-than-eating-raw-chili, caustic burning-hot-violent reactions inside my brain for no conceivable reason.

I say visions because there were some vague impressions of pulsation, flow, and movement, all within pitch-black darkness. And then, as if arising from the perimeter of the cloud-shrouded space, came shrieking sounds as loud as I imagined Jawiris' atomic booms designed to kill. Each time they occurred, the punishment was so grossly horrid that the anticipation of another dose never left me a moment's calm.

My sleep patterns had been disrupted since my incarceration. But that evening after Josea had met with Jivin, shortly after I drifted off, I was awakened by a dream, an obvious cousin of the daytime vision. I must have shrieked because one of the guards rushed to my cell to check on me and discovered me lying on the floor, pounding my hands on the concrete.

Before leaving the jail I cautioned Josea about these new interlopers. She assured me I'd not be alone.

"You'll be at a hotel with people there twenty-four seven to protect you. Your mom has already been moved into a nearby suite. Any medical care you need, we'll have someone on call day and night."

"What good are doctors going to be now?"

"Sometimes things can be more difficult after the fact, but you'll be well."

Josea showed me papers indicating my "unconditional" release and that all charges had been dropped. The two of us strolled down a long hallway with cells on both sides and then came to an iron gate that opened electronically. I felt as though I was being born after a long, near-fatal ordeal, being evacuated out the birth canal like a newborn with congenital neural, heart, gastric, and limb deformity.

We entered a guard station where Josea presented documents to two uniformed, armed men. They checked them as carefully as the Hamdallahs had been searched entering Gaza. Before we exited the jail building, there was a small waiting area. My mother was waiting there with rapt anticipation. This time she fully opened the faucets; they probably needed a mop and pail to clean up after we left. I didn't blame her. The only thing preventing me from adding to the mess was the screeching sound. It had devilishly selected that minute to attack me again.

I recall her embracing me for an eternity and me standing there while a sound associated with the vision took on language for the first time. *"You can't go back. You had your time."*

All I could think was that it was telling me I was out of jail and not going back—for the thousandth time I was wrong. It would be days until my analysis would interpret the crucial message.

As we were about to leave, I recognized the man standing in the corner of the room speaking with Josea. It was Nasir Danish. I presume Josea felt it would be inappropriate for her to disclose to me my mother's relationship with him. He came up to me and hugged me. He voiced only two sentences. I remember both precisely, but at the moment I hadn't any inkling that he and my mother were rocking and rolling together. I wouldn't until later that evening, when I was finally settled at the hotel.

"I'm Nasir; I've been helping your mom. We're together now."

33

LUXURY HOTEL WITH NO TIME TO LUXURIATE

I WENT DIRECTLY FROM jail—chauffeured by limousine—to the Carlton Tel Aviv...talk about culture shock. What I wanted most was to be alone. That may sound like loose screws, since for an eternity I had been almost entirely by myself. But I was nutty, no doubt about it. I found it took time before I could be around anyone without experiencing feelings of paranoia and terror. The insecurity one develops in isolation is treated best with time and tenderness. I had the latter, but the former had a way of setting its own pace.

Awaiting us at my suite was Josea's boss Hazut, who by now had been briefed by Nasir and my mother on the added findings. After introducing himself and apologizing for the "unfortunate misunderstanding" pertaining to my "detainment," he informed Josea that we needed to get going quickly; so much for freedom.

I was told that a sport coat, shirt, and slacks were in the closet and I needed to get dressed immediately. I was so used to following orders that I never questioned why. Within minutes of arriving at my luxury suite, I was back in the limo. Off we went—Josea, Hazut, and I. It was quiet in the vehicle. We soon arrived in front of a large building, rectangular shaped, about thirteen stories high, the windows reflecting the sun with pastel blue and purple, white and black. There were large fountains outside. Off to the left I noticed an attached structure, a thin tower several levels higher spindling off the main edifice. We pulled up and were escorted to the side of the foyer to a small door that was opened for us by a male wearing a suit.

Everything moved with tremendous rapidity. In seconds, we'd passed through doors with uniformed guards positioned at each juncture. Then, we were loaded into an elevator and taken up several floors. Exiting, I noticed a long corridor. Josea was holding a briefcase in her right hand, swinging a large arc in harmony with her speedy pace. Hazut was straining to keep at her heels and I lumbered behind, not even trying to keep up. Just before the two of them entered the room, Hazut whispered in Josea's ear. His words were inaudible to me, but I believe I read his lips to say, "It's your show."

When I did finally get to the room, Josea was already at the front, standing at a small lectern with four men seated opposite her; she had handed them booklets with "TOP SECRET" stamped on each. Hazut was sitting next to where Josea was standing. I entered and he motioned for me to sit next to him. Josea appeared strained, suggesting this was not a task she looked forward to.

The men must not have been prepared for what was coming because they were chatting merrily with one another. There were two armed female soldiers standing rigidly at the rear of the room. Following my entrance, I saw another military man close the door. I imagined these were important dignitaries of Israel. My supposition proved correct.

After requesting the armed guards to step outside, Josea went to work like a soldier armed with something more powerful than any of the weapons that had in the past confronted any of the men present.

"I wish there was even a shred of doubt about the veracity of what I have documented for you but the terrible reality is that unless we have a miracle in little over a week from today, there will no longer be a State of Israel."

The four men were Aviv Barak, President of Israel; Yoni Shamil, Prime Minister; Yashay Zahavy, Minister of Defense; and Gal Posner, Minister of Foreign Affairs. None had been prepped; Hazut had called the meeting and made it clear that it was for a matter of the utmost urgency.

After the unmelodious message from Josea, the room turned deathly still. There were several glances from one man to another as the leaders' thumbs heavily plodded through the report. The period of muteness, a sickly eternity of silence, was finally broken by Hazut's words.

"Mr. Miller," he said, pointing informally to introduce me, "while here on vacation with a family in Jerusalem, inadvertently stumbled upon a file containing details of this planned attack on our country. That was a while ago. Unfortunately, he was…detained for a period of time. It seems now we are under the gun to respond in a timely manner."

"Uri, how well substantiated is this?"

"Mr. Prime Minister, it's ninety-nine point nine percent. I'd say irrefutably accurate, but if I could take an admission from one of the members of their club I'd feel even better about what we already know with certainty."

"What's to stop that?"

"Sir, we'd have to go into one of their countries and…kidnap them. That wouldn't be too difficult, but I would need your permission. Ms. Roth has already detailed an undercover operation that could have any one of them here in Israel within hours."

"Then what?" chimed in Yashay Zahavy.

"Yashay, if I knew that, I probably would have taken care of it myself," Hazut responded sorrowfully. "We wouldn't be having this meeting."

"We don't know if something like this is feasible. I'm looking over the report and I can't believe this can be pulled off with the level of damage they're anticipating. I'm going to have to let my people take a look at this," cautioned the defense chief.

"I've already consulted with our experts in the sound munitions program and they affirm it is possible. In fact, we've worked on sound warfare for years ourselves but have never been able to accomplish what they're claiming to have done. That said, I think it's best you still have your experts take a look. This is too big to take chances," Hazut stated agreeably.

"Let's go back to Yashay's question. Assuming this is legitimate, what will our plan be?" asked the prime minister.

"We don't know if we can abort this or, for that matter, if anyone can. We went to the home where the file was kept in a safe, but by the time we got there the contents had been removed.

"According to Mr. Miller, and we'll be detailing more with him in the coming hours, the design was such that at a point in the implementation it might become impossible to stop. But that remains to be seen. I find there is always a way," answered Hazut.

"What about a preemptive strike? This is the survival of our country and we're not about to take it on our butt," Zahavy roared.

Gal Posner reacted angrily toward Zahavy. "Yashay, what are we going to do, kill half a billion people, radiate our own backyard? We can't do it."

"We can't?" the minister shot back. "No, we can and will if it comes down to it."

"From what I see here in the material Ms. Roth prepared, there's no proof that any nation is backing this. This is a private operation and right now I don't see against whom we can even retaliate, except a few Arab big shots," Posner struck back. "So, let's keep our heads."

"Gentlemen, please, cut it out. We need more than ever to put aside personal differences and work together," the prime minister asserted. "Before we even consider resorting to extreme measures, we have some time. Now, Mr. Miller, from what you read, does it seem possible that we can muscle anyone in a way to interdict this matter?"

Let's see, I've been out of jail about two hours twenty minutes. Over the past couple of months, I've been close to death more times than Kansas has had tornadoes. I've been told I'm going to spend the rest of my life in jail, and if I get lucky and become a real good Jew-boy and go to synagogue every Friday night during my stay at prison, I might, just might at some point be released. I'm merely hearing the word "debrief" and I'm urinating in my pants. But the Prime Minister of Israel is ingratiating himself to me, soliciting my opinion? Can I have permission to tell this P.M. hotshot to shove it? It was a speech never delivered.

"None of the men whose names I know and who funded this operation would be able to do that," I meekly responded. "They were intentionally excluded from any knowledge of how this was to be carried out. That was a mandate insisted upon by Jawiris. These men don't even know who their partners are.

"I would determine the backers useless, in terms of a strategy to stop this. There is a person in charge of what they called the implementation stage," I informed them, "but I don't know who it is. In my opinion, there really is only one chance and that is Jawiris. But the problem may be that he already removed the power to terminate from his own hands; all the teams would then be operating independently, not responsible to anyone."

"You're saying that if that is the case, we're finished," retorted the prime minister.

"I'm not sure of that. I know Jawiris is the key. But from what I read about him, there's no way he'll have a guilty conscience, crack, and call it off…even if he could at this late date." I paused for a moment. "It's going to take something else, but I don't know what that is. I'm working on it."

The last sentence of my reply flowed out even more thoughtlessly than those at The Book Junkie. "*I'm working on it*," was a statement of absurdity, earning at best pardon by the group, at worst—as turned out to be the case—fury by the minister of defense.

"You're working on it? Who the hell are you, some damn Arab sympathizer? We have our own nuclear weapons here to settle this if we have to."

He slammed his file on the desk, stood up, and walked out of the room.

The prime minister asked me what I meant by my statement but my mind shut down; could barely hear him and at the same time was incapable of formulating a thought. Josea came to my defense, proving to be a faithful sidekick, just as she'd promised.

"I'll be delving into it with him later. He's been through quite an ordeal. We need to appreciate the fact that he's even here with us trying to solve this matter."

Posner continued as if she hadn't uttered a word.

"We have to bring the Americans in on this *soon*. It's their ass as well as ours."

His words coincided with a door slamming and the warmonger—what else would you expect from a minister of defense—reentering. The break did little to mitigate Zahavy's anger. He proceeded without even apologizing for his Arab slur to me.

"It's their ass, but it's our existence. We've planned for contingencies like this for years. I say we tell the damn Arabs to call it off or we're launching a full attack. There'll be nothing left of them."

"True, Yashay," Posner responded, with a twinge of sarcasm. "The problem is we haven't even analyzed what we might accomplish by doing that. The likelihood is that their capacity to harm us will not be reduced by a crumb and we'll be responsible for the lives of more people than we want on our conscience. Now, I think we should get in touch with Caplow in America. I'm going to stress that we cannot make mistakes here."

"Nobody outside this room is to know about this except those who already do. Let's not risk them finding out we're on to the scheme and have them move their target date up in response. Caplow has to understand this. In fact, Gal, can you get him here immediately so we can brief him in person?" Hazut said, trying to soothe the tension.

"No problem. If I have to pick him up myself, I'll have him here by tomorrow."

"Then, let's all consider this from every angle we can until we meet next. Let's say about eight o'clock tomorrow morning. Uri, bring one of these billionaire terrorists in. Just to be sure, okay?"

"Yes, Mr. Prime Minister. We'll take care of it immediately."

The mid-afternoon drive back to the hotel contrasted sharply with the trip there. Hazut and Josea were urgently discussing a number of issues; most prominent for them was which one of the sponsors they were going to "pluck" and bring back to Israel for interrogation.

Nasir had arranged to have each of the men shadowed continuously. Hazut had been routinely in touch with him for updates. While they easily could have moved against any of the men and were prepared, if necessary, to take each in rapid succession, they decided on the Saudi Arabian, Jaffer Al-Yassin.

It was purely a matter of convenience. Al-Yassin was vacationing with his family in Lebanon; the geographic proximity made the operation simpler. Also, it was a resort setting. It's not unusual for people to drink too much, or in the case of some guests enjoying recreation with the local ladies, even disappear for periods of time. It would be a while before his absence would alarm anyone.

Josea had not prepared a contingency plan for this partic- ular operation, but she assured Hazut it would be simple, that she'd have it accomplished by that evening. Hazut then went over the details he'd learned from his consultants who had evaluated the feasibility of the sound detonation strategy. Their conclusion was that it was probable within eighty-one percent. He was sure the Americans would have addressed the matter as well; they would have their own statistics.

The driver dropped me off at the hotel; Josea came in with me. The privilege of plush wealth had abandoned me several signals back, replaced harshly with knifing pain that gruesomely split my head down the center, the left eye and ear taking the brunt of the visionary attack. This time, during the latter portion of the car trip back to the hotel, I thought I saw a pool, or what looked like water in an enclosure. There were tiny amphibian-like creatures whipping their tails to propel themselves through the liquid. The sound was a silence so pure it amplified. It caused my ears not only to heat up but also to feel the immense pressure of fullness. It was as if the drums were about to burst. Standing in the sun blinded me. I was hardly used to natural light and the strength of the rays caused me debilitating dizziness.

Josea must have noticed my pained state and walked me inside. The large glass door automatically opened to welcome us. The lobby—which I hadn't noticed when I'd first arrived that morning—had an expansive bleached wood floor, enhancing my oceanic sense of disequilibrium.

"What is it, Zach?" Josea asked as she directed me to a sofa off to the side of the room.

"Nothing. It'll pass," I answered tentatively.

"Tell me what you see. Maybe I can help you with it."

"Nothing makes sense, so I don't know what you can do."

I told her as best I could what I was experiencing. She asked me to write down every detail I could whenever I had an episode. She instructed me to keep a pencil and paper nearby when I slept so I could record my dreams. She cautioned me that if I didn't, by morning, the content would fade beyond recovery.

"Zach, you did fine today. Don't worry. They were shocked and scared. Listen, these visions as you call them, when did they start?"

I told her how they coincided with her visit with Jivin—even accounting crudely for the change of time between Israel and New Mexico—and how they'd graduated in frequency and intensity ever since.

"Zach, I've studied at length hallucinations and that's not what you're experiencing. I want you to know that." Her response was intended to comfort me, but really wasn't necessary in that regardless of what I had been through I never genuinely doubted my sanity.

"I can't explain it but something deep inside me wants to escape, as badly as I wish to go back to my normal life. Where it's coming from is the mystery."

"That's what we have to solve and the more data you give me the more I'll be able to help." Then she hesitated, as if she was unsure if she should share her thought. "You know, it's possible that there are forces in the universe that we are just not aware of, that we are not supposed to be aware of, but that communicate to us at times." She bobbed her head as if examining her point. The grimace on her face then disappeared, a refreshing smile taking its place. "On some deep unconscious level you might just be sorting out a solution. You're the one who just announced you're working on an answer."

"I have no idea why I said that in the meeting," I argued. "I swear it was not a thought I consciously constructed. In fact, it floored me. I don't blame the minister for getting peeved at me. Josea, I suspect that if there is a way out of this hell, it's on you and your people to find it."

"I know I may be grabbing at straws, but just stay with me

here until…we explore these images that are coming to you. Now, do you need anything?" she asked.

That was a dangerous question. If I prepared a list of my needs, she would wish she hadn't posed her query. I let her off easy.

"No. I want to go up to my room now. I still haven't had time with my mother and I'm dying from fatigue."

"Good. I'll see you in the morning. And don't be alarmed if you think people are following you—they are. Remember, you'll have round-the-clock protection."

I dragged myself to my room, noticing as I entered that on the table in the living room was a platter with an Israeli salad that had grown tired waiting for me and a pewter dish filled with my least favorite snack, walnuts. It didn't matter. My appetite must have jumped out of the elevator on the trip up. It was now so irretrievable that the thought of food was as appealing as licking my finger and then placing it in an electrical socket.

The long ceiling-to-floor grey window shades were drawn open, and my corner suite offered a full ocean view through two giant windows. The vast Mediterranean Sea was still. Its deep marine color reflected so close to the windows, I imagined I could open the sliding door and walk right into its warm water.

As I stared at the beach, however, I felt as if I'd entered a deep hole. On a table overlooking the outdoors was a huge display of live red lilies, the petals darkening to a bloody color and drooping in spite of the sun's rays heating the glass; they seemed intentionally to disobey their purpose of bringing brightness and color to my heart.

I stood for a moment, trying to get oriented to what I truly felt was no more than a continuation of my detention: the ocean's voice spoke no words to me. Even the children playing on the sand and running in the surf hushed when I glanced their way. There was a brass statue of a female ballerina sitting on a cabinet near the television. When I looked in her direction, she sneered at me. The furniture, all tan and brown fabrics and woods of varying shades, ignored me like a stranger. The only noise I could hear was the faint sound of air filtering mockery through the air conditioning ducts. I felt more alone than ever in my life.

Humor had always been like a sedative pill for me, but it didn't work all the time. When it failed, I sank into horrid sadness. I had shed more tears on a daily basis since my incarceration than for decades before. One of my big insights was that when comedy fails you're in trouble—and I knew I was.

I went to my bedroom, all similar disimpassioned tones of grey and tan; with disregard, they magnified my sorrow. The stereo system had been assigned to monotonously fill the volume of space with soft music, but it was soulless to my mood, treating me as an intruder. I terminated it as I would an enemy.

Scanning my new home I observed to the right of the bed a wall fully windowed like the living room; it was a copycat version, shunning me a second time, adding insult to my injury. I closed the curtain to hide from the affront.

I dropped into the bed with only the memory of Zach Miller grinning at me in the mirror to hold on to. Thankfully, the softness of the comforter, the smell of lavender, and the coolness of the sheets didn't betray me. Amazingly, I crashed into a magnificently deep sleep for what must have been at least a few hours. What awoke me was not a nightmarish vision, but a joyful rendition, the first time in my life rising so pleasantly from a dream. The clock read nine in the evening.

From the large sitting area I looked out at the darkness of the night, noticing that the hotel exterior had taken on a trim in a deep blue color with a paler tone of the same hue filling in big sections of the glass. It was an elegant structure and made no attempt to deprive me of its pride and pleasure; for a moment I felt reborn, as if the world's magic was translating itself into signs of friendship and greeting—a good sleep makes a fool of a sorry mood.

My mother came to mind. I picked up the phone and asked the operator what room Kaye Miller was in and if she could ring her. Seconds later, I heard my mother's voice, setting an infantile remembrance skipping along an abandoned limbic pathway, keying open a door to a chamber so ancient my first whiff was musty and moldy. But the air quickly freshened. As I entered, sensations of safety and security enveloped me. I knew I had been there many times in my life and that it was where I felt love—I sucked at the milky whiteness of peace that energized me enough to breathe gently.

There are people who believe in angels. I don't. But I would like to ask one of those who do if their messengers actually fly, because my mother was at the door before I could hang up the line. Her emotions were draped on a clothesline, blowing as high in the wind as earlier in the day when I'd been released. Between us, it was a scene Nasir would no doubt be relieved to have not witnessed; besides, I never used to cry; and in front of men?

A lot had changed for me. I knew I would never be the same male I had been. Now, I understand better that healthy people let the circumstances of their life set the rules rather than trying to establish dogmas that restrict their range of response to whatever situation they encounter. I had no awareness of what these changes were at the time, but I admit that there were limits I had in my past placed on my behaviors and emotions. Had the events of my trip to Israel not happened they would have ensured my missing perhaps the greatest opportunity of my life.

34

TYING UP VERY LOOSE ENDS

I GREW UP ON A street named Canyon View. My admiration for the developer of the community stemmed from his daring imagination, for there was neither canyon nor view. The street was as flat as the surface of a lake on a calm morning, though these missing elements didn't subtract a smidgen from my fine childhood upbringing.

I raise this point only because, had I been aware of the twin misrepresentations pertaining to my past history at any prior time in my life, I would have thought it thoroughly rational that I would be raised a devout atheist when the truth is I possessed the seeds of two religions. In other words, my surprise discovery about my background may have tipped me to a clue that I should be looking for repetitive patterns of absent pairs, though I'm not betting too heavy on this pristine insight having saved me the joint imprisonments.

Sessions at all hours of the night, when I would gaze endlessly at walls capable of projecting from my memory vault wonderful old performances, from rock concerts to my favorite movies, were welcome companions during my incarcerations. As my mother started to talk, I had a sick sensation that I was in for a new presentation; it was one I didn't need at the time. She opened with "I'm sorry," accompanied by a gushing of tears she could have drowned in. My words of consolation only increased the outpouring of sorrow and regret.

"Mom, what is it? I don't care what you did. I love you," I pleaded.

When she finally ceased the self-flagellation, we talked, though it took her longer than I would have bet to come to her senses. "None of this would have happened if I had told you our history from the start," she painfully concluded.

Listening to her atonement for her perceived sin, I felt worse for her than myself, and that's saying something for a guy with a Ph.D. in self-pity. Fortunately, she paused. I took it as an opportunity to cleverly test whether or not I could lighten her mood.

"Mom, did you ever think about the name of our street, that we didn't have either canyon or view?"

She roared, disproportionate to what the humor deserved, but the exaggeration added weight of forgiveness. Finally, we were able to get down to business.

My personal and family history as taught to me by the Israelis was accurate. She explained that she had chosen my name out of honor to her parents; my great-grandfather's name was Zachary. But my mother refused what she knew to be an obvious Hebrew name and shrewdly negotiated Zacchaeus as a compromise, the name selected for its meaning, "pure of heart," but more importantly, for having its origin not only in Hebrew, but Greek as well.

My grandparents on my mother's side were what my mother labeled as nothing other than Zionist extremists. She described the dose of religion injected early in her upbringing as comparable to gulping gasoline.

"Before I had even become Bat Mitzvah, I felt like I was gagging on the beliefs being force-fed me every day of my life. We lived in the Fairfax district of Los Angeles. It was the center of Jewish orthodoxy. Most of the girls who were my friends accepted the teachings, but I couldn't. I questioned every lesson, all the rules and laws, and rather than encouraging my precociousness, my instructors punished me; later, I was ostracized by my peers. Zaci, my childhood was really a living hell," she said sadly. "It wasn't until I started reading outside the traditional Hebrew material in which I was indoctrinated that my spirit was born.

"One day, I ventured outside the confines of our neighborhood and found a small used bookshop. I went in and asked the owner what he would suggest. I remember I specifically told him that I wanted to 'explore life, philosophy'—what a big shot I was at such an early age. I admitted to him that I only had a few dollars. It didn't matter—he treated me like a dignitary.

"I walked out that day with copies of Kafka's *The Trial*, Spinoza's *The Ethics*, and Gertrude Stein's *Tender Buttons*. I knew they cost far more than my allowance permitted. The irony was that all three of these authors were Jewish, but their work was nowhere near the material I was barfing on in my school. I was about twelve at the time and never looked back. I had to hide the books, but I imbibed them with the thirst a drunk has for alcohol.

"I can't tell you how bad things got at home. They never found what I was revving my soul on, but they were astute and educated people and knew my ideas were polarized to their own. It was warfare every day at home and just as bad at school. But I had my comrades to guide me through the pages of a never-exhausting supply of material.

"The man in the bookshop repeatedly took back the books as I finished them and then gave me others, no different than a library. He was a very shy, timid man, who wore on his arm indelible tattoo work designating him a Holocaust survivor. His name was Mr. Katz, and many times I talked with him, enough for him to sympathize with my plight and keep funding my rebellion.

"It's true that by the time I went to Israel, it was a last ditch attempt by my parents to rescue me from what they saw as a guaranteed path to self-destruction. I know I hurt them by rejecting what was precious to them, but it was not my responsibility to reassure them of their faith by capitulating to what I knew in my heart was damaging.

"I went on the trip trying to have an open mind. I spent quite some time exploring the history and culture. But here I am rambling, when I suppose what you most want to hear about is your father."

"Really, it's not important. You don't have to."

330 | M<small>ISTAKEN</small> E<small>NEMY</small>

I was sincere that I didn't want her to prostrate herself before me. Frankly, I was concerned mostly for her safely, given what I knew was coming only days in the future.

"I always told you that no matter who it is—a parent, a spouse, best friend, therapist—they would never be able to come close to understanding your inner experience. As much as I wish I could get that close to you now, to help in some way to heal you from all this, it would not be possible, even if I were willing to exchange the remainder of my life to bear one simple moment of this nightmare for you.

"So, for what I did in Israel I am not asking your approval or criticism or any type of judgment, and I don't expect you would want to do that regardless. I only want to explain from my perspective what happened and give you a couple ideas about the man who was your father."

Abruptly, she stopped her presentation, interrupting for a concern she had brought with her to my room but had forgotten. "Zach, I'm going to get you to a doctor tomorrow."

"It's okay, Mom. They checked me out at the prison hospital."

That did not go over well with her.

"Rot. Those prison doctors are butchers. I wouldn't let one of them pull out a splinter. I already have an appointment with a Dr. Allan Schwartzberg at Tel Aviv University."

"Look, I know there are fractures that were never set, but they healed. I have a lot of pain, but it will get better; I'm already a bit improved. Let's say the Israelis weren't as physical with me. The mental aspect is another story." I was reluctant to disclose more of the trauma inflicted on me, further embarrassed about my emotional state, but I babbled on. "To tell you the truth, that's where I'm not doing so well. My inner self is a little curious."

"I can't imagine what they did to you, but I know it will get better with time. We can talk to the doctor about that too."

"We'll see. Why don't you go on with what you were about to tell me?" I urged, with admitted curiosity about my father.

"Are you sure this is a good time? You have to be exhausted."

"I slept for a couple of hours before I called you. It was the most refreshing rest I've had in months. No, go ahead."

"I didn't come to Israel looking for love—at least, I wasn't aware of it if that was the case. I was visiting the Old City of Jerusalem and looking around in an old bookshop. I bought several items that I thought I'd read in my spare time and tucked them in my sack. As I was leaving, I failed to notice a tiny step leading down to the street. I fell forward and landed with such force that my free hand was bloodied and my nose badly scraped; I was in a bit of shock. A man, who by chance was passing at that instant witnessed my fall—I nearly hit him on my way down.

"He picked me up, took some tissues out of his pocket, and began wiping my wounds. He asked me to follow him and I did. He took me a couple of blocks to a small building and led me up a stairwell to what was a medical office run by a physician who, as I would learn later, was his uncle. My hand must have grazed a corner of the stone surface, and I had a laceration that was bleeding profusely; it took six stitches. But my face was undamaged, apart from a few bruises.

"He introduced himself as Abbas Ashrawi and that night I had a date with him. Zach, what's important is that this was the kindest man I had ever met, a gentleman in every way, and we fell in love. He was a writer, very much like you, but most of his work was political.

"Sure, I was aware of his sentiments regarding Israel, but you have to understand that for him it had nothing to do with religion. He adored me as a person, appreciated that I had a mind and could think. He was a liberated man in a world treating women as second class—he was emancipated and humane, a truly heroic figure, especially if you think about the values of his culture.

"I hope I'm not making him out to be more than he was, but I doubt I am. Some people are special, and I had a jewel of a man. The closest I've ever known since is Nasir, but I'll get to that later. Your father would have adored you. I never told you about him because I didn't want you to know there was tragedy in your background, that there was violence. He died for what he believed, but in my mind it was senseless. We could have left the chaos of Israel. And that's the only thing I hold against him, that he refused to hear my pleas to get the hell out before it was too late.

"I knew he wrote anti-Israeli material, but it's a blatant lie to say it was anti-Jewish. It may surprise you but Abbas really didn't have much interest in religion, no more than I, in fact. It was land. He loved the dirt, sand, sea, mountains, and streams. He felt bullies were robbing his people of what was rightfully theirs. That was his Achilles' heel. In spite of the love he had for me, he couldn't give it up.

"After he found out I was pregnant, it excited a monstrous passion in him, as if he was consumed with putting the matter of Israel's incursion to rest so that you would have a peaceful place to grow up. I only wanted for us to get out and leave the battle to others because to me risking our life to fight over ground was idiocy, especially because we had something far more valuable—love.

"When you said you were going to Israel, it was an awakening of old pain. I knew nothing good could come of it for you. Now, look at you, what they did to you."

She couldn't go on without sobbing, weeping her eyes dry. I grabbed her and we hugged for several minutes. Then we sat quietly.

I was glad she'd told me the story, and I had not a shred of resentment toward her. She was correct. I had no right to judge her life choices. And as far as my father went, he had died before my birth and nothing she could have done would have changed that.

My father might come up casually in subsequent conversations, but this was the last time we directly discussed him. After some time I veered the discussion in a different direction.

"Mom, what about the Hamdallah family? Have you heard anything?" My tears were surprisingly irrepressible. "I was very close with them…they're my only relatives…"

She gave me time to compose myself before responding.

"I've been very busy since I came here. Zev Feld owed me big and he knew it. He admitted that after I went—while pregnant—to the American embassy to leave Israel, they started a file on you. The Israelis were ridiculously obsessed with security, and they monitored any potential risk. So, you having an Arab father who opposed Zionism and was killed defending his beliefs and a Jewish mother not supportive of Zionism either, you were considered a potential threat.

"Zev was the one keeping an eye on the situation. He never knew if I had told you about your father, but he assumed I had and that someday you would come back—if not seeking revenge then at least to contact your roots. Your visit to Israel set off a sick reaction by these assholes, and it's because of it that the second half of your imprisonment happened."

At that moment, the picture crystallized as to why I had been followed in Israel, and why Feld magnanimously was attempting in the only way he knew to send me a message to leave—I still had no generosity toward him.

"The point in my telling you this is that in return for his mistrust—for spying on you, getting you involved in this journalist credential business—Feld gave me Mr. Hamdallah's contact information. I called him."

Then she stopped, no doubt recognizing how upset I was. After a moment, she resumed. "Since all this happened, I thought that after so many years I should at least get in touch with him. He's living in Paris temporarily. He remembered me quite well. I was surprised there was no animosity. Zach, I'm afraid he has much greater problems.

"I have to tell you, he never knew who you were. He wept like a little boy when I told him. He said he adored you and had prayed you would be husband to his Bahlya. The man is broken. Both of his children have taken to hiding someplace in the Middle East, though he has no idea where. Zach, he had no knowledge of this plot against Israel. He told me the Israelis had found out about Amir and Bahlya's Hamas connections. As far as he knows, that's why they're being sought."

"It's better to let him believe that. Besides, it's true for Bahlya. She never knew what her brother was doing."

"His only joy is that his other daughter just gave birth to a baby boy, but he's crushed that the husband still insists on leaving for Syria and taking his wife and newborn with him. I think he said they're leaving on September 8th or 9th. Isn't that date odd?" my mother asked.

"No, Mom. The husband is Dr. Efron, and he's steeped in terrorism as deep as the son, Amir. When I finish going over the full details of what was planned with the Israelis, they'll pick him up. I'll guarantee you that neither he nor his wife and baby will ever leave Israel," I said confidently. "Mr. Hamdallah… he's such a kind man. He's a bit dense about his children, but he doesn't deserve this."

"He asked me to say hello to you," she interjected.

"I wish I could see him. Damn it, Mom, I got screwed here, didn't I? You were right. I never should have come."

She said nothing. That's what the regret-comment deserved.

My mother fell asleep on my couch. Sometime later, Nasir knocked softly on the door. I opened it, and he came in and sat next to her, holding her in his arms.

He helped her up and walked her to their room. My relationship with Nasir was still limited to two single sentences.

35

MR. PRESIDENT, LET'S HEAR WHAT ZACH HAS TO SAY

IT WAS NEAR TWO in the morning when my mother left my room. I had more meetings and consultations to face in a few hours. I thought I'd get some added rest, but that was not to be. I was struck by the fiercest mental vision yet.

This time the imagery focused more clearly, as I peered within what still looked like an enclosed chamber containing water or some similar fluid. I was sure I saw objects moving, a number of them, but they were nebulous except that each was distinct from the other. Then I noticed tethers; it appeared a rope was pulling each figure.

They would successively come forward and then recede, presenting in series like football players poking their heads toward the television lens to be introduced to the audience. Finally, they began to move at higher speed, merging into one another, all the while with blazing acceleration transforming in size, smaller and then larger like a phantasmagoria. I had the sensation once again of needing to pound my head to get the swiftly careening images to cease, to relieve me of the sickening wooziness.

Accompanying the visuals was a soundtrack, a musical cacophony, the intertwining tones and pitches tipping me into a rotating, whirling dizziness. It was a piercing, hideous sound, yet it beckoned me to lend my ear to what I could only make out to be a devil chanting madly, welcoming sinners to hell.

I wanted to run from the shrieking, but to where could I go without it shadowing after me? Then, in the time it takes to flip the page of a book, it stopped—similarly to what had transpired with earlier episodes. A gentle piano sonata with subtle variations in tempo and rhythm replaced the unmelodious piece; it best fit a highbrow afternoon tea.

That's when I heard it. It was a cry, not one but many, each with a distinct signature; some lingering through several cycles; some long, unbroken monotones; some gradually rising in pitch; some a swift, successive repetition of short exhortations. But the cries were associated with breathing, assuring me each distinct object was alive.

My first thought was that it was my weeping again—a billion types, styles, models, and brands of tears, either for all the pain I was enduring, or as a plea for clemency from the mercilessness of my various captors, or even another indulgent expression of again feeling sorry for myself. Disgusted, I drifted into an unpleasant state of semi-sleep. That lasted until the phone rang.

"How are you?" Josea's voice called out.

"Terrible." Rather than a platitudinous response typically mandated by convention, I felt my dire circumstances granted me permission to speak the truth. "I had one more unpleasant episode, but I suspect I've figured it out. It was another whimpering session."

Josea chuckled. "I know this is hard, but it won't get any easier by you beating up on yourself."

"I'm frustrated," I shouted what was obvious. "There are things dangling at the tip of my tongue and I can't retrieve them."

"Dreams can be quite elusive so don't be alarmed…let me do the psychoanalysis. I'll be there in ten minutes. I ordered breakfast to your room, so we can eat and get going. We have to be at the ministry at ten."

I couldn't wait.

I was naked and had no idea what had happened to the clothing I'd been wearing when my mother left. Looking around the room, I found my pants and shirt lying on the floor near the bed; I put them on. It never dawned on me that I hadn't showered—a pro forma morning grooming task remote to me now. A few minutes later another knock at my door, and like magic, there was Josea. Right behind her came the Carlton version of Pizza Man making a delivery, a meal fit for a lot more appetite and status than I had.

*****

Governments are known to make snails into track stars. They're so pathetically slow at addressing matters even of great urgency it's shocking to its own citizens. Not this time.

This assembly of officials must have been up all night—and looked it—which made my creased attire chic.

There were two additional faces not present at the meeting the day before. The first new attendee was Theodore Caplow, the U. S. Secretary of State. After the briefing he received by his Israeli counterpart, Gal Posner, he must have thought better of coming unprepared, inviting U. S. President Calvin Upshaw to tag along. For me, this was an odd circumstance. In hours, my life had gone from pauper to prince. I was about to meet with two presidents at once; and I was the surprise celebrity.

What a dream! I was onstage with the greatest actors on planet Earth. They commanded audiences of millions, breathed incantations erasing the spells of sorcerers, stroked pens with more authority than words spoken by ancient kings, and they peed—but only in gold urinals. Now, I was being called to act my lines next to theirs, and they were going to listen with eager anticipation, hang on to each word of my performance.

Hazut began the meeting.

"We brought Al-Yassin to Israel last night. Within an hour of his being assured at best he might save his family if he cooperated, he puked the Argentine steak dinner he was in the process of digesting and then validated every detail Zach has reported. Unfortunately, also as Zach told me, he was of no use in terms of the operational plan."

Al-Yassin probably had a savage night of interrogation, but if not for me, it would have been far worse. My assurance to the Israelis that he truly wouldn't be able to reveal the information they wished for was my unintended gift. It was determined that there would be no immediate gain to capturing any of the other conspirators. The dangers of alarming Jawiris that he had been found out were portended too severe a risk. Zahavy added that he was sure, based on his experts' reporting; theoretically, what Jawiris had planned could be accomplished.

Caplow then interjected, "If I may add, I've been consulting throughout the night with our experts on noise and sound warfare. They have also completed extensive research and experimentation in the area. They're sure we are only a few years at most from accomplishing something similar to what we think Jawiris has already; they believe it's highly probable."

Needless to say, the tone was somber, owing to the fact that these powerful leaders, with all the resources known to modern man, hadn't a clue how to cope with this threat. It was Zahavy who championed his position with greater authority.

"We have to make a quick, deliberate, and decisive strike on one country in the region immediately. That's going to serve as notice that unless someone calls it off, the rest can bet on what's coming to them."

Posner wasn't ready to capitulate to Zahavy's bellicosity.

"Can't you compute that the perpetrators are beyond the reach of any regional leaders? What you're advocating will accomplish nothing other than a senseless first-strike death scenario."

The foreign minister retained reason, but the fact remained that Zahavy had a plan and no one else did. Upshaw kept his hands in his pockets throughout the discussion. I wondered if he was playing with himself. Or maybe he was holding the funny nuke button to make sure that if Zahavy had any idea he was going to beat him to the punch by pushing Israel's first, he was mistaken. Upshaw had never indicated he would grant permission to the Israelis to take the offensive…yet. He never said he disagreed with Zahavy either. What he did do that relieved me was to survey the group, gauging their opinions on striking first and what the possible outcomes might be.

While my initial impression was that the other Israeli leaders objected to the extreme measures suggested by Zahavy, as the dialogue ensued, I noticed the president and prime minister gradually gravitating closer to his position. They countered Upshaw's possible reluctance with the argument that several cities in America would indeed be damaged, but Israel would be obliterated as a country and would lose nearly all its population.

I had always heard that Israelis had the mentality of, "If you hit me with a peashooter, I'll crack you over the head with a bat, and if you shoot me in the leg, I'll blow up your whole family." I'm not judging. I've never had someone threaten to kill me, at least when I wasn't bound and gagged. But that may be the point. Israel understood that they could never exist if options were lost; and they could never allow themselves to be in a position where they could not act in their own defense.

They knew what it was to live with survival constantly on the line. Thus, they were polite to the American president while they also knew he had little influence over what the

Israelis decided to do. They had their own buttons to manipulate. I believe both Caplow and Upshaw got the point—the former agreeing that it was too late for diplomacy and that there was clearly no one with whom to negotiate.

This led to a crucial disclosure by Hazut, one that concerned him greatly and contributed to his increasing allegiance with Zahavy's reasoning.

"Danish Nasir, a reporter working with Zach's mother to gather information aiding her son's case, has associates of his watching all the billionaire participants, including Jawiris. He called me early this morning to let me know they couldn't find Jawiris. It's not likely he knew he was being watched, but for whatever reason he's disappeared. I've put several agents on it; however, so far his whereabouts remain unknown."

For Zahavy this added information only increased the tension.

"If this Jawiris did sense he was being followed and fled for that reason, he might advance the date of attack. We need to act, and soon."

"That would detract some of the satisfaction from having it occur on 9-11; they've been counting on a big celebration since planning this. Giving up that date might be a decision they'll resist making," President Barak responded.

It was the American president's turn to take the lead. "Miller, is there anything else you recall about Jawiris that might provide a lead as to where he might have gone and why?"

"It was my understanding that by this date his role would have been completed. I have no clue where he might have taken off to."

Mr. President wasn't finished with me. "If we can pick up this Jawiris, you're saying he's the only one who you believe can call this off. But if we can't get to him, we're out of luck. Is that what you understand?"

"That file I saw was comprehensive and thorough. I doubt anything has changed since. Jawiris is the key to all of this," I explained.

"Then we'll have to find him, young man, and we're hoping you'll recall something else that will help."

The way he used "young man" was belittling, but it didn't stop me from disclosing a potentially important piece of information I remembered just as he was speaking. "His wife was pregnant with their first child, I know that. Did he take them with him?"

"Oddly, his wife and their newborn are home. We haven't done anything to alarm his family," Hazut said.

I couldn't account for what stimuli might have set off a visual reaction for me at that instant. However, the next thing I knew, an electrical bolt lit the interior of my head. It brightened the inner regions of the brain so vividly that I wandered inside. I stood and gazed. I knew I was exploring the dwelling place of all the visions that had been torturing me. They were hiding in this impermeable darkness…and as sure as I was breathing, I knew the experience not a creation of my imagination or some sort of abnormal mental state. I was aware at that instant of my physical presence in the room with these leaders as well as the existence of my own personal self.

The spotlight, presumably switched on by Hazut's words, beamed first to the rear region of my brain. It was there I saw the vast pool loaded with little swimming creatures still tethered. They seemed to be smiling at me, as if they had a secret and were mocking my inability to unravel it.

Then, the bearer of the beam changed the angle ninety degrees to the left, to another subdivision of my brain. I advanced a few steps closer, noticing a distinct structure that was intense and burning hotter than a carbon arc light. The sounds I had heard in each of my prior visions began playing, one after another, archived recordings stimulated by illumination, similar to an actor in the limelight on stage.

The familiar repertoire lingered on as the beam gradually dimmed. A second later, the light flicked on again, aiming now at a more central location of the brain: it set off a tickling sensation that enveloped me. This funny feeling yielded an outpouring of giggling, strangely emanating from every one of my organs, joints, and orifices.

It seemed for an instant the bosom of my mind was revealed to me. The conductor of the spectacles that were thrusting themselves on me at will commanded the liquid to swish, bubble, and boil; the smiling creatures to swirl, whip, and beam from their ropes; the sounds to enter and exit in symphonic order; and even to force me to roar, chuckle, and laugh on demand. It was the first time I wasn't devastated by the experiences. I felt...I don't know what, but it wasn't torturous.

When I returned to the meeting, I realized nobody had witnessed as much as a twitch of a muscle on me, for the episode had been wholly embedded somewhere on a subtle level, as if in my soul. The expedition in search of these enigmatic statements and images had failed to bring closure as to any deeper meaning that might be ascribed to them, but I had peered into the structural setting where they resided and authenticated their reality.

I noticed the Israeli president, Barak, becoming more active in the meeting. He was reinforcing Upshaw's assertion that every effort should now be made to find Jawiris, since he represented the only lead with some prospective value. Zahavy persisted in displaying the desire for vengeance against me; I assumed he still saw me as an Arab. He continued to hurl sarcasm like a shot put ball aimed at my head.

"Our guest witness is working out the problem, so what's all the concern? Aren't you ready yet to tell us the solution, Mr. Miller?"

His words were nearly inaudible, but I did sense his scorn. I must not have fully emerged from the experience just described, because at that instant the conductor struck up the orchestra, changing the tune to a renewed hideous concoction of pitches and tones. The sounds burst in on me like a pride of lions on the kill. This time, it was an oceanic swishing and there was a sensation of teetering.

At first, I thought it was like being on a seesaw, but then I recognized it more precisely as swaying, reminiscent of a ship's motion in a storm, the noise and stirring movement was causing disequilibrium. I dropped off my chair. I lay on the floor. I was gripping my head, trying to rock to the motion in an attempt to align myself with the vertiginous disorientation, hoping to cease it.

"Get a doctor," President Upshaw called out.

I was captive to a different sound than the order of Upshaw. My perceptions were of the percussion section as it was ordered by the conductor to play a rondo movement. This was a noise detached from body, free to move at light speed. The acoustical monster slammed me face down, pressing me flat and squeezing me like a sponge with the fullness of its weight. It whispered in my ear, "You had your time, and you can't go back."

It repeated the message a million times in a microsecond, lasting until I heard Josea shriek at Upshaw, "Just give him a minute—I'll take care of it."

I felt her hands softly rubbing my scalp, the voice reducing to a murmur in my ear and then halting. Gradually I started regaining my balance, blurriness faded, and I was finally able to stand. To spare me added embarrassment, Josea stood up for me again.

"If any of us had been through what he has…"

That was it. The incident deserved no added commentary, not even by Zahavy.

By the time I fully composed myself and was able to rejoin the group, they were moving on to a topic none wished to address, but all knew had to be examined. What if? What if they could not produce a prevention strategy and the lives of millions of people would be at risk? With only about a week left, would evacuations be possible?

Then, about the time the meeting was coming to an end, Josea posed a question to me. "Zach, what about Dr. Efron? Could he be helpful in finding Jawiris?"

"I don't believe so. He was definitely Jawiris' right-hand man scientifically, but he had no role in the operation itself. He's planning to go to Syria any day now."

I'm sure it was then I sealed his fate. Hazut took down a note and later that afternoon asked me what else I knew about Efron. It was decided to let him have free reign until just before he was scheduled to flee Israel, in case his activities might reveal something of worth.

Thus, it was not until about a day before he was to leave for Syria that a commando squad entered Gaza and packed the doc into a van. His wife and baby boy…we'll get to that shortly, but what happened was not pretty and speaks to the unfortunate fact that in war bullets ricochet and unintended people are damaged or killed.

It was agreed that everyone would meet again the next day to discuss the pros and cons of striking early against the enemy. They concurred that waiting a few more days, while in the meantime commencing an all-out pursuit of Jawiris, would be the best strategy. Finally, all parties promised to refrain from attempts to contact regional Arab leaders, agreeing that the risk was greater than the potential return.

The tension was thick. I could see these men were terrified. Whatever their motivation for assuming positions of power within their respective countries, it's not likely any of them seriously imagined they'd be in the pickle they were. I could tell that each of them felt the burden of mankind had suddenly taken a royal dump on their shoulders; not everyone could be protected, there would be casualties—these brash, arrogant, and empowered men were acquainting themselves with the experience of humble love.

I knew I never wanted to be a world leader. I hated these meetings.

36

LET'S GO TO THE BEACH

JOSEA AND I LEFT the session together, with her driving. It was very quiet in the vehicle, and I noticed she didn't seem to be going in the direction of my hotel. Ten minutes later, we were by the seaside. She parked.

"I never come to the beach. I've been here all this time and not once have I gone swimming in the ocean. Remember I swam in high school?"

I didn't. I refrained from interrupting with a false yes.

I hadn't paid attention to Josea's physical appearance that morning, but as she started walking I beheld her wearing a cute little blue and white vertical stripe dress styled with a rounded neckline, revealing a small portion of her breasts, the cut adding a couple of inches' appearance to her figure; she looked adorable. She was wearing a mossy green bonnet she had grabbed from the back of her car. We wandered to the water's edge.

Together we sat on the warm sand and she leaned back. Lying supine on the surface, she began to cry. It must have been her first tears in ages, because she was a neophyte compared to me. Little drips. That's all she was able to produce as she labored to hold in as much of her grief as could. I was sitting up. I took her hand and held it, rubbing her arm with my free hand.

I knew what it was without her saying a word. Time was running out and the situation was dismal. Josea did not like messy. Pure and simple, this was a filthy muddle with no constructive options she could turn to for success. It's my opinion that she had believed all along she would nip this crisis like all the others, but she was just now sucking in the sad reality that it might not happen. I had accepted that long before.

"I wish I had the answer. I can't imagine what you must feel like," I said to comfort her.

"Zach, I've decided. I'm not leaving. I'm not going down under to the shelter. I took on a responsibility to this country. It's not right to back out if there may be a last-second chance to stop it."

This was not what I wanted to hear. Over the past few days she had become an integral part of my life. I cherished her. I was living an experience that for the first time heightened my need for intimate and trusting relations. I simply didn't have that many people I could count on; I knew after this, we would be blood-bonded for life.

"You know Josea, sometimes things work out differently than we think, just by chance or luck. What if we can't do anything about this but it never happens? Say Jawiris or his people realize it's purely evil and quit? What if by chance it doesn't work, or at least only works to a small degree?"

"I don't see that. Zach, this war will never end. We'll lose this one, but from all over the world Jews will unite to preserve our faith. It'll make us stronger, and we'll come back again and retake our land."

For this cause she was willing to die, hurt her parents by causing them to suffer the loss of their child, deprive the world of one of the greatest minds ever to live, and cheat me of her friendship for the rest of our lives? As I rehearsed the last portion of that thought sequence, for the first time I dwelled on my father, who had also deprived me of his love for precisely the same motive as Josea's. Was I to endure a destiny of bullying threats repetitively assaulting me? Might I slap it down?

"Josea, what is with this land thing? You know that's how I lost a father."

"You don't understand," she said solemnly.

"Hell, no, I don't," I battled. "And truthfully, I don't want to. I've never comprehended it since I first arrived here. Sometimes I think these people deserve each other. They're all bound to perpetuate this conflict to eternity, as if they need it, as if it's a meal they'll starve without. It's not your war!"

"That's similar to what my parents say to me."

"If I could, believe me, I'd find an eleventh plague for this conflict and inflict it on both sides. That infestation would ravage the region, locking every single combatant together so tightly they couldn't damage each other. That's what I wish to do. But I'm only Zacchaeus, one man born in Los Angeles and going back home as soon as I can get out of here."

Josea sat up, looking at me quizzically.

"I'm tired. If by a miracle I'm living next week, I want more in my life. I didn't mention it but when I was talking with Preeti on the reservation, I shamefully admitted that the last date I went on was our graduation night. It seems I slipped into my career and never paid attention to the things other girls were addressing, like intimacy. And can you blame me for hanging on to the memory of us going out?

"I was on a special assignment for two weeks. I was so involved that I had little time to keep up on what was happening at home. But when I came back and heard you were in jail, my heart screamed out in pain. I knew it was impossible that what they were saying about you was true. That's why I called your mom. I never knew it would turn out like this.

"I know I'm in love. I'm in love with the idea of falling in love, with the thought of making it happen, with having a family of my own. If I live, will you be my friend and help me? I'm afraid to be with a man." She made the disclosure like one might admit to being a drug addict. Then she rambled on. "I can measure the light years between galaxies like you can reach for your wallet. I can find black holes like you can use a cell phone. I can discover new moons rotating a planet like you can find a friend's phone number.

"Can I hold a man's hand, kiss his lips, look in his eyes and see if he loves me? Can I hear the cry of a child? Can I believe I could have one? Can I even spell sex? I've got a lot of learning to make up for."

"I'll get you the top sex therapist in the world, and the best men on earth are going to have to audition for beta testing your love machine," I humorously assured her.

"Promise?" She asked earnestly.

Wow, wow, wow. This was not what I'd bargained on. How wild and crazy my life had become! I wasn't dead; I heard my heart groaning, but my spirit was alchemically making laughing gas out of agony.

We lazily made our way back to the car, hand in hand.

37

BABY, HAVE I GOT A SURPRISE FOR YOU

OVER THE NEXT FEW days, nothing substantive was accomplished. I attended several meetings, listening to more of the top analysts and leaders of Israel and America debate the possibilities. What it came down to was two options. The first was to take it in the shorts and let the damage go unanswered, hoping international treaties would be negotiated afterward to preclude additional attacks. The second was to launch an all-out assault on the enemy with the understanding that, even if Israel and parts of America were destroyed, the Arab world would be decimated and left in ruin, unable to enjoy any benefit of victory. The latter option was heavily endorsed...but with opposition.

More and more energy was being devoted to damage control, how the crisis was going to be handled after the fact. What astonished me was that these people had addressed the prospect of mass destruction to such an extent that they were convinced it was going to happen someplace at some time. Even more amazing was that their line of thinking incorporated who would survive, what would be done to protect select leaders and valued individuals. If one was in the wrong category, and most people were, they were toast—there would only be room for a small number on Noah's Ark, and even the bathroom cots were presold.

Jawiris was being sought, but his whereabouts had yet to be determined. The same went for Amir and Bahlya. Efron was only a day or two from his final moments of freedom, and an equal time period separated Mr. Hamdallah from more tragedy.

In the meantime, the visions were increasing in frequency. Josea was consumed with the hope that they would have meaning relevant to the upcoming crisis. Thus, while the giants of destructive retaliation were polishing their nuclear buttons, Josea hovered over me like a devoted analyst doing an intensive in-home treatment—with a brain like hers I can't imagine how anyone could have done better.

Josea kept meticulous notes on the dreams and visions I was having and was continually referring back to them in hopes of detecting a pattern or connection, themes that might clue her to the deeper meaning of the experiences. I participated as best I could.

One evening while I was sitting alone, I had another odd visual experience. It presented the opportunity for me to again rummage through my brain with the aid of what seemed like a flashlight. The findings were bizarre.

The next morning when Josea came over, she was quick to pursue the investigation. "Zach, tell me what you dreamed last night, every detail," she insisted.

"It was strange. I recall being on another exploratory journey to the interior space of my brain. The inside area was well organized. Each structure had its own shelves, drawers, and cabinets, and there were pulleys between each of the lobes and sections that were used to draw materials together from disparate areas at the same time.

"Listen to this. There was someone or something there, like a guide, and I was told it was a unique privilege I was being given to search a particular tiny cavern. I followed the flashlight's beam to an obscure region with a sign labeled 'Mesiotemporal Area.' It was boarded up haphazardly and the entire thing looked dead.

"There, I saw remnants of cords and connectors, and I even noticed a pile of old busted eight-track tapes scattered helter-skelter. In this area, there were no live cables making contact with the other loci; its day had passed—the whole mess may have been the calamitous result of a Saturday night binge. I was grateful I never abused drugs."

"Stop making a joke of this," she growled at me, assuring me that she was in no mood for foolishness.

"I'm not. You told me to tell you everything and I am," I assured her. "This dream was similar to the experience I had when I fell over at the meeting a few days ago. It's like the visions are being manufactured inside my brain. Gradually, I'm getting the chance to see and hear more."

All this ransacking and hunting about ancient and deceased brain matter was designed for me to dig up clues for the process of dream analysis. Josea was already building premises.

"Now, the lake that serves as the perimeter harnessing the liquid is alive but it's not permanent. The objects are tied to the outside wall by some sort of flexible line. We know for sure the objects are alive. They are also transforming, possibly evolving. It seems they're all at the same stage of development.

"The figures are being swept into the vortex of the swirling and violent mass, while at the same time emitting their own utterances, their frequency of vibration defining a higher pitched, shrill tone standing apart from the background auditory material. Is that correct?" Josea asked.

I used to be enchanted when Bahlya would tease me with allusions and vague insinuations. Josea had her own pattern of communication, far more intellectualized, but equally captivating. When she finished with her supposition regarding the sounds, I jumped in on her imagination.

"You mean, like the orchestra is playing tolerable music but the objects themselves are superimposing all the jarring material?"

"Yes, because they're distressed and need help," she deduced.

"So, it's all the people who are going to die wanting me to save them? Isn't that just my conscience feeling responsible, and probably guilty, because there is nothing I can do?"

"No. That is not it. You're taking the easy way out. That's too obvious."

Precisely what I wanted…the easiest way out.

In the middle of the night on September 6th, I awakened like a sprung spring. I sat up and snatched the paper and pen from beside the bed.

Exterior portion of pool started to crack. Slow motion. Reconstructed into a hundred smaller identical pools. Each is attached to the same vague object. Now each a separate pool— has one distinct item. The subdividing is occurring—each of the hundred in turn is dividing over and over to what seems infinity. A tiny portion of the new pools contain more than one object—hardly any have three.

What importance these details would or would not have I left to the scientific genius of Josea. My job was to follow her instruction, not to leave out an observance just because I deemed it unessential. I had barely finished scribbling the above note when I fell back asleep. But when I awoke, I found myself repeating the only decipherable sentence in any of the dreams: "You can't go back; you had your time."

I couldn't recall dreaming it that night. Furthermore, it wasn't written on the pad. Yet, I couldn't stop rehearsing the words. I went to the bathroom and, unwittingly violating Josea's instruction, forgot to write down the iteration of the phrase. It passed from my mind; in a flash it had been abandoned by conscious thinking.

Later that morning, I had breakfast with my mother and Nasir in the hotel café. It was the first time I had taken a meal outside my room. I was nervous being in this type of public setting. They both sensed it and arranged for a quiet table off to the side on the patio. Under normal conditions, it might have been a breathtakingly romantic setting; the dark wood deck practically kissing the ocean's surface, with the air still and cozy.

We talked casually for quite a while awaiting our food. My mother had more to discuss about her past life. Since her once obscured history had been brought out into the open, a new round of introspection had unleashed within her. She found it beneficial to go over periods of her life she hadn't dusted for decades, especially because she wanted to share them with Nasir.

One of the topics she discussed was her courtship with my father, and her mourning how it ended. At one point, she looked at Nasir and attempted to dismiss her feelings philosophically. Her exact statement needs quoting: "That's over. Nasir, I can't go back. I had my time."

The words didn't compose an oft-used expression, nor were they particularly unusual. But they were nearly identical to those used to compose the phrase from my early visions, and expressed in the dream I'd had the previous night. Like a key being twisted in a lock, they let loose a huge door that swung with such force it reminded me of how Alwari entered my cell. The opening permitted access to a chamber. It was filled with an infinite number of separate enclosures, each containing their own little screeching objects.

I was compelled to enter by the same impulse that had instigated my exploration of Amir's room. But the second I was within I wanted to "go back." I ran, pushed, shoved, muscled, banged, and lunged, but the door had recoiled from the slam. Then it locked, trapping me inside. I bellowed, "let me go back," but my ability to force a retreat was rejected.

So hurtful was the sense of exclusion, that I began crying out the words, "Why can't I go back?" It was simultaneous, in the vision of my mind and live in the restaurant. I heard a human voice competing with my cries.

"Kaye, we have to take him out," Nasir said with urgency.

I felt like a little baby being removed from the establishment because I was throwing a tantrum. There had to be a twinge of comedy, though I was not in a state to judge it—I really did feel naughty. My good fortune was that Nasir and my mother moved swiftly. In so doing, they earned me the leniency of the staff and customers witnessing my outburst.

Just as they were able to get me to the lobby, Josea walked in. I must have ratcheted up the alarm level for my mom, because when I saw Josea my eyes were wet. All I could say repeatedly was, "I want to go back. I know I had my time. I want to go back. I know I had my time. I want to go back."

Proving me wrong, that I could go back, they rushed me back to my room. Fortunately, they had no restraints, white jackets, little blue pills, or telephone numbers for local inpatient asylums. Oddly, I would have refused all of the above—I still knew in my heart that I was entirely sane. In my repetition of the words, I was peeling away the layers of gauze obscuring me from a final perfect clarity. Yet the more I tossed aside obfuscating material, the faster the imagery moved.

Once in the room, I was still highly emotional, hyperventilating but trying to control my breathing. My mother took one of the ten washcloths this hotel felt were needed for one person and put a cold compress on my head; it helped me regain control. I motioned Josea to look at the pad on the nightstand, and she tried to read what I had jotted down.

"Tell me, Zach. I can't read it," she pled.

"They're separating; each one is its own…millions… millions."

"Keep going." Josea was affected by my unexpected exuberance.

"I just started to see it in the restaurant." My words were unrestrained, fully escaping the mental prison in which I had held them captive. "It's their time, not mine." I was yelling and prancing about the room like a rock star on stage.

"They're alive! Can't you see? They have little eyes, noses, and mouths. They're breathing, but the noise is too loud. It's deafening to them. It's time, they had their time, and they're ready. Once they leave they can't go back," I sung out as if performing. "But they're ready. It's their time; they're finally ready. Can't you tell?"

"Who are they, Zack? Who are they?" Josea was near hysterical.

I felt like every morsel of energy I had ever possessed in my entire lifetime was at my disposal, and more. I had harnessed the power of armies upon armies, all in formation for the greatest event known to mankind. I was floating weightless, about to commence the attack, to burst out.

I cried, "I'm giving birth!!!!!"

They all stood gazing at me with unspoken pity.

None of them got it. I was far ahead of them, alone in my own zone of transparency. It was my baby. How could I expect anything other than for them to think I was making a severe infantile regression from which I might not return; that the trauma I had been through was more deleterious than at first thought, and that my physical and mental systems couldn't tolerate the insults suffered one on top of another? They had to believe I was broken.

Now, I might be able to empathize a bit with women, because I know birthing babies takes vast amounts of strength and energy. You feel alone, and nobody can understand. You feel exhausted. Still, I continued.

"Josea, they're babies. They're in the amniotic sac, growing and ready for birth. They're being born."

"Okay, but what does it mean?" she asked, her question conveying both frustration and impatience. "Go on, what?"

I started laughing, giggling. The genius was hooked. Even she didn't compute. Oh, how I delighted to think of shoving this so far up Zahavy's rectum he would choke on it.

"Zach!" my mother shrieked out frightfully.

"Mom, this whole journey has been about nothing but babies, and specifically…well…let me get to that in a minute. My mom is pregnant, and they don't want to let her leave. Mr. Hamdallah wants Bahlya to get married, to have a baby. His other daughter, Lilya, is having a baby, and he's distraught because Efron is taking his baby to Syria. Efron, as a baby, is blasted to smithereens and adopted out, and his family, in spite of having more children, can't patch the hole in their souls because their baby is gone. Want me to go on?"

Their collective muteness instructed me to continue.

"Sure, I will. But listen, birth is the single most essential experience to human beings, and the product most treasured.

Take a person's baby away and their soul is dead. They'll beg for mercy from their most hated enemy, pray to gods they despise, give their fortunes to strangers, walk on hot coals to repent for sins they never committed, spit on land that a moment earlier they would have killed to keep, all hoping for a sight, touch, smell, taste, or sound of that baby.

"Look, lots of facts have come out about the principal billionaire backers of this plot. Jawiris recently had a baby born. Rami Majeed and Jawiris' wives shared almost identical due dates for their firstborn babies. Basem Uddin's son's wife had her baby, and Asif Pervaiz was waiting for two new grandchildren near the same time."

"Zach, am I hearing you?" Josea asked tentatively.

"You're talking about millions of lives and the right of a country to survive. These leaders are earnestly deliberating wiping out half a billion people as a preemptive strike. This is cupcakes, ice cream, and pure vanilla milk in comparison.

"You use those commando teams of yours to steal babies, plant the newborns in the areas where the attacks are planned, notify the world, and hope to god somehow Jawiris gets the news and *can* still call it off. They'll never let it happen if they know their babies 'have had their time' and it was so short."

My mother and Nasir were speechless. Josea must have processed the variables in her supercomputer in seconds and was more than intrigued. "We have to figure out how many and which babies."

"Remember at the beach yesterday, I told you I wished I could give the whole region an eleventh plague? Well, if we reenact ten, eleven follows. Josea, is there a bible here? Don't they always have them in hotel rooms?"

We all went through the drawers—Nasir finally found what we were looking for.

"I remember one year going to a friend's house and they did Passover. You know it, Josea, the ten plagues. The tenth, here it is.

"'This is what the Lord says: About midnight I will go throughout Egypt. Every firstborn son in Egypt will die, from the firstborn son of Pharoah, who sits on the throne, to the firstborn son of the slave girl who is at her hand mill, and all the firstborn of the cattle as well. There will be loud wailing throughout Egypt—worse than there has ever been or ever will be.'

"Jawiris and Majeed's babies just born are boys; Pervaiz had his first male grandchild just born. Uddin's grandchild is a firstborn boy. Efron's wife just had a boy. If anyone can reach Jawiris, it might be Efron—and they would have a lot to talk about after both of their babies are plucked.

"How many other male babies can you find throughout the region, intentionally selected from the families of high officials, leaders, and businessmen? More than you need, I'm sure.

"Taking the babies will be the simplest assignment your troopers have ever had—just make sure their copters are fully stocked with Huggies and formula and that the boys know how to change a diaper."

Josea was on the phone immediately. She called Hazut to set up an emergency meeting. "If it works, it is the eleventh plague. It locks the Israelis and Arabs tight and they'll have to make peace."

I was compelled to insert a nonpartisan penny. "Josea, it's not about Israel winning or the Arabs losing. It's about compelling both sides into a position from which they can't harm one another. The Israelis at some point have to give back the babies, and the Arabs are going to have to recognize the State of Israel, which they will in exchange for their blood."

"Zach, you just may have done it!" Josea shouted exuberantly.

"I doubt it."

"You don't think it will work?"

"I'll pray it does, but if so I'll doubt it was me."

"We'll get to that later. If it works, you'll be a hero, like it or not."

"If it works, Josea, let me go home. Please, I can't handle gallantry right now. My pieces are barely holding together and I want to 'go back,' back home."

"Let's go. We'll be meeting soon."

I knew I had my story to write in the future and these leaders would be setting the operation in place in moments. I was beyond worn out. "Let me off on this one, please."

Josea kindly granted me a pass. After she left, I asked Nasir and my mother if they would mind me having some time to myself. After all, I felt like I had gone through a delivery, a hard-fought one—my pregnancy had been juiced by one hell of a fertility clinic; I'd hatched not one baby, not twins, triplets, quadruplets, but billions of new living humans.

I was certain that the resulting babies really weren't mine. I had no responsibility for their care. I had no choice but to give them up. I was not in the same boat as those unfortunate selected parents about to be parted from their firstborns—the solution I had presented seemed a hell of a lot better alternative to what I had already calculated would be the beginning of World War III.

Mother and Nasir readily agreed to leave. They appeared as tired from the morning's ordeal as I. My room had a refrigerator with drink, and on a table were snacks, a bowl of fruit, and a plate of fresh-baked oatmeal cookies. I took a Perrier water and cookie and sat back in a soft leather chair, chuckling as I contemplated how swiftly my life could go from spy to mole to possible national hero, from having my head shoved in buckets of puke and piss to sipping sparkling water in a luxury hotel, from a nation promising me life imprisonment to footing the bill for medical care, and a suite at a Carlton with more washcloths than in a spa.

None of this to the slightest degree had I planned or contributed to; it all unfolded independent of my volition. My perception was that my life prior to this time had been determined by my direct efforts, dedicating energy to accomplish one endeavor after another. But now, looking back I wondered if I had essentially done no more than run in circles. *All those roads, did they lead anywhere? Would I have ended up in the same place regardless?*

I wanted to conclude that all the searching was in vain, that there was no use trying because a greater force made all the decisions for me. I wanted a copout, a way to give up and surrender my life to the vagaries of fate. But I knew it was wrong. I wouldn't give up one of the back road gravel paths I'd roamed.

Sure, my highways had turned around on themselves. I'd traveled some of the same ones repeatedly, sometimes only to try and master the challenges hidden in their potholes and crummy diners, but they all comprised my life. This was just another point on a multidimensional cosmic map.

We still were far from out of the woods, light years from it. Sure, I'd survive, but if the attacks were to be set off, there was no doubt that Israel and America would retaliate harshly against the Middle East region and from there…it had to escalate to envelop the entire globe.

For some reason, that afternoon I wanted to eat. I called room service.

38

PRIVILEGED?

ON SEPTEMBER 10TH, THE world spun dauntlessly on its axis. A late monsoonal storm in India's Andhra Pradesh state resulted in massive flooding of the Krisna River, killing thousands. A little girl, who had been missing and presumed dead after four days in Jasper National Park, was magically found alive and healthy under the supervision of a sloth of grizzly bears.

America braced itself—as it had every year since 2001— for a possible repeat performance, alerts rising to the triple red zone, with more reports of terrorist schemes than actual terrorists in the world. At ten that Wednesday evening, most of the residents of Chicago, New York, Washington, D.C., Los Angeles, and San Francisco were sleeping. At the corresponding time in Israel, the population at large went about their normal routine.

In all the targeted areas, innumerable officials, many unapprised of the situation until moments prior, were taken to underground bunkers for safety. Nuclear launching capacity for both Israel and America went on full alert; many pads in Israel moved to safe regions. Submarines carrying enough explosives to wipe out every major city in the Middle East ten times over were moved into strategic positions in preparation for a full retaliation on Israel's neighbors in the event that the next day turned disastrous. These American Trident monster subs were at the same time stealthily roaming in regional waters, capable of inflicting equal damage on literally every major city in the world.

I sat in a comfortable and safe shelter, along with many other privileged souls. I'm not sure the word "privileged" was the most fitting term for the people I was temporarily sharing space with. Each had left loved ones behind, never given an opportunity to say goodbye. That is, in order to avoid the chance of panic, those who were taken to bunkers were abducted similar to the selected infants.

Most were suffering guilt, regret, and terror—they were on a theme park ride, stuck on the top of Hell's Ferris wheel— yet sober enough to know not to jump. Those left in the potential battle zones on the ground, at greater immediate risk, were oblivious to the danger they were facing, and probably better off living in ignorance. I was blessed to have the tiny world of people most precious to me sitting within a few feet, but even that couldn't protect me against the immense force of emotion suffusing through our room like a poison gas.

All around me were what would be considered grossly important people. Yet, under the circumstance, they were tearfully reduced to tiny specks of humanity. A man later identified to me as Samuel Abraham, one of the leading industrialists in Israel, wept in a corner by himself like a little kid who'd lost his mommy. I'd never in my life seen one particular woman, but she looked into my eyes from across the room and then ran over to me, grabbing me and crying on my shoulder. Another man walked aimlessly in a circular pattern, all the while bowing his head repeatedly like a rooster pecking at seeds.

I surmised he was one of the better adjusted of the group, having found a method to escape mentally from the horror of the moment. I felt overwhelmed by the circumstance, but watching these people set off an inspiration to travel. I wanted to venture as far as possible from the death cell I found myself in once again. I instructed my Kid Kraft make-believe rocket ship to take off—it wouldn't. I silently cursed—reality was cursing me. The next thing I recalled was Josea's voice.

"You seem distant," she whispered while she jammed her foot into my leg.

"No, I'm here. I was just thinking."

"So was I." She was still talking in a hush. Her eyes were imploring and her heart was pounding so hard it was inflating her breasts.

"About what?"

"Zach, I think I figured something out, something very important. All this fighting over land is wrong. The land we live *on*, it'll never belong to anyone. The only land you can ever possess is where you live within yourself. That's why I changed my mind and came down here," Josea disclosed.

"I can't tell you how happy I am that you did."

"Thanks. I needed to see that my land is *what* I am, not *where* I am. Wherever I am, I bring the only land I'll ever own with me. The rest of the land…let them fight over it. I don't know how I got into this."

As she finished her sentence, a loud banging sound occurred, so intense it rocked the structure. If I might have thought it was an element of another vision it could have only been for an instant, because it set off a purely human panic inside our hellhole. It was a single blast but sufficient for an immediate reaction assuming the worst of all possibilities.

I suspected one of two events had taken place. The first was that we were hearing the repercussions from the intense sound blasts Jawiris had promised. The second, far worse, was that we were experiencing the residuals of a massive nuclear strike. If we had struck the Middle East region, was it possible that the extreme act caused panic by the Russians or Chinese, or both? Were each of the nuclear powers joining the party and unloading their arsenals?

I could see in the eyes of every person in my space that both options were conceived. The wailing suggested that the end of civilization had taken place. What the hell could there be left for us? It was a scenario nobody was prepared to deal with.

What was interesting was that after the initial volley of anguish, the room quieted to a most eerie hush. You could have heard the sound of a sparrow perched on a phone line dropping his load on the hood of a car. For the next ten minutes, breathing ceased. There was no clue what had happened.

As it turned out, we finally received a communication from outside informing us that an elevator cable had busted and was being repaired. Similar pandemonium set in again for several minutes after the announcement had been made explaining the nature of the loud sound we had heard—relief proved it had every bit as much punch to cause a heart attack as shock.

I went and hugged my mom and Nasir. We had nothing to say. I sat back next to Josea and finally spoke to break the terrible spell left from having lived through the end of the world and then its rebirth in less than fifteen minutes.

"What do you think will happen with all the babies? I mean, if all this works out," I asked Josea tentatively.

"That depends how they handle your eleventh plague." She smirked. "If they're smart they'll get the message, but I'm not holding my breath. They're continually finding new ways to hate."

"You know, Josea, I've heard the story, twice from opposite viewpoints, and in the end I don't believe either side is right. I remember when we were growing up; it was not uncommon for boys to get into fights. Well, we had a headmaster at our school and to settle disputes of that sort he'd put gloves on them and have them clobber each other. The combatants of this conflict behave like children and need one of those plastic guys who manufacture silicone tits to make them one for their fists and let them go at it."

"Yeah." She paused, about to inform me of a decision. "Zach, if there's anything left of it after this, I'm going back home."

"Good. What are you going to do there?"

"I plan to stay with my sister for a while. I don't want to be alone right now. What I plan to do is take yoga classes, learn to cook—if you promise to come test it out—take morning walks by the beach. Oh, and I have to educate myself about men.

"I might write also. Not like you, but poetry or maybe musical lyrics. I have to see. There's a lot in life and I've missed much of it. I know it won't be forever, but I need to be normal once in my life, even if it's just for a while. Then, I'll probably use my head and go back to science. I really do like it."

I smiled at her, my muteness speaking the simple joy I felt sitting next to her.

"What about you? What will you do?"

"I don't know. My mother wants me to come home for a while, until I'm stronger. I'm not sure, though, if going to my place will be better."

"Are you going to write about what happened?"

"I couldn't now. It would kill me, literally. You do it. I give you permission."

"No way! I couldn't anyway."

"You'll see what you can do," I said encouragingly. "You may be surprised. "

"When will you go back and see Jivin?"

"Josea, what are you talking about? Why on earth would I go there?"

"I don't know." She had a puzzled expression, as if she was stumped why she had raised the question. "Maybe because that's where all this began; for closure?"

"Getting out of here will be all the closure I need. Besides, the last thing I want in my life is a kid that eats soup for breakfast."

I put my arm around her shoulder and she rested her head on mine. I thought I remembered her doing that for a moment in the car on the way home from grad night. She must have read my mind, because her dark, round eyes with those long lashes looked up at me and she nodded her head.

"We did this on our date. I dreamed we would do it again."

Some women are too precious to fall in love with. I only wanted her to stay in my life as long as I lived. I know she felt the same. Wouldn't it ruin everything trying to get intimate?

I glanced right—for the first time in my life a witness to my own mother enjoying the warmth of a man she loved, a man she planned to marry. Wow, she was definitely having sex way more than I. I was pleased to see her so happy. I'd say the entire experience I went through was worth it solely for her to find love…but I'd be a cheat-notes-written-on-my-palm liar.

I never saw a wink of sleep for anyone I shared that evening with in the underground fortress. The hours passed like years, the minutes like decades, and the seconds loitered like guests who wouldn't get the message to leave. When the clock in New York registered midnight, September 12th, we had no idea whether or not millions of people in America, Israel, and all over the world were sleeping and going about their daily business without more care than any other day.

Was the irony of the story to be that the heartbreak had been inflicted on the privileged only?

39

SO, WAS IT A HAPPY ENDING?

AS IT TURNED OUT for those of us in the safety shelter, many of the final hours were an added precaution. In the early morning of September 10th, Jawiris, through contacts in Egypt, had negotiated his surrender. The Americans and Israelis coordinated a major operation launching thirty teams into various Middle Eastern countries, literally stealing as many newborns as possible, including, of course, all the baby boy relatives of Jawiris, his billionaire backers, and Efron.

Thus in a short timeframe, their mutual efforts made the firstborn males of princes, prime ministers, presidents, premiers, and pea-packers vanish. By then God's warning, of wailing louder than ever had been or ever would be heard on earth, was proved true.

The families would not find out until shortly after that their treasures were in safekeeping. The Efron baby, for example, had been transported to Washington, D.C. Under the nurturing of Marine Captain Joan Washington and her husband, Melvyn Washington, the little tyke was guzzling formula, listening to *The Mozart Effect*, and pissing through Pampers; the babe was princely peaceful.

It seems after the babies were snatched, and the irate and appalled victims collected their reasoning power, an urgent attempt was made to reach Jawiris. As it turned out, he had not disappeared. His wife, who had not been contacted, knew exactly where he was. Jawiris was so exhausted from all the effort required to pull off his caper that he had wanted to relax while awaiting his plan's execution. A close friend of his had arranged a suite at the Grosvenor House in Dubai, but it was registered in the friend's name.

The suffering parties sent out the word that Jawiris was about to lose more than his baby if he didn't reconsider and call off the show. Fortunately, the mastermind had not been foolish enough to fail to develop an escape plan just in case abortion was warranted as the time approached to implement the plan.

The deal agreed to when Jawiris finally surfaced was that he would hand over information for the hundred-plus locations where the installations in America and Israel had been placed. In return it was guaranteed that his baby would be returned to his wife, "within reasonable time."

He, on the other hand, had to turn himself over to the Israelis unconditionally and face a trial for crimes against Israel, America, and the Jewish people. The Israelis told Jawiris that there would be no compromise under any conditions—whether this was a bluff can never be known, because it was a decision made at the highest level of Israeli leadership and they refused even after the affair to show their hand.

It was eleven in the evening on September 10th when a special operations team of the U. S. Marines made a surprise visit to a flat on the thirty-second floor at East 54th Street in New York. The three heavily armed men guarding their sonic treasure were overwhelmed without a shot being fired. Their equipment was still disassembled, but all the components necessary for the attack were accounted for.

A similar scene was taking place simultaneously at over a hundred locations; there was resistance at only a few of the sites and casualties were minimal. By eleven fifty-nine in the evening, all reported locations had been disarmed.

Efron, as already disclosed, was arrested and would stand trial. There would be no comfort for either Efron or Jawiris in the fact that Israel had only executed two people since established as a state. It does have the death penalty for crimes against humanity, as well as against the Jewish people.

The remaining billionaires were all imprisoned within Israel. Between all of them, they couldn't borrow a single shekel. None of their governments had the nerve to come to their rescue and all of their funds, assets, and properties were frozen. They would each be standing trial as well—at a minimum, none of these conspirators would ever have a day's freedom for the remainder of their lives.

Amir and Bhalya as of the time of this writing have never been found. Did they join in a suicide pact? Did they hook up with a renegade terrorist group in Pakistan, Yemen or Somalia? Did they simply outsmart the Israelis who, in hot pursuit, couldn't catch a scent? I don't have the answer.

I know the sorrow I've selfishly endured for the loss of family. But as time passed, I dwelled on them less frequently and their lights faded like so many of the expiring stars I visited on my planetary excursions. My mind had switched to the birth cycle of life. I had no interest in decay and death.

I felt the worst for Mr. Hamdallah. He lost the most. If one were cruel in judging him, one could only justify a sliver of the redwood-log-sized punishment he suffered. All he was left with was one daughter, grief-stricken for the loss of her husband and little baby, with no reason to hope that she would ever see the infant again. Her reaction was understandable but thankfully unjustified, for the baby eventually would be returned. I thought of calling Mr. H. but realized I could do nothing but intensify his hurt—maybe at some point in the future.

At one minute past midnight, the elevators accessing the underground were activated. Like miners from the bowels of the earth, we were brought to the surface inside the ministry building. We were then able to exit to the street.

An elderly lady was sweeping the foyer. I watched as she pushed the broom across the floor, never an idea how close she came to fertilizing the new Palestinian state. I envied her for the ignorance she enjoyed.

My mother, Nasir, Josea, and I walked the two miles back to the Carlton. We all wanted to bolt the country as hastily as we could. Josea had several matters that needed attention before she could leave; her departure would be postponed for a couple of days.

The three of us went to the airport that afternoon. It wasn't as simple going through customs as I'd hoped. Believe me, I hadn't called President Barak to tell him I would be leaving as soon as possible, but it was Israel. If they wanted they could find out when anyone blew their nose.

We were prohibited from entering customs. Instead, an Israeli representative informed us that private transport home had been arranged for later that evening. In the interim, we were to be taken to the ministry where we were met by Barak and Prime Minister Shameel.

My president, Upshaw...I never heard from him again. "You had your time, you can't go back," held true for my association with our leader.

It still astonished me that after everything that had happened I wouldn't at least receive a gesture of appreciation, but since it couldn't be publicized on national television what value was there in it for our national leader? I was just as happy with that arrangement. Besides, I wasn't impressed with him. I was looking forward to the upcoming election in November, rooting for him to lose to that tough little lady from Ohio who was a hell of lot better looking.

As hard-ass as the Israeli brass seemed, they were genuinely grateful. They told me I was an unsung hero of Israel, but I would have to forever remain without music, lyric, fanfare, or celebration. If what happened were to be made known, panic could still set in for the millions who had been a whisker from demise. Both the Israelis and the Americans determined it was best to keep the entire affair tucked in their secret archives, not to be opened for at least fifty years.

What they did do, however, was insist I receive a pension of five thousand dollars per month for the rest of my life (answering the question of how I came home financially better off than when I left), first-class free passage, and expenses for life anytime I wanted to visit Israel in the future— I wouldn't have insulted them, especially with my mother watching…but what I wanted to do was ask if they were out of their f-in minds; about the only way I'd ever return to Israel would be if…

Finally, it was back to the airport and…let's get the hell out of here.

40

I'M HOME—WHERE'S HOME?

NASIR AND MY MOTHER insisted I stay with them at least for the first week. Reluctantly, I agreed. They truly appeared to enjoy one another. I wondered if they would have a child but quickly dismissed it. My mom was fit, but not foolish. She'd have to settle for a week of looking after me and then become a volunteer grandparent for some young out-of-town couple with a baby...or wait for me to embrace parenthood.

I spent the days with them resting. Of course, I also allocated sufficient time toward ruminating on every detail of what had occurred. The newspapers were selling out at the stands with biblical-themed stories about missing babies from Egypt, Syria, Palestine, Iran, Iraq, and Saudi Arabia. People were guzzling Facebook, CNET, and other Internet news sources and social networks like beer and wine. The world was abuzz with rumors. It was all about breakthroughs in negotiations between the Israelis and the Palestinians, as well as the rest of the Middle East countries.

Upshaw, beaming as if he himself were the chief architect of the greatest peace plan ever in the history of mankind, told the world that a new round of Camp David accords would soon to be announced, insinuating it was a done deal that in the very near future the State of Israel would be formally recognized by the Arab world and Israel was in agreement with the formation of a new Palestinian state with enough land to join the West Bank and Gaza.

I wondered if I would ever be able to make sense of what had happened to me, if I'd ever be able to recover. I was certain of one thing; in terms of "isms," I was as comfortable as I ever had been that I had no use for any of them. Regardless of expressed intent, encouraging divisiveness between groups, advocating superiority of faith or god, arguing that a right god can express preference for one group over another, providing a platform for prejudice, professing an inside track on truth, building intolerance for others with dissimilar beliefs, and permitting killing in the name of laws, rituals, and belief in a supreme power, they all belonged in a toxic dust pail to be eradicated by repeated nuclear assault and then buried in the furnace of earth's hell.

The whole affair left me pondering if there actually could be a new way for people to cope with the inescapable unknowns that force mankind into a state of fear. At an even larger level, I contemplated whether we humans might have backed ourselves into a corner from which we have no choice other than to defer to a new type of world order, one with real order.

Josea arrived home a few days later and called me immediately, needing assurance I would follow up on my promise to her. I know there's more intelligence than some entire nations possess in that one head of hers, but she's got issues too—she's insecure and…scared.

Well, I would have given her my Israeli pension, all the royalties from the writing of the book I hoped to someday craft, and my collection of Nike shoelaces to assure her but figured the best way to convince someone that your love is sincere is to just to tell them, and I did. She giggled.

Two days later, we met. We were both apprehensive about seeing one another. Neither of us could have explained it but we knew the subject of romance had to be addressed. She picked me up and we drove to the beach, perhaps she had in mind to use the familiar scene to stimulate intimacy.

We walked, talked and had lunch. Then we flipped off our shoes and let the surf splash on our feet. Finally, facing her, I reached for her hands. I encountered no resistance. The god of sun was chaperoning from the west and the moon goddess peeked from the east. We were looking into one another's eyes, neither of us taking note that our companions were laughing.

At last I kissed her. It might have been the strangest embrace of my life. I desperately wanted our first act of love to be passionate, for the sky to light up with Fourth of July fireworks—it didn't happen. Instead, instinctively we both pulled back. We looked knowingly at one another. Then we hugged the hug of a thousand lifetime friendships.

My earlier thought about ruining our bond by introducing intimacy was on the mark. Hot passionate love would never be on the menu for Josea and I. The wonder of our sun and moon overseers was that they permitted us to quickly accept a reality that might otherwise have cost us months of agony.

We strolled along the edge of the waves. Our hands grasped tightly. Our souls were inextricably bonded but our hearts were free to wander. Forever we would have a special unbreakable connection.

No words passed between us and no time in the future did we feel the need to discuss that one kiss. As if the experiment had never been conducted, Josea needled me.

"When are you going to see Jivin?"

"As soon as my diarrhea stops running marathons, my heart quits accelerating prestissimo, the headaches untie the knots in my eyes, and the aches go away further than I can travel in space…" I looked at her for a sign of jest but it wasn't there. "Why do you ask again?"

"I don't know. I really don't. But I do have to share a secret," she disclosed with a glint in her eyes.

Then she proceeded to inform me that as part of the negotiation over my benefits for helping Israel, she had insisted I be provided a private jet roundtrip to New Mexico and a limo to drive me to and from Jivin's home.

To this day I can't explain why but a few months after coming home I made my second trek to Mescalero. When I informed my mother that I was going she thought I was crackers; still, she objected only seventeen-and-a-half percent what she had over me going to Israel, especially knowing I had private transport door-to-door.

I was picked up by a chauffeur to take me to Van Nuys airport. A Gulfstream G-150—I was the only traveler in the four-seater craft—streamed off the runway and in about an hour we landed in Albuquerque, New Mexico, where another limo driver awaited me. His name was Sandy.

"What do you say we get a bite to eat first?" I suggested.

"You're the boss."

We stopped at a small roadside café. I ordered a hamburger with fries. I was sure I'd be suffering dyspepsia from the grease, but my appetite was gradually coming out of hibernation. Although I could only handle small portions, I noticed I was eager for several meals a day.

"You must be a big gambler," Sandy commented early in the ride.

"Actually, I don't even buy lottery tickets. I'm not a fan of chance."

I started laughing out loud. Like it or not, fortuity had played with me like a tool.

"I'm the type of guy, Sandy, who likes to keep things under my own control. I believe…actually, I'm not sure I can tell you what I believe anymore."

"Know what that's like, sir. Had a few heartbreaks myself."

"You might have a point. Something did break in me."

"It heals, son, always does. Just give it time."

Sandy was a good twenty years my senior. I interpreted his "son" reference as an attempt to give me some fatherly comfort. He was African-American, a tall but very skinny man. Getting into the car, I had noticed that he limped off his left leg, an old injury no doubt, because he ambulated as if it didn't exist. Yet, it caused him to thrust the right side of his body upward each time he bore down on the left; it ached me worse watching him move than it seemed to bother him.

"If I'm being inappropriate please don't answer, but I couldn't help noticing your limp."

"Proudest moment of my life," he answered.

"What do you mean?"

"You were probably a little tyke in diapers, but in 1981 I was in the Secret Service. My assignment was to guard President Reagan. This young man named Hinckley tried to assassinate Reagan. You read about it in history, right?"

"Sure, I did. In high school."

"I was the agent who jumped over the president and used my body as a human shield. The bullet actually entered my gut, but the damn thing exploded into my back and groin. I'd do it again in five minutes for Mr. Reagan."

He left me more breathless than listening to Jerry Lee Lewis rockin' the song with that name. There were real heroic people out there, just like Sandy…lots of them. They were rewarded with nothing but their own pride and self-respect; few would ever know of their bravery and sacrifice.

Sandy represented a different breed of man, one I had never been able to understand but I respected.

"You did something great," I openly praised. "You're a hero."

"No, that's a label they pinned on me until I bled."

I knew if the circumstances were different, my picture would have been plastered on every newspaper and magazine cover, every website and television newscast for months to come. I knew I didn't want it either. But my reasons were different. I didn't see where I'd done anything heroic.

"But you directly risked your life to save a man you thought was a great leader," I said.

"That sounds romantic, all right, son," he responded. "But I did what anyone, including you, would have done. You see, when a situation like that happens, instinct takes over and you react without volition or choice. That's why so-called heroes who let exaltation pour on them in the end become severely depressed. They're just normal guys being paraded like fools in front of millions of others who feel shame that they aren't as courageous as them. Not me, sir. I'm right where I want to be."

I wished I could have told him my story, just because I knew he'd be one of the only people who would genuinely treat me as I wished, like Zacchaeus Miller. But I let him do the talking.

"Well, if it's not the local casino—and they have a first class joint there—what brings you?"

"There's a boy who lives there who played an unusual kind of role in my life."

He bellowed knowingly, assuming this child an offspring produced along a one- time traveled road earlier in my life.

"It's not like that. I just need to see him one more time. My friend thinks it will help bring closure to a life crisis."

"Whatever you say," Sandy said dutifully. "But are we going to have a little time to visit the gaming house or you in a hurry?"

My phone rang and I excused myself. It was Preston. I had kept him abreast of my status since coming back. Once I'd gotten back in my home, the man visited me almost daily and looked after me like a second mom. My mother told me she'd had to beg him not to come to Israel when she first decided to make the trip. He was ready to take on the whole damn Israeli military, and might have died trying.

"Hi, I'm okay. Couple hours more and I'll be there," I updated him.

"I bumped into Josea over at your mom's place a couple times. What a hot number. Too bad, though, she's a bit too much on the brainy side to want a slacker like me."

"We'll see. She needs some time to settle in."

"Now, you'll call me as soon as you get out of there, right?"

"Yes, Mommy. Later."

"Sorry about that," I said to Sandy. "It was my closest friend. Now, I'll make a deal with you. Give me a half hour at most with the boy and I'll be out. Then you can gamble a couple hours before we head back."

"That's fine. I feel lady luck this time."

"Let's go."

I paid for lunch and he thanked me.

We began our ascent. I felt like I was returning to the scene of a crime—I don't know whose but I noticed my gut tightened.

Strangely, turning onto the dirt road leading to Kuruk was a different experience than when I'd come the first time. Perhaps it was being a passenger that I was able to take in the scene. As we headed north, I noticed an old dilapidated wood gate. It had permanently positioned itself open, proving the point by indolently bowing its weight with such persistence that the low end farthest from the hinges could be accused of sticking its tongue out at anyone dumb enough to try moving it. The distal point was dug deep into the ground. So fragile did the termite-eaten frame and cross-members appear that any attempt to free it would have surely collapsed the entire structure. What was most attractive, besides its antiquity, was the green moss heavily blanketing portions of the oak like fur on a lion's mane.

As we drove, I noticed off to the side of the road the shell of an abandoned vehicle. It had become home to a giant-sized privet indifferent to deteriorated seats and rotted metal. Its heartily growing trunk flexed to lift the carcass off the ground while its limbs were waving out the windows like a jubilant group of gypsies welcoming me.

Next, we came upon a small garden, one so carefully tended it had to be the work of a pro. It came into view after a few hundred yards of the entrance. It was adjacent to both the wood corralled parking area and a building. Attached to the latter was what must have been born a hothouse but had long before collapsed to a heap of rotting wood and glass.

The main structure's exterior paint was coiffed by the fluttering hands of decades of wind strokes, a dull limey-green shade. The roof had baked in the sun's intense rays. Alternating periods of intense heat with ice and freezing had corroded the long planks of metal into rusted marbling patterns of orange, charcoal, and pink, each piece defined by blackened channels seeming about eight inches apart.

At the far eastern end was a large brick chimney of old used material that nearly matched the color of the rooftop. In fact, due to the high pitch, if one looked straight on at the building, they might miss the fireplace altogether. But on this fine day it was unmistakably alive; the cool air was sucking smoke as joyously as an old gent puffing his pipe. Three partially decomposed steps led up to a small, uncovered landing presenting the front door.

Why had none of the quaintness of Kuruk impressed me on my earlier visit? I didn't dwell on the question. Instead, I noticed the wrenching feelings in my stomach as they increased. Sandy sensed it too.

"You're tense, man. You need me to go in there with you?" he volunteered.

"No. Just wait here. If I'm not out in half an hour, call the sheriff."

"You sure about this?"

"I'm joking. There are no sheriffs here. It's an Indian reservation."

"Watch out for those Indian women. They can be a handful." He slapped his thigh gleefully.

"Seriously, I'll be right out."

The parking lot was nearly empty. Lunch was over by the time we arrived. Sandy pulled the limo right up to the front door. I scanned the area, noticing that the garden looked abundant with vegetables and fruits. I especially noticed some of my favorites, orange cantaloupes and light green honeydew. The Kuruk sign was in its same battered shape.

I went in the door and looked around at the vacant tables. It was eerily quiet. If it weren't for a faint aroma of fried potatoes dawdling after lunch, I might have taken it for abandoned.

As I glanced to the rear, where I had seen Jivin on my prior visit, I noticed him in the same chair. He was covered with a wool shawl and reclining back at a forty-five degree angle. There was one man sitting across from him with his head limply hanging down. Then as if déjà vu, Josea's new buddy, Jivin's mom, Preeti, appeared from a door off to the side of the room.

She was wearing jeans—they were an old-fashioned Levis brand that had been washed to that perfect point where the heavy material had long ago worn down to a soft and thinning fabric that makes the owner never part with them, even as the knees tear and the cuffs wear ragged, treasures deserving of a weepy funeral when finally shoved in the trash—a black tank top with no space vacant, white tennis shoes with pink and green laces, and a funny silver bear pin on the left strap of her top.

Her hair hung in dangles, swirling and glowing brunette radiance to below the neckline, affording a broken view of turquoise and silver drop earrings. Her skin illuminated, turning the angelic darkness a lighter shade of amber, her eyes sharp and black. I estimated her to be five foot two and her weight about a hundred ten pounds, her figure distributed wisely by the maker.

Jivin's mom's physical appearance was similar to that of the woman who had rushed in briskly to attend her son when I first visited. Now, in the short instant she and I stared at one another, I could tell she was transformed. She was promoting temptation and seduction better than a crew of Madison Avenue ad men. This adornment couldn't have been in my honor, but I was grateful just the same. She hesitated for a moment before cautiously moving forward into the room.

The space we were now sharing was motionless. When I peered into her eyes, exactly as when I'd done the same with Bahlya, another piece of myself came into focus—but then the procession continued, one image after another, until a total familiarity emerged, as if I were seeing me for the first time. I had the feeling that I was coming home, was home, after a long, torturous journey, but this time was different. I wanted to embrace all the missing elements of me I saw in her, to never stop exploring—I wanted to call my mother and ask if by chance there wasn't something else she hadn't told me, some Apache blood in my veins?

Those moments when I lay in prison trying to capture the impression that was taunting and teasing me but refused to come into focus, those times I battled the prankster yanking me by a tether to see the joyous appearance that would have comforted me in my torture, merged in a single image. It was Preeti! She had harpooned my heart during that brief moment when she glanced "incuriously" my way during my virgin visit to Kuruk—that was the reward my blind eyes were unable to own.

Unwittingly, I had returned to Kuruk, not to discover a mystical explanation as to how or why her son instructed me to go to Israel but to find the love of my life.

I walked outside to Sandy, handing him an obscene tip. "If I don't call you in the next two hours, take off." I reached to shake his hand. "I wish I could tell you this will be the luckiest day of your life but that may be up to your destiny."

Sandy took off. He was eager to play humankind's most popular game of spitting at odds guaranteed to eventually whip him.

As for me, well…it was going to be a long visit to Kuruk.

The unexpected amour between Preeti and me may sound corny, a romance made for television, a childish tale of fate and destiny ending a journey of searching and wandering for a mixed-up young man with the discovery of love forever after. Come on! Why this woman…with whom he shared no past history, no common heritage, no familiar roots?

Why wouldn't it have been Bahlya, who on the run would still find a way to meet up with her lover and then devote her life to him in some obscure corner of the planet? She was only a distant cousin.

And what about the most likely lover, Josea? Why after so many years, just when fate had brought our two lives together again to face a challenge that had built between us a powerful respect and dedication, couldn't we have fallen in love? Isn't this the romance we would have all been betting on…rooting for?

Sometimes we don't get answers.

Most important is that Preeti and I knew we would spend the duration of our lives together. Sure, we'd just met, but really, how long does it take to know when you've found your soul mate? For me, I can only attest that from the moment I looked at Preeti a second time around, I was aware I'd found mine.

The sad part of the ending is that Jivin was ill and dying. In the coming weeks I'd watch as his skin became translucent and thin, his hair appeared dry, lacking luster. His face drew in, making his features more pronounced. He rarely spoke owing to each time he did he'd cough and gag. Preeti's home remedies ceased to curb his symptoms, ones in the past she had assumed were asthmatic. Instead, he suffered from interstitial lung disease with cytomegalovirus.

Oddly, he never complained and was always smiling. The few times he spoke of his condition he might have been discussing dust. His detachment didn't suggest fear but rather a physiologic nihilism, as if he really didn't exist.

One afternoon we had a bizarre encounter.

"Don't go feeling badly," he lectured paternally as my sadness over his suffering came to the surface. While he talked his breathing was lazy, longer than normal gaps between inhalation and exhalations. "There's a lot more to life than most people stop to experience. They don't pay attention." I was unprepared for his next statement. "Zach, I had my time, and there's no going back."

The words made me laugh. Was I on Candid Camera or some similar new unreality reality show? I tried to forward the conversation as quickly as possible but...

Every word he spoke appeared to strain him but he was in the mood to talk. "Most people have to have it one way or the other, don't they?"

"What are you referring to?"

"Being the commander of ones life verses powerlessly bowing to the forces of fate." He began expressing himself in generalities before narrowly pointing at me. "Did you ever think it might be both? You are responsible for many aspects of your life, yet at the same time there are elements, like your role during the trip to Israel, that are part of a deeper destiny you will live out regardless of your own volition—and they each may be equally important." He paused to emphasize a point. "Life is not about using the underlying order of the universe to absolve ourselves of duty and obligation."

I'll never forget that talk, or the one just before he passed. It was early morning when I was wiping down his brow. He opened his eye, offering a few words.

"You'll have more stories, don't worry. They'll come to you right here."

I didn't know what he was referring to, but it dawned on me later that Kuruk could be a magnet for people from all walks of life to stop in for a meal. I'd have plenty of grist for my writer's mill—Preeti and I had decided we would run Kuruk together.

Later that morning I noticed Jivin's breathing slackening noticeably. The time was expanding between the taking in and letting out of oxygen—sometimes a minute or two elapsed within that span. The process was gentle, making the movement of air nearly inaudible. Then he opened his eyes and spoke his last human words.

"When I saw you that first time I knew you would love her. Take care of her. And tell my mother I love her."

Josea was convinced he was a child mystic. Preeti admitted she'd birthed an odd creature from another universe. I prayed that when the time came we'd not duplicate her effort. In the meantime, I was overjoyed to be breathing and alive.

*****

Completed and Upcoming Zach Miller Stories:

Insatiable Hate
Mescalero Blood
Crushing Steel
To Protect The Guilty

If you enjoyed *Mistaken Enemy*, please write a review on your favorite site(s)—and tell your friends. The success of any author rests in the hearts of their readers. Your feedback is appreciated so feel free to visit my website and contact me—time permitting, I will reply.

The next book to be published in this series is *Insatiable Hate*. The truth is that I wrote this manuscript as the fourth Zach Miller story. It never dawned on me until two years after completing the first book that what happened in Israel had a sequel—never registered with Zach either that Israel would come back to make another run on his life.

Insatiable Hate is due to be published in the spring of 2016. For more details regarding the date of release visit:

www.dennisnehamen.com

For a preview of *Insatiable Hate*, turn the page.

INSATIABLE HATE

By

Dennis A Nehamen

PROLOGUE

I THOUGHT IT WAS the morning of my life. Past horrors had graciously bid me adieu. My shoulders were light and I had no cause to look over them anticipating tragedy. Then I sneezed. As I blew into a Kleenex a ghastly smelling stringy substance streamed out of my nose. It flowed like vomit from the bowels of evil.

I couldn't stop it. *What is this?* I shouted into an echo of irreverence. I had my answer even before I finished posing the question. It was hate. It was the worst sort of hate, the type that wants revenge, the type that won't be satisfied without a rampage of murder, the type that will kill millions to punish one.

Rueben Cloud and his wife, Josea Roth-Cloud, were causelessly buzzing back stage, trying to appear to be addressing last minute details in preparation for the lights to go up for the first time on their latest musical—in truth, they, as well as the remainder of the staff, were panic-stricken, gravely incommunicative like parents whose teenage daughter hadn't returned home on time from her first date.

The audience, composed of those privileged souls fortunate to have a ticket for the kick-off performance of what the couple believed to be their greatest work, was seated, impatiently waiting the unveiling—they would never serve as witnesses to the grand opening.

After fidgeting in their chairs for over half an hour the announcer informed this eager group that due to a undisclosed tragic event they would all receive refunds, along with the right to see the work as soon as it was next scheduled. That would never happen; the piece would never be staged at The Center for the Performing Arts at Kuruk.

The lead female character, an eight-year-old girl taking the role of Star, had gone missing. The spokesman for the theater must have sensed a worse crisis than any participant of the show would have allowed themselves to imagine when he referred to a "tragic event," yet that is exactly what accounted for the conspicuous absence of the budding young prodigy. While resting late in the afternoon following the final dress rehearsal she was lured out of her room and then abducted. The mystery of her missing the curtain call was solved at sunrise the next morning.

The killer had hung sweet Adina Bernard like Christ from a cross. He had driven the stake into the ground deep enough to support her limp body, drenched in blood from a visible puncture to the heart. The site where she rested was half way along the private road leading to Kuruk.

I recall the first time I drove the quarter mile stretch leading to what was then not only our restaurant but also my wife's home. The earth paralleling the road on both sides had been stingily landscaped by nature. Scattered randomly were a few large yucca, tall figures with their sword-like leaves shooting out in every direction like the frizzy hair of a mad scientist. The older, lower growth was thick and drooped downward from the trunk, the overall impression suggested this family of cactus had been awakened too early and needed a cup of coffee to perk up. Less notable were clumps of mescal plants interspersed with Alaskan Ginseng, the latter creeping their dark green, maple shaped leaves like tortoises across the blackened loam-covered ground.

Most memorable for me was the wooden gate that at some past time might have proudly permitted or denied entry. Yet as I passed it I noticed it was so badly eaten by termites that its miracle was having wrestled with the earth around it such that it had managed to stay standing upright—during my first fall season at the New Mexico Indian Reservation called Mescalero an early windstorm finally terminated the stubborn structure like a bullet fired into its brain.

At first I felt like weeping but my wife, Preeti, consoled me that all objects, animate and inanimate, have their time and it was our calling to construct not only a new gate but a fence of similar style spanning the entire length of the road. That wasn't all. Additionally she surmised, correctly, that with the volume of traffic it now served we needed to pave the entrance to our place of business.

I used to smile reminiscing the ticklish sensations I had stored like gems in a leather pouch from my maiden voyage to Kuruk.

Now, if any person had by chance turned onto the road leading to Kuruk the morning Adina's body was found, they would have been welcomed by a spiffy split rail open gate with matching fence. Resting under the crossbars were clumps of blooming coneflowers, their pink petals submitting gracefully to feature the perfectly round-shaped orange jewels cloistered in their center, these bursts of color so bright that each possessed as potent an effect on the senses as a field of California golden poppies. Dandelions, in their supporting role, covered the adjacent ground.

That very morning the wonder of this precious and beautiful strip of earth was looted from the rooftop of my memory like tenderness from a warrior.

I was already, owing to the unsolved mystery of what happened to Adina, in a gloomy mood when I left home just before daybreak to look into a couple matters at the restaurant. I had proceeded only some two hundred yards before the remains of our lead lady came into view; the image burns eternal agony in my heart to this moment.

I slammed my car to a stop, sending my companion, the esteemed English Cocker Spaniel family pet, Henry Higgins, unpleasantly head first into the dashboard.

He yelped. I screeched. The next thing I recall was the sound of a damn fleet of pickup trucks roaring along the road. Then I heard sirens. The noise of a procession of police vehicles racing toward me was deafening. Successively each skidded to a stop before the officers bolted from their cars. After the near fatal events I had lived through during the few years prior to this tragedy, I felt doomed.

It would not be until some time later that I would come to understand that this adorable little girl was savagely murdered owing to two crimes, neither of which she could have had knowledge or averted. Putting aside that she was an unusually talented child who was going to bring joy to thousands of people during her career and had been a delight to all of us associated with her at Mescalero, she was sentenced to death for the offenses of being associated with me…and being Jewish.

This was not to be a common hate crime. The evildoer of this act was a rabid animal who had stuffed his belly with viciousness but could never be sated. He wanted me, and everybody and everything precious to me, to suffer or be destroyed. He landed in town with vengeance. He wanted to play with me like an alley cat with a field mouse, terrorizing me with pinprick impalements by his wicked incisors before releasing me to scamper away, but only to then mouth me with just enough grip to let me know that at any moment the fatal tightening of the jaw could bring about my termination.

Adina Bernard was only a warm up exercise for this sick monster. I would soon learn that the man wasn't bred for the role of cold killer but acquired it out of an irrefutable faith— the worst equation for the devil's work in that the horrors he commits are in his demented mind permissible, rational, necessary and justified.

The end game would come much too late for many inno- cent people. I'm not sure to this day what other acts of terror were on his agenda when we did finally meet. I do know that his enterprise was futile to him unless at some point he would be able to encounter me face-to-face. I surmised this to be the case as time went on but it wasn't until the moment he embraced me that my suspicion was confirmed.

After everything, he wanted to kiss me—twice on each side.

ABOUT THE AUTHOR

Dennis A Nehamen, Ph.D. is a forensic and clinical psychologist who has authored novels, screenplays and musicals, including the award-winning musical Wrapped. He lives in Los Angeles with his wife and has two adult children.

www.ingramcontent.com/pod-product-compliance
Lightning Source LLC
Chambersburg PA
CBHW030545260626
47157CB00006B/2198